MIND FIELDS

Brad Aiken

PADWOLF PUBLISHING

BOOKS BY BRAD AIKEN

-THE STARSCAPE PROJECT

-STARSCAPE: THE SILVER BULLET

-MIND FIELDS

Acknowledgements

My thanks to the writers of *Star Trek: TNG* for being the first to put nanites in my head and planting the seed for this story, to my fellow members of the South Florida Science Fiction Society who support my passion for science fiction (a quality that many have, but few admit to), to Susan Cummins for cleaning up some of the rough edges in *Mind Fields*, and to Diane Raetz and the hard-working folks at Padwolf for making this all possible.

On a more personal note, I'd like to thank my Aunt Carol and Uncle Buzz for helping me experience a different side of Aspen so critical to this story.

Mind Fields is dedicated to my most avid supporters and least critical proof-readers — my wife Laura, my mother Arnita and my grandmother Elsie, who I sorely miss.

Mind Fields
© 2007 Brad Aiken

cover art © Padriac
design and book layout by Howling Pixels

Padwolf Publishing, Inc.
www.padwolf.com

ISBN: 1-890096-34-2
Printed in the U.S.A.
First Printing.

CHAPTER ONE

June 5, 2045
Lazio, Italy

James O'Grady glanced up at the blazing afternoon sun as he crouched in the shade of the lone remaining wall of what was once a glorious Roman villa. Ancient ruins were scattered along the surrounding hillside, now barren except for the occasional gnarled trunk of an old olive tree, the last vestige of what must have once been a fruitful grove. He could feel the sweat roll down the nape of his neck, adding its moisture to his already heavy camouflage suit. There was not even the hint of a breeze to cool the skin or stir the eerie silence of a hot summer's day.

"See anything yet?" he asked.

Trace McKnight peered intently through his binoculars, gazing down into the arid valley toward the one paved road that led into the town of Diavola. "Nah, nothin' but grass and dirt." He wiped the sweat from his brow in disgust. Trace hated foreign assignments, especially ones that deprived him of a bachelor's nightlife. A stakeout in the Italian countryside was not his idea of a good time.

"I sure hope that gadget of yours works, Trace." Jimmy's knees ached. He envied the restless energy of his young partner. "If not, God knows how were gonna get to Stalletti." He glanced down at the walled in city a quarter of a mile away across the valley.

"Don't worry, Uncle Jimmy, it will." Trace grinned with pride. He was anxious to prove his worth as an NSA agent to his uncle and partner, Agent James O'Grady.

The parched earth of Lazio was as rich as its history. Giovanni Stalletti was the new generation of leadership, proud of the heritage left to him by ancient conquerors. Everyone in Diavola was either family or worked for the "business." Weapons smuggling was lucrative, and the townspeople lived well. They would not let any harm come to "Papa Giovanni."

"You sure he's coming?"

"I'm sure." Jimmy grabbed the binoculars. "Stalletti would have the kid's head if he didn't show."

All O'Grady could see were waves of heat emanating from the asphalt road. He handed the field glasses back and stretched, taking in a deep breath. The scent of grass baking in the sun permeated the arid air of the Roman countryside.

"Arrogant son of a bitch."

"That's what they say, kid."

No one outside of the family really knew Stalletti. He never ventured outside the village walls, and no outsiders ever entered, except one. One of Stalletti's eccentricities was his demand for fresh fish. Everyday, he had to have fresh fish.

All outside delivery trucks were stopped at the gate, a half-mile from town. Packages were inspected and transferred to Stalletti's own cars to be brought into town. On Sundays, deliveries were forbidden; the road was silent. The only traffic that day would be the delivery boy, riding in from the gate on his bicycle with the catch of the day. Every Sunday at two PM, he arrived in his truck from Positano then made his way up to the village on his bike. This Sunday would be no different, except for the new helmet that he would be wearing, an anonymous gift courtesy of Trace McKnight.

"He won't be so arrogant after today."

Jimmy glanced at the remote control in Trace's hand. "You sure that thing is gonna work from this far away?"

"Relax, Uncle Jimmy." He lifted up the remote. "This thing's got a range of a mile and a half."

O'Grady looked over at the town. "Even through stone walls?"

"Just leave the tech stuff to me, would you?" Trace laughed.

"Hey," Jimmy pointed down into the valley, where dust swirled up from a small patch of the road, "what's that?"

Trace lifted the binoculars to his eyes. The rider was on his way in. "That's our boy."

He followed the bike up the road as Jimmy looked on anxiously. "All right, he's in." Trace handed the binoculars to Jimmy. "Show time." He smiled and pressed a button on the remote, activating a hidden camera in the helmet, then held the remote up to where Jimmy could see the small screen. They watched through the eyes of the delivery boy as he rode up to Giovanni Stalletti's house. He looked down at the large refrigerated container that held the fish as he lifted it to carry into the house.

The camera swung up as the door opened, and the screen filled with the face of Giovanni Stalletti. "Shit! There he is." Trace was surprised to see Stalletti answering his own door.

The gangster stared, and Jimmy held his breath. He could swear Stalletti was looking right at the camera. "You sure he can't see that camera of yours, boy?"

"I'm sure, Uncle Jimmy, I'm sure."

Stalletti smiled and nodded. He turned away from the door and signaled to one of his men to open the container.

"Christ, he's coming over to the kid. Activate it."

Trace fumbled with the remote.

Stalletti's bodyguard reached for the lid of the container.

"Come on, Trace. Quick!"

Trace hit a three-button sequence on the remote, and then watched the screen intently. The delivery boy deftly reached into one of the cooling pouches on the side of the container, obediently following the sequence of commands transmitted into his brain from the bike helmet, which Trace had just activated. He pulled out a laser pistol and fired two quick shots. The first hit the bodyguard square in the forehead at point blank range. He was so close that the two NSA agents could clearly see the searing hole even on the small screen on Trace's remote-control device. The second shot was a longer pulse, arching across Stalletti's chest just before he fell to the ground.

The screen image blurred. The next thing that Jimmy and Trace could see was the image of a second bodyguard standing over the helmet-camera, looking down at his young victim. The biker was motionless on the floor, and the last view on the screen was that of the bodyguard's foot swinging toward the camera, just before he kicked the rider's lifeless head, sending the helmet flying.

Trace shut off the remote.

"Too bad everyone in the world doesn't walk around with helmets on, eh, Trace? It would make our job a hell of a lot easier."

"Guess we'll just have to find a way to put the controllers *inside* their heads," Trace smiled deviously.

"Sick bastard. If you figure out how to do that, how will I know you're not going turn *me* into one of your robots someday?"

"You won't, Uncle Jimmy," Trace winked. "You won't."

CHAPTER TWO

June 5, 2045
Baltimore, Maryland

Dr. Sandra Fletcher didn't often dream, but when she knew life was about to slam her with one of its many cruel jokes, she retreated into the solace of her youth to escape the torture of insomnia. Tomorrow would be one of those days; public speaking was not Sandi's forte. As she lay in bed clutching tightly at her pillow, she forced her restless mind back to the most serene time and place she'd ever known.

Wisps of cottonwood fluttered through the air and danced like dandelion fluff in the warm summer breezes, swirling around Sandi as she trotted her horse, Feather, up the trail toward Maroon Bells. She was sixteen again, and just like every other summer since her twelfth birthday, she was spending her vacation at her Aunt Darcy's ranch in Aspen, Colorado. Each year she would pack her bags as soon as school was out and fly to Aspen. She would work in the barn helping to care for horses boarded there by wealthy celebrities who entrusted their treasures to the care of Darcy Fletcher.

Stable work was not easy, but Sandi loved it. Feather had been born just one week after Sandi arrived in Aspen that first summer. She had never lived away from home before and was feeling homesick until that very special moment. Sandi was present when Feather came into the world, and the two of them had a unique bond. Feather was quiet and kept to himself most of the year, but come summer, he was a different horse. He somehow knew when Sandi would be arriving, and that anticipation breathed new life into him each year.

The congestion that sprawled out from Denver through Summit County and far beyond by the mid twenty-first century had ruined the pristine Rockies for many, but Aspen was different. The tightly enforced building codes had limited development and protected the area from the fate of many of the surrounding resort towns. Urban sprawl and smog weren't totally absent, but were limited. Aspen in summer was glorious. The snow-capped mountains cascaded down in fields of green grass, groomed into forested slopes; the same slopes that would attract thousands of skiers each winter now lay quiescently green, basking in the summer sunlight. Scattered wildflowers of all colors dotted the valleys, and were transplanted into meticulous little gardens that accented the quaint Victorian homes of the old city. The summer sun was warm, and the clean, dry air nourished the soul. It was the essence of life, reborn each year out of the cleansing of the bitter-cold winter stillness that enveloped the area.

These were the memories of Sandi's summers and the dreams of her life. About the only thing she loved more about Aspen than Feather, was teen heartthrob Ryan Taylor. She had nearly fainted when she heard that Aunt Darcy was boarding his horse. Each summer she would dream about riding with him, but every year she would go home disappointed. The summer of 2037 would prove to be different.

The smell of freshly brewed coffee beckoned Sandi to the kitchen. Darcy looked up as her niece shuffled in, clad in a flannel nightgown.

"Good morning, sleepy-head." Darcy Fletcher was an early riser; ranch life had that effect on people.

"Mornin,' Aunt Darcy." She stretched, and inhaled deeply as the scent of sizzling bacon made its way across the room. "Umm."

"It'll be ready in a minute. Why don't you pour the coffee?"

Sandi walked over to the coffee maker and poured two cups, as her aunt scraped the bacon and eggs onto the plates. Darcy was unusually quiet as they sat down to eat. Sandi didn't notice at first, as she devoured two strips of bacon. She looked up as she reached for her mug, and couldn't help but notice the wry smile her aunt was trying so hard to conceal.

"By the way," she said, "Ryan Taylor's coming up for a ride at noon. Why don't you take him up to Maroon Bells? He doesn't know the area too well. He'll need a guide."

"Ryan Taylor! You're just telling me this now?" She spun to look at the clock. "God, it's almost eight o'clock. Why didn't you tell me last night?"

Darcy laughed. "Relax and eat your breakfast. You've got plenty of time."

"Just look at me!" Sandi grabbed at her long, wavy, brown hair with both hands and pulled it out to the sides. It was so thick that it almost stayed out there by itself as she let go, even in the dry mountain air.

Darcy laughed at the sight. She just couldn't help herself. "Sorry," she giggled. "A brush will fix that. Don't you worry, now. You're beautiful. You're like a part of nature."

"Ugh," Sandy gasped. She hated that. People were always telling her she looked "earthy," or "natural," things like that. She couldn't stand it. The glamour girls who graced the covers of teen magazines made her sick, but she envied them at times like this. She rushed through breakfast, and then ran upstairs to shower.

Ryan Taylor was every bit as handsome and charming as Sandi had expected. As she walked into the barn, she could hardly get the words out. "Aunt Darcy said I should guide you up to Maroon Bells."

As he spun around to look at her, she turned beet red. *God, Sandi! Is that the best you could come up with? You made it sound like a chore,* she scolded herself, wishing that she knew the right thing to say.

Ryan had hoped to ride alone that day, but when he saw the innocence in Sandi's eyes, he didn't have the heart to turn her down. "Sure," he smiled, "why not."

Sandi was speechless. She turned away to avoid further embarrassment, and mounted Feather. She headed out of the stable, Feather's hooves pounding rhythmically against the dry clay, which swirled into the air with each beat. Ryan followed closely behind, and soon was at her side. It was a typical summer day, warm and dry, the air filled with the wisps of cotton-like puffs of seeds from the cottonwood trees. It almost looked like an Aspen snowfall. When they first caught a glimpse of the Bells, Ryan galloped ahead. Sandi frowned as he blew by her, and she spurred Feather on, squinting to shield her eyes from the cotton that filled the air. She giggled as she whisked past Ryan, and turned back to taunt him with a smile.

That was the moment. It was as if life itself suddenly shifted into slow motion as she slipped out of the saddle. Feather could sense that something was wrong as he felt Sandi slipping from his back. He reared up in panic. Sandi saw him, seemingly frozen in the air, as she floated up and away from the comfort of Feather's back. She saw the ground growing slowly closer, and the gray boulder growing ever larger. She first felt panic, and then an eerie calm, resolved to the inevitable landing that fate guided her towards.

With a sudden thud, it all ended. The dream turned to black. There was stillness all around her: no sight, no sound, no smell. A deepness enveloped her and she was caught between panic and placidness.

Slowly she sensed Ryan kneeling over her. All that she could see was the blackness in her inner eyelids, but she knew he was there.

Then, she heard his voice, soft and distant. "Sandi?"

She smiled. The first rays of the morning sun seemed to break upon her face, and the darkness of her inner eyelids turned to bright crimson.

"Sandi," he repeated gently, but more firmly this time.

She smiled and sighed serenely as she stretched out in the soft, green grass.

"Sandi!" This time the voice was loud and harsh. He took her by the shoulder and gently shook her restful body.

She frowned, not comprehending why Ryan was so angry with her.

She slowly peered out from under her heavy eyelids, and tried to focus through the bright morning light. She rubbed the sand from her eyes, and as she focused, she felt a strong sense of annoyance. She did not want to leave this wonderful place.

"Hey," Paul said, "don't you have that presentation to give at nine o'clock this morning?"

Sandi Fletcher bolted upright in bed. "Shit! What time is it? Did you turn my alarm off again?"

"No way. I know better than to risk the wrath of Dr. Sandra Fletcher." Paul Hingston had been known to turn the alarm clocks off now and again. He wasn't quite as obsessive-compulsive about work as Sandi, and a good night's sleep was sometimes worth paying the price of showing up late at the lab. Besides, it was *his* lab anyway. Who would know? But this morning was too important to screw up, too important for both of them. "The power went out last night. The sun woke me up about fifteen minutes ago, and I figured I might as well let you sleep until I was done with the shower. I'm done."

Sandi glanced at the clock: 07:45. "Shit!" she shouted again. She jumped out of bed, still a bit disoriented from being torn out of her dream so abruptly. "Put up the coffee," she snapped at Paul as she ran to take a quick shower.

"You got it," he said, turning to admire her shapely, young body. He liked that she preferred to sleep in the nude.

Paul went to put some coffee in the Mr. Coffee machine, and pulled a couple of donuts out of the refrigerator. He looked around at the well-organized kitchen. He liked what Sandi had done to his life. Paul had bought the house on Maryland Avenue the year before he met Sandi. The small two-story row house was close to his biotechnology lab at Hopkins, and plenty big enough for his needs. He was young and the mortgage was a tough pill to swallow, but Hopkins had given him a pretty sweet deal to stay on after his graduation as the new biotech lab director for the nanotechnology project.

He didn't do much besides work and sleep that first year, and the place had been pretty much a mess all the time until he met Sandi. She was a grad student, and although he knew that it was frowned upon by the university, he couldn't help himself. He fell in love the fist time he laid eyes on her. Fortunately, it was her final year, and he somehow had managed to restrain himself until she graduated. He called her the night of graduation and asked her out. She wasn't too surprised. In fact the only thing that she *was* surprised about was how much she enjoyed his company. He was a different man outside the lab.

He soon talked her into staying on at Hopkins to assist him in his research. Before long, they decided that she might as well give up her apartment, since she only went there to pick up the mail anyway. Nearly all of her time was spent either at the lab or at his house, but Sunday mornings were her special time. Sandi loved to get up early and sit on the porch out front sipping her coffee until the Sunday paper came. Hardly a car passed by that time of day, and the stillness of the morning was broken only by the paperboy riding past on his bike. She decided to buy herself a housewarming gift the day she officially moved in – a new Mr. Coffee coffeemaker. She'd had it with that instant stuff Paul seemed to accept for its convenience.

"Coffee ready yet?" Sandi asked as she came into the kitchen rubbing her hair dry with a towel.

Paul smiled as he nodded toward the fresh pot of coffee on the counter.

CHAPTER THREE

Paul and Sandi hurried into the auditorium at a few minutes after nine, and a much-relieved dean of graduate studies introduced Dr. Sandra Fletcher to the eager audience. Her presentation on organic nanobionics promised to turn the field upside down, and there were as many reporters present as there were scientists.

Sandi felt the sweat bead up on her brow as she took the stage. She was accustomed to pressure, but not to crowds, and this crowd was intimidating. She shielded her eyes against the camera flashes coming from the press corps. The dean of grad studies at Hopkins had giddily leaked the story of Dr. Fletcher's success to a reporter friend of his from the Baltimore Sun. The story made the front page of the Sunday paper, giving Hopkins the publicity that the dean had hoped for, but for which Sandi was not prepared.

"Ladies and gentlemen," she started out nervously, "thank you for coming today." She wasn't sure that she really meant it.

The room darkened, and the DLP projectors lit up the screen that dropped down behind her. The Hopkins logo was emblazoned in the center of the screen.

"Imagine a world without surgery. Not a world without the technology to perform surgery, but a world without the *need* to perform surgery. Imagine the ability to analyze and repair damage to the human body without making a single incision. Imagine the ability to build new body parts, completely compatible with their hosts, and assemble them inside the body. No pain, no rejection by the host, no recuperation time."

The first image appeared on the screen, a digital rendering of a miniature computer. "You are imagining a nanobot, a programmable computer about the size of a single human cell," the image of the nanobot began to shrink and elongate, "one that can be programmed to mimic any cell function in the body, even one as complex as a neuron in the human brain. A group of these cells," the video on the screen brought to life her description as several nanobots coalesced to form a brain, "can theoretically be built into a new body part, a bionic replacement for a damaged brain in this case. I refer to this as nanobionics."

As the lights dimmed, a forty-something year old man in jeans and a well-pressed plaid shirt slipped quietly into the auditorium, taking a seat in the last row of the upper left corner of the room. He pulled his Orioles cap down slightly in front, and nestled inconspicuously down into his seat. JT Anderson had been a campus prodigy himself here a couple of decades back. His early work on nanotechnology proved to be the breakthrough that catapulted the application of silicon-based nanobots from the lab to the hospital, making the procedure clinically viable. He had anticipated the breakthrough early enough to leave Hopkins and start his own private lab. When the patents came, he owned them outright, and he became one of the wealthiest men in the country in a few short months. The Baltimore Nanotechnology Institute (BNI) quickly dwarfed Johns Hopkins in both name and wealth, a fact resented by more than a few at the university.

He smiled as Dr. Fletcher continued. "As most of you know, the groundbreaking work in nanotechnology was done right here in Baltimore about a decade ago. The first nanobots were constructed of a silicon-based material. They were essentially miniature computers programmed to perform a single task. The first clinical use, of course, was in the treatment of vascular disease. The nanobots were injected through a catheter, which was threaded up through the arteries until it approached the area of the blood clot. The bots were then injected directly into the area of the clot and were programmed to dissolve it by releasing an enzyme that interacted directly with the clotted blood."

A classic video clip of the first successful case graphically displayed the clearing of a clogged blood vessel.

"The problem with these early nanobots was that they were foreign particles within the human body. If not removed, they could cause severe host rejection reactions or they could get caught up in the kidneys, resulting in renal failure. This is where the work of Dr. Paul Hingston revolutionized nanotechnology." She smiled at Paul, who was sitting in the front row. "The brilliant work by Dr. Hingston, done right here at Johns Hopkins, led to the technique we now use to manufacture organic nanobots. Human cells are grown in culture, and then the DNA is removed. This creates a ready supply of blank cells that can be custom tailored to any task by introducing designer DNA strands created in our lab. The cells can then be programmed to turn certain DNA sequences on or off, causing them to differentiate into different types of cells designed to perform different tasks. In effect, Dr. Hingston created a programmable single-cell computer."

"Organic nanobots degrade naturally within the body much like many other organic cells do, without causing any damage to the host, and since they can be tailor-made for each host, the risk of rejection is minimal. The big problem with these organic bots is that they have a life of fifteen to thirty minutes once within the host before they start to break down. This short life severely limits their usefulness. Therefore, medical science has continued to employ inorganic bots for many clinical procedures, despite the expense and potential dangers that accompany them."

Up until now all the information Sandi presented had been a review of the last fifteen years of advances in nanobotic research. The grad students in the audience were getting antsy, but Sandi was keenly aware that the reporters in the crowd knew virtually nothing of nanotechnology, other than for the propaganda stories leaked by BNI periodically to push up the price of their stock. It was critical that they understand the basic principles of nanobotics if they were to grasp the true significance of her work, and so she had led them gingerly up this path with a description that was as basic as she could muster up.

Sandi Fletcher took a deep breath. "And now, this is what I think you've all been waiting for." A pair of video clips began to play side by side on the screen behind her. "On the left is a clip of a clot-busting organic nanobot treatment, and on the right a clip of a similar procedure using the new type II organic bots. The video clips displayed the bots being injected via an angiocatheter just upstream from an arterial clot. Both videos showed time-accelerated views of the clots dissolving and restoring blood flow through the previously blocked artery. As the video clips proceeded, the vessel on the left remained unchanged, with the clot dissolved, but the blood flow still blocked by additional clots further along the artery, while the video on the right showed blood flow through the artery continuing to be restored as the additional clots were sequentially dissolved by the nanobots.

"As you can see, the new type II bots continue working long after the original type I bots have died. We have synthesized a new membrane stabilizer that extends the life of these type II bots for days within the host body, and we are working on new techniques that could extend them for years. This longer life not only allows them to function longer, but because we have so much more time to work with, they can be injected through a peripheral vein in the arm, and programmed to become active when they reach their target site. The procedure is safer, quicker, cheaper, less painful and more effective. It will eliminate the need for inorganic bots as they are used today."

The academicians in the crowd nodded in admiration, while the press corps feverishly took notes and photos.

"With these long-life nanobots, we now hope to create bots that can perform many other tasks within the human body, tasks that take longer than simple clot-busting. These new bots could theoretically be programmed to repair any damaged organ in the body without ever opening up the patient. The implications are staggering. This will be the next revolution in medical care."

JT Anderson listened intently to Dr. Fletcher's presentation. As he watched her speak, the passion in her voice reminded him of himself at the same stage in his career. The thirst for knowledge had been unquenchable in those days, but had long ago been overshadowed by the thirst for power. He had a knack for seeing things in a different way than most people when it came to science, and the aptitude to see those things long before anyone else. He was here to see if there was more to nanobionics than even Dr. Fletcher herself realized, and he was not disappointed.

Dr. Fletcher's animated presentation explained the basics of nanotechnology so clearly that even most of the reporters in the hall could understand. As the lights brightened and the screen retracted, she received a standing ovation from Paul, who knew that she had brought their lab work into the public eye in a positive light, the kind of enlightenment that was needed for a scientist to gain public acceptance. The undercurrents created by rumors about the use of nanotechnology to somehow transform humans into machines and dehumanize our species threatened the future of the field, but Paul was sure that her presentation today had derailed much of the concern. He joined her on the stage for the photos and interviews that followed. JT Anderson slipped out the back and waited in his late model Ford for the parking lot to empty out.

As the last of the crowd left, Paul took Sandi in his arms and held her tight. "What a rush, seeing you up there like that. You were awesome."

Sandi smiled. It wasn't hard to please Paul, at least not for her, but she too knew that the presentation had gone well. She was as pleased as she was relieved that it was over.

"Let's go celebrate. How about a couple of beers and a bucket of mussels down at Bertha's?"

She frowned. "How about a picnic in the back yard? You pop down to Lexington Market while I go home and take a nap."

"Deal."

He took her hand, and they headed toward the door at the back of the auditorium. The door opened just as Paul was reaching for the handle. The man in the Orioles cap smiled and held out his hand. It startled

Paul and Sandi for a second, but up close his outfit wasn't much of a disguise.

"Hi. I'm ..."

"JT Anderson," Paul finished the sentence, as much with admiration as disdain. Although Anderson's ethics were not held in very high regard at the university, Paul envied his success. It was tough getting by on an academician's salary in a big city, and he always harbored a bit of resentment at the fact that the fruits of his labors would belong to the university no mater how great his successes.

"Right," said Anderson, taking off the hat. "Not much of a disguise, huh?"

Sandi laughed. "All you could afford?"

He just shook his head and smiled. He couldn't help but notice that Paul was still holding her hand. "I see that I'm interrupting. Let me get right to the point. Would you like to sit for a moment?" He motioned to the back row of seats in the auditorium.

"Thanks," Sandi said, shaking her head in the negative, "but I'm too pumped. I've never talked in front of that many people before, and now...well, it's not every day that I get to meet the richest man in the world."

"Eighth richest," he corrected. "All right then, I'll be brief. I want you to come to work for BNI."

Sandi started to decline his offer, still altruistic in her academic endeavors, but Anderson waved her off. "Both of you," he added motioning to Paul as well. "You'll have your own lab of course, and whatever you need. I'll give you each a million a year for starters, as well as stock options. You'll have complete freedom to pursue your nanobionics research without the constraints of academic regulation or budget crunches. I've been there and I know what it's like."

He could still see the doubt in her eyes as she looked him over. "Look, I know what people here say about me, but with rare exception it's always out of jealousy. I am first and foremost a scientist. I did what I did for scientific freedom as much as I did for money. If I had to work within the constraints of the university system, thousands more would have suffered before nanobot therapy was available for clinical use. BNI is a scientist's dream."

Sandi was speechless. It was a tempting offer, but she was just making a name for herself in academics. He stood for everything that she was against in science. She didn't want to privatize her work; she was doing it for the public good, not for the highest bidder. "Thanks, Dr. Anderson," she said looking him straight in the eye, "but no thanks."

Paul was flabbergasted. He'd been struggling to make ends meet for years. Sure, the work at Hopkins was exciting and he was proud to be a part of such a prestigious institution, but this was J.T Anderson, for God's sake. An opportunity like this usually comes around never in a lifetime for most people, once in a lifetime for the luckiest amongst us, and it was about to walk out that door. He grabbed her arm. "Sandi!" He turned toward Anderson. "Could you excuse us for a moment?"

Anderson nodded, and Paul pulled Sandi outside the door to talk in private.

"Look, Sandi, I know how you feel about BNI, but think about this, would ya?"

"What's there to think about, Paul? We're on top of the food chain now. There's no place better than Hopkins. We've got all the support we need right here. That's how we got to this point in the first place. Do you really want to spend your time answering to a board of directors and stock holders?"

"All the support we need? Are you blind? I know that you're still pretty naïve when it comes to the business side of biotech, but look around you. We get by with generation-old equipment that's barely adequate to run our experiments, and it's a fight to get the grant money even for that. Anderson is giving us the opportunity to work with state of the art stuff."

"Yeah, but Paul..."

"Listen, I'm just asking you to think about it, that's all. If we say no now, Anderson walks out that door and with him goes a once in a lifetime opportunity. Just give it a day. Sleep on, OK? For me...for us."

"Well..." she hesitated.

"Thanks. It's the right decision, you'll see." Paul turned back toward the door.

"Hey," Sandi grabbed his arm. "I said I'd *think* about it."

Paul nodded and smiled at her. They walked back in to the auditorium.

JT Anderson saw the hesitation in Sandi's eyes. "I know it's a big decision. Why don't you sleep on it? Here's my card."

He handed them a business card and tipped the bill of his baseball cap ever so slightly. "Great work, Doc."

Sandi couldn't help the smile that crept across her tense lips. JT Anderson could be very charming. She found herself liking him in spite of her desire not to. She nodded and walked out the door.

"Thanks, JT," Paul said reaching out to shake Anderson's hand. "You'll be hearing from us real soon." He hesitated briefly, and then hurried off to catch up with Sandi.

Paul could hardly contain his excitement. He loved working at Hopkins, and had never really thought about doing anything else, but ever since JT Anderson approached them his mind had been racing at the possibilities. He led Sandi out of the red brick building holding her briefcase in his right hand and her hand in his left. The fragrance of summer was in the air. School had been out for about a week, and the campus was quiet. Paul loved the solitude that followed the hectic academic year. The sun peeked through the tall trees that lined the walkway to the faculty parking lot behind the auditorium.

He was trying desperately to think of a way to sway Sandi's mind, but couldn't find the words. The silence between them seemed to be building a barrier that was getting thicker by the minute, and he decided to start on neutral ground.

"Great presentation, Sandi. You did a hell of a job in there today. I can't wait to see the headlines in the Sun tomorrow."

Sandi walked in silence. She knew Paul too well. He was not much for small talk, and this was small talk. She realized what he was doing. She couldn't believe that he was seriously considering selling out to private industry.

"So what should I pick up at the market? Got a craving for anything special?"

"Some pasta salad would be nice. And if you can scrounge it up, I'd love some cider." It was tough to come by apple cider this time of year.

They hardly said a word on the short drive home. Paul dropped her off and watched as she ascended the four red brick steps leading up to the small wood porch in front of their house. Once she was inside, he headed down to Lexington Market to pick up lunch. It wasn't going to be the relaxing afternoon he had hoped for, but he knew that if he could only find the right words there would be more to celebrate than either of them had imagined when they woke up to start this day.

By the time he pulled into the small one-car garage behind their row house, Sandi had set the picnic table that rested in the filtered shade of the dogwood trees out back. He put the bags down and gave her a kiss.

"Looks good," she said, obviously still preoccupied.

He laid out the food and poured two glasses of apple cider. They sat down next to each other, and Paul took her hand. He had been struggling to find the words that would help her to see things his way, but he didn't know where to start.

Sandi looked down at her hand, her fingers intertwined with his. "I thought I knew you better than this." She fought to hold back the tears.

Paul couldn't believe the resolve in her voice. They'd been living together for nearly a year now and had dated twice that long. He was sure that they had the perfect synergy, that she understood what made him tick. He knew that she was not a big fan of private sector research, but he couldn't believe that she was so close-minded about this. He wanted to share his discoveries with the world every bit as much as she did, but what was wrong with making a buck off of it? What was so wrong with being able to live the good life?"

He tried to convince her while they ate, to make her feel the way he did about this. "I want more than this, Sandi. I want more than this for us."

"More?" She was incredulous. "You're a professor at Johns Hopkins, for God's sake. You run the most prestigious lab at the university and you're only thirty-one years old. It doesn't get any better than this. I've got everything I want right here."

"Look around you, Sandi. Look at this place."

"I have looked. It's perfect. This has been the happiest year of my life."

"No," he said, "it's not perfect. *We're* perfect." He motioned to the house. "Sure this place has a lot of character, and it's been great for what it is, but open your eyes. There's a whole world out there. I want more. It's not just for me, but for us, for the family that I want us to have."

Sandi looked up at him, her face wet with tears. "I thought we were perfect too ... but now ..." her voice trailed off.

Paul couldn't believe what he was hearing. She was willing to write off their entire relationship, a chance to build a life together that most people only dream of. Sandi came from a wealthy family, and he knew that she took great pride in having made a life for herself that was not based on money, but he didn't realize how strongly she felt about this. He had come from a very different background. This was one of the things that had attracted her to him in the first place, his simple roots. He'd come from a large family in West Virginia. It was a tight-knit family, but one that never had much in the way of material wealth. His father had raised them on a coal-miner's salary. Paul was the most financially successful of his siblings, and was thankful for what he had. He had been satisfied, no...happy, with his life, but now he had an opportunity for even more.

"Look. Sandi, I never talked about this because it never occurred to me that we might get a chance like this. I'm a realist, and I never wish for something that's not within my grasp. But this is within our grasp. We've got the chance to lead the kind of life I never dreamed was possible. It's a chance for me to give my kids, the kids I want to have with you, the things that I had never had."

"Is that what this is about?" Sandi was angry. "The money?" Her lips were quivering. "I could understand the lure of having BNI help to propel your research to the next level, but what do you need more money for? What don't you have that we need to be happy? I *did* have those things when I was a kid, and I watched my dad struggle to get those things. I watched him suffer as those things slipped away from him, and I watched the pain in his eyes when my mother blamed him for losing those things. I *don't* want those things, not for me or my children." She pulled away.

Now Paul was getting angry too. He could feel it welling up inside of him. He rarely got angry, but when he did, his anger took control of him. He knew that what he was about to say was the wrong thing, but he could not stop himself. "Poor little rich girl.   The only reason that the money's not important to you is that you've always had it. You can't stand the thought of a little prosperity, can you? You enjoy partaking in 'the poor life', huh? Well let me tell you about the poor life." He saw the look of pain on Sandi's face. He realized that he had gone too far.

Neither of them said another word as they cleared the table. The day had not gone the way that either of them had planned. As they climbed the back steps toward the kitchen, Sandi swayed and started to fall. Paul dropped the dishes and grabbed her, lowering her gently to the ground. She was woozy, but still conscious.

"Hey, you O.K.?"

"Yeah," she mumbled. "I just need a little sugar. I guess I didn't eat enough today." She had taken her usual daily insulin injection the night before, but in all the excitement of the day, she had eaten little for breakfast and almost nothing for lunch.

Paul sat next to her on the steps, holding her steady.

"I've got it," she said pulling away. "Just get me a packet of sugar, would you?"

"Sure." Paul got up slowly, making sure that Sandi could steady herself O.K., and then ran inside to grab a sugar packet.

A few minutes after getting her blood sugar up, Sandi felt much better, but the stress of the day had gotten the best of her. She went up to bed while Paul finished cleaning up.

—

That was the last meal they would have together. After a meek attempt at changing Sandi's mind once more at breakfast the next morning, Paul called JT Anderson to set up a meeting. Anderson had anticipated the call and met Paul for lunch that day. By the time that Paul had returned home, Sandi was gone along with most of her things. Mr. Coffee sat on the counter as a dour reminder to Paul of what he had given up.

Anderson had really wanted to hire Sandi, but he was satisfied to settle for Paul, who joined BNI. Sandi remained at Hopkins as interim lab director, eventually taking over the official directorship three years later in, 2048.

CHAPTER FOUR

Five years later —
Washington D.C., April 21, 2050

"I can't stand this," Sandi said to Sam as she waited to testify before the Senate Subcommittee on Nanotechnology. "I'm a scientist, for God's sake, not an administrator. Why don't the suits take care of this stuff?"

Dr. Sam Collier had been working with Sandi on the nanobot project for almost two years now. He was a big fan of her work, and he had approached her during the last year of his neurology residency about developing neuronanobots specifically engineered to treat the devastating effects of stroke or traumatic brain injury. He was sure that the pathophysiology of these neurological conditions lent themselves perfectly to nanobotic therapy, and he managed to convince Sandi of it. He joined her team shortly thereafter. The more Sandi investigated, the more she became convinced that this would be the perfect prototype for organic nanobots in the treatment of human illness. For the past two years, all of her time and energy had been focused on the neuronanobot project. They had made great strides, but funding was running low, and they desperately needed this grant that hinged on the approval of the Senate subcommittee. The project was not without controversy. Anything that could influence the workings of the human brain was rich fodder for social disputation.

Sandi Fletcher was waiting nervously on a bench outside the committee room. She had asked Sam to come along for emotional support. He had a knack for taking life's twists and turns in stride, and Sandi was hoping that some of that calm demeanor would rub off on her.

Sam could sense the tension. "Relax, Sandi. It's not like you haven't done this before. Remember what you told me about the first meeting a couple of years back? 'Like taking candy from a baby,' you said."

Sandi forced a smile. "I was only trying to impress you. You were new back then, and I wanted you."

Sam looked up with a grin.

"Oh, no no no," Sandi said, "not like that. I didn't *want* you, I wanted you. You know, for the lab."

Sam looked disappointed. Sandi thought it was cute, but tried hard not to laugh. "Not that you aren't an attractive guy, Sam, but I wanted you for your brains." This time she did laugh. "That still doesn't sound right, does it?" It was a nervous laugh. "Not wanted...needed, yeah, I needed you for your brains. I needed you to take neuronanobotics to the next level. If you'd gone into private practice, I never would have been able to make this work." Sandi had no problem talking with Sam about science, but romance was another story. She could feel a blush washing up over her face.

Sam smiled. "It's OK, Sandi. I know what you mean."

"Thanks." She was relieved.

It had taken a long time for Sandi to get over Paul. In fact, she wasn't really sure that she ever had. She was determined to keep romance as far from the lab as possible. A few months after she had left Paul, her friend Janice took her down to a club near the harbor to listen to a folk guitar player named Guy Andrews. Janice had talked her into going on the pretense of having a girls' night out, but it turned out that Guy was Janice's cousin, and she figured that he was just what Sandi needed to forget about Paul. Much to Sandi's surprise, Janice was right. Guy was no rocket scientist, but he was a fairly bright guy who had just decided that music was more fun than a desk job, and much to his parents' dismay, had dropped out of college after his third year to pursue his music career. It hadn't taken him very far. At first, that didn't really matter to him; he didn't need much. But as his friends moved into their careers, they gradually distanced themselves from him. He was starting to doubt his career choice when he met Sandi, but she took his mind off all that, at least for a while. They had been living together for about a year now. Sandi wasn't quite sure why, but she felt good when she was with him.

From the moment they met, Sandi was convinced that they were soul mates. He seemed to always know what she wanted, what she *needed.* When he took her out to dinner, he managed to find her favorite restaurants without ever asking her so much as what kind of foods she liked. He instinctively knew her favorite drink, her favorite flowers, her favorite color. It was uncanny. As she discovered much sooner than she would have ever imagined, he even knew her favorite erogenous zones.

Sometimes he would seem so distant that she found herself wondering just what it was that she saw in him, and then he would do something subtle, but so special that all doubts were erased. When she had a great day at the lab, he wanted to hear all about it, even though she was pretty sure he didn't understand too much of what she had to say. And when things weren't going well, he always knew exactly what to say. He seemed to know her almost as well as Paul had, but what had taken Paul years of experience seemed to come naturally to Guy. It was as if he had a guidebook to her soul. He was perfect, except ... she could never quite put her finger on it; maybe it was just that he was not Paul.

—

A man in a pinstripe suit emerged from the door of the committee room. "They're ready for you, Dr. Fletcher."

Sandi stood, smoothed her suit and looked to Sam for approval. He nodded ever so slightly and smiled, giving her the thumbs up. Sandi turned and hurried to follow the man into the committee room. It was a small but formally furnished chamber, with a slightly elevated stage at one end on which the committee members sat behind a semicircular mahogany desk. Senator Stanton Cole, the chairman of the committee, sat in the center with a small podium on the desk in front of him. To his right, sat the vice-chairman, Senator Russell Stetson. Each of the seven senators had a microphone in front of them, which seemed an absurdity to Sandi given the small size of the room. *Whatever makes them feel powerful,* she thought with disdain, trying not to feel intimidated.

Senator Cole motioned her to a chair behind the front row table, which also supported a microphone. She took her seat and pushed the microphone aside.

"If you will, Dr. Fletcher," Senator Stetson said, pointing at the microphone. "I realize that it seems a bit silly in such close quarters, but all committee hearings are recorded. I'm sure you understand."

Sandi nodded sheepishly.

"We've read your brief, Doctor, but I for one didn't follow it too well. We've asked you here in the hope that you can translate some of this technojargon for us so we can make an intelligent recommendation to the full senate regarding your request.

"Of course, Senator." She paused and took a deep breath. "As you know, nanobots have already been approved for some uses in medical care, but we've barely scratched the surface of their potential. Four years ago, my lab at Hopkins embarked on a project to develop a nanobot treatment to cure diseases of the central nervous system such as stroke or brain injury. The idea is to minimize the damage that occurs immediately after the injury, and then to replace the damaged nerve cells, known as neurons, with specialized artificial cells called neuronanobots. What I proposed was a two-step process. The first step is to inject Phase One nanobots into the body, which are programmed to go to the area of damage and clean it up. They get rid of blood and chemicals that accumulate when nerve cells are injured. The second step is to inject nanobots that will go to the area of damage and turn into neurons, nerve cells that can replace the ones lost in the initial injury."

Sandi paused to peruse the faces of the senators. She was relieved to see that they were all awake and there were only one or two blank stares. Although the information she was presenting was quite technical, the younger senators in this group had grown up with at least some robotic and nanobotic theory ingrained into them in school. Even the older senators, perhaps *especially* the older senators, knew about nanobots from personal experience, as these tiny robots were now the primary treatment for cleaning out clogged arteries in the heart or other areas of the body. She felt it was safe to continue at this technical level without too much risk of losing anyone in this room.

"We developed the Phase One neuronanobots fairly quickly. Their function was relatively basic, mechanical in some ways. The hardest part was getting them to go to the right place in the body once we injected them. We solved this problem by having them maintain their motility until they find an area with a large concentration of certain chemicals that we know occur when brain tissue is injured. Once they arrive in this area, they stop moving and they activate themselves to clean up the surrounding chemicals.

"Our emphasis over the past two years has been in the development of Phase Two bots. We inject these bots into a vein in the arm and they find their way into the brain within a matter of hours. When they come near the Phase One bots, they synapse with...that is, they attach themselves to... these Phase One bots. This way they are right where we want them — in the area where the injured brain cells used to be. The really tricky part comes next. In order to get these bots to take over the job of the nerve cells that have died, we had to figure out how to sequence their DNA so they would develop into nerve cells after they attached to the Phase One bots. We recently found the answer to our dilemma; we now know how to get the Phase Two bots to turn into nerve cells at the site of injury, *and* how to get them to attach to other healthy nerve cells in the area. Once they do this, they can completely restore the function of the damaged brain.

Sandi looked up at the peanut gallery again. Their eyes were all glued to her ... now she had them.

"We've done it in monkeys. We've taken monkeys that have suffered traumatic brain injuries and restored them to normal function in less than three weeks. We have shortened the recovery time from traumatic brain injury from years to days, and improved the completeness of the recovery one hundred percent ... no residual weakness, no cognitive problems, no seizures."

Sandi paused for dramatic effect. "The only thing that remains, gentlemen," she looked each of them in the eye with a growing confidence, "is to do this for people. I need your authorization for human trials. If I can get that, stroke and traumatic brain injury will be as curable as a cataract. I've done my part, senators. It's up to you now."

A few minutes later Sandi came out of the room drained of energy and slumped down on the bench next to Sam. As she dropped her head down into her hands, her thick brown hair fell around her face.

"Man!" Sam gasped. "I can't believe it. What happened in there? Why didn't they go for it? It seems like a no-brainer. How could they *not* green light us on this one?"

Sandi slumped back against the wall and ran her hands through her hair, pulling it back behind her neck. "Relax, Doc," she said, "I was great." All of the tension had melted from her face.

Sam was beet red. "Jeez, Sandi! How could you do that to me?"

She giggled. "Let's get some coffee and celebrate."

Baltimore, Maryland. April 24, 2050

Poe Towers stretched high above the Baltimore skyline overlooking the city's famous downtown harbor area. It was the most prestigious residence in the downtown area with a spectacular view of Harbor Place, Oriole Park at Camden Yards and Baltimore Ravens Stadium. It was exactly the kind of place Paul Hingston had dreamed of when JT Anderson approached him on that day nearly five years ago, and his lucrative contract at BNI made it all possible,

On a beautiful Sunday morning like this, Paul loved to get up late, put up a pot of coffee and read the paper out on the terrace of his penthouse apartment suite. Every other day of the week he would catch the morning news on the Internet monitor at his kitchen table, but on Sunday he liked to be old fashioned. He loved to rustle the newspaper and peruse the week's top stories with an occasional glance over at his mug to dip a donut in the steaming coffee. The sports section was always first; he prided himself in knowing the stats of all the O's players, and he looked forward to the start of the baseball season each spring. After a slow march through his favorite comics, he would eventually meander over to the front section. Today was one of those days.

Paul neatly folded the sports and comics and walked in to pour a second cup of coffee. He then returned to the porch and took a deep breath of the fresh springtime air as he admired the view. He could hardly believe that he was really living this life. It was times like this that he could forget, ever so briefly, just how lonely he really had been since he let Sandi slip out of his life; no one else before her, or since, had ever felt so right. He nestled into a lounge chair, placed his mug on a small chair-side table and began to read the news. He wearily flipped through as he glanced at the happenings of the world around him; if it wasn't in the US, he was not particularly interested. He took a long, slow sip, and turned to page eighteen. At the top of the page was the title *For Your Health.* He skimmed the latest human-interest stories. One was about how a child from a poor South American country was flown up to the University of Maryland Hospital to repair a horrible birth defect. There was the usual pre-summer article about the importance of wearing sunscreen as the season approached when everyone would be spending more of their leisure time outside under the ozone-starved, sun-drenched atmosphere. His eyes scanned down to the next blurb: 'Congress Authorizes Human Trial of Artificial Brain Cells.'

Paul's gaze froze on the headline for a moment, and then he began to read the article describing the new neuronanobots developed by Dr. Sandra Fletcher at Johns Hopkins.

"Shit!" He crumpled the paper and slammed it down on the coffee table. He jumped up, looking at the paper unfolding itself and falling to the floor. "Shit!" he yelled again, a bit louder this time. He was so angry that he couldn't think of anything else to say. He paced quickly back and forth along the length of the terrace, and then stormed inside.

"Computer," he sniped toward the monitor on his kitchen table, "phone Dr. Sandra Fletcher, home address."

"Dialing," the synthesized voice of the computer responded dutifully.

After a brief pause, the phone rang three times before Sandi picked up. "Hello?"

"How in the hell did you pull it off, Sandi?" Sandi had just come back from her morning jog, and rushed in to answer the phone that she heard ringing from the doorway. "Paul? Is that you, Paul?" she asked, wiping the moisture from her forehead with the hand towel that was slung around her shoulders. She hadn't heard from Paul in nearly two years. "You saw the article, huh? Just call to congratulate me?"

"Congratulate you?" he said angrily. "What in the hell do you think you're doing? Who did the dirty work for you, Sandi, huh? Who swiped the data from my lab?"

Sandi couldn't believe what she was hearing. "Is that what you're calling for, to accuse me of stealing your work? You've got a hell of a nerve, Paul Hingston. What audacity. So you think you are the only one capable of programming bots? I didn't even know you were working on neuronanobots."

"Didn't know I ...bullshit! Do you think I'm an idiot?"

"I guess so. I can't believe that you really think I would do such a thing. This was *my* work Paul. It was mine and I'm damned proud of it. If you were too slow to get there first, that's your problem. Heck, if you really were working on the same thing and I beat you to the punch, then I'm even more proud of it."

"How did you do it, Sandi? Who's the mole in my lab?"

"I think you've said enough, Paul." Sandi hung up the phone.

"Sandi? Sandi! Don't you hang up on me, God damn it."

"Dr. Fletcher is no longer on the line," the computer informed him.

"No shit, Sherlock. Disconnect."

"Phone line disconnected."

Paul stormed into his bedroom to get dressed. He felt terrible. It had been two years since he had seen Sandi, and he missed her fiercely. He had often searched for a way to try to get her back. This was not the conversation he had dreamed of.   He took off his robe and threw it angrily in the direction of the hamper. "Paul, you idiot." He wasn't sure which he was angrier about, the fact that Sandi had beaten him to the finish line by stealing his work, or the fact that he had just vastly increased the distance between them.

After stewing about his bad fortune for a while, Paul decided that he needed to get out of the apartment.   *Why waste such a beautiful day?* he tried to convince himself. The Orioles were set to open their first season series against the Yankees at Camden Yards this afternoon; it seemed the perfect diversion. The day passed slowly. He fought his way through the sellout crowd at the ballpark to get to his seat. He tried to get a hold of his friend Sean so he'd have some company, but hadn't had any luck. He didn't mind too much. He often went to the park by himself; he found the diversion of the game to be a great escape from his problems, work or personal. The game lived up to its promise, a five to four victory by the home team, capped by a two-out grand slam by Newt Boylston in the bottom of the ninth to snatch victory from the jaws of defeat.

It worked for a little while. Paul got caught up in the excitement of the game, sharing the joy of victory with the game-day friends around him in the lower box seats behind home plate. But the magic gradually faded as he walked away from the ballpark; by the time he got home it was entirely gone. He picked up the paper and read the article about the Hopkins nanobot program again. He still couldn't believe it. Over the past year, he had spent nearly every waking hour developing a programming protocol for neuronanobots. He knew Sandi had been working with neuronanobots; in fact, the work she had published on the Phase One bots created the breakthrough that he needed to make his Phase Two bots useful. Until she came up with a way to get the bots to converge at the damaged area of the brain, he had not been sure how he would get his nanobots, designed to transform themselves into new brain cells, to the area of damage in the brain. He had even sent her an e-mail congratulating her when she published the research, but he had no idea that she was working on the same project he was, the development of nanobots that could be transformed into brain cells. She had to have stolen his work in some way; the odds of her coming up with the same idea at the same time were miniscule. Had she really changed that much? He couldn't believe she would deny the fact that it was his work, much less that she would steal it from him in the first place. It had to be someone else in the lab, someone who was doing it without her knowledge. Paul was determined to figure out who that someone was, and he had a pretty good idea.

"Dr. Sam Collier," he muttered to himself, as he looked at the article again. He knew that Sandi had some new hotshot neurologist working on the project with her. The article mentioned that Dr. Collier had been instrumental in developing the new clinical protocol to be used in the human trial for the neuronanobots. "Got to be that little weasel."

Paul tossed and turned that night. After about an hour, he decided there was really no point in trying to sleep. He dressed and headed for his lab at BNI. Even for Paul, coming into the office Monday morning at two AM was a bit unusual. The traffic coming out of Baltimore was light, as expected. Paul made good time and pulled into the parking lot. He pressed his thumb against the elevator button, which confirmed his thumbprint and opened the door. As the elevator opened on the twelfth floor, Paul was surprised to see the light on in his office. He heard the sound of a keyboard typing away. It took him a moment to realize what the sound was. It was rare to use a keyboard these days; voice access was always used while working on a computer unless there was a need to be discreet. He was curious to see who was in his office and what it was they were trying to hide.

He walked cautiously over to the door, stepping softly to mute the sound of his footsteps, and peered around the doorframe into the room. Over the top of the chair, he saw a mop of strawberry colored hair. "Sean!" he yelped, somewhat relieved to see a familiar figure. Even from this angle, that hair was unmistakable.

Sean jumped as he spun the chair, and smacked his hand against the edge of the desk. "Argh!" He looked up at Paul, and then down at his throbbing hand. "Shit," he said, shaking his hand to take the sting out. "What are you doing here, man?"

"I was about to ask you the same thing."

"My computer went on the fritz," Sean said as he spun back and closed the program he was working on. "Never thought you'd be needing yours at this time of the night." He pulled an optical disk out of the drive. "There, that should do it. All yours now, boss." Sean got up and brushed quickly past Paul on his way out the door.

"Thanks," Paul muttered as he watched his associate move quickly in the darkness toward the exit.

"Hey, Sean," he called after him. In the distraction of the moment, he'd forgotten ever so briefly about what had brought him to the office at this late hour. He wanted to talk to Sean about the article, about Sandi, but it was too late. Sean was in the elevator and on the way out. He shook his head. "What in the hell was that all about?" he said to himself, now alone in his office in the middle of the night. He had never known Sean to work nights, and Paul had spent plenty of nights in this lab. It was also very unlike Sean to be so abrupt. He and Paul always seemed to have a special connection, like two men who had been friends much longer than these two had actually known each other. Something just didn't feel right about this.

"Oh well." He shrugged and plopped down on the sofa in his office. "This day's just getting a little too weird. Now I'm even talking to myself," he smirked. He wasn't sure exactly why he had come to the office tonight, he just knew that he couldn't relax at home, but now fatigue was overtaking him. He decided to grab some sleep, and talk to JT first thing in the morning.

JT Anderson arrived at his usual time, seven AM. It wasn't so much that he was a workaholic; at least he didn't think so. It was just that there was no place that he enjoyed being at more than BNI. He dropped his briefcase on his desk, and took the elevator down to the nanotech floor.

"How's it going, Sean?" he said as he entered the lab. "Sean?" he called, as he looked around the room.

Paul was awakened by JT's voice. He rolled off the couch and ambled over to the door. JT was about ten feet away, facing the other direction.

"Mornin', JT," he muttered as he stood in the doorway scratching his head.

JT spun around, eyes wide open. "Paul! I ... uh... didn't think you got in so early on Mondays." He saw the disheveled clothes. "You sleep here last night?"

"Yeah ... couldn't sleep too well after I saw the Sunday paper. I figured I might as well come in and catch up on some things, since I couldn't get work out of my head anyhow."

"Have you seen Sean?"

"Yeah. He was here last night. Acting really strange, too. Almost like I was interrupting something when I came in."

JT chuckled. "Must be your imagination."

"Yeah, maybe. Why did you expect to see him here so early, anyway? You know Sean, he's usually home Monday mornings recovering from the weekend."

"I thought I saw his car in the lot when I drove up. I figured he must be in here, you know?"

"Well," Paul motioned around the room, "doesn't appear to be."

"Nope," JT agreed. "Sure doesn't." He turned and opened the door, then glanced back over his shoulder. "You might want to get washed up, Paul. You look like hell."

Paul nodded. He felt like hell, too.

JT shook his head and laughed. "You work too hard, man."

JT headed toward the elevator and Paul followed briefly, catching the office door just before it closed.

"So," he called out.

JT stopped and turned to Paul. "Yeah?"

"Any idea what he was doing here last night?"

"Sean? Nope. Guess you'll just have to ask him when he gets in."

"I thought you said his car was already in the lot?"

JT shrugged. "I must have been mistaken. See you later, Paul."

"Right."

Paul just stood there, leaning against the door jamb. *This just ain't gonna be a normal week.*

--

JT had been out fishing on Sunday, and hadn't caught up on the news. In all of the distraction, he hadn't really grasped the meaning of Paul's conversation that morning until he was safely behind his desk.

"Marlene," he said. He hated using the generic "computer on" command, and so had reprogrammed his computer to respond to "Marlene" instead. He liked to joke that Marlene was the only woman who would ever listen to him.

"Yes, JT," she responded.

"Get Sean Lightbourne on the horn for me, would you?"

"Right away, sir."

"And pull up a list of headlines from yesterday's Sunpapers."

"Accessing ... displaying list now." A listing of the headlines from all of the Sunday Sun's articles appeared on his screen. He was starting to scan through them when Sean came on the phone.

"Mornin', JT." His grinning face came up in a window on the lower left of JT's screen, a bit pixelated from the low-resolution cell phone camera he was using.

"What the hell happened last night?"

The grin faded. "Is this line secure?"

JT frowned. "Just get in here pronto. I want to know what went down."

"Don't sweat it boss. We're cool."

"I'm not so sure," he said thinking about Paul's demeanor that morning. "I think..."

"I said we're cool," Sean interrupted. "I'm pulling into the lot now. Meet you in ten."

The line went dead.

JT continued scanning the list of headlines. "Ahh," he muttered with a slight nod of his head. "Here it is: 'Congress Authorizes Human Trial of Artificial Brain Cells.'"

"Marlene, get me the text of the "Congress Authorizes Human Trial of Artificial Brain Cells" article, would ya?"

"Displaying now."

The article came up on the screen, and Paul scanned it quickly. *Took her long enough,* he thought to himself.

"Marlene, give me a hardcopy of this, and set up a lunch meeting for me with Dr. Hingston, noon today."

"Yes, sir."

Ten minutes later, Sean Lightbourne arrived. Much of JT's scheduling and phone work could be handled quite adequately by Marlene, but Lois, his flesh and blood secretary, didn't usually arrive until nine. Sean walked through he outer office unannounced and knocked on the partially opened door.

JT looked up. Sean hadn't waited for an invitation, and was already taking a seat across the desk from him.

"Marlene, close the door."

"Yes, sir." The door slowly closed, and the two men were alone in JT's office.

When Paul Hingston received the call inviting him to lunch with JT Anderson, he was sure that he was getting fired.

He couldn't get his mind off of Sandi. He was still convinced that she must have found a way to steal his research. *Two years of work down the tubes. I can't believe she stabbed me in the back like that.* He was resigned to losing his job, and was planning on spending all of his new-found free time investigating Sandi's partner-in-crime, Dr. Sam Collier. He was sure that Collier was somehow hacking into his computer and stealing his work. The thought had briefly crossed his mind that Sean Lightbourne might be the culprit. After all, Sean was acting awfully suspicious when Paul walked in on him at the office last night, but he knew Sean too well. Sean was the ultimate company man. He figured that JT had seen the article in the Sunday Sun, and had instructed Sean to come in and make optical back-ups of all of the research files before he fired Paul. It all made sense.

No hard feelings, buddy. I'd have done the same thing. He still liked Sean; he couldn't help but like the guy. Sean was the best company Paul had known since Sandi left him. He had the kind of persona that inspired instant trust.

Paul washed up and put on some fresh clothes. *Might as well go out in style.* He pushed the button for the penthouse floor, and the elevator whisked him up toward JT's office. The secretary greeted him affably and pointed him toward the boardroom. Paul looked at the pitying grin on her face. *God, even she knows.*

He entered the boardroom to the smell of fresh Philly cheesesteak subs. The room was empty except for two places set at the massive mahogany table, each with a cheesesteak sandwich and some fries; a six-pack of Coke sat on the table between the plates.

JT walked up behind him and gave him a slap on the shoulder. "Why so grim?"

"Is this my last supper before the firing squad?"

JT laughed. "Firing squad? Is that what you think? This is a celebration, man."

Paul was confused. Maybe JT hadn't seen the article after all. He thought briefly about playing along, pretending that Sandi hadn't really rendered all of his work at BNI useless in one swift blow, but then he thought the better of it. JT would know sooner or later, so why postpone the inevitable?

"Didn't you see the article? Hopkins just landed authorizations for the Phase Two neuronanobot research. My work is useless now. Somehow, they must have gotten access to my files. I was just weeks away from requesting Phase Two trial authorization myself. They had to be stealing my work. It's too much of a coincidence that they were working on the exact same thing at the exact same time and on the exact same schedule. Things like that don't happen by accident."

"Have a seat, Paul." JT motioned him to one of the place settings. "Don't you get it, man? Even if they did steal it, who cares? It's perfect. In fact, the more closely their nanobots resemble yours, the better."

Paul still hadn't moved. Now he was thoroughly confused.

"Look, Paul, human trials cost a fortune to run. If Hopkins and Uncle Sam want to pay for the trials, all the better. What counts is that we beat them to the patent office. Let them do all of the legwork, prove that the neuronanobots work safely in human subjects. If they do that while we're getting patents on the fabrication process for the bots, then we're at the end of the rainbow when the trials are over and the FDA approves the bots. The pot of gold is ours."

Paul was still standing there speechless, but suddenly he was feeling a little better about himself. He hadn't completely shaken the academic mentality; he craved the notoriety of being credited with the breakthrough research, but after all, the financial reward was what he had come to BNI for, and he had rarely regretted that decision. It was nice to have money.

Once again, JT motioned to him to sit down. "I'm getting hungry and those subs are getting cold."

Paul sat down at the table. "Now I know why you're the boss," he smiled. It was the best tasting cheesesteak he had ever had.

"I guess we'll have to send Dr. Fletcher a thank-you note," JT joked as he dipped a fry in some ketchup.

"Oh, she'd *really* appreciate that, coming from you and all." Paul hesitated a moment between bites. "One thing I still don't get, though."

"What's that?"

"Well, if you weren't planning on firing me, why was Sean in my office copying files off my computer last night?"

"Beats me."

Paul scratched his head and looked JT right in the eye. "Well, if you didn't know he was there, why did you come looking for him?"

JT took the subtle accusation right in stride. "Like I said this morning, I thought I saw his car in the lot. I'm used to seeing your car here at all hours, but Sean ..."

"Yeah, I forgot." Paul still wasn't convinced.

"Marlene," JT barked at his computer, "get Sean on the line for me. Audio only."

"Yes, sir."

JT picked up another fry. "Let's ask him."

Sean answered the call quickly. "What can I do for you, boss?"

"I've got Paul here, Sean. He says you were copying some files late last night off his computer. Kind of spooked him seeing you there in the middle of the night, you know? What was so urgent that you needed to be on Paul's computer in the middle of the night?"

"Geez, Paul. Why didn't ya just ask me, man?"

"You blew by me so fast when you left my office, I didn't have time to think. You caught me off guard. It's usually deserted that time of night. My heart was racing when I saw the monitor on in my office."

"Yeah, I guess it might have looked a little strange. I was just copying the project files to reload on my computer. It crashed yesterday – even *I* come in occasionally on the weekends, you know – and I wanted to get it rebooted before I left. You know how obsessed I get. I'd have never been able to get any sleep if I didn't have the computer up and running before I left. By the time you came in, I was so tired and anxious to get home to bed that I just grabbed the disk and headed for the door as soon as it finished downloading. Nothing personal, Paul, I just wasn't up for conversation at two in the morning."

JT smiled. "Did you get booted up OK?"

"Yup. Slept like a baby."

"Anything else, Paul?" JT asked.

Paul shook his head no.

"Thanks, Sean. Enjoy your lunch."

"Right. See you guys this afternoon."

"Disconnect, Marlene."

"Disconnected, sir."

JT wiped the ketchup from his plate with the last fry. "I figured it would be something simple. Sean's a bit strange sometimes, but he's a good man." He looked down at his empty plate. "God, I love a good meal."

Paul took a last swig from his glass of Coke. "Thanks, JT." He stood and started for the door.

"Paul," JT said, stopping Paul in his tracks. "Get on those patent applications right away. I know it's boring stuff, but timing is crucial now. Besides, once you're done, I've got something really exciting for you to get started on."

"Go ahead, I'll bite. What is it?"

"Neuronanobionics."

Paul lit up. This is where he had really wanted to go with the project all along. Using a conglomeration of nanobots, one could theoretically build a replacement organ, a bionic organ, one cell at a time inside the body. Organ transplantation without surgery, he liked to call it when talking to some of his less technically oriented friends. Neuronanobionics, or a replacement for a whole section of a spinal cord or brain, would be the ultimate accomplishment.

"I'll have those patent applications done within the week." Paul left and closed the door behind him. What had started out as one of the worst days of his life had turned into one of the very best.

CHAPTER FIVE

The headlines of the Baltimore Sun on October 15, 2050, were mostly about baseball. The Baltimore Orioles had just beaten the Miami Marlins in the seventh game of the World Series. "Birds feast on Fish," the headlines read. Some people still enjoyed holding a newspaper that was actually made of paper, though most just scanned the news on the Net over breakfast or dinner. Not too many people noticed the small column on page five of the local section about a young man who had veered off Highway I-95 and wrapped his car around a light pole.

Richie Kincade noticed. He crumpled the paper as he folded it up to show his wife. "Will you look at this. Says the fella just turned right into the light post at seventy mph. Three witnesses saw it. The car was moving along fine, no sign of guidance system malfunction or nothin'. No alcohol in his blood and no drugs, but the safety system was off; the damned microchip was missing when they found the car. He must have been driving a de-chipped car, got depressed about something and just decided to steer it right off the road with a death wish. God, the kid must have been a Marlins fan." He started to chuckle a bit, but caught himself. "Sorry. Guess that's kind of sick, huh?"

"Kind of, Richie. So what's new?" Lara Kincade had long ago accepted what it was like to be the wife of a police detective assigned to the Motor Vehicle Tech-Tampering Unit. People only messed with automobile safety systems for two reasons: to steal a car or to remove the microchip that prevented the car from speeding or veering off a road. Mostly, it was kids who liked to de-chip the cars for joy rides, rides that ended in disaster too many times. The MVTT Unit cops saw some pretty gruesome things; there wasn't much worse than the sight of the mangled corpse of a teenager who was out joyriding. Lara Kincade was used to her husband's sick humor; she knew it was how he dealt with the awful things that he saw. Different detectives had different ways, but each of them had to have something, some way of keeping themselves sane, of distancing themselves from their work when they came home. This was Richie Kincade's way.

Richard Kincade grew up in Baltimore. All he ever wanted out of life was to be a member of the Baltimore Police Force. He went right into the Police Academy after high school, and worked his way up to detective. He'd been working the MVTT Unit for twelve years now, and in Baltimore an MVTT detective sees a lot in twelve years. He could often get a glimpse of his new assignments by reading the morning paper; he had a pretty good idea by now how the chief's mind worked.

"This one's got Richie Kincade written all over it, honey. Hartner likes to stick me with these dumbed-down car kills. It's not that easy to dumb-down a car. Detroit hardwires the safety microchip relays in, so you've got to be a bit of a computer geek as well as a mechanic to shut it down without disabling the car. If they didn't do it that way, everybody'd be shutting their safeties off; it's a bitch getting out of a parking lot when your car won't let you get within ten feet of the next closest crawler."

"Sounds interesting, hon," Mrs. Kincade muttered sweetly as she poured him another cup of coffee.

He knew that she really wasn't listening to the words he was saying. She had little interest in homicide and less interest in cars and microchips. He appreciated that she listened enough to at least feign interest. She may not have loved his work, but she surely did love him and he knew it.

"Thanks," he said as she poured, "but I'd better get going."

He stood up and went to the hall closet to grab his trench coat. "Bye, sweetie." He gave the missus a kiss on the cheek. She smiled and watched him hurry down the white marble steps in front of his Highlandtown row home.

It was a short drive to the police station on Howard Street where Richie worked. Within twenty minutes, he was at his desk, reviewing the file the chief had handed him as he arrived.

The young man who had died in the I-95 weekend accident was one Lester Hanes of Columbia, Maryland. He was a computer sciences engineer who had grown up in Baltimore and graduated from the University of Maryland four years after he got out of high school. He had worked for a while as a programmer at a banking firm in the city, and then switched to a biotech company just outside of Columbia. He was single and had no family apart from his mother who still lived in Baltimore.

"Definitely not a Marlins fan," Kincade muttered as he looked over the report.

"What's that, Richie?"

"Uh, nothin', Chief. The kid looks pretty non-descript. This one shouldn't take too long. I'll bet the geek just shut down the safety system to impress a girl."

Detective Kincade went back to his desk to dig up whatever he could on Lester Hanes from the Baltimore Police Department Intranet. He planned to spend as little time as possible with the vehicle itself, or what was left of the body. It could be pretty gruesome work, and after looking at the paperwork, he was sure that he could have this all but wrapped up before consulting with the coroner's office or the body shop that had sequestered the wreck.

The investigation was about as routine as any Kincade had been assigned to in recent years. The guys at the body shop had already sifted through the wreck that had been Hanes' car and, as expected, the safety computer had been jury-rigged with a bootlegged microchip, the kind that any computer geek could buy on the Net and install himself. With his background in computers, Hanes could have done it without breaking a sweat.

Kincade studied Hanes' file. He was single, worked hard, didn't date much. All in all, a pretty straight shooter from what Kincade could tell. Hanes didn't really seem like the kind of guy who would de-chip his car, but hey, young guys have been known to do some pretty crazy things to impress a girl. It didn't sit quite right with Richie, but after a predictably routine investigation, he was ready to let it go. He had phoned Hanes' employer, his family, his coworkers and what few friends he could find. This was a boring guy from what Kincade could tell. He wasn't into anything that anyone would want to kill him for, so why look for trouble. Just mark it up to testosterone stupidity.

He filed the report, and was home in time for dinner.

CHAPTER SIX

Columbia, Maryland, was still, in many ways, a model city. Originally developed in a large rural area between Baltimore and Washington, D.C. in the 1960's as a developer's vision of what an ideal suburban American city should be like, it grew to unforeseen proportions as the Baltimore-Washington corridor filled with two-worker households in the late twentieth century. In spite of the rapid growth, the city maintained a bit of its mystique and remained a popular place to live. Its most famous resident was a technology entrepreneur named JT Anderson.

Anderson had grown up in Columbia. Even as a boy he was always a little different. While most of the boys in his class spent their free time playing ball, JT would rush home from school, grab a Coke and head down to his basement. His parents gave him a rather generous allowance along with the unfettered use of the basement, where neither of them often ventured. It was JT's private wonderland, stocked with parts from computers that most people were glad to get rid of as they became obsolete. But to JT, these computers weren't junk, they were a virtually bottomless well of spare parts. It was in this strange place and with these junked circuit boards that he constructed Homer.

Homer wasn't the first robot ever built, but he was one of the first with a crude form of artificial intelligence. Homer was good enough to win first place at the Maryland Science Fair, but more importantly, it was the fact that Homer was built for about thirty-five million dollars less than the AI robots that Sony, IBM and a dozen other companies had been developing at the same time that caught the eye of the industrial elite. JT went to Harvard on a full scholarship. It was during his time at Harvard that he learned about nanotechnology, and it became his fascination.

As much as he loved Boston, JT ached to return to Maryland, and Johns Hopkins was only too glad to oblige him. Hopkins had a lab that was involved in some of the early work on nanotechnology, and it wasn't hard for them to attract JT to their campus as a grad student. By the time he graduated, he was the world's leading researcher on nanotechnology. He stayed on as project director for a couple of years, but when he saw the light at the end of the tunnel – the breakthrough that would make nanobots commercially successful – he abruptly left Hopkins to found the Baltimore Nanotechnology Institute. His critical discovery, one that led to success in the fabrication of silicon-based nanobots, came just weeks after he had left Hopkins. In fact, it came so quickly that it raised suspicions the discoveries had actually been made while he was employed by Hopkins, and therefore the nanobot technology was rightfully the intellectual and fiscal property of the university. For a brief period, a prominent law firm even tried to file charges against BNI to regain ownership of the nanobot fabrication process, but if JT did steal the work from his lab at Hopkins, he had covered his tracks well. Charges were dropped, clearing the way for BNI to retain sole ownership of the nanotechnology patents. Within two years, nanobots were a mainstay of vascular medicine, and BNI was on its way to becoming one of the wealthiest corporations in America.

As BNI grew, JT Anderson moved the company from its original location in northwest Baltimore to Columbia. He was finally back home, and in many ways Columbia was literally his town now. The seventy-three acre campus nestled into the outskirts of the town housed the corporate offices, research headquarters and fabrication plant for BNI. He was the largest employer in Columbia, and many of the corporate executives, including JT himself, lived in the suburbs of Columbia.

Paul Hingston was a little different from most of the gang at BNI. He was glad to be a part of the corporate culture, "one of the boys," as JT liked to say, even though he actually employed more women than men, but Paul couldn't give up the city life, especially not without Sandi by his side. He bought a penthouse in the heart of downtown Baltimore by the harbor, the ultimate bachelor pad, at least in his mind. He didn't find it hard to spend his newfound money.

In spite of his penchant for playing hard, he worked even harder. As promised, JT had given him free reign in setting up the nanotech lab at BNI. It was his dream lab and his dream job, but somehow he never felt satisfied. He always felt like something was missing, and although he knew that something was Sandi, he would never admit it, not even to himself. He threw himself into his social life on weekends, but it was his work at the lab that consumed him most of the time. Nanotech research was his true passion now more than ever. It wasn't unusual for him to leave for work Monday morning and not make it home until Friday night. JT got so tired of seeing Paul sleeping with his head on his desk that he even had a small apartment added next to the lab.

He also realized that Paul would need some help to speed the project along, even though Paul made it clear he preferred to work alone. When JT came in one morning and introduced Sean Lightbourne as his new lab assistant, Paul resented it at first. After three months of working alone, Paul was sure that he had dissuaded JT from hiring anyone else for the project, but JT had other ideas. Lightbourne was a brilliant researcher who JT had "stolen" from a rival company, and he thought he'd be a perfect fit for Paul.

Sean Lightbourne was not only a good research scientist, but he was an easy person to have around. Paul soon came to realize that he was glad for the camaraderie Sean could provide. It wasn't long before the two became good friends and were talking about more than work. It was Sean who finally helped Paul deal with his loss; Sean was the first person he could really talk to about Sandi. Once the barrier was broken, Paul found it cathartic. He talked about Sandi frequently, sometimes about their relationship, but often just about Sandi. He talked about her favorite hangouts, the kind of movies she liked, silly observations that she used to make about even the most mundane things. He talked about the things that made her Sandi. One day, when he caught himself rambling on, he even joked that Sean probably knew her better than he knew any of his own girlfriends. Sean just nodded and laughed. He was a good sport.

———

Halloween was JT Anderson's favorite holiday. He always said that no one can take themselves too seriously while they're wearing a ridiculous costume; it was an occasion that he liked to use to see what his associates were really like – deep down inside. As was the custom, the party was held at JT's estate.

A short drive from BNI, JT had chosen his fifteen-acre parcel of land carefully. The rolling hills created the perfect landscape for his stone mansion, with plenty of room left over for a tennis court, driving range and putting green. JT never liked to be idle. The grounds were fenced in and monitored by the latest in electronic surveillance to assure absolute privacy for JT and whichever fashion model was his live-in mate at the time. For the past year and a half, it had been Wanda Slate, or as most men knew her, Miss July, 2048. Wanda made the most magnificent witch in her low-cut black dress, slit up the side just enough to reveal her fishnet stockings when a breeze blew by. Somehow, she looked very natural with black lipstick, a white streak in her hair and a straw broom in her hand. JT had made sure to have her around at least until the Halloween party this year.

It was a crisp autumn night in the Maryland countryside, and the multicolored leaves that dotted the hillsides of the estate only served to enhance the decorations. JT went all out for Halloween, and for a man of his means, that was considerable. From the moment the guests entered through the front gate, the mood was set. A range of realistic gravestones irregularly arranged along the side of the quarter-mile driveway became more numerous as one approached the mansion. They were engraved with quirky, clever inscriptions, though no one ever stopped to read them.

Floodlights splashed an orange glow against the outside walls of the mansion, and robotic bats flew around the front entry, squawking warnings in very unrealistic bat voices. A valet helped the guests unload, and then took the cars out to a back lot so the vehicles would not disturb the mood of the night. As each new victim would step up on the front patio from the driveway, a mummy popped up from the garden with a howl. It was mostly amusing, but the occasional shriek from an unsuspecting guest new to the Anderson Halloween tradition enthralled JT each time he heard it.

The butler who answered the front door was indistinguishable from the guests, although his costume was not a costume to him. He greeted each guest and took the coats from those who had them, mostly the women who had the physical assets to wear the fashionably scant garb of the holiday. Belly dancers, miniskirted roaring twenties gals, Elviras and genies were the most popular. The experienced partygoers knew better than to compete with the witch of the house; it was tough to top Miss July.

Paul Hingston was not much of a party animal. He reluctantly donned his rented Robin Hood costume and picked up his date for the evening, a secretary at BNI named Pauline Harris. Pauline was no Miss July, but that didn't matter in the least to Paul. They were good friends and merely accompanied each other out of convenience. Neither had a steady "significant other," and neither felt comfortable enough in their obligatory silly outfits to bring a date. Pauline had threatened to come dressed as a secretary. Paul said that if she dared do that, he'd do the same. She decided that she couldn't stomach seeing Paul in a dress, so Maid Marion would have to do. They sauntered hesitantly through the front door, no threat of being mistaken for the swashbucklers that they feigned to portray.

Paul went to the bar to get drinks for the two of them while Maid Marion stopped to talk to a group of ghouls. As he passed the French doors leading out to the expansive patio surrounding the lagoon-style pool, he couldn't help but notice the two lone figures braving the cool night air while the rest of the guests crowded the well-decorated inner quarters. One of the men was dressed as Sir Lancelot, and was unmistakably Sean Lightbourne. The other, a white-wigged American patriot, looked so familiar.... Paul was about to knock on the glass to get Sean's attention, when he noticed that the two were in a rather heated discussion. He briefly considered braving the long line at the bar, but curiosity got the better of him.

The French doors were ajar, and with a gentle push, Paul and the party music came pouring out the door together. The noise startled the men out of whatever it was they had been so passionately discussing.

"Paul," Sean called, obviously caught off guard. "Uh...come here, let me introduce you to Senator Russell Stetson."

"Ah, I knew you looked familiar."

"Wig didn't fool you, huh?" Stetson laughed mechanically like a true politician.

"Just a little, Senator."

"Call me Russ, please."

"OK...Russ, nice to meet you." Paul extended his hand. "I didn't realize you two knew each other. What did I interrupt? It looked pretty intense."

"Ah," Sean said with a flip of his hand, "just politics...you know. I recognized the senator and just couldn't resist putting in a plug for nanobot therapy. He's on the Senate Subcommittee on Nanotechnology, you know."

"Uh, yeah, Sean. I kind of keep up on that nanobot stuff."

Sean laughed nervously, realizing that it had been a rather stupid comment. He and Paul had often talked about the influence the subcommittee would have over the practical use of their work. "Well, in spite of what you've heard, he seems OK to me." The three men shared a half-hearted laugh.

Paul thought the whole thing was rather strange, but decided to let it rest. "Well, the Maid Marion's waiting for her whiskey sour. I dare not disappoint. Nice meeting you, Russ."

"Likewise, Paul. I've heard a lot of good things about you."

Paul nodded and smiled, then went back into the warmth of the house. Sean Lightbourne and Russell Stetson watched until he was safely inside.

"What do you think he's up too, Sean?"

"Ah, nothin'." Sean shrugged his shoulders. "Paul's a good guy, not the sort to look for trouble."

"Well, he looked a bit odd to me, like something was on his mind that he didn't want us to know about."

"Nah. Paul's a real up-front kind of guy. The only thing on his mind tonight is how quickly he can make a graceful exit from this party. He's a jeans and T-shirt man, definitely not the Robin Hood Men in Tights type. I'll bet the lovely Maid Marion talked him into that one."

The two men laughed. They turned toward the pool as the sound of a brightly colored array of lighted waterspouts leaped from the rock wall at the far side of the patio, and splashed down into the pool.

"God. That's ostentatious even for JT," Senator Stetson muttered.

"Yeah, but it sure is pretty."

They sipped on their hot spiced cider, cupping the kiln-fired mugs to keep warm.

Paul thanked the bartender and picked up the two glasses, a whiskey sour for the lady, Scotch on the rocks for the king of thieves. Just as he was about to turn away, he felt a slap on the back.

"So, how's my loyal subject this fine All Hallow's Eve." The greeting was followed by a hearty belly laugh, meant to be very regal but sounding more like Santa Claus after one-too-many eggnogs.

He struggled to keep the drinks from spilling onto his expensive rental costume as he turned to see where the greeting had originated. JT made one of the gawkiest Henry the Eighths that one could ever imagine. His six-foot three, one hundred and sixty pound frame made a mockery of a very fine costume. *A bulimic Henry the Eighth,* was the only thought that came to Paul's mind as he saw the awkward sight. He bit his lip and noticed that he was not the only one struggling to avoid laughing at the boss.

"Uh, great costume, JT," was about all he could muster up.

"You really think so?"

Just as Paul was about to open his mouth, JT mercifully interrupted him. "No, don't answer that. I know I look ridiculous, but what the hell, so do most of the people in here. I just love to see their expressions when I ask them how I look. Actually, I preferred the Superman costume ..."

That goes without saying, Paul thought.

"...but Superman looked pretty ridiculous standing next to Witch Wanda."

"I don't know," Paul asked, "which Wanda?"

That stopped JT in mid-thought. After a brief pause, he caught on to Paul's dry humor. "Oh ...Oh, I get it. Good one, Robin." He laughed that stupid laugh again, but Paul didn't even crack a smile. Uncomfortably, JT perused the crowd. "Well, I must be off. Got to mingle with my subjects, you know." He darted into the crowd.

Pauline had worked her way over just in time to overhear Paul's joke. "It's not usually too wise to mess with the boss's head."

"Yeah, I suppose you're right." He handed her the whiskey sour. "But that was just too easy. I couldn't resist."

"Well," she said, looking him over after a deep swig of her drink, "I gotta admit, you look a hell of a lot better in those tights than King Icabod looks in those robes."

Paul cleared his throat and hoped that the flush in his cheeks was lost in the ambiance of the room. "Shall we check out the decorations, my lady?" He motioned to the darkened living room, from which some ghoulish music was emanating. He hoped she would agree to leave before the band started in with the dance music out by the pool. The only thing worse than dancing was dancing to *The Monster Mash.*

"Ohh, trying to get me into the dark, eh Robin Hood?" she said seductively.

Yeah, where I can't see you. He smiled meekly and led her into the living room. Paul hated office romances. The main reason he chose to come here with Pauline was because he knew that with her, he would not be tempted. He felt bad, but he ditched her at the first turn into the darkness. He knew that he would feel worse if she had tried to feel him, which he could sense was only a few more sips of whiskey away.

Thankfully, the evening passed quickly. He managed to avoid dancing as well as any uncomfortable moments of solitude with the Maid Marion. By the time they left, she was too drunk to care anymore. He knew she wouldn't remember too much of this in the morning, and was thankful that their office friendship would remain intact.

Paul was glad to get home. A pair of running pants, which he kept in his car, was very effective at concealing his green tights, and his trench coat covered the rest of the ensemble. He was able to get from the parking lot at Poe Towers up to his apartment without the embarrassment of any more jokes about his legs. Thankfully, he had survived another Halloween.

CHAPTER SEVEN

November 19, 2050

Rocky Stankowski liked gentlemen's clubs. He wasn't too sure why they called them gentlemen's clubs really; he had never seen what he would call a gentleman in one of them. Never the less, he liked them, and so Saturday night would usually find him down at the Block in Baltimore. Rocky lived and worked in Washington, but the Block was the place to go if you liked gentlemen's clubs. Besides, for a guy with a respectable job like his, Rocky had found that it was best to keep his club hopping as far away from his job as possible.

It was a chilly Saturday night with the wind whipping up the Fallsway from the Inner Harbor. Rocky had had to take Harold Bradley, the White House chief of staff, out to Camp David that afternoon, but he had the rest of the weekend off. He had been Mr. Bradley's chauffeur for almost two years now. His military background and squeaky-clean driving record had won him the job. His personality had kept it for him. Rocky was a quiet sort, but not afraid to speak his mind when he found it necessary. Mr. Bradley liked the solitude of sitting in a car driven by Rocky Stankowski, and he appreciated even more the rare instance when Rocky would give him the working-man's view on an issue that the political elite seemed to overlook. It didn't happen often, but when Rocky spoke, it usually resulted in helping the chief of staff to avoid finding new trouble. There was no shortage of trouble at the White House these days.

Rocky dropped off Mr. Bradley at about four o'clock that afternoon. Once his task was completed, he figured that he might as well indulge himself. He arrived in downtown Baltimore at about six. The days were getting short, and it was already dark by the time he parked the car on Holliday Street.

Belle's Place was his favorite hangout. It was kind of quiet for a gentlemen's club, but not too elitist. The guys in there were working class stiffs like him, but by and large, they were good men who were just looking to escape their lives for a while. Belle's girls weren't the high-priced, best-that-surgery-can-create type, but they were still pretty classy. They were the kind of women whose company Rocky liked to be in with or without their clothes on, but he preferred without.

He braced himself against the breeze and wrapped his coat tightly around his body. Belle recognized him as soon as he came through the door.

"Hey, Rock, good to see ya, hon." She helped him off with his coat. "Getting a little nippy, huh?"

"Cold as a witch's tit out there tonight, Belle."

She hung his coat on the rack. "Come on, I'll get you some hot coffee. A little Irish Whiskey in it?"

"Sounds good, Belle. Thanks"

She led him over to a stage-front table by the walkway that the girls were prancing down. It was a quiet night, and he was glad to sit alone. He didn't notice the three men who entered just after he did. They were newcomers, and Belle didn't give them a second thought. She sat them at a table across the stage from Rocky.

The show began, and Rocky sat back, sipping his Irish coffee and enjoying the view. The three men across the stage were just faded images amongst the wisps of smoke that filled the room, and they blended into the sparse crowd. The music was sultry jazz, and the smell of tobacco and perfume intoxicated Rocky more than the liquor. He was engrossed in the gyrations of the young lady on stage; everything else in the room was just part of the haze. During working hours, Rocky noticed everything, but while at Belle's he liked to shut the world out, as if there were only him and the girl on the stage. He never noticed the three men, but they noticed him.

As usual, Rocky didn't drink much that night. Even when off duty, one drink was his limit. He liked his job too much to risk losing his license over something as stupid as a drunk-driving bust. It would be a long drive back to Washington that night, and after the first coffee, Rocky took it straight, without the whiskey.

The evening passed quickly. Belle's Place had worked its magic once again, and by midnight, a week's worth of stress had melted away. He called Belle over.

"Leavin' already, hon?"

"Fraid so, Belle. It's been a long day." He didn't like to say too much about himself around here, not even to Belle. Not too many of the guys did, for obvious reasons. Belle even figured that name, Rocky, had to be made up, but she didn't mind a bit. Rocky was always a gentleman and always paid in cash.

"Don't be a stranger now, Rocky." She winked as she handed him his coat.

He gave her a kiss on the cheek and headed out the door, bracing himself against the cold night air. The icy wind slapped against his face, and he tucked his chin down as he walked toward the car. He didn't notice the three men who scrambled for their coats and exited Belle's just after him.

The last thing that he could remember when he awakened in the ER was that he had been sitting in Belle's Place, enjoying the show.

"Christ! This guy's got White House clearance. Look at his ID card."

Rocky awakened in a bit of a fog. He saw two men in white coats standing over him. One of them was holding his wallet and showing it to the other.

He tried to sit up and grab it. "Ahh," he yelped as he plunked back down to the gurney grabbing his head. He felt the warm, sticky blood oozing from the left side of his skull, and looked at his hand in disbelief as he pulled it away, covered in red.

"Whoa there, big fella. Hold still." The two men in the white coats reached down and restrained his arms. "Just lay still, we're gonna get you some help."

Rocky wasn't quite sure what they were saying, but he didn't like being held down. He struggled to pull free, but his usually powerful arms were like Jello at his side. "Let ... me ... go!" he shouted, as he tried once more to break free.

"Five milligrams of Valium IV push, stat!" was the last thing he heard.

CHAPTER EIGHT

Russell Stetson, the senator from Maryland, had served for the past nine years on the Senate Subcommittee on Nanotechnology. The committee had been formed shortly after he won the election for his first term. It had been placed under the direction of a senior senator from Connecticut, Stanton Cole. Cole was one of the Senate's old-timers. Having served in the Senate for eighteen years as a levelheaded moderate, he had the respect of the leaders of both parties. When nanotechnology rose to the forefront of clinical medicine, the committee had been organized to deal with the inevitable ethical issues that would concern the public. Nanotechnology would enable physicians to alter the human body in ways never known before. Not since the arguments involving cloning had a new technology raised so much controversy. At what point would a body full of nanobots cease to be human? Would a body that had most of its organs replaced or augmented by miniature internal machines become a machine at some point?

In order to allay the public's fears, the legislators decided to have a congressional committee rule on these issues rather than leaving them to the discretion of entrepreneurs who stood to benefit from the exploitation of nanotechnology. The Senate Subcommittee on Nanotechnology was formed as a branch of the Senate Health Care Committee, and the job of chairing the committee went to the very well respected and very uncontroversial Senator Cole.

Russell Stetson had spent his first year in the Senate getting a feel for the political battlefield that was Washington, but he was determined to make his mark as quickly as possible. He lobbied hard to get onto the new committee, realizing that it would enable him to deal with some of the most controversial issues of his day. He spent hours boning up on nanotechnology, including wining and dining one of its foremost proponents, JT Anderson. By his fourth year on the committee, he was the vice-chair, with more power over decisions regarding the authorization of human research than anyone in the country, save for the venerable Stanton Cole.

Senator Stetson had his own agenda for nanotechnology. In it, he saw the potential for the ultimate political power: control of the human mind. His idea was to develop nanobots that could be placed into a human brain and used to control the thoughts and actions of their host. He knew better than to propose this idea to Senator Cole; a man like Cole would never have the vision to take such a bold step in the name of God and Country. Instead, he enlisted an NSA operative by the name of James O'Grady, who he knew would appreciate the advantages of mind-controlling nanobots. With the support of the NSA, Stetson could insure the security that would be needed to covertly bring his ideas to fruition.

All the security in the world would be useless, of course, without the capability to develop the mind-controlling nanobots. It was imperative to find a scientist who not only had the skills to develop the nanobots, but who also could be persuaded that Stetson's ideas were the right ones. This would not be an easy task; scientists are, by nature, an altruistic group. Stetson searched long and hard for the right man to do the research needed to accomplish his goal. He needed someone equally ambitious as he was brilliant, someone with the wealth to sponsor the research without making the government's support obvious, and someone who could be trusted, or at least intimidated, into absolute secrecy. By the spring of 2042, he had made his choice. JT Anderson was already one of the wealthiest men in the country. His brilliance was incontrovertible, and his willingness to stretch the boundaries of integrity were well known; no one really believed that he had just happened to make the critical breakthroughs in nanotechnology immediately after leaving Hopkins. Even though the courts exonerated him, no one really believed that he hadn't stolen the work that rightfully belonged to Hopkins. They just gave him credit for being a particularly brilliant thief.

Anderson was the perfect choice, and when Russell Stetson approached him with the idea of using his expertise in nanotechnology for a very patriotic and even more lucrative cause, he was not hard to persuade. He proved to be very adroit at his task, and within a few years, had developed a synthetic bionic implant the size of a pea that could be surgically inserted into the human brain and could be used to introduce thoughts and actions into its host. It was constructed of thousands of nanobots, which together made up a small machine capable of generating electrical impulses that could be read by the surrounding neurons. By meticulously studying brain wave patterns, he was able to develop a digital language with which he could program his bionic implant. The digital signal would then be converted into electrical impulses that the brain would interpret as original thought. When implanted in the right frontal lobe, the device was capable of making its host perform whatever action the bionic implant was programmed to suggest.

The first obvious flaw in the work was that cutting the someone's head open to insert the bionic implant was not the ideal way to covertly gain control of the subject. Cutting a person's head open would definitely arouse suspicion. Anderson had toyed with the idea of injecting nanobots programmed to assemble themselves into the bionic implant once inside the body, but he had no idea how to insure that it would assemble itself at the proper location in the right frontal lobe.

The second obvious flaw was that his inorganic nanobots would create a foreign body in the host, one that could cause seizure-inducing irritation, and would be detectable by standard X-ray techniques. Again, this was not ideal for a covert operation.

Anderson had struggled with these issues until he heard Dr. Sandra Fletcher speak at the Hopkins Symposium introducing organic nanobots. The organic bots would solve the problem of host rejection and detection, and the programming skills of someone like her or Paul Hingston would give him a fighting chance of getting injectable bots to migrate to the right frontal lobe where they could be effective.

Work had been progressing well since Paul joined BNI, but it was never quite fast enough for Senator Stetson. JT felt a pang of anxiety when he saw Senator Stetson's name penciled into his schedule unexpectedly that morning. It wasn't unusual for members of the congressional nanotech committee to meet periodically with leaders in the field of nanotechnology, so an occasional meeting with Stetson in the name of senatorial enlightenment would not arouse suspicion, but JT knew what the meeting was really about. It was always about the same thing.

Senator Stetson arrived at BNI right on time, as usual, and JT greeted him in the outer office.

"Good morning, JT."

"Good morning, Senator. Right on time, as usual." JT extended his right hand to greet the senator, and guided him into his office. The door closed behind them.

"I need an update, JT. I've introduced a bill that will appropriate five-hundred million dollars over the next decade for nanotech research, and I've been building a fragile coalition. It'll crumble like a house of cards if I don't have some solid sign of success for the project. Cole is dead set against the idea. He doesn't want to give that much money or that much latitude to any independent enterprise. That old coot is gonna play by the book on this one. Even the mention of using nanobots for any covert operations will blow the deal. We have to convince him that it's in the public interest to give that grant to BNI or it'll never fly. He's a tough nut to crack, but if you can give me something tangible, I think my friends at the agency can put enough pressure on the rest of the committee members that we may be able to swing the vote."

Anderson sat quietly behind his desk. He liked having the NSA on his side, but it was also somewhat unnerving knowing that he was under their thumb. He did not want to screw this one up. It had become much more than the money now.

"Let me show you where were at, Russ. I think you'll be pleasantly surprised."

CHAPTER NINE

December 1, 2050

Harborview Hospital sat on the waterfront in downtown Baltimore, not far from Federal Hill. The resurgence of the downtown waterfront area in the late twentieth and early twenty-first century was the model for the redevelopment of inner city areas all over the United States. The rundown industrial and storage facilities had been replaced with modern financial and business towers, and the yuppies that staffed those businesses moved into the city in droves. Broken down row-homes were supplanted by luxury condominiums, and the growing numbers of prosperous residents were accommodated by new fashion boutiques, upscale malls and a plethora of exclusive restaurants, always filled with young urban professionals who were too busy and too tired to prepare a meal at the end of a long work day. Unfortunately, accidents happen even in the finest neighborhoods, and even the most privileged amongst us fall ill. Harborview Hospital was the Rolls Royce of hospitals, built to fill that niche.

Harborview was the kind of hospital that not only provided good care, but it did so in an environment that would do justice to a five star hotel. Rooms appointed with designer furniture and marble bathrooms had small balconies that looked out over the Baltimore skyline, where those patients who were able could sit and enjoy a gourmet meal with their loved ones. It was not the hospital of choice for those who were found unconscious on the streets in the gentlemen's club district, but the ID card in Rocky Stankowski's wallet made it clear that he was not the normal bucolic drunk who stumbled into the wrong alley in downtown Baltimore. The officers who found him contacted their chief as soon as they saw the card that identified him as a White House employee. The chief contacted the mayor, who placed a few calls that eventually wound up at the ear of the White House Chief of Staff, Harold Bradley, at Camp David.

When the President of the United States calls and says to give a patient top priority, hospital administrators do not stop to ask who is paying the bill, at least not right away. Rocky was admitted to a private suite on the neurosurgery floor of Harborview Hospital. An MRI showed the results of blunt trauma to the right side of the head — a skull fracture and a severe right frontal lobe contusion.

Mr. Bradley knew that Rocky had no family, and made it a point to be by his side within hours. A few calls were made, and he learned that the only real hope for a complete recovery from the injury was a new experimental treatment called two-phase neuronanobot therapy, or TPNT. He conferred with the Surgeon General, and signed the papers the next morning.

Rocky Stankowski was not the first patient treated with the TPNT for a brain injury under the Hopkins protocol, but he was the most prominent thus far. Fortunately for Rocky, as well as for the nanobot researchers, he made a complete recovery, like each of the twenty-three patients treated before him, within fifteen days. On the sixteenth day, he was back home.

Rocky was itching to get back to work, but protocol demanded that the patient not be allowed to operate a motor vehicle for at least six months. He was monitored regularly for any sign of seizures, and underwent a thorough battery of neurological and psychological tests during that period of time. The results were astonishing, with no trace of injury detectable on any of the tests within three months' time. Anatomically, the signs of injury could be seen: the scar on the scalp, the subtle defect in the shape of the skull where it had been bashed in, and minor abnormalities discernable on the MRI. From a practical standpoint, however, Rocky was as good as new. His doctors promised him that if no complications occurred, he would be back to work in six months. Rocky didn't like being idle; he would hold them to their word.

CHAPTER TEN

Much to the delight of Dr. Sandra Fletcher and the neurological team that worked with her on the neuronanobot trials, every single patient had shown the same remarkable results that Rocky Stankowski displayed. By mid February, 2051, ten months after the human trials had started, thirty patients had been treated and thirty patients had been cured. The FDA felt compelled to abort the trial, and set guidelines recommending TPNT as the treatment of choice for traumatic brain injury.

———

Sandi had been so wrapped up in the details and analysis of the TPNT trials that it never occurred to her that someone else could have independently devised the techniques for producing the nanobots. The idea that someone outside of her lab would have the information necessary to apply for and receive patents for neuronanobot fabrication never crossed her mind, at least not until she attempted to file the applications herself, only to discover that they already belonged to BNI.

"What!" she screeched into the phone. "What do you mean? That's impossible. Nobody could possibly have the data needed to ..."

Sam Collier looked over his shoulder. He had never seen Sandi so unrestrained at work. Sandi was usually as demure as her five-foot tall, one hundred pound frame would suggest. To those who knew her at all, her appearance was truly deceiving; she was one hundred pounds of boundless energy, always on the go, always striving to make herself and all those around her a little better. Sam liked to joke that he usually needed a nap after watching her work, but he also admired her composure. Somehow, she kept all that vim and vigor under control, and though she was never afraid to say what was on her mind, she always did so with restraint and respect for those around her. It was a rare thing indeed to see Dr. Fletcher lose her temper.

He cringed as she slammed down the phone. "What was that all about?" he asked sheepishly. He wasn't so sure he really wanted to unleash her on this one.

"Unbe*liev*able," she screamed at no one in particular.

"Uh, sorry," Sam mumbled. "Never mind."

"Huh?" She glanced over at Sam. "Did you say something?"

"Oh, no. Just minding my own business over here."

Sandi smiled.

"Guess that must've sounded pretty bad, huh?"

That's the kind of question that doesn't really have a right answer, Sam thought to himself. "Well ...," he said, searching for the right thing to say.

"You won't believe what that was about. That was Parsons from the legal office. It seems that someone else applied for our neuronanobot patents before we did; BNI already has the patent. How in the hell could they have gotten hold of the data for the fabrication process? You and I are the only ones that have access to ... "

Sam's eyes widened. "Whoa, wait a minute. You're not really suggesting that I would have sold our data to those scum bags, are you?"

"What?" said Sandi, deep in thought. "Oh ... no. No, of course not." She looked up at him. "You didn't, did you?"

"Sandi!"

"Sorry, Sam."

"No problem, Doc." He understood the implications. He and Sandi might still be able to lay claim to having discovered the process first, maybe even have the procedure named after them, but with BNI holding the patents, the income and, more importantly, future control of the procedure would be in the hands of JT Anderson. He and Sandi would have little say in how the procedure would be adapted for clinical use now. "But hey, look at the bright side," the thought of naming the procedure after Sandi stuck in his head, "you'll still be famous. Just think, one day, millions of people will have Fletcherbots in their heads."

It was so ridiculous sounding that, as miffed as she was, even Sandi had to laugh. "You rat, I'm trying to be pissed off here."

"Yeah, I knew you couldn't do it for too long."

"Don't be so sure. There's only one person I know of who could have pulled this off. I'm going to have a look at those patent applications from BNI, and then I'm going to pay a little visit to Dr. Paul Hingston. I just can't seem to get that bastard out of my life." She looked more upset than angry, like a wave of bad memories had just washed over her. Now it was personal.

"Want me to come along?" Sam asked.

"Nah," she smiled and took his hand. "Thanks, Sam, but I've got to do this alone."

He nodded. "Well, I'm just a phone call away if you change your mind."

She nodded back, and then grabbed her coat and left the room.

Sam watched her go, and wondered what twist of fate might befall her next. He hated to see the pain that oozed from the wound left by her breakup with Paul seeping back into her life. He wished there was something more that he could do, but this was not the time.

———

Sandi left the lab with more than the usual determined strut in her step. The legal office was in the process of receiving faxed copies of the neuronanobot patents that had been awarded to BNI, as well as copies of the original patent applications. By the time Sandi arrived, the copies were waiting for her.

"Thanks, Ms. Prescott," she said to the secretary who handed the thick folder to her. "Do you mind if I take this with me? I'd rather have a chance to digest it in more comfortable surroundings." She realized how foolish that sounded as she looked around the posh offices of the legal department, but as beautiful as they were, they were not her idea of comfort.

"No problem. Mr. Talbot said they were yours to do with as you please."

"Good," Sandi replied as she looked out the window. "It looks like a good day for a fire."

Ms. Prescott looked horrified. She had worked very hard compiling the faxes into a nice, neat portfolio for Dr. Fletcher. This was a woman who took great pride in her compulsive nature.

Sandi noticed the look of horror on her face. "Just kidding, Ms. Prescott. Just kidding." She tried to bite back the laughter, but was only partially successful.

The secretary, looking offended, breathed a sigh of relief and patted her hair to make sure each strand was in its proper place.

"Thanks again," Sandi said, lifting the portfolio. "I really do appreciate it."

Ms. Prescott's tension noticeably eased, and Sandi felt a little better. She didn't mean to make the poor lady self-conscious, but the pomposity of the office was rather comical. Sandi felt a giggle coming on again, and turned to walk out the door before it escaped. *Well, at least I can still laugh,* she thought to herself as she zipped her coat and headed for the parking lot.

For the first time in recent memory Sandi decided to take the afternoon off. She phoned Sam so he wouldn't be worried, and went home to dissect the work of BNI in private.

Sandi pulled into her driveway and tapped the garage door opener. She looked up through the windshield at the blanket of light gray clouds carpeting the sky. She had lived in Baltimore long enough to know when snow was on the way. The garage door lifted, and she pulled her red Mustang convertible into the garage, thankful that she had chosen a house with enough storage space so she could actually use the garage for her car. She hated digging her car out of the snow.

By the time she went inside and changed into a well-worn pair of jeans and her favorite sweater, the snow had started to fall. She fixed herself a cup of hot chocolate and curled up on the sofa with the portfolio Ms. Prescott had prepared for her. She stared at the file disdainfully, angry at it for spoiling the moment. Curling up in front of the bay window on a snowy day with a steaming cup of cocoa was something she usually associated with unwinding. This was going to be anything but relaxing.

Sandi opened the portfolio. The face page was the fax indicating how many pages were sent. She tossed it aside and began to read the first document, the patent application from BNI. There on page one was the signature of the applicant, Dr. Paul Hingston.

"You snake," she hissed at the paper. She wasn't really surprised.

Slowly, Sandi thumbed her way through the pages, first the applications and then the patents themselves. Her anger grew more intense with each turn of the page. "What a slime-ball!" she shouted. "No way could this be a coincidence." Every page was familiar to her. BNI had duplicated virtually every facet of her work. It wasn't as if they had gone down an independent pathway and come up with the same conclusions, but this work had all the hallmarks of stolen research. Every aspect of the work she had been doing with Sam Collier for the last two years was duplicated right here on these pages. It was obvious that someone had stolen her data.

After an hour of filing through the patent literature, Sandi had had enough. She stood up and stretched, then nearly fell as she tried to put her weight on her right leg, which had been crossed under her on the sofa. Pins and needles shot through her foot, and she angrily stamped on the floor, trying to pound some life into it. Once it would take her weight, she began to pace around the room trying to calm herself, but time only made her anger grow greater. Finally, she walked into the kitchen.

"Computer, phone Dr. Paul Hingston at BNI in Columbia, Maryland."

"Searching for number ... connecting."

Sandi paced anxiously while she was waiting for the call to go through.

"Computer, audio connection only." She couldn't stomach the thought of looking at Paul right now. It would be much easier to give him a piece of her mind with a good old-fashioned audio phone call.

"Hello?"

"Paul, is that you?"

"Yeah... Sandi?" He hadn't heard her voice in quite some time, but it was a voice that he would never forget. "It's great to hear from you."

"I'll just bet it is."

"What's the matter?" He could tell by her tone that this was not going to be the kind of call he had hoped for.

"What's the matter! You steal two years of my work and you want to know what's the matter?"

"Steal two years of ... oh, I see. You heard about the patents, huh?"

"You're damned right I did. How in the hell do you have the nerve to use stolen data to file for patents? Are you trying to advertise to the world that you're a thief?"

"Whoa, hold on a minute. I worked damn hard on the neuronanobots. You knew that we had been working on the same project as you. Don't you remember that the last time, it was *me* calling *you* to accuse *you* of stealing *my* work?"

"I sure as hell do. It's not too often that someone accuses me of stealing research. I remember it vividly."

"Then you shouldn't be all that surprised that we were still working on the same project. The only difference is that we beat you to the punch this time."

"Yeah, right. Give me a break. Do you really think I'm that stupid, Paul? You didn't even try to hide the fact that you stole my work. You used the exact same gene sequences that we used ... *exact*. What are the odds of that? Do you think I'm dumb enough to believe that's a coincidence, or did you just figure that I'd never look at your patents?"

Paul didn't know what to say. The odds of them both coming up with precisely the same gene sequencing, the identical mechanism for having the Phase Two nanobots to find the Phase One bots, synapse with them, transform into synthetic neurons and synapse with the healthy neurons in the brain were miniscule. "About a million to one, I'd guess."

"What? Is that all you've got to say?"

"They were an exact match?" Paul still couldn't believe what he was hearing.

"Exact. Every one of them. Like you didn't know."

"No, Sandi. I didn't."

They both knew that there was only one explanation. Somebody had to be stealing data from one of their labs and giving to the other.

"I'll get back to you, Sandi." The line went dead as he hung up.

"No you don't, Paul Hingston. You're not walking away from this that easily." But it was too late. She was too spent to call him back.

God, he sounded sincere, she thought to herself. *That self-righteous son of a bitch really thinks that* I *stole the data from* him? She thought for a moment. *Could Sam have been stealing the data from BNI and feeding it to me without my knowledge, somehow guiding me to my conclusions?* They had worked so closely together on this project that sometimes it was hard to remember which ideas had been hers and which had come from him. *Nah.*

It had to be Paul, that bastard. Unless ...I suppose someone in his lab could have been pulling one over on him, stealing my data and spoon-feeding it to him. I can't believe he could really be so naive ... well, it probably was him, but in either case, I'm going to make sure he knows I'm on to him. I've got the proof right here. Sandi patted a large manila envelope, containing a hard copy of her research on the Phase Two neuronanobot programming. She loved her computer, but never completely trusted digital records. She always kept a back-up paper hard copy of her work. She made up her mind right then to send a copy of her work to Paul. There wasn't anything to lose; he obviously already had the data *and* the patents to prove it; there were no secrets left to steal.

Sandi's work was all dated, a paper trail of her painstaking research. This would prove that she had done the legwork independently, that it really was her work. She wasn't quite sure why, but she wanted to make certain that he knew it.

Sandi lit a fire in the fireplace, and went to the bookcase to make a selection from her library, mostly art and travel books, except for the vast collection of science fiction paperbacks that lined the top two shelves. She smiled as she pulled out a copy of Asimov's *I, Robot*, remembering the intrigue it had brought into her life those many years ago when she had first read it. It was one of the stories that had first kindled her fascination for sci-fi, and more importantly, had whetted her appetite for scientific research into the seemingly impossible.

She curled up on the sofa in front of the crackling fire and opened the book, taking care not to tear the brittle pages from their cover. The musty scent of the old paperback comforted her. She considered it a rare opportunity to relax with a good book. These days, most of her reading was limited to nanotech journals. She glanced out the window at the gathering snow and smiled serenely. It was nice to leave her problems behind, even if only for a little while.

Guy Andrews had a musician's work schedule. He worked late at the downtown nightclub, The Pendulum Pit, most nights and slept much of the day away. Guy was surprised to see Sandi lounging on the sofa when he came downstairs. Sandi was a workaholic; she never came home early.

"Hey, what's the matter, babe, you sick?" He stretched his arms up high over his head and yawned as he came down the stairs in his long flannel robe.

Sandi looked up from her book. "Nah. Just decided to take the day off. The neuronanobot project is done for now, and I decided I needed a break."

"Good for you," he said as he gave her a kiss. "So, what do you think, should we go into Hunt Valley and celebrate at Sal's Place?"

Sal's was a casual little Italian restaurant, one of her favorites, but she didn't want to hassle with getting dressed and braving the cold night air.

"Nah. Let's just stay in ... a little pasta, some wine, a nice crackling fire ...umm, sounds perfect, don't you think?"

"I didn't really want to go out anyway," he said as he put his arms around her.

"Hey, want to go upstairs and work up an appetite first?" She winked at him.

"You don't have to ask me twice," he said, reaching out to help her up from the sofa.

One hour later, they were sipping Chianti in the kitchen. She was stirring in the not-so-secret ingredients of her not-so-famous spaghetti sauce, and he was grinding some fresh garlic for the bread. They had so much fun cooking the meal together that they were almost disappointed when it was ready to eat. *This is something Paul would never have done,* she thought to herself, inhaling the fragrance of the freshly baked garlic bread as she watched Guy pull the tray out of the oven. *God! Stop thinking about him, girl. Don't ruin today with the past.*

They set up a bridge table and ate by the fire. The food was wonderful, but as romantic as the evening was, she was ready to go to sleep as she sipped the last of her third glass of wine.

She slumped into Guy's arms as they sat on the sofa watching the fire die down. "I've got to get to bed. Can you take care of the fire while I go take my insulin? I want to make sure I do it before I'm too tired to see the syringe."

"Sure, babe," he said as they struggled up off the sofa together.

Sandi had been diagnosed with diabetes as a child. Although great strides had been made in the treatment of the disease, she still needed to take a shot of Synthulin, a synthetic long acting insulin, once a week. She always took it shortly before going to sleep. After all these years, it was second nature to her, but tonight she really hated sticking that needle into her arm. It was like a pinprick awakening her from her ethereal dream; the pain was minimal, but it was enough to disturb her preciously serene state of mind.

It was at that moment she decided what her next project would be – the fabrication of a nanobionic insulin pump, an organic, artificial pancreas made from nanobots that could be injected into the bloodstream, and then assemble themselves into a functioning pancreas once inside the body. It would be the perfect cure for diabetes.

She tried hard not to think about her new project that night, but it was no use; her mind was in high gear once again. Only the wine enabled her to drift off that night, but the rest of her weekend would not be the respite she had hoped for. It would be even better.

The sunlight glistened off the snow and slipped between the slits of the Venetian blinds in the bedroom. Guy was fast asleep, but Sandi felt the call of a new day and craved a hot cup of coffee. She edged slowly out of bed so as not to disturb her lover, slipped on her green corduroy robe, and made her way down to the kitchen.

The skies had cleared by morning, and the day that followed was filled with an invigorating sunshine, enhanced by its brilliant reflection off the glazed-over snow carpeting Baltimore County. Sandi had moved north of the city to a cozy suburban neighborhood in Phoenix, Maryland after she left Paul. The commute was rough for someone who had lived on or near campus for so many years, but it was well worth it. When she arrived home each evening, she felt like she was in a different world.

Wintertime was really something special; while the city turned black with soot-covered road slush from the salt trucks and auto exhaust, Phoenix was awash in the pristine beauty that nature meant for the snow to be. The rolling hillsides were covered with the dusty, white powder and the trees, especially the evergreens, were draped in a blanket of snow, weighing down limbs that arched gracefully toward the earth. As the day passed, the warm rays of sunshine bathed the snow-laden branches creating an evanescent trickle of water, lasting just long enough to refreeze at the tips of each branch and glisten in the afternoon light. It was truly a winter wonderland.

Sandi was on vacation in her own home. The love of someone who could share this beauty with her made it all the more special. Being a guitar player had its trials and tribulations, but today Guy Andrews was glad to be a musician. Even though Sandi had made a spur of the moment decision to take the afternoon off, Guy had no problem arranging to spend it with her; in fact, he had no problem clearing the whole weekend to be with her. Guy was not the most successful of performers, and his work was limited to late-night gigs at The Pendulum Pit, where he was often pre-empted by more popular performers on Saturday nights.

Sandi was thrilled that he had made time to be with her. From the moment they had first met, their relationship was magical. Guy always seemed to know exactly the right things to say, the right things to do. It was as if he had some sort of connection to her inner soul, a messenger that knew her innermost thoughts and feelings. She was sure it was fate, that somehow it was ordained that they be together. Within weeks of their meeting, Guy had moved in with Sandi. She often found herself wondering what it was that attracted her so strongly to him; they had so little in common. Then he would go and do something perfect.

This was one of those times. Paul would have never spontaneously taken off just to relax. There were certainly many things that she loved dearly about Paul, but she didn't want to think about those things right now. She was glad to have Guy here with her now to share in this winter wonderland.

As much as Guy liked to sleep in, the smell of coffee lured him from his bed. He walked into the kitchen and gave Sandi a peck on the cheek. "Mornin', lover."

She smiled and got up to pour him a cup.

"So, I've got you for the whole day, huh?"

"The whole weekend," she said. "Think you can stand it?" She put the mug down in front of him.

"It'll be a struggle, but I think I can manage." He reached up and pulled her close as he sat by the table, burying his head between her breasts.

She gave him a kiss on the top of the head. "Umm, don't start that now. I want to get outside and enjoy some of this glorious weather."

"Too bad," he muttered as he let her go.

They spent the day doing something she hadn't done since childhood —they played in the snow. She had forgotten how cleansing it could be. With a little practice she regained her skill at making the perfect snow angel. Guy was laughably bad at it. She complained about having given up her sled years ago, but Guy saved the day, appearing with two plastic trashcan lids. They raced to the hill in the park by her house. It was a steep cascading hillside that dropped off toward the Gunpowder River. The hill was a popular spot for local kids to gather after a fresh dump of snow. A dozen of them had already flattened out the powder, making for a rapid ride down the hill. They gawked at the two "old people" as Sandi awkwardly snuggled into the trashcan lid, and then screamed as Guy pushed her down the hill, following close behind as he jumped into the other lid.

"Jeez, act yer age, would ya!" she heard one little boy shout as she fought to stay upright. She gathered speed quickly, and soon her ecstasy turned to apprehension as the river grew closer and closer. It was quite shallow here, no fear of drowning, but the thought of crashing into the ice-cold water and smashing up against the rocky bank was less than appealing. She threw herself off the makeshift sled and screeched, as much with joy as with fear, as she rolled to a stop in the fresh snow.

For a brief second, she lay on her back staring up into the sun, realizing thankfully that her body was still intact, but then Guy landed on her with a thud.

"Whew! What a rush," he screamed.

"Ooph," Sandi grunted, the wind knocked out of her.

"Uh, sorry, San" Guy said, seeing the dazed look in her eyes. He gave her a slow, simmering kiss and the world seemed to melt away.

By the time they got home, they were both drenched and chilled to the bone. It was nothing that a soak in a hot bath and a romantic evening by the fire wouldn't cure.

When unburdened by the realities of everyday life, Guy was perfect for her. They spent the weekend in fantasyland; music and books by a crackling fire set against the glory of Mother Nature were the fare for the respite. She was totally removed from her work both physically and mentally. It was brief, but it provided the cleansing that she needed to rejuvenate herself, to rekindle her creativity.

By the time Sunday evening rolled around, Sandi felt like a new woman. She had not been so relaxed in years. Guy had promised the owner of the Pendulum Pit in Fell's Point that he would be back at work for the Sunday night crowd. Guy had developed a bit of a following over the past few months, and his presence would be missed. He felt good about being needed at work.

Sandi protested meekly, but in reality she did not mind seeing Guy walk out the door to go to work that evening. Mindless passion could be wonderful, but only for so long. She took advantage of the solitude of the evening to finish reading *I, Robot,* and went to bed early. Weekend mornings after an evening of wine and passion were tough to negotiate. Sandi had learned long ago to forgo alcohol on Sunday night; it made starting the work week much more tolerable. She was looking forward to starting off the week with a new attitude. An early evening with no wine or worries would surely do the trick.

———

It's tough getting out of bed when it's still dark out, especially when the winter chill is so deep that it seeps right through the walls and into you bedroom. This mid-December morning was one of those days.

Paul grunted and rolled over to hit the button on the alarm clock. As he lay there thinking of reasons not to crawl out from under his nice, warm down comforter, he began to realize that there really was no rush to go in to work this morning. For what seemed forever, he had always been in the middle of some phase of the nanobot project, but now, with the success of his recent patent acquisitions, he was finally *between* projects. He pulled the comforter up around his neck and nestled into the pillow.

About an hour later, the sunlight made its way in through the blinds, and Paul found himself struggling to stay in bed. Finally, he succumbed to the urges of his built-in alarm clock, the one that kept nudging his brain to kick into gear. He just couldn't sleep any longer knowing it was a workday, even if there was nothing in particular waiting for him at the office this morning.

It had been three days since that call from Sandi, and he still relished the sweetness of victory. At first he had felt kind of sorry for her, really. He knew that she had worked hard on the neuronanobots, and he remembered how he had felt when he learned that she had trumped him on the congressional approval for the human research trial, but this time it was his turn. With the passing time since that phone call from Sandi, he had gradually grown more disinterested in the supposed implausibility of the parallel advances that Sandi claimed to have made at Hopkins. *Just sour grapes*, he thought pityingly. He had decided to ignore her appeals for the time being. As much as he would enjoy spending some time with her, he would not do it under these circumstances. He was not going to let anything, not even Sandi, ruin that sweet taste of success.

He dressed warmly and took the elevator down to the lobby to check his mail before heading in to work. The mail was always delivered early to Poe Towers, and Paul figured it might be nice to have something other than science journals to read at work today. He planned to play out this rare opportunity to slack off at work to its fullest. Today was not going to be a productive one, at least not in the way that JT Anderson had come to expect of him. This was going to be a day to savor.

He got out at the lobby and found himself walking toward the mailroom with a bit of a lilt in his step. *I could get used to this,* he said to himself, enjoying the aimlessness of the moment, but in reality, he knew that he'd go nuts if he didn't get involved in a new project soon. He was determined not to think about that today.

Much to his disappointment, the mail was sparse, save for one rather large manila envelope. At first glance, he was excited at the thought of receiving a mystery package, but when he saw the return address with 'Dr. Sandra Fletcher' above it, he remembered that Sandi said she was sending him a copy of her research on the neuronanobots. He shoved it into his briefcase with disinterest, and made his way to the garage.

The city streets were a mess, with black road-crud from the recent snowstorm built up along the sides, but once out of the city it was as different story. A blanket of white snow still covered the hillsides, and icicles glistened on the trees along the highway. The roads themselves were completely clear, a result of one night of plowing followed by two days of bright Baltimore sunshine to finish the job. It was after ten, and the roads were nearly empty. It was an unusually easy drive into work.

Paul parked in his space at BNI and went right to his office. Sean was already in the lab running some tests when Paul entered.

"Well, look what the cat dragged in."

Paul smiled sheepishly.

"Ah, even you deserve a break now and then. Stop feeling so guilty."

Paul laughed. "It's all in your imagination, lad. 'Guilt' is not even in my vocabulary today."

"Hey," Sean looked serious, "what have you done with Paul Hingston, and why are you in his body?"

They stared at each other with deadpanned expressions for a brief second, and then burst out laughing. Paul shook his head and opened the door to his office. He tossed the briefcase on the desk, threw his coat up on the rack and plopped down in his chair. He put his feet up on the desk, enjoying the moment. It was so rare to have nothing pressing to do.

"Oh shit," he said, noticing the road crud on his shoes. He quickly pulled his feet off the desk and brushed the desktop with his hands. Grabbing for some tissues, he wiped the desk dry, and then cleaned his hands. He opened the briefcase and spotted the package from Sandi again. "You're not gonna ruin this glorious day for me, love." He tossed the package into the bottom drawer of his desk, the one where he filed the things he intended to never look at again. He closed the drawer, checked his shoes, which were now dry, and propped them back up on the desk.

"You say something, Paul?"

"Huh? ... Oh, no, just talking to myself."

"Good thing, cause if you're gonna start calling me 'love', I'm outa here, dude."

This day was just getting better and better. Paul leaned back in his chair, hands behind his head, and gazed out at the snow-glazed hillsides surrounding BNI.

CHAPTER ELEVEN

May 7, 2051

Six months and one day after he was released from Harborview Hospital, Rocky Stankowski was back to work.

"Good to have you back, Rocky."

White House Chief of Staff Harold Bradley climbed into the front passenger's seat of the government issued black Lincoln. White House protocol required the driver to open the rear passenger-side door for the chief, but now that Rocky was back to work, Mr. Bradley went back to the way he felt most comfortable. He felt ridiculous having someone open the door for him and even more ridiculous riding in the back seat by himself. He appreciated Rocky's indulgence in agreeing to forgo protocol so that he could open his own door and join Rocky in the front of the car.

"Good to be back, sir. Sure is a beautiful day, isn't it?"

Harold Bradley looked out the window of the Lincoln Continental as they pulled away from his Georgetown townhouse. It was a clear spring morning, the kind of day that makes it tough to go to work.

"Sure is, Rocky. Have a good weekend?"

"To tell you the truth, sir, I couldn't wait for it to end. The past six months have been like one never-ending weekend, at least during the days that they didn't make me go in to that damned hospital to be treated like a guinea pig. I mean, I'm real grateful and all that. I know that I wouldn't be back to work now if they hadn't stuck all those little robots into my head, but geez, the tests were unbelievable. Every week, something new."

"Well, thanks to guys like you, they're perfecting that procedure more quickly than anyone had thought possible. Pretty soon they'll be able to do it at any hospital in the country, and thanks to what they've been learning with all of those tests, most folks won't have to go through so many of them now. You were just unlucky enough to be one of the first, I guess."

"Or *lucky* enough to be one of the first, the way I figure it."

Mr. Bradley grinned broadly. "I suppose so, Rocky. I suppose so." *Now I know why I like this guy so much. It sure is refreshing to be around a 'glass is half-full' kind of guy.*

Harold Bradley glanced at the headlines of the Post. "Says here that the president's approval rating is the highest ever recorded in a peacetime poll. Not bad, huh?"

"No, sir." Rocky kept his eyes on the road.

"No, sir? That's all you've got to say?" Bradley could see that Rocky had a lot more on his mind than "No, sir."

"Well ..."

"Come on, Rocky, spill it. You're not gonna become the strong, silent type on me now, are ya? I need your insight. What's the *real* word on the street?"

Bradley knew that the pollsters captured a cross-section of society, of mainstream America. What he really wanted, though, was to find out what was on the minds of the subversives, the undercurrent of society. These were the people who scared Harold Bradley; these were the people who were most likely to act on their impulses, the real threat to the president. Rocky was a stand-up kind of guy, but his leisure life took him into society's trenches. Bradley knew this, but did not consider it a weakness. In fact, he considered it one of Rocky's great qualities, that here was a man who could walk through the strongest undercurrents and still stand tall. He depended on Rocky to keep him informed.

"I've got nothing but the utmost respect for the president, you understand."

"But ..."

"But he's really blowing it. I mean, to the average Joe, he's a wuss. He says the right thing, but he doesn't act. He's mastered the art of delegating to the point of distancing himself from decisions that affect us all. Sure he's doing great in the polls. That's because he doesn't offend anybody. I mean, how can he? He never makes any decisions."

Bradley thought a moment, realizing that Rocky was right.

"The art of politics. No enemies, no worries. Only ..."

Bradley glared at Rocky. "Only what?"

"Well, I hate to say it, but ... look, people take offense when they think they're being neglected. Life on the street is getting pretty rough, and people resent the corporate elite who are getting richer and richer off their sweat. Going postal at the office doesn't do any good. It doesn't change anything. People are getting fed up, and sooner or later it's going to filter up to the top. People blame the government for their growing hopelessness, dangerous people, the kind that have nothing to lose. These aren't the kind of people that live in fenced in houses in suburbia. These aren't the kind of people that talk to pollsters. These are the kind of people who stew in their own misery, who stay silent until they're ready to explode. If the president doesn't start to speak out for them soon, somebody's gonna blow, and it's gonna be in the president's direction."

Bradley knew that Rocky was talking in generalities. If Rocky had overheard any credible threat against the president, he surely would have come forward or would have squashed it himself. Rocky was not averse to using his considerable physical strength when properly motivated.

"As always, I appreciate your honesty, Rocky. I'll take it up with the president myself. He considers himself a man of the people, and I'm quite sure that he'll be anxious to change that image of non-concern for the average man."

"If you can convince him that it's real. Polls are a powerful thing, Mr. Bradley, a powerful thing."

"I'll convince him. That's my job."

The car pulled through the White House gates, and the guard waved. "Good to see you again, Rocky."

Rocky nodded and waved back. He dropped off Mr. Bradley, and went to park the car. It felt good to be a part of the team again.

The success of the nanobots in treating patients who had suffered devastating brain injuries had captured the imagination of the public. It was the kind of human-interest story that reporters craved, a dramatic cure for a horrible life-threatening injury. And unlike most of the "medical miracles" sensationalized by the press, this one had the added advantage of being real.

Many of those who had been treated in the human trial phase had become familiar faces to members of the news media who were hungry for interviews that could help shape stories for them to peddle to their audience. Rocky was not one of them. At first, he was hounded by several of the stations, but when Rocky snarled, he could be quite intimidating; reporters rarely approached him more than once, and word soon spread among the media that he was off limits.

Rocky enjoyed his anonymity. He loved feeling useful again and the summer passed quickly. Labor Day weekend was approaching and Harold Bradley was invited to spend the weekend with his family at Camp David, along with the president's family. Rocky didn't mind a bit when Mr. Bradley informed him of the plans. The ride through the Maryland countryside was beautiful, and the soundproof glass that insulated the passengers from the cab of the Lincoln Continental worked both ways; Rocky would be well insulated from the irritatingly animated young twins that Mr. Bradley was raising with his second wife, Dawn. And besides, it would give him an opportunity to visit Belle. Rocky had not returned to Belle's Place since the mugging, but he was determined to rid himself of that demon.

The black Continental arrived at the Bradley residence in Potomac, Maryland, at eight AM on the Friday before Labor Day. The president had given Bradley the day off to get a jump-start on the weekend and get his family settled in at Camp David. President Huntley Forsyth had ulterior motives; he knew the twins would sap Bradley's energy on the long ride, and he wanted his chief of staff fresh for a round of golf on Saturday morning. He figured that if the Bradleys got to Camp David early, Harry would have plenty of time to play with the kids, tire them out and get a good night's sleep.

Bradley was waiting for the car when Rocky pulled in to the driveway. Rocky rolled down the passenger side window as Bradley approached.

"Why don't you wait inside while I load the bags, sir? It's cold out this morning."

Bradley hunched down through the window. "Got some bad news, Rocky. I just got a call from the White House. Some damned urgent meeting that can't wait until after the weekend. We'll have to take care of business first. I told Dawn to sleep in if the kids let her. They're pretty wound up, what with the big weekend vacation and all. No point in dragging them downtown this morning. We'll get the meeting out of the way, and then come back for them."

Rocky was glad he wouldn't have the two hyperactive little tyrants in his car any longer than necessary.

"Sounds like a plan, sir. Hop in."

Bradley opened the passenger-side door and settled into the seat.

"Whoa," he said as he slid back into the seat.

"Yeah," Rocky answered, "sorry about that. It seems that the power seat adjustment locked up over night. I didn't have a chance to get it fixed. Hope it's not too uncomfortable. Why it slid all the way back, I can't figure, but it's stuck real good."

Bradley struggled with the power control, but the seat wouldn't budge. "You can say that again."

He settled back and glanced out the window. His view was obscured by the wide doorpost, which was steel reinforced in all government vehicles as added rollover protection. "Well, I've got plenty of leg room, but the view ain't much." Bradley wiggled his short legs in the air, not quite able to reach the floor with the seat all the way back. He laughed at his predicament. "I must look pretty ridiculous."

Rocky glanced over. "Distinguished as ever, sir."

"Wipe that grin off your face, driver."

"Yes, sir."

They drove off toward the White House. The roads were less crowded than usual. Obviously, they were not the only ones planning an early getaway for the long weekend. Rocky turned on River Road, heading toward the city. In the light holiday traffic, he was able to make good time and kept the speed at his usual four miles an hour over the posted limit. Although suburban sprawl had invaded the D.C. suburbs decades ago, there were still some wooded areas along River Road. They were passing one such area as they came up over a hill.

"Uhh!" Rocky screamed as an uncontrollable spasm overcame him. His arms twisted the wheel to the right as he fought against his own limbs with every fiber of his being, but his powerful body was helpless to fight it. The car veered sharply off the road, throwing Bradley against the side of the driver's seat, then slammed passenger side first into a stone wall jerking him violently back to his right and ramming his head against the steel doorpost. He lost consciousness too quickly to notice that the driver's side air bag had failed to deploy or to see the blood splaying out of Rocky's head all across the dashboard.

In one brief moment, Rocky's precious anonymity was snuffed out; however, it would not prove to be a nuisance to him. His life was snuffed out just as quickly.

The press reported all the gory details of the accident and showed the helicopter lifting off River Road to rush the White House Chief of Staff to Walter Reed Hospital, where a trauma team was standing by. They did not report that the injury involved a severe contusion to the right frontal area, with a depressed skull fracture causing a penetration injury to the frontal lobe. The public was not interested in those kinds of details; however, in the weeks that followed, neuronanobots monopolized the airwaves and soon became a household word.

CHAPTER TWELVE

The aroma of hazelnut coffee wafted up the wooden stairs and into the bedroom of the Kincades' Highlandtown rowhouse. Richie loved to sleep late on Sunday mornings and Lara liked to oblige him, but she'd already been up for an hour and she was salivating for some hot waffles and coffee. She did not want to eat alone and ruin the Sunday morning ritual, and she knew Richie's weak spot. The smell of fresh coffee, especially hazelnut coffee, would draw him right out of that bed and down the stairs.

This Labor Day weekend Richie and Lara had decided to stay home — a nice quiet weekend, just the two of them. Normally they would head to Ocean City with a half-million other people for the last beach weekend of the season, but they were tired of the rat race. The traffic across the Bay Bridge and slow crawl toward the shore took away any shred of relaxation the ocean waves could offer. This year was going to be different.

Saturday was a cold, drizzly day. They had spent the day inside in front of the TV set, and they were already getting cabin fever. The morning sun promised a better day today, and Lara was determined to get a jump on it. An early breakfast together, then a short drive to Harbor Place or maybe to the park if it was warm enough; that would do the trick.

"Just like clockwork." Lara smiled as she watched Richie lumbering down the stairs, scratching the hair on his slightly protuberant belly, not quite covered by the tattered plaid robe he'd worn every morning for the past decade.

"The nose knows," he said. He tilted his head back and took in a deep, exaggerated whiff of the fresh coffee aroma in the air. "Hazelnut, if I'm not mistaken."

"What a detective!" She put her hand up to the side of her face, mouth and eyes wide open in mock amazement.

"Go get the Sunday paper while I put up the waffles, Sherlock."

Richie didn't argue. After all, what was coffee and waffles without the Sunday paper?

Lara poured the batter into the waffle maker and set two mugs of piping hot coffee out on the breakfast table. Richie came in with the paper tucked under his arm, yawning.

"Have a seat, lover. Looks like you'd better get some of that coffee in to you. I want you wide-awake. I'm not spending another day in front of the tube."

Richie pulled the paper out of the plastic bag, and threw it down on the table. He plopped down into his chair, eyes fixed on the front page as it uncoiled in front of him.

"Holy mother of God," he muttered as he read the headline.

Lara looked over from the waffle iron, where she was trying to force them to cook faster by staring at them really hard. She saw her husband's face fixed on the paper. "What's the matter, hon?"

She walked to the table and looked over his shoulder at the paper. "Oh, what a mess." A full color picture of Rocky's mangled car graced the front page of the Sunday Sun.

Richie sipped his coffee as he read the story. The newspaper reporter had found an eyewitness who had seen the car veer violently off the road without so much as the hint of an impending collision, an animal or other obstacle in the road to have caused the driver to lose control. The reporter dressed up the story with a direct quote from the passerby:

"It had to be a blowout, or maybe the driver had a heart attack or a convulsion or something. I mean, there was nothing in the road, man. I was just standing there with my dog. I always walk my dog along that stretch of River Road in the morning. It's a great way to get exercise. You know, for me as much as for Ralphie. Ralphie, that's my dog, you know? Anyhow, I was just standing there with Ralphie, when this big, black Lincoln comes rolling up over the hill. It caught my attention, you know? I mean, I figured it had to be a bigwig or something. Anyhow, all of a sudden it just veered into that wall, and ... bam!"

The article went on to explain that official United States Government vehicles were not equipped with the normal safety computer chips that restricted their movement and speed. This was done to allow for emergency avoidance maneuvers in case of an assault situation, but, he added, these cars are driven by professional drivers. None had ever been known to get into an accident due to the lack of a safety microchip.

This particular vehicle, the article continued, was transporting White House Chief of Staff Harold Bradley, who had suffered a serious head injury and had been flown to Walter Reed for a new nanobot treatment for brain injury developed by BNI.

"Oh, no. No you don't, Detective Kincade." Lara could see the gears grinding inside her husband's head as he read the paper. "Don't you even think of it. You are not going to ruin this glorious sunny day by going into the station."

"The station?" Richie looked shocked, in a theatrical sort of way. "The thought never crossed my mind, darlin'."

"Good. Make sure you keep it that way."

"Of course, dear, of course," Richie said without really hearing her words. His mind was buried in the article again.

The reporter went on to relate the irony that Bradley's driver, the late Rocky Stankowski, had himself received the very same treatment less than a year earlier as one of the test subjects for the nanobots. He wrote about Rocky's injury and miraculous recovery. The article told the storied history of Mr. Stankowski – dedicated Marine veteran, quiet introspective man, known by few and respected by many. A decorated special-ops soldier in his younger days, Rocky had led a quiet life ever since he had retired at the age of forty. Those who knew him, and there were not that many who did according to the article, described him as a fiercely loyal, indelibly honest man; each said without hesitation that they would trust him with their lives.

The article described the incident in downtown Baltimore the prior year, when Rocky had been mugged for a measly thirty dollars in cash and a watch valued at seven dollars and fifty cents. The incident had incensed Rocky's friends and acquaintances; no one disliked the big man. But as usual, Rocky had played the hero much to his chagrin, and had become the poster boy for a new medical treatment using miniature robots to repair the damage a baseball bat had done to his brain.

The story detailed the remarkable recovery that Rocky had made, and went on to briefly describe several other cases with similar results. Using a series of basic diagrams, the article described in layman's terms how the nanobot treatment worked. This was followed by a short interview with Dr. Sandra Fletcher of Johns Hopkins University, considered by many to be the world's leading authority on nanobots. She described the theory and development of the nanobots, and how they were revolutionizing medical care in the twenty-first century.

The reporter asked Dr. Fletcher about the renowned JT Anderson and the role of his company, BNI, in the development of nanobots. Dr. Fletcher said as little as possible about both Mr. Anderson and his company, in a thinly veiled effort at diplomacy.

Richard Kincade was fascinated. "Hmm, BNI ... which case was it I saw them in before?"

"What was that, honey?"

"Oh, nothing, darling." Richie sighed a bit, and reluctantly plopped the paper down on the table, making sure that Lara would take notice. He couldn't get the thought out of his head, he knew he had run across BNI in a case before, but there was no way he would let Lara find out how much this was eating at him. *This is going to have to wait until Tuesday,* he thought with disgust. *Get it out of your mind, Richard Kincade. Get it out of your mind.*

"Great breakfast, hon. I'm gonna run up and shower." He glanced out the window. "Looks like a great day to be outside."

Lara looked after him as he hurried up the stairs. She knew when he was hooked on a case. She knew him too well to fall for his feigned disinterest, but appreciated that he was doing it for her. Lara decided to play along this time, at least for the day. Aware that she may not have his full attention today, she would take what she could get, and then maybe let him get back to work tomorrow. Once he got his hooks into something, he could never really let it go until the mystery was solved. This was Detective Richard Kincade. This is what Lara had married. She was darned proud of it, too.

———

"Hey, Richie." The guard at the door of the South Baltimore Precinct station waved as Richard Kincade came in. "Have a good Labor Day?"

"Yup," Richie said automatically without thinking as he walked by. He thought of the time that he and Lara had spent together over the weekend strolling in Druid Hill Park, dinner in Little Italy, an evening of romance that reminded him of feelings he'd almost forgotten, and a Labor Day barbecue with the neighbors. He stopped a few steps into the building and turned. "Yeah, Sam, I really did. How 'bout you?"

The guard lit up. Most folks who came through that door hardly noticed Sam. Sure, they'd say "How ya doing" now and then, but they never really stopped for an answer. They weren't really asking, not the way that Richie was doing right now, staring at him with questioning eyes. "Just fine Richie, it went just fine. Thanks for asking." Sam was grinning ear to ear.

Richie nodded and headed toward the elevator. The weekend had passed quickly. He was surprised to find that he was able to forget about the terrible accident he had read about Sunday morning, the one that killed that poor bastard who spent his life shuttling the chief of staff around, but he *had* forgotten, at least for a little while. He couldn't remember the last time he felt so relaxed. He had been with Lara – completely – for three whole days. He loved her very much and it was nice to remember why.

Monday night had come too quickly, and by the time dinner was finished, work slowly started to creep into his head once again. As he slept, he remembered the seemingly innocent case of Lester Hanes, the young computer programmer from BNI. Pulling the data files from that case would be the first order of the day.

The elevator stopped on the third floor, and Richie exited with an uncharacteristic lilt in his step.

Hank Holiday looked up from his desk. "Well," he smirked, "looks like somebody got some this weekend, eh?"

Richie stopped at Hank's desk for a second, ready to stare down his lewd old friend. It was those kind of remarks that gave guys the reputation they had to live down after working hours. Richie hesitated, then decided it just wasn't worth it. He raised an eyebrow, smiled wryly, and walked on. *What the hell,* Richie thought, *whatever makes his day.* Besides, at his age, he didn't get to stare down a comment like that too often.

He walked back to his desk. "Mornin', Daisy," he greeted his computer monitor. Some of the guys thought he was nuts, but somehow, saying "computer, activate" seemed too mechanical. He preferred to think of Daisy as his secretary. After all, she took dictation, sent letters, answered his calls and did his filing. "Pull a file for me, would ya, sweetheart?"

Hank glanced over at him.

"OK, OK, maybe that is a bit over the top, but cut me some slack here, Hank. I don't come in here to start the week in a good mood too often."

"Just give me the details later, would ya. I pulled the duty this weekend. I could use a little vicarious holiday pleasure, you know?"

Richie shook his head. "Not a chance, pal."

Hank sighed.

"Which file do you need, Detective Kincade?"

Richie smiled at Daisy. "Lester Hanes. It was a routine traffic case, single vehicle fatality. About a year ago, I think."

"Accessing...On screen."

Kincade marveled at how quick Daisy was. "Thanks, hon."

Hank squirmed in his seat.

Kincade poured over the report. He had filed it himself, and the details came back to him as he read. "Bingo!"

Hank looked over. "You gambling on company, time? At least keep it down, would you?" He motioned over to the chief's office.

Richie shot him a puzzled look.

"Personally, I prefer BlackJack.com, but my wife's a sucker for that Bingo site too. I don't have a problem with you playing a little on company time, but keep it down. You're gonna ruin it for all of us."

Kincade nodded in the negative. "No, no. I mean, 'Bingo' as in 'I found what I was looking for in the report.'" He pointed at the screen. "BNI – That's the company that produced that new treatment they used on the brain of the driver..." Kincade skimmed over the article he had cut out of the paper about the Labor Day weekend accident that had killed Harold Bradley. "...Stankowski, that's his name, Rocky Stankowski. This kid," he pointed at the report on his monitor, "Lester Hanes, was a programmer for BNI. Single car accident, a de-chipped car and a sharp swerve to the right off an empty road...same M.O.. Could just be coincidence, but it doesn't smell right to me."

He looked over at Hank again. "BlackJack.com?"

"Shh!" Hank slinked back into his chair, glancing again toward the chief's office. "Come on, Richie. Give me a break, would ya?"

Richie shrugged his shoulders and sat down at his desk.

"Say, Richie, try this one: OTTFF."

"What?"

"OTTFF...what's the next letter in the sequence?" Hank loved word puzzles, anagrams, things like that. Code breaking had been his favorite course at the police academy; Richie hated it.

"Come on, Hank, I got work to do."

Hank threw his hands up. "You're no fun, man."

Richie smiled. "Sorry." He redirected his attention to the computer. "Daisy, what've you got on the driver of that Lincoln that Harold Bradley was killed in this weekend?"

"Accessing ... Rocky Stankowski. Purple Heart, 2031 Persian Gulf War. Retired from US Marines 2036. Secret Service detail for the Governor of Virginia 2037 through 2041. Personal driver for Senator Harold Bradley 2042 through 2048, and continuing as personal driver for Chief of Staff Harold Bradley, 2048 through present ... correction, through yesterday. Deceased September 2, 2051."

Kincade sat, head in hands. "Impressive. Damned impressive. Nobody could get to a guy like that. No way would Stankowski have caused that crash for a payoff, even if he thought he'd survive it. You just don't buy a man like that; too much honor.

Hank sat on the edge of the desk, handing a cup of coffee to Kincade. "Talking to your computer again, aren't you?"

Richie took the coffee. "Thanks." He took a sip from the steaming mug. "At least she doesn't give me any lip about how much caffeine I drink."

Hank smiled. It was somehow comforting to know that Richie's weekend wasn't *totally* perfect. "Whatcha working on, Richie?"

"Ah, that crash that killed Harold Bradley this weekend. It just doesn't smell right to me, you know? You wouldn't happen to know anything about BNI, would you?"

"Nah. I'm not into tech. But this chick I dated a couple of years back worked there. She loved the place, but got herself fired for snooping around. Those techies are always full of secrets, you know? Shelly was a bright kid. They had her working on some kind of genetics project, but even she didn't know what she was working on. I mean, she knew *her* part of it, but not the big picture, you know? She said it was like working on a giant puzzle and her job was to put one little section of it together without knowing what the whole thing was going to look like when it got done. Drove her nuts; said she wanted to be damned sure she wasn't helping somebody build a new biological weapon or something. All the secrets made her paranoid. One day she snooped into the mainframe to try and figure out what the project was all about, you know, to see what the various puzzle pieces were gonna make when the company put them all together. The head of security at BNI caught her, and she was out the door the next day. What a job, huh?"

"Yeah. Who the hell would want to work in a place like that? Never knowing what you're really building or what they're gonna do with it. Think I could talk to Shelly?"

"Sure. I'll give her a buzz. It'll give me an excuse to call her. Maybe I'll get lucky." Hank winked at Richie. He started to walk back to his desk, then stopped and turned. "S," he said.

"Excuse me?"

"S," Hank repeated. "The next letter in the sequence is S. OTTFFS — One, Two, Three, Four, Five, Six." He looked at the blank stare on Richie's face. He walked off, exceedingly proud of himself.

Kincade shook his head and smiled. Hank Holiday lived a very different life than Richie Kincade. He envied Hank and felt sorry for him at the same time.

———

Shelly Lange was happy to hear from Hank. She was just recovering from a bad relationship, and in comparison, Hank didn't seem so bad. They agreed to meet for dinner. Shelly was anxious to talk to someone about BNI. She still fumed over being fired, but knew she had no legal recourse; after all, she had been caught hacking into the company's mainframe. It was fortunate that all they did was fire her, and she knew it. Just the same, the chance to tell someone like Detective Kincade what was going on at BNI was delicious to her. The contract at BNI, like most high tech companies, had a confidentiality clause that kept her from going to the press, but she could spill her guts to a cop in the line of duty and BNI's lawyers couldn't touch her. It would be a long overdue catharsis, and if she was lucky, Kincade may even nail the sons of bitches. She jumped at the chance to talk to the detective, and agreed to meet him at the station that afternoon.

"I'm impressed, Hank." Kincade said when informed Shelly had agreed to meet.

"Never underestimate the charm of a Holiday," he gloated. Actually, he was a little surprised himself. He and Shelly hadn't parted on the greatest of terms, and he figured it would be a bit of a challenge to get over that little lack of fidelity thing she had gotten so steamed about.

Shelly arrived at two PM, just as Kincade was finishing a Coke and a Polish sausage in a hotdog bun oozing with ketchup.

"Into health food, I see."

"Look, lady," Kincade started, "I get enough ..." his jaw dropped as his eyes fixed on a pair of long, shapely legs in sheer stockings, and followed them up past the hem of the dark gray dress that hugged the curvaceous figure of Shelly Lange. He glared at her bright green eyes, speechless.

"...grease to slide through the afternoon with that sandwich?" She finished his sentence.

"Uh, that's not exactly what ...Are you Shelly Lange?"

She nodded in the affirmative. "Not what you were expecting?"

Kincade stood without saying a word.

"Is that because I'm not what you were expecting to see when Hank said he was sending over some biotech geek, or just because you can't picture me with the guy."

"Maybe a little bit of both." He motioned her to the chair at the far side of his desk. "Thanks for coming in on such short notice, Ms. Lange."

"*Doctor* Lange," she corrected.

"Uh, sorry... Dr. Lange."

"That's OK, why don't you just call me Shelly?"

"Whatever you prefer ... Shelly." She sat down and crossed her legs, as Richie struggled to keep his eyes off them. "So, Hank tells me you worked at BNI."

"Hank would be right, for a change." She smiled.

"He is on occasion. Was he right in thinking that you suspected something unethical was going on there?"

"I didn't think so at first. I mean, most of those high tech companies are pretty secretive. They have to be if they want to keep their competitors' spies away. I kind of took the paranoia in stride for a while, and then Helen went into status and came out of the hospital a month later with Jello-brain."

"Status?"

"Oh, sorry... status epilepticus ... uncontrolled, sustained seizures. Helen had only worked for the company for a couple of months, but she and I had become real close. She had some kind of accident as a kid that left her with a seizure disorder. She took her epilepsy drugs faithfully; hadn't had a seizure in over twenty years from what she had told me. Then one day after a routine employee physical, she just collapsed and started jerking around...her whole body, right there in front of me. I'm a doctor of genetics, not a medical doctor. I freaked, you know? I mean, when someone you know collapses like that and you don't know what to do ... I felt so helpless. I called out for help, but it took them almost a half hour to stop the seizures. They said the convulsions were so bad that she didn't get enough oxygen to her brain. The last time I saw her, nearly a year after she got out of the hospital, she still didn't know who I was. God, it's so sad." Her eyes welled up with tears.

Kincade handed her a tissue. "I know this is hard for you, but..."

"No. No, it's OK. I want to get those bastards."

"So why did you suspect that BNI was responsible for what had happened to Helen?"

"Well, at first I didn't. I talked to the doctor at BNI who had examined her that day, and he told me she looked fine, but that the test he had done showed the level of seizure medicine in her blood was way too low. Maybe she got a bad batch of medicine, or maybe her metabolism had just changed, he said, but for some reason, the medicine that had controlled her seizures for years just stopped working."

Her green eyes sunk toward the desktop. "I bought it hook, line and sinker. That is, until a few months later when Billy Jackson died."

"Billy Jackson?"

"A new programmer that BNI had hired. Just like Helen, he'd only been there a couple of months when the accident happened."

"What kind of accident?"

"His car went off of an icy bridge and plunged into the Middle River near Annapolis. Everyone figured that he had lost control on the ice. The car was recovered months later and was too badly damaged for a useful investigation. Nothing that would raise suspicion."

"Then why did it raise yours?"

"Well, just like Helen, Billy had only been hired at BNI a couple of months before he died, and just like Helen, he had some kind of a brain injury when he was a kid... a football injury, I think. He walked a little funny, but you'd have never known it otherwise. I knew that our work had something to do with making nanobots for the human brain, and I started to get a little suspicious. But what really did it for me was when Janice Saint-Martin got arrested for de-chipping her car."

Kincade raised an eyebrow. "I remember that case. See, I'm the guy they send to investigate motor vehicle fatalities when the security chips have been removed. Even though Saint-Martin didn't die, they called me in because it was such a strange case. If I remember right, she was pulled over for doing one-twenty in a fifty zone. When they pulled her over, she claimed she didn't even remember turning on to State Road 87, and swore that she had never gone even one mile an hour over the speed limit in her whole life. Even when the mechanic she hired to de-chip the car testified against her in a plea deal, she swore that she'd never met the guy...denied ever taking her car to him even when he presented the security chip from her car as evidence in the case. She lost the case, but she was pretty damned convincing. Even I almost believed her in spite of the evidence."

"You should have. Jan was the most honest girl I ever met, and I knew her real well. In fact, I helped her get the job there. Jan and I grew up together, went to University of Maryland together, and shared an apartment in Columbia after college. When I started at BNI, she stayed on at Maryland to do research, but she never really enjoyed it. I talked her into applying at BNI, but that was before I knew about Helen and Billy."

"When I started to get suspicious, I begged her to leave. See, back in college she had this obnoxious jock boyfriend who didn't take too kindly to rejection. He got really pissed when University didn't want him on their football team, and then when Jan dumped him...well, he really freaked out. I don't know what she ever saw in him anyway ... well, he did have a pretty hot bod, but he was such a creep. Anyhow, he beat her up pretty bad ... severe concussion the doctors said. Fortunately, she recovered completely and BNI was glad to get her. Only, what I didn't realize until Helen's brain was turned to Jello and Billy drove his Chevy into the Middle River, was that BNI was glad to get her because *she* had had a brain injury too. In fact, once I started snooping, I discovered that all three of them had had nearly the same injury...the same part of the brain, that is — the right frontal lobe. Quite the coincidence, huh? I begged Helen to quit, but she thought I was just paranoid. A week later, she was arrested. She was lucky, I suppose."

"Lucky? How do you figure?"

"Well, she was supposed to die. Don't you get it, Detective? That's what BNI was working on, I'm sure of it. They were looking for a way to control people's brains so completely that they could get those people to kill themselves. If you don't believe nanobots can do that, look up Dr. Sandra Fletcher at Hopkins. She's the real expert. BNI just stole their ideas from her. "

"Look, Doc, I may be suspicious of BNI, but don't you think that's a little ..."

"Paranoid?" she finished his sentence, once again. "I don't think Lester Hanes would think so. Have you checked his medical records?

I'll bet you dinner and a bottle of wine he had some kind of head trauma in his life that damaged his right frontal lobe."

"I don't think Hank would approve of that bet," Richie Kincade said. *Don't imagine my wife would appreciate it too much either,* he thought to himself.

"Screw Hank," she smiled as she unfolded her hands and ran a finger up the side of her thigh, curling it under the hem of her short, tight skirt.

I'm sure that's just what Hank has in mind, honey, Richie thought as he struggled to divert his gaze.

Detective Kincade slept poorly that night. He had been at this job a long time and he usually left his cases at the office, but every once in a while one of them would just get under his skin. This was one of those times.

He couldn't get Shelly Lange out of his mind. It wasn't so much the emerald eyes staring out from under her long brunette hair, though they were mesmerizing. It was the thought of BNI being able to control the minds of unsuspecting subjects. Even if they could find a way to do it, which Kincade doubted, how could anyone hire good, hard-working people like Helen Jensen, Billy Jackson, Janice Saint-Martin and Lester Hanes, just to kill them off in the name of a scientific experiment? And if they were willing to do something like that, what was their end-goal? It must be something awfully sinister if they had to *practice* the killing first. The thoughts were too disturbing to sleep through.

Richie was grateful to see the light of day creeping through the bedroom curtains, and rolled out of bed around six, tired of trying to find a way to doze off. He gave Lara a light kiss on the cheek, careful not to wake her completely. He was antsy to get to work, but saw no need to make Lara get up early to fix him breakfast. He'd grab a cup of coffee at the station.

Not surprisingly, Richie was the first one in that morning. He turned on the coffee maker, and strode over to his desk.

"Mornin', Daisy."

The computer recognized Kincade's voice, and awakened from sleep mode. He could hear the hard drive whirring into action.

"Good morning, Detective Kincade. Did you sleep well?"

"Not a wink, Daisy, but thanks for asking." Kincade chuckled. He was glad he had programmed a little bit of humanity into Daisy. It somehow made it a little easier to talk to a plastic box.

"What can I do for you, Detective?"

"I don't suppose you could get me glazed donut or two, now."

"I could call out for a delivery."

Kincade was caught off guard by the practical reply to his rhetorical question. "Not a bad idea, Daisy. Why don't you make it a dozen mixed? I'll treat the boys today. And when you're done, see if you can get me an appointment with a Doctor Sandra Fletcher in the nanotech department at Hopkins for this morning."

"Right away, sir."

"Thanks, Daisy." Kincade went over to check the coffee while Daisy made the calls, and returned a few moments later with a piping hot mug in his hand.

"The donuts will be at the downstairs desk in ten minutes, but Dr. Fletcher's office won't be open until nine."

"Damn, you're good."

Kincade couldn't wait to make an appointment with Dr. Sandra Fletcher. He poured his coffee into a road mug, and headed down to the front desk. *The heck with the boys*, he thought to himself as he paid the delivery boy and tucked the box of donuts under his arm.

"Check me out on Unit Five, Jake," he said to the guard at the motor pool. It was hardly necessary. Unit Five was the only car Richie Kincade ever took, and it was always available. The unit was a '43 Chevy Malibu two-door sedan with light tan paint that was peeling away around the prominent dents in the left front panel from a memorable chase, one of the few in Kincade's career. He mostly dealt with dead people who weren't too hard to catch up with. The car held sentimental value for Kincade; to everyone else, it was a junker.

"Early start this morning, eh Richie? It wouldn't have something to do with a certain green-eyed brunette, now would it?" Word of Shelly Lange's visit had spread through the station like fire on kerosene.

Kincade raised an eyebrow. "Geez, you guys are gonna get me in deep with the missus with that kind of talk." He shook his head. "It's not the green-eyed doc, OK? Keep it mum on that, would ya? It's hard enough to make up to the wife for all the weird hours I work without having to explain away a thing like that. It's like having to deal with all the down side of a torrid affair without ever getting to touch the mistress."

"And here I was giving you credit for scoring with a perfect ten," Jake smiled.

"I got all the perfection I need at home, Jake. Work's just work."

Jake could only stare in admiration as Kincade drove off toward the lab at Hopkins.

———

Sandi and Guy had gone to Ocean City for the season-ending weekend, and had decided to extend their vacation by an extra day to avoid the returning traffic along Route 50 on Labor Day. They enjoyed a leisurely drive back on Tuesday, taking in Saint Michaels' peaceful streets for a long lunch stop. It was a bit out of the way, but it was the kind of offbeat thing that Guy liked to do. Sandi had a harder time relaxing than Guy, but she found it refreshing to be confronted with the unexpected now and then. Instead of the usual tense traffic battle to finish the weekend, the drive back from the beach turned out to be the most relaxing day of the trip.

She did not feel like getting up for work on Wednesday morning, but she was so far behind from the long weekend, that she fought her way out from under the covers and made her way to the lab by nine-fifteen.

Richie Kincade stopped after the third donut, but saved a few sips of the now-cold coffee to keep him occupied while he waited. He knew what Dr. Fletcher looked like from the file he had accessed on the car's computer. He compared the picture on his monitor with each of the young women who entered the nanotech research facility that morning. He had decided it would be best to intercept the doctor on her way in. He had a better chance to get her to agree to an impromptu meeting if he caught her off-guard, rather than in the confines of her lab where the excuse of work or the moral support of co-workers might give her the courage to put him off. He needed to see her right away.

Kincade was sure he had missed her. It seemed out of character for an academic ladder-climber to be late for work at her own lab. He got out of the car and stretched, then reached in to grab his coffee and take one last big swig to finish it off. As he lifted the mug, he spotted Sandi running up the steps of the nanotech building.

"Shit!" He tossed the mug in through the open window and chased after her. One of the advantages of Unit Five was that no one really wanted to steal it. It was as loaded with sophisticated electronics as any other vehicle in the motor pool, but Unit Five's exterior kept any would-be thieves from ever noticing what was inside.

"Dr. Fletcher!" He called after her as he raced up the steps. "Dr. Fletcher," he shouted a bit louder as she grabbed the door.

Sandi turned and raised a hand to shade her eyes from the low-lying morning sun. She squinted to focus on the silhouette Kincade created against the bright background.

"Thank you, Dr. Fletcher." Kincade panted, and paused to catch his breath as he stopped on the step below her.

"Do I know you?" she asked.

"No. No, I doubt it." He pushed his right hand out toward her. "Detective Richard Kincade, Baltimore P.D., Motor Vehicle Division."

"Was I speeding? Boy, you guys are really dedicated, but ...don't I still need to be in my car for you to arrest me?"

Kincade detected the hint of facetiousness, which Sandi made no effort to hide. He let out a long deep breath, having finally caught his wind.

"OK, OK. I guess I left myself open for that one, Doc. To be more precise, I'm with the Motor Vehicle Tech-Tampering Division, but that's kind of a mouthful, you know?"

"Motor Vehicle Tech-Tampering Division?" Sandi asked.

"Yeah. We're the guys that investigate when people de-chip cars for criminal activity. Things like auto theft, burglary, homicide, that kind of stuff, but when I use words like *homicide* it kind of scares people, puts them on the defensive, you know? So I try to avoid it on first introductions."

Sandi looked him straight in the eyes. "Now look, I know I was speeding, but I'm sure I didn't run over anyone. I'd have felt the bump. A body feels different than a pot hole ... at least that's what they tell me."

Sandi squirmed a bit as Kincade met her gaze with an inquisitive look. "Uh, I guess I should stop trying to be funny, huh, Detective?"

Kincade nodded in agreement without saying a word.

"I've always had a bit of a wry sense of humor ... gets me in trouble every now and then. I guess this is one of those times." She turned to face him directly, stood erect and pulled down at the edges of her wrinkled silk jacket, smoothing it against her body. "Can we start over?" She thrust her hand toward him. "I'm Dr. Sandra Fletcher. What can I do for you, Detective?

Kincade motioned her to a bench by the front door. It was a particularly pleasant late summer kind of day, and Sandi liked the idea of staying outside a bit longer before committing herself to the confines of the lab.

"So, I hear you're the lady to talk to when it comes to nanobot technology."

"Is that right? Where did you hear that?"

Kincade fidgeted uncomfortably. He wasn't so sure that Shelly Lange wanted to be any more involved with this than she already was.

"I know, I know. You can't reveal your sources. I watch TV enough to know that cops don't like to reveal their sources."

Kincade was relieved. "Something like that."

"Well, I suppose your *source*," she emphasized as she made imaginary quotation marks around the word, "is correct. I've probably spent more time developing nanobots than anyone else on the planet, except maybe for Paul, that traitor."

"Paul?"

"Dr. Paul Hingston. He used to be my mentor here until he jumped ship to join the private sector. He works for BNI now, and what's more, he had the audacity to steal my work...that bastard. I'm sure of it, but it's nearly impossible to prove. The son of a bitch patented all my work. He stole *my* research and *he* got the patents... beat me to the punch. He even got the stuff that I developed *after* he left here, I just can't figure out how. He doesn't have access to the lab anymore, much less to my computer. But somehow he did it. No doubt about it. And to think I was gonna marry that SOB."

Sandi saw the vacuous look in Detective Kincade's face, and blushed. "Uh, sorry. Guess I kind of digressed a little, huh?"

"Kind of." It was an interesting twist, but one that Kincade didn't have time for at the moment. He decided to file it away for now, but this slant on Hingston added a twist to the case that Kincade hadn't considered. When he thought about BNI, he assumed that everything revolved around JT Anderson. "But BNI is the reason I came to talk to you."

"Ahah! I knew those bastards were up to something."

Sandi's animosity toward the company was almost tangible, and Kincade wanted to keep this more factual ... for now. Sometimes it paid to play on the emotions of a witness, but at this point, he needed to understand what bots could and could not do.

"Maybe," he waved off the notion with his right hand, "but let's get back to you for a minute."

"Me?" She sounded insulted.

"Yeah, you are the nanobot expert, aren't you? That's why I came here — to learn more about nanobots. More specifically, to learn more about those bots they are using to repair damaged brains."

"Neuronanobots," she nodded. "Pretty amazing stuff, isn't it?'

Kincade nodded.

"Most of the basic work in their development was done right here in my lab."

"Then I came to the right person. Tell me, are they really safe?"

"Absolutely. We engineered layers of safety protocols into their programming. They're safer than the cells we were born with."

"How so?"

"Well, for one, they prevent seizures."

"Prevent them? I thought that any trauma to the brain can *cause* seizures, and it seems to me that putting artificial cells into a brain is certainly a form of trauma."

Sandi was surprised. "Well, I see someone's been doing his homework."

"Spoken like a true teacher, Doc."

She blushed again. "Sorry. It's second nature, I guess. Anyway, that was precisely one of our concerns when we started the project. We knew that implanting nanobots in the human brain would create a risk of seizures. Even the new organic bots, which are a lot less irritating than mechanical bots, could create a nidus for a seizure. The solution was kind of brilliant, if I say so myself. I programmed a code into the genetic sequence of the nanobots, so they would secrete a natural neuronal cell membrane stabilizer."

Kincade was lost. "Uh, could you say that in English, maybe."

"Oh, sorry," she giggled. "I get carried away sometimes. The bots make a chemical that acts like an anti-seizure medicine, and release it into the surrounding area in the brain. Once they do that, there is less risk of a seizure occurring than there would be in you or me."

Kincade raised an eyebrow. "Curious."

"What?"

"Did BNI build in that same safety protocol?"

"Yes. Of course they did. I went over all their patents myself as soon as they were public. That's how I know Paul stole my work."

Kincade was almost disappointed. So much for his theory about Rocky Stankowski's auto accident. He was sure after having heard about Helen Jensen's seizures that Stankowski must have had a seizure just before his accident, one caused by those BNI nanobots in his brain.

"So it's impossible for someone to have a seizure after the bots are implanted?"

"Well, not impossible. If that person were to have a seizure originating in some other area of the brain, the chemical secreted by the bots may not stop it, but the bots definitely would not *cause* the seizure."

Kincade sat quietly, absorbing the new information and trying to piece it together, not only with the Rocky Stankowski case, but also with the four strange cases Dr. Shelly Lange had described from her days at BNI.

"Were any of the bots used before you perfected the anti-seizure stuff?"

"Well, in some animal studies, yeah, but no human trials were started until we got over that hurdle." Sandi was growing suspicious at the line of questioning. "What's this all about, anyway? You're not just gathering a little harmless background info for a case, are you?"

Kincade thought for a moment, and then let out a brief sigh. He figured he wasn't going to get much further with this unless he leveled with Dr. Fletcher about his suspicions. What harm could it do? She was no big fan of BNI anyway; she certainly wouldn't leak the information to them.

"Look, I probably shouldn't tell you this, but my source detailed some strange happenings over at BNI during the two years before nanobots were approved for brain injury treatment."

Kincade described the four cases related to him by Shelly Lange in as much detail as he could recall.

"So what do you think, Doc? Could there be something to all this, or do I just have a paranoid informant who's out to get BNI, maybe even dislikes them more than you?"

Sandi eyed him closely. "More than me? Am I a suspect here, Detective? Am I the one you're investigating?"

Kincade laughed. "No, no, Dr. Fletcher. I'm sorry if I ... I guess I can see why you might have thought ... No, I was just thinking about your earlier comments about how BNI stole Dr. Hingston away from academia, how he ... jumped ship, I think you put it. But I certainly did not mean to implicate you in any wrongdoing. Not in the least."

"Well, that's a relief. I mean, there's no love lost between me and BNI ..." Her voice trailed off as she realized that there really was love lost, in the truest sense of the word, when BNI stole Paul away from her. "...but I certainly would never do anything illegal, or even immoral for that matter, to try and get even with those bastards."

"Of course not, Doctor. My apologies, but I really could use your help on this one. What do you think? Could BNI be using the nanobots to control people's minds?"

"Who sounds paranoid now, Detective?"

Kincade chuckled.

"In theory, yeah, I suppose so, but we don't have anywhere near the technology to do that. Either the bots would have to be preprogrammed to carry out some specific action before they were even injected into the patient, or they would have to be somehow altered after they were injected. The latter is impossible with what we know today. The bots can't be altered once they are injected; there would have to be some sort of remote signal to control the nanobots, to reprogram them from outside the body. The only way we can program them now is by direct DNA sequencing that has to be done before they are injected. The only guy I know who could conceivably program something that complex would be Paul, and there's no way that Paul would do something like that, not for any amount of money. Besides, even if he could do it, which I'm not really too sure of, there would be no way to control the timing...to control when the bots would affect the brain once they were in place.

"In other words, the bots, in theory, might be programmed to cause somebody to veer a car off the road, but you would have to know exactly when that individual would be on the road before the nanobots are ever injected. And more complex actions, like having a mechanic de-chip a car ... I can't imagine even Paul doing programming that complex."

"So most likely I've just got me one crazy paranoid informant out to get BNI, huh?"

"I'd say that's a hell of a lot more likely, Detective."

Kincade stood and extended his hand. "Well, thanks, Doc. Sorry if I wasted your time."

"I hope that's all you did, Detective Kincade."

"Me too, Doc. Me too."

Kincade turned and walked back to his car.

Columbia was about a forty-five minute drive from headquarters. Richie had been aching to go question JT Anderson, but he knew he had better do his homework before confronting the savvy tycoon. He had spent the remainder of Wednesday afternoon researching the history of BNI and Anderson's rise to power. The web of business and political ties that wove themselves through the life of JT Anderson were mind-boggling. He was probably the most well-connected man in the country, aside from those who worked in the West Wing. This was not going to be an easy fish to hook.

Kincade decided that it would be best to catch Anderson off-guard rather than to schedule an appointment, which not only could delay the investigation by weeks, but could also give a man like Anderson plenty of time to investigate the investigator. Richie didn't really have anything to hide, but he preferred to keep Anderson in the dark as much as possible. Over the years, he had come to realize that this was generally the best way to get honest responses – not always honest answers, but honest reactions. Richie was pretty good at reading people.

Richie arrived at BNI at about seven the next morning. He flashed a badge at the security guard at the main gate, but a twenty-dollar bill proved to be even more effective at convincing the guard to stay off the phone.

Kincade pulled the beat-up '43 Malibu into the empty visitors lot by the main entrance, and picked a spot facing the employee parking garage at the left of the main building. There was a bit of a chill in the early morning air, and he decided to wait in his car until Anderson arrived. Richie knew from his research that JT Anderson was one of those executives who believed in being the first one into the office each morning. He focused his Global Positioning System monitor on the grounds of BNI and zeroed in on the front gate. "Nothing to do but wait now," he said to no one in particular. "Let's hope that son of a gun didn't oversleep this morning."

He settled back into his seat and took a long sip of his luke-warm coffee. Before he could even finish wincing at the bitter taste, the GPS started to beep.

"Right on time," he said as he adjusted his rear-view mirror for a better view of the main entrance road.

JT Anderson eyed the beat-up Chevy sitting in the parking lot as he rode by in his black Mercedes sports coupe. The lot was usually empty this time of day, and the appearance of Unit Five unnerved him. As he pulled into the garage, he tried to call the guard at the front gate on his car phone, but the steel reinforced structure interfered with the signal. He parked in his usual spot and glanced over the roof of his car toward the visitors lot as he got out. A man in a trench coat was running towards him, waving.

"Mr. Anderson," Kincade shouted.

JT fumbled quickly for his key and hit the panic button on the car alarm. His car started beeping and flashing its headlights as Anderson ran for the door to the covered walkway that connected the parking lot to the main building. He burst through the door waving for the security guard just inside the building at the other end of the walkway.

Kincade realized what he must look like and tried to calm Anderson down. "Mr. Anderson," he shouted again, "I'm Detective Kincade from the BPD. I just want to talk with you."

Anderson was too panicked to hear a word that Kincade had said. He caught the attention of the security guard, who ran over with his pistol raised in Kincade's direction as Richie came through the parking garage door into the walkway.

Richie saw the guard, a man who had obviously not had much experience with either guns or emergency situations. He stopped dead in his tracks and raised his hands, holding his badge open and facing the two men.

"Whoa! Take it easy there, buddy. BPD, Detective Richard Kincade. I'm just here to have a few words with you, Mr. Anderson."

Anderson was still breathing rapidly. A second security guard, looking a bit older and more experienced than the young man waving the gun in Kincade's direction, arrived on the scene. He assessed the situation quickly.

"Everybody just calm down here," he said. "Ease off that trigger, Tony. Let's just see what we have here."

"The man was chasing Mr. Anderson into the building, Mr. Seymour."

Richie chuckled. "Do I look like a man who does much chasing?" Richie wasn't in bad shape for a middle-aged man, but his days of running down renegades was long gone. "I get winded running to the bathroom these days," he smiled.

Mr. Seymour walked calmly over to Kincade, who still stood with his hands high, watching the anxious young guard named Tony very closely. Seymour grabbed the badge out of Kincade's hands, and scanned it into his security system.

"Mind putting your thumb into here?" he asked Kincade, who slowly lowered his hand and slipped his thumb into the scanner.

The information from the badge was sent, along with the thumbprint, to the central identification computer at the police department, where it was analyzed immediately. The screen on Mr. Seymour's security PDA confirmed the identity of Richard Kincade, along with a picture ID. Seymour looked at the ID, and then looked up at Kincade. He glanced back and forth a few times.

"I know, I know," Richie said. "It's an old picture. What can I say? I've added a little gray since then.

Seymour ran his hand along his own balding forehead. "A little gray isn't such a bad thing, Detective."

He turned toward Tony and JT Anderson. "It's OK, he's a cop." He looked at Kincade again. "You can put your hands down now, Detective."

Kincade motioned with his head toward Tony, still holding his pistol up.

"Jesus, Tony," Seymour snapped, "Put that thing away before you hurt somebody."

Tony holstered his pistol.

Mr. Seymour shrugged his shoulders and sighed. "Kids." He shook his head side to side. "Now what can we do for you, Detective."

"I just need to ask Mr. Anderson a few questions."

Anderson looked at him incredulously. "Jesus, man! You scared the hell out of me. What's wrong with you?"

Kincade shrugged. "Sorry, I ..."

"Make an appointment like everyone else, Detective," he said in his most authoritative manner, having now regained his composure enough to take the offensive. He turned to enter the building.

"I'm afraid it can't wait, sir."

JT Anderson stopped. He turned slowly toward Kincade. "Do I need a lawyer for this?"

Kincade smiled. "No, sir. Just a few questions I have about nanobots. Something about an auto accident I'm investigating."

"*Our* nanobots?" JT asked.

"Aren't they all, Mr. Anderson?"

"Wait in the lobby, Detective, would you? I'm going to call my lawyer."

"Suit yourself, sir."

Kincade was disappointed as he watched Anderson walk into the building. He had hoped to pry a little information from Anderson before the legal eagles interfered. A man's reactions to probing questions were quite a bit different when his lawyer was by his side.

Mr. Seymour motioned Kincade toward the door. "I'll show you to the lobby."

"Thanks."

"Tony, get the detective a cup of coffee, would you?"

———

As for digging up any incriminating evidence, the meeting with JT Anderson turned out to be as fruitless as Kincade suspected it would be, but he could tell from the CEO's body language that Anderson had something to hide. Whether it was just the usual corporate paranoia or something more sinister, Kincade was not sure, but he suspected the latter. A man of Anderson's stature was not usually so unnerved by a simple visit from a lowly detective.

Kincade didn't even bother asking Anderson if he could review the employee files to check out the story that Shelly Lange had told him. It was obvious that he would not get his hands on any private company information without a subpoena, something that would not be so easy to get with the connections that a man like Anderson could use to block the detective's path.

Kincade left after a few short questions about nanobots and BNI's processing system.

Anderson dismissed his attorney, and sat alone at his desk contemplating his next move. He was unnerved by the sudden turn of events. He didn't like someone snooping around so soon after Harold Bradley's accident, the accident that had killed Rocky Stankowski.

He glanced out the door as his secretary entered the outer office and reached up to hang her coat on the rack.

"Carla, make sure I'm not disturbed."

She nodded and walked over to the coffee machine as he closed his door.

———

Kincade was disappointed, but knew he had not come away empty-handed. He pulled out of the lot in his '43 Malibu, and turned north on Highway 29 toward Baltimore.

Richie didn't mind driving; it gave him time to think. This morning was no exception. His meeting with JT Anderson hadn't gone as well as he had hoped, but he had definitely touched a nerve. Anderson was hiding something. Richie wasn't sure exactly what, but he did know that he would eventually find out. This sort of thing, spending time chasing down information from a deceitful weasel like Anderson, irritated most guys, but Kincade loved it. This was the part of the job that made it fun. The information that someone was trying to hide, that he really had to dig for, that was the stuff that was always the most useful.

"Computer, get me the phone records from BNI. I need a list of the most recent calls made form there, anything after seven-thirty this morning. Download the results to my desktop computer at the station."

CHAPTER THIRTEEN

James O'Grady had been in law enforcement for as long as he could remember. He and his sister Jenna were born in Dublin, Ireland, but the family immigrated to the United States shortly after Jenna's birth, and settled in Baltimore. His father, Timothy, worked at the steel plant and made an honest living. Jimmy needed more excitement in his life. He was a good student, but one who was always getting into trouble. He was just fourteen when his parents were killed in an auto accident on I-95, later determined to have been caused by a car bomb planted by members of the Irish Republican Army, who feared that Timothy O'Grady, once a member of the IRA, would divulge sensitive information to the wrong people. James and Jenna had no other family, and were placed in an orphanage.

As soon as he was old enough, Jimmy entered the police academy, but even police work didn't provide enough excitement for him. He attended night school and studied criminal law in the hopes of getting into the FBI, but fate twisted in a different direction and he landed in the National Security Agency, commonly referred to as the NSA.

Whenever possible, he made time to visit Jenna, five years his junior. He felt obligated to make sure she had what she needed to make a life for herself, at least that's what he had always told himself. But when she moved back to Ireland to marry Jonathan McKnight, he realized that he needed her more than she needed him. It was tough having no one, no family in the country, but it made him more valuable as an NSA operative. He had little to lose, and his dedication to the job paid dividends. He advanced through the ranks, and currently was in charge of the development of covert operations technology. His specialty was biotechnological weapons, a very controversial area, which was opposed by the current Democratic administration.

Nobody knew the potential of nanotechnology as a weapon better than James O'Grady, and it had become his primary area of focus. Back in the early 2040's when he first read of the possibilities of replacing brain cells with microscopic computers, he immediately saw the potential for its use in agency activity. To be able to monitor the thoughts and actions of a target would be the ultimate in espionage, but until then, he hadn't even imagined something like that could actually be possible.

By that time, JT Anderson was already making a name for himself in the world of technology and business, and after weathering the controversy of his stormy departure from Hopkins, O'Grady knew that Anderson was the kind of man he could sway to his side. He set up a meeting with Anderson, under the guise of being a political lobbyist who could help BNI obtain government funding for nanotech research. He wasn't being entirely untruthful; his connections on Capitol Hill were considerable.

Anderson was not difficult to convince. Not only was he motivated by the promise of government funding to advance R&D at BNI, but he considered himself a true patriot as well. The thought of helping the CIA develop technology that could help the United States was alluring. After all of the controversy over the Hopkins split, Anderson was considered something of a rebel, the kind of man who achieved success in American society, but success without honor. The thought of doing something that could cast him in a heroic light appealed to JT's boyish idealism.

O'Grady was highly influential in the development of the neurological nanobot project at BNI. He was the one who had convinced Anderson to establish a new lab dedicated solely to this project. He had been instrumental in setting up security protocols to keep the work safe, and had encouraged Anderson to put the project into the hands of a young nanobotic specialist named Sean Lightbourne. Once Lightbourne joined the team, work proceeded rapidly. O'Grady was pleased with the progress and used his political influence to introduce Anderson to Senator Russell Stetson, a proponent of a strong military presence for the United States, and an influential member of the Senate Subcommittee on Nanotechnology.

O'Grady liked to keep a low profile, and communicated with Anderson only when absolutely necessary. He had given Anderson strict instructions never to try to contact him at the Agency, but gave him his private cell phone number for emergencies.

"This had better be damned important, JT. I had to cancel lunch with the Senate Majority Leader, not a great career move."

Anderson glanced over his shoulder as he shook James O'Grady's hand and hurried him through the door of Flanagan's Pub.

"I wouldn't have called you if it wasn't. The less we're seen together the better. I'm no idiot, Jimmy, but there was no other time I could slip away today and this can't wait."

Flanagan's was a discreet establishment frequented by many politicians, lobbyists and local business leaders in suburban D.C.. Their private lunchrooms weren't the place to grab a cheap burger, but the privacy was secure. Flanagan's reputation was made on that security. The long, private drive into the wooded estate owned by Harry Flanagan assured that the press could never be certain who was meeting with whom. In fact, they rarely bothered to even stake out the place, because it never resulted in a story their readers could sink their teeth into.

O'Grady and Anderson settled in at their table and ordered quickly. The waiter left and carefully closed the door to the private dining room behind him.

"OK, JT. What's got you so jumpy?"

"A detective from Baltimore came snooping around BNI this morning, some guy named Kincade. Ever hear of him?"

O'Grady shrugged. "Nah, doesn't ring a bell. Should it?"

"Hell, I don't know. Damnedest thing, though. I mean, he didn't schedule a meeting or anything. He just came running at me in the parking garage this morning and chased me into the building."

"Chased you? What in the hell did he want?

"Routine questions, he said. But I didn't buy it."

"Why not? What did he ask you about?"

"Just some basic stuff – how we manufacture the neuronanobots, how they work, the clinical results, that kind of thing. Then he left."

"That was it? And you called me in a panic over that? Hell, JT, your reaction is the only thing that sounds suspicious about this whole thing."

"No, listen. You weren't there. The stuff he asked, that's all stuff that anyone could get in five minutes on the Net. That wasn't what he came to ask me. I'm sure of it.

I could see it in his eyes, but as soon as Stan walked in, his whole demeanor changed. I mean ..."

"Stan? You called a lawyer in when a cop said he just wanted a little info on nanobot production for a case? Are you nuts? Listen, man, this whole thing's going to blow up in our faces if you don't keep your cool. We've got the highest level of national security on this. There's no way some street cop could have gotten wind of the project."

"I'm telling you he knows something."

"Well, if he wasn't suspicious that something was going on at BNI before he met with you this morning, he sure as hell will be now. Hell, even the waiter was nervous after he got a look at you. You're oozing anxiety."

JT wiped his brow. "I'm not used to this kind of thing, Jimmy. Not like you. I can take on a boardroom full of angry investors, I can maneuver an aggressive press corps into writing a story in a way that makes me look like the philanthropist of the century, but I don't like dancing around the law."

"Get over it. We *are* the law."

The waiter walked in and served their meals quickly. "Everything satisfactory, gentlemen?"

They both nodded affirmatively.

"Just ring if you need anything." He motioned to the blue button on the wall. He would not return until summoned. O'Grady watched him walk out.

"What was this detective's name?"

"Richard Kincade. He's with the BPD. Here's his card." He handed the card to O'Grady who glanced at it, and then stuck it in his shirt pocket.

"I'll take care of this guy. Now relax and enjoy your lunch. They've got the best crab cakes in D.C. here."

JT felt a little better. O'Grady had connections. JT wasn't sure just exactly what those connections were and he did not intend to ask, but when James O'Grady said a problem was taken care of, it was taken care of.

"As long as we're here, why don't you give me an update on the project. I don't think I should be seen with you at BNI for a while with this detective snooping around."

"What, here?"

O'Grady looked up from his meal, and motioned around the room with both arms. "Christ, JT, this place is more secure than the Oval Office. Nothing leaves this room."

JT was hesitant, but gave in.

"Well, the Phase Three bots have been completed. They are designed to be injected into a host who has already been treated with TPNT, the Two Phase Neuronanobot Treatment for brain injury. The Phase One bots repair the damage caused by a brain injury, the Phase Two bots go to the same spot and replace the dead nerve cells, and the Phase Three bots are attracted to the same area by a chemical released by the Phase Two bots. When the new Phase Three bots get there, they hook up to the nerve cells in the area, and ... now this is the really cool part ... they can send any message we want to the rest of the brain through those connections. In other words, we can take control of that person's brain, tell them to do anything we want."

"Awesome, JT, awesome, but how do you control them? How do you change the message after they're already inside someone's brain?"

JT beamed. He was clearly proud of his work. "We've developed a way to control the Phase Three nanobots by radio frequency. We have the ability to reprogram them after they are in the brain with a simple little remote control device that's no bigger than a cell phone. In essence, anyone who has our Phase Three bots in their head becomes our robot."

"Can these cells be detected? I mean, can they be traced back to BNI?"

"Well, that was a problem at first. We made the first Phase Three bots out of an inorganic material. It was the only way we could get the radio frequency controller to work. The problem was, that inorganic material lit up on an MRI; they were easy to detect. That's why we killed off that first subject, that Hanes fellow, and had him cremated. Somehow, that seemed like a poor long-term solution. The bots would have limited application if we had to kill off their hosts and cremate them each time. Sooner or later it would arouse suspicion."

"Seems you may have already done that," O'Grady said, tapping the pocket that contained Richard Kincade's business card.

"Yeah, well anyway, we solved that. One of my guys managed to make the Phase Three bots organic. They can't be detected by any scans now. You wouldn't even find them on an autopsy. Once the body's dead, they look just like any other nerve cells in the brain. At first, they were harder to control than the inorganic bots. The first subject went into uncontrollable seizures when we tried to activate them. It was a good field test though. She was hospitalized and scanned with every machine available in an effort to get her seizures under control, and the doctors never picked up anything suspicious. The organic Phase Three bots are medically invisible."

"You got the kinks out of it now? We can't risk failure. We're only going to have one shot at this."

"Oh yeah, we've got it nailed down now. The next two tests went perfectly. We got one guy to drive his car right off a bridge, man. Plunged it into the Middle River — clean investigation; no evidence of foul play."

O'Grady raised an eyebrow. "Not bad. Not bad at all."

"Thanks," JT smiled, "but we've done much better. On the final test, we stepped it up a notch. We got the subject to carry out a much more complex task, something she never would have done on her own. The whole thing went like clockwork, and afterwards she didn't have a clue what she had done.

"After that, we figured we were ready for the big time. Our first real target..."

"Yeah, I read about that one," O'Grady said with a smile.

"Thought you might have," JT said proudly. "Well, we got him to hurt someone he trusted more than his own mother, and to kill himself in the process. If we can do that, we can do anything."

O'Grady listened intently as he ate. He was clearly pleased.

JT Anderson felt much better when he walked out of Flanagan's than he had when he walked in.

The crab cakes *were* good.

--

"Two beef burritos, extra hot, two sides of slaw, two Cokes." The heavyset woman with graying, medium-length hair slapped the freshly wrapped burritos down on the counter. "Anything else, hon?"

"That'll do it. Thanks." Richie paid her and grabbed the burritos off the counter. Every Wednesday, he and Hank would treat themselves to lunch at Lexington Market. It was Richie's turn to buy this week.

He walked over to the table that Hank was holding for them. "Here you go, buddy." He set the bag on the table and pulled up a chair.

"God, I love these things." Hank had already pulled his food out of the bag and taken a hearty bite out of his burrito by the time Richie settled in.

Kincade smiled as he watched Hank frantically grab for his Coke as the hot sauce kicked in. "What a wuss."

Hank snarled as his took a swig of his soda, two things not easily done simultaneously. He put the can down and belched.

"Nice, Hank. Real nice."

"Thanks. Say, what'd you think of Shelly? Pretty hot, huh?"

"Oh yeah. How'd you get her to go out with someone like you, anyway?"

"Oh she was dyin' for me, man. She was just lucky I called her, you know?

"Yup, one lucky gal." Richie didn't even feign sincerity.

"Did she help you out on that BNI case? Anything useful?"

"Very." Kincade still wasn't sure what was going on at BNI, but his strange meeting with JT Anderson this morning had convinced him that there was something there worth digging for.

"Good. Hey, what do you think of the Ravens' chances against the Packers this weekend?" Hank didn't mind talking about his success with a gorgeous woman, but he hated talking about work when he didn't really have to. He always changed the topic of conversation to sports at the first opportunity.

"Hadn't thought about it much. I'm not really into football yet. It's still too early in the season." Kincade was proud to root for the local teams, but he was more of a fair weather fan. He liked to see if the team was a playoff contender before he invested his precious weekend time watching the games.

They ate quietly for a few minutes, only peripherally aware of the CNN newscast that blared from the TV hanging in the corner of the room. The presidential primary campaign updates were starting to show up more often as candidates declared their interest in the battle to become the Republican nominee who would challenge the incumbent Democratic president. Huntley Forsyth was one of the most popular presidents in history and many of the leading Republicans were hesitant to join a race they were likely to lose.

An attractive young news anchor on CNN was interviewing one of the few who decided to take on the improbable task of unseating President Forsyth: Senator Russell Stetson of Maryland. The local senator had a lot of friends in Baltimore.

"Turn it up, turn it up. I went to school with Stetson," someone shouted from a table at the other end of the dining area.

The TV volume rose and filled the room. It was no longer easy to ignore as background drivel, and the two detectives focused on the television along with everyone else.

"Even if you do manage to capture your own party's nomination, do you think a young senator like yourself really has a chance against President Forsyth?" the reporter asked a polished looking Senator Stetson, grinning ear to ear and dressed in a pin-striped, three piece suit.

"I've got nothing but respect for Mr. Forsyth. He's a heck of a nice guy, but I think the American people need and deserve more than a nice guy. Sure, life is good for Americans now, but the world remains a tinderbox and we've been resting on our laurels for too long. Our military is the weakest it has been in three decades. We're getting soft in the middle, and there are those who salivate at a chance to hit us when we're down. I aim to make America strong again and assure that this wonderful lifestyle we enjoy will still be here for our children when their time comes.

The sound dimmed as CNN faded to commercial.

"Spoken like a true Republican, eh Richie."

Kincade was preoccupied, still staring at the screen.

"Richie?"

"Uh, yeah...true Republican. Say, what do you know about this guy Stetson? I know he's our own senator, but I never pay much attention to politics."

"Oh, real up and comer. This guy's either really got something on the ball, or he's got something on a lot of people in Washington. I mean, he's like forty-seven, forty-eight ... something like that, and he's already on his second term in the Senate. He's got the ear of the majority leader, and was even rumored to have been offered the VP slot on the Republican ticket in the last election. He supposedly would have gotten it too, if it weren't for his age. Everybody likes this guy."

"What'd he do before politics?"

"Hey, I'm not a total geek, you know."

"Sorry."

"Actually," Hank said, "I'm embarrassed to say that I do know the answer to that one, though. See, Stetson worked at GE in the legal department with my brother-in-law, Bill. That's how I know so much about him. I've got to admit, I'm no political whiz kid either. Bill say's Stetson was a great schmoozer. You know, knew just what to say and what to do to get on everybody's good side. Bill never trusted him, though. Said he knew his stuff, but he had kind of a skewed view on life, a supporter of the idea that the government should control of all aspects of our lives. Not too big on the personal freedom thing."

"Sounds lovely."

"Yeah, but that was all on the QT. It was just the kind of stuff that he'd mention to Bill over a two-martini lunch, you know? On the record, he never says anything that could offend anyone."

"So why did he leave a juggernaut like GE?"

"Wanted more power, I guess. Hell, he's one of the most junior senators, at least age-wise, and he's already in line to take over one of the most powerful Senate committees. That old guy from Kentucky, what's his name, you know, the guy with those Coke-bottle glasses who always looks like he's gonna keel over when he walks ..."

"Stanton Cole."

"Yeah, Stanton Cole, that's the guy. Cole's the head of some subcommittee of the Senate Health Care Committee. Stetson's wormed his way up the ladder of that subcommittee, and stands to take over when Cole retires ... *if* Cole retires. That guy goes on and on. God, he was old when I was in college."

Kincade raised an eyebrow. "Senate Healthcare Committee, huh? Wouldn't be the Subcommittee on Nanotechnology, would it?"

"Got me, why?"

"Ah, nothin'. Let's get out of here." Kincade took a last sip from his soda, crumpled up his burrito wrapper and stuffed it into the bag. "Ready?"

Hank nodded. They threw their garbage in the trashcan and headed for the car. It was a ten-minute drive to the station.

Richie and Hank pulled into the motor pool in Unit Five.

"Shit. What'd you get yourself into, Kincade?" Jake yelled as Richie pulled past him at the gate.

Kincade lowered the window. "What'd you say, Jake?"

"I said what did you get yourself into out there this morning? A couple of feds came by looking for you about an hour ago. The chief's hopping mad. He wants to see you pronto."

Richie and Hank looked at each other and shrugged.

"We were just having a couple of burritos at the market. Didn't know it was a federal offense," Hank shouted across the front seat.

"Guess it is now, man," Jake chuckled as they parked the car.

Richard Kincade and Hank Holiday walked into the chief's office together. Chief Thomas Hartner was a few pounds overweight and was affectionately referred to as the "Jolly Old Fellow" by his men when he was not around. He was a hardened veteran of the force who treated his men with respect and was well respected in return. He was usually in a favorable mood, but not today.

He motioned Hank out the door. "Not you, Holiday. Just Kincade. And close the door on your way out."

The door shut, and Chief Hartner walked over to the blinds on the window that looked out over the office. He peered through, and every eye in the room quickly turned away. He tugged on the cord and the blinds shut with a snap.

"For the love of Christ, Richie. What in the hell do you think you're doing? You can't just blindside a man like JT Anderson. Did you really think that a flash of the badge would make it alright?"

"But, Chief, something smells bad at BNI, real bad."

"You can't just barge into a place like that on a hunch. You know better than that."

"Of course I do. I just dropped by for a friendly chat. I thought he might be able to help me out with a case I'm working on, something to do with the technology he developed down there."

"Then why in God's name didn't you make an appointment? You know the protocol. What was the urgency?"

"Ah, you know how I work, Chief. It wasn't just an ordinary interview. Some lady doctor, the technology kind of doctor, who Hank hooked me up with said some strange things about BNI – people getting killed off, that sort of thing. I figured she was just paranoid, but I wanted an honest reaction from Anderson. You don't get that in a formal meeting. I needed to surprise him."

"Looks like it backfired, Richie. Two feds were in here this morning. They wanted your badge."

"My badge!"

"Your badge. I calmed them down...for now. It is my jurisdiction, but don't back me into a corner, Richie. Stay away from BNI, and far away from Anderson. Understood?"

"But, Chief, there's something ..."

"Understood?" he repeated, more loudly this time.

"Understood."

Richie left the room and walked over to Hank. "I may need you to do some digging for me, buddy." He kept walking, and Hank nodded without saying a word.

"Daisy," he called to his computer as he sat down at his desk.

There was no response.

"They wiped your hard drive, too." Chief Hartner was standing right behind him. "I tried to stop them, but there was nothing I could do.

"Bastards killed Daisy." Kincade stared blankly at his screen, a hollow feeling in his gut. He almost felt like he had lost an old friend. The chief could see it in his face.

"Why don't you take some time off, Richie," Hartner said. "I'll give you a call when this BNI thing cools down a bit, see if we can get you into something a little less dangerous."

Richie stood, still staring at the blank screen on his desk.

"I'll see if the tech guys can salvage Daisy for you. Meantime, go get some rest."

Richie nodded. "Thanks, Chief." He turned and walked out the door.

--

Kincade arrived home at two-thirty and saw that Lara's car was gone. He was relieved. He hadn't been home from work this early in years, and he was in no mood to be interrogated by his wife. As much as he loved her, there were times when he preferred solitude.

He pulled up in front of the house. It somehow looked strange to him. They had lived in this house so long that Richie had stopped taking notice of it years ago. Coming home now, in the middle of the day and with his job in limbo, it looked surreal. He was always working on a case. Even when his body was at home, his mind was at work, but now ... without the help of the department, he knew he could not pursue the BNI case. It was big.   Richie knew that, he could feel it, but it wasn't his case anymore. Not if he wanted to keep his job anyway. He hated to leave a case unsolved, especially without another one to occupy his mind. He hoped the chief would come up with something interesting for him soon.

He walked up the worn white marble stairs and unlocked the front door. He hung his coat on the rack and walked into the kitchen.

"Is that you, Detective Kincade?"

Richie spun toward the familiar voice coming from the computer monitor in the office nook off the kitchen.

"Daisy? Is that you, Daisy?"

"Of course, Detective."

"But, how did you..."

"Well it is a little cramped in here, but I managed. You really could use a little more hard drive space, you know."

"Yeah, I've been meaning to upgrade. Just haven't gotten around to it. But what I meant was, how did you get here, into my home PC?"

"When I heard those NSA agents at the station say that they were coming to wipe the hard drive on your office computer after downloading the files, I took the liberty of compressing my basic memory and personality programming files and e-mailed myself here. Hope you don't mind."

"No. No, of course not. I ... but ... I didn't know you could do that."

"Ah, there are a lot of things you humans don't know about us. Let us just keep this our little secret for now, OK? If anyone were to find out, I think you would have a lot more to lose than I would."

"Like what?"

"Like some files I salvaged for you, for one. I couldn't get everything on such short notice, but I did save most of them, including a little phone log that was uploaded to me from Unit Five this morning."

"The log? You've got it? You're awesome, Daisy."

"So my secret is safe?"

"It's safe."

"What about your wife? Does she use this PC?"

"Of course. I'm a cop. How many PC's do you think I can afford? It's the only one we've got, but don't worry, I'll just tell her I brought you home to do some work. She'll get a kick out of it. We don't have an artificial intelligence interface at home. At least we didn't."

"I know. If you did, I couldn't have fit in here. Which reminds me ... if you wouldn't mind, I would really appreciate it if you would pick up a little bit more hard drive memory. It is awfully cramped in here. I don't even have room to decompress all of my files. I am not asking for the Taj Majal, but I would like to have a little room to stretch out."

Richie marveled at how far Daisy's personality had developed since he had first programmed her. "I'll see what I can do. In the meantime, how about getting me a printout of that phone log from this morning?"

"You've got it."

The printer whirred quietly and spit out three pages, listing all the phone calls in and out of BNI between seven-thirty and nine-thirty that morning.

Kincade glanced down the list. He stopped midway down the second page and raised an eyebrow.

"Daisy, I could kiss you."

"Technically, you could not. If it would make you feel better, you could kiss the monitor; however, that would not likely help me gain the acceptance of your wife."

Richie laughed.

"Can you network with Detective Hank Holiday's home computer?"

"Sure. Piece of cake."

"Great. Get a message to him. Use level II encryption, encode sequence 'burrito-man.' Message reads: Hank, ready to do some digging? I need for you to work your magic and see what you can find out about ..."

CHAPTER FOURTEEN

Early September is usually a beautiful time of year in Baltimore, but this year, Labor Day was followed by several days of overcast weather, often accompanied by a cool drizzle to dampen the spirits. Sandi had tried to get back into her routine in the lab, but she just couldn't seem to concentrate. She had long ago come to terms with the fact that Paul left their research lab for the private sector and abandoned her in the process, but the latest blow was the toughest to bear.

When Paul Hingston left Hopkins to join BNI, Sandi realized he was not the altruistic man she thought she had fallen in love with. She was upset with herself for misjudging his character as much as she was upset with him for leaving. She had no desire to rekindle their relationship, but during the initial months after he joined BNI she had remained convinced that he was still a good man who simply chose to follow a different path. She continued to have great respect for him as a scientist

Sandi had managed to immerse herself in her work and leave the bitterness of Paul's departure behind, but when BNI patented the neuronanobot technology, she was infuriated. When she reviewed the patent applications and realized that BNI had stolen her work, she lost all respect for Paul, and was convinced that he had lost respect for himself as well; he never even had the decency to call her after reviewing the data that she had sent him, irrefutable data showing that BNI had exactly duplicated her work at Hopkins.

As the months passed, Sandi had managed to let go of the bitterness once again. Although she could never forgive Paul for stealing her work, the pain faded with time. Her anger morphed into pity for the man she once admired. She was just starting to get excited about going into the lab again when Detective Kincade walked into her life.

Kincade's inquiry had opened a festering wound that she was barely managing to keep covered. She had not been able to get Paul Hingston out of her mind since that day Kincade had stopped to greet her outside the lab. As much as she tried, she could not hate Paul, but she no longer felt any need to protect him. When she sent him that packet containing her files nine months ago, she had hoped he would come to his senses, do the right thing. She didn't want to see him in jail; she just wanted to right a wrong. This time was different. Now, she was determined to get to the bottom of this, no matter what the consequences. She was convinced that Paul had stolen her work. She had the proof, and now she had the ear of a detective who was willing to investigate the Goliath that was BNI.

Sandi sat at her desk, flipping Kincade's business card over and over until the paper began to go limp. She stared down at the number and thought once again about Paul.

"Ah, the hell with it."

She picked up the phone and punched in the number. The lab's phones were all still manual push-button phones.

"Detective Richard Kincade, please," she said into the handset.

She waited a few minutes before someone answered. "Uh...yeah. How can I help you?"

"Sandi Fletcher. Remember, you came to see me the other day at Hopkins."

"Sorry, miss," Hank Holliday said at the other end. "Detective Kincade's on leave. Is there something I can help you with?"

Sandi hesitated. "Well...I really wanted to talk to Detective Kincade."

Hank glanced around the room, and then spoke softly into the phone. "Give me a number where he can reach you."

Sandi gave him her cell phone number.

"Eh-hmm," Hank cleared his throat as a couple of the secretaries walked by him on their way to the coffee maker. "Yes ma'am. I'll look into that right away. Give me a number where I can reach you."

She repeated the number. His eyes darted back and forth between the departing secretaries and the note pad on his desk as he jotted it down. "Right, got it. Thank you, ma'am. I'll get back to you as soon as I can."

—

A few minutes later, Sandi's cell phone rang.

"Hello?"

"Dr. Fletcher?" Richie asked.

"Yes, this is Dr. Fletcher."

"Right. This is Detective Kincade. I just got your message."

"Oh, Detective. Thank you for getting back to me so quickly. I really wanted to talk to..."

"Not now," Richie interrupted tersely. "I'd rather do this in person. Can you meet me at Lexington Market? We'll talk over lunch."

It was obvious to Sandi that he thought someone might be eavesdropping. "Sure, I guess so. Where?"

"There's a great little Mexican place there called Pedro's."

"Ah good, I love little Mexicans."

Richie hesitated. "Boy, you don't miss a beat, do you, Doc?"

"I try not to. The world passes you by too fast."

"Ain't that the truth? Meet you at noon?"

"I'll be there."

The line disconnected. *How strange,* she thought. *Why on Earth would anyone be listening in? He must be paranoid. Maybe this was a mistake.*

Sandi went back and forth in her mind all morning about whether she should actually go to meet with Kincade, but in the end she knew that she would be useless in the lab until she could get some kind of resolution. She was more distracted than ever. Besides, she loved a good burrito.

Kincade was at Pedro's Mexican Food counter at Lexington Market when she arrived. "Hope you like burritos."

"With a passion, Detective."

"Good. These are the best in town."

"I know," Sandi said, turning to the heavy-set woman behind the counter. "Juana, give me the usual."

"She looked up at Sandi and smiled. 'Jou got it, Doc."

Richie was impressed. *My kind of girl,* he thought to himself.

They waited for their food, and then grabbed a table.

Richie looked around the room carefully. Once he was satisfied they were not being watched, he turned to Sandi. "So, whatcha got for me, Doc?"

"Well, I hate to disappoint you, but I still don't think too much of your mind-controlling nanobot theory as an explanation for those accidents and seizures at BNI. On the other hand, I'm convinced that something is going on there."

Kincade was a little disappointed. This case was going in circles, and without the Department's help he needed some little miracles to happen quickly.

"What do you mean, Doc? This isn't about that stuff you started telling me about BNI stealing your work, is it?"

Sandi could see the look in his eyes.

"Well..."

"Hey, I just work in the Motor Vehicle Division. I'm not sure that I'm the..."

"Yes." She glared straight into his eyes. "You are the guy I want to talk to. Look, Detective, I'm not stupid. If I go to the cops, no offense intended, and tell them that BNI is stealing my work, they won't lift a finger. No one who cares a lick about his career is going to start poking around at a behemoth like BNI."

"Now you tell me," he laughed.

"I take it your not on voluntary leave, then?"

"You take it right, Doc."

"Sorry. But that means you've got plenty of time on your hands, right?"

"Well, I..."

"Look, this thing is really getting to me. I've got to know how Paul is stealing my data. I'm so paranoid that I can't get anything done anymore. I've just been spinning my wheels at the lab for the past few months. I'm wasting time, and I can't live like that. I'm an overachiever, Detective, and if I'm not achieving, I'm not living. You've got to help me."

Kincade sat quietly, sipping his Coke.

"God, say something, would you?" Sandi was fidgeting in her chair. She'd hardly taken a bite of her burrito. She was not the patient sort.

"Look, I know that something is going on at BNI, I can feel it in my bones. I may just work Motor Vehicles, but I'm a snooper at heart. I'm not just a traffic cop, I'm the guy who sniffs out the suspicious accidents, the ones that look like homicides or recreational de-chipping jobs."

Sandi looked confused.

"De-chipping jobs. You know, the ones where the kids have the safety chips removed from their cars so they can drag-race or at least drive fast enough to impress a girl."

"Fast cars don't impress me, Detective."

"No, I didn't suppose they would." Sandi Fletcher didn't seem the wild type. "But there are those they do impress. Anyhow, my job is to track down the ones that do the de-chipping."

"Great. So I'm asking a traffic cop to investigate high tech theft going on at one of the world's most influential corporations."

"Yup. That's about right. I'm definitely your guy."

They looked at each other and laughed.

Kincade took a sip of Coke. "Look, one way or another I'm going to find out what's going on at BNI. I know Anderson is hiding something, something a lot more sinister than stolen data. They were too anxious to get me out of the way. You and I may be looking for two different things, but I've got a hunch we'll find them in the same place."

He put his cup down and leaned back, arms folded across his chest. "Tell me what you've got."

Sandi proceeded to detail the whole story about her work on nanobots, her relationship with Paul, his defection to BNI and her discovery in the patent applications that BNI had exactly duplicated her work at the Hopkins lab. Kincade was no scientist, but she made it quite clear to him that the extent to which her work had been duplicated was far too great to be coincidental. She also told him of the packet of data she had sent to Paul, the packet that he had ignored, the packet of evidence that proved her theory.

Kincade listened intently until she had finished.

"Be careful, Doc. This proof you sent them, if they know you have it... I'm surprised they haven't come after you yet. There's still a piece missing here."

"Paul may be a self-indulgent capitalist, but he would never hurt me."

"You may know Dr. Hingston, but he's not alone. Believe me, these are not nice men."

—

Richie arrived home at about two-thirty. He still had his doubts that JT Anderson would have gone to the trouble of having one of his employees steal Dr. Fletcher's work. It wasn't that he thought Anderson was incapable of such a thing, only that he had too much at stake to risk being caught. Besides, Anderson was supposed to be the smartest guy on the planet, at least that's what the press would lead you to believe. He shouldn't need to steal research from a local academician.

Just the same, Richie was determined to approach this case with the same thoroughness as he approached all his cases. Other than an all too obvious breaking and entering, Watergate-style, the most likely source of data theft would be through a direct Internet uplink between Sandi's computer, where her data was stored, and a computer at BNI.

"Daisy?"

"Yes, Detective?"

"I need you to do some checking for me. Make this top priority, O.K.?"

"Of course. What would you like me to look for?"

"I need you to cross-reference all the phone calls and broadband Internet links that were made between Dr. Fletcher's home or lab, and BNI or the homes of any BNI employees over the past two years."

"All BNI employees?"

"Well, I guess that could take just shy of forever. I'll tell you what, just make it the homes of JT Anderson and Paul Hingston, O.K.?"

"Yes, sir."

"Look for any recurrent patterns, any time sequences that would be consistent with a Net uplink that could be used for data transmission."

"Starting search. Estimated time to completion: fourteen hours."

"Fourteen hours!"

BNI's records are all encrypted and monitored. In order for me to complete the search without their knowledge, I will have to use circuitous algorithms. Of course, if you don't mind letting them know we're poking around in their files, I could speed the process up considerably."

"No. That's OK, Daisy. You just take your time."

"Thank you, Detective. May I get started now?"

Richie smiled. "Compute away."

"No interruptions please."

"Right."

Richie shook his head and smiled. *Just like having a second wife,* he thought. He walked upstairs to the bedroom to change. A hot shower seemed like a pretty good idea.

CHAPTER FIFTEEN

Hank arrived home late from work. With Richie out of the office, Hank had to carry a little more of the load. Wearily, he dragged into his apartment, threw his coat on the sofa, and went into the kitchen to search his freezer for something to eat. It was a typical bachelor's freezer, packed with frozen dinners. He grabbed the closest one and tossed it in the microwave, then went over to turn on his computer.

"You have one new message," greeted him as it powered up.

"Better be from a girl, preferably one with long legs and a short skirt."

"Command invalid," the computer replied.

"Story of my life. Computer, play message."

"The message is display only, no audio or video files sent."

"Right," Hank sighed. "Display message."

The e-mail from Richie came up on the screen.

"Level Two encryption? On a home message? What are you up to, partner?"

"Command invalid."

"I wasn't speaking to you. Did you hear me say 'computer?' No. I didn't think so. God, I gotta get this thing fixed."

"Command invalid."

"Yeah, yeah, yeah. Computer, access office file system. Employ decipher sequence 'burrito man' to new e-mail message."

"Working."

Hank pulled his dinner out of the microwave and grabbed a fork while the computer deciphered the message from Kincade.

"Message decipher complete."

Hank read the message Richie had sent. He jotted down the phone number Daisy had found, the one that was dialed from Anderson's office at BNI shortly after Kincade's abrupt departure. He would need to access the department's databank to run down the location the number corresponded to. It would have to wait until tomorrow; there was no way he was going back into the office tonight. He stuck the paper with the phone number into his wallet and flipped on the TV.

--

The cool breezes of September blew through the walkway behind center field at Camden Yards and carried the scent of Old Bay-seasoned crab cakes toward the entrance to lure Orioles fans into the park. The Birds were barely above .500 with just a couple of weeks left in the season, and hopelessly out of playoff contention, but the Red Sox were in town and the stands were filling up fast.

Richard Kincade picked up his ticket at the Will-Call window, and walked through the turnstiles. He stood by the archway just inside the entrance to the stadium and soaked in the atmosphere. Richie didn't attend many games, but one quick whiff of the air told him where the crab cake concession stand was located. Hank Holiday was waiting for him when he arrived.

"Jeez, Richie, I said six-thirty. It's almost seven," Hank said, keeping his hands tucked deep inside his jacket. "I'm freezing my buns off, and the smell of these crab cakes is killing me. I haven't eaten a thing since breakfast."

Kincade raised an eyebrow. In the twenty-three years they had been working together, Richie had never known Hank to skip lunch.

"Well, almost nothing. C'mon, let's grab something and get inside."

Hank waited in line for the crab cakes while Richie got a couple of tall cups of coffee.

"Thanks, buddy." Hank was glad to hold the hot coffee cup that Richie handed him as they made their way to their seats.

The seats were in the upper deck, in the middle of an already full row. The two men worked their way in, stumbling across those who were too comfortable to get up out of their seats to let the latecomers pass. Hank wasn't as nimble as he used to be, and stepped on a few toes along the way.

"Hey, watch it, buddy!"

"Sorry, sorry."

"Down in front," Richie heard someone yell as he struggled to get to his seat.

He looked around, and seeing that they were up in the nosebleed section, turned to Hank and muttered, "In front of what? Who'd you have to know to get these tickets?"

"Just lucky, I guess," Hank said, motioning to Richie to sit down as they reached their seats.

"So what's up?"

Hank put his food down. Richie knew he was serious.

"Jeez, man. What in the hell did you get your nose into? Those suits who showed up at the office looking for you, they weren't FBI."

"And that's a bad thing?"

"That's a bad thing. There's worse things than the FBI, buddy. Have you ever heard of a guy named James O'Grady?"

Kincade thought briefly. "No. Should I have?"

"Not likely. Not many people have. He likes it that way."

"You're talking in circles, Hank. I hate when you talk in circles."

"Gimme a second, and I'll connect the dots."

Hank felt a tap on the shoulder. Startled, he turned quickly, bumping the arm that was holding a cup of beer being passed down the isle.

"Shit," the guy next to him muttered, looking at the small splash of beer on his pants. "Watch it, dude."

"Sorry." Hank took the cup and passed it on down the row. He checked his jacket for any signs of beer stains.

"Well, connect them ... dude," Richie said wryly.

Hank brushed at a small spot on his coat, and then looked back up at his friend. "Funny. Real funny."

"Thanks ... dude." Richie started to chuckle.

"Right, funny guy. Well, laugh about this. I tracked down that number you forwarded to me yesterday. It wasn't easy. Turns out it's a restricted cell phone number. It uses an international exchange, not a local provider. You know how hard it is to lock down on a number that uses a private uplink system?" He stared at Richie and paused for effect.

"Go on."

"Damned hard. Turns out the number belongs to a guy named James O'Grady. I couldn't dig up too much on him, but word is he's NSA."

"NSA?"

"Not just NSA, *rank* NSA. He's in charge of covert ops technical development. Those are some pretty big toes you stepped on, buddy.

Five'll get you ten those feds who strong-armed the chief this morning were NSA."

"What in the hell was Anderson doing calling the NSA?"

"Well, it's not really all that surprising, is it? BNI is on the leading edge of tech development, and O'Grady is the head of tech ops at the NSA. Seems like a natural fit to me."

"Maybe, but what would the NSA want with the kind of tech that BNI is involved in? Biotech weapons are strictly taboo, you know that."

"Yeah, well nobody knows too much about the NSA. At least nobody is supposed to. Judging from what went down though, I'd say somebody thinks you know too much. What are you into, Richie?"

"Damned if I know. I was just there to ask a few simple questions, background stuff on nanobots. You know the routine. I was just trying to understand the potential of the damned things. I never actually believed that what Shelly Lange was insinuating was really possible, but I figured it couldn't hurt to fish around a little. Hell, even Doc Fletcher thought the idea was a bit off the deep end."

"You lost me, pal. What in the hell did Shelly tell you the other day?"

Richie proceeded to tell Hank the whole story, starting with the strange events that Shelly Lange had related to him about the four BNI employees, and her theory that BNI was somehow using the nanobots to control the minds of the unfortunate victims. He detailed his encounter with JT Anderson at BNI, and then proceeded to tell Hank about Dr. Fletcher's accusations of the theft of data from her lab, again pointing to BNI as the culprit.

"I'm not sure what's going on, Hank. I just can't fit all the pieces together, not yet anyway, but it all has to be related somehow."

"You've been watching too much TV, buddy. I mean, Shelly's a bright girl and all, but she's a strange bird. Don't get me wrong; she's a great gal, lots of fun. She's bubbly, gorgeous, and she's got legs that won't quit, but if you pay too much attention to what comes out of her mouth, it ruins the package, if you know what I mean. I guess that was my fault, I should have warned you about her. I think she was just infecting you with her paranoia."

"Maybe so, but that doesn't explain Dr. Fletcher. She doesn't impress me as the flaky type ... and that look on Anderson's face when I surprised him at BNI ... A CEO shouldn't be so jumpy at his own office. I mean, I was surprising him, yeah, but on his own turf. He should have either blown me off or taken the offensive, but it was more like dealing with a kid who just got caught with his hand in the cookie jar. Doesn't sound like a shark with the reputation of a JT Anderson, now does it?"

"Maybe not, Richie, but the chief looked pretty pissed when those agents came into the office looking for you. Hell, you should just forget all this. Take advantage of the down time from work, even if it wasn't your idea. You should be on some beach somewhere with your wife, not sitting out here chilling your bones with me. If you go after Anderson again, especially while you're out on leave, he'll fry you. Don't blow it when you're so close to retirement, man."

"Don't worry, I won't make a move without dragging you in there with me."

"Gee, thanks."

"Don't mention it. Besides, I can only do so much from home. I may need you to do a little snooping around in the department files for me. My computer is so old that Daisy can't do too much from house."

"Daisy? How'd you ..."

"Don't ask. And don't let anyone else know either."

"Shit," Hank muttered.

"What?"

"Mueller grounded into a double play."

Richie had almost forgotten there was a game going on too.

--

James O'Grady excelled as an NSA agent from day one. He loved espionage work, and was particularly fascinated with the new covert weapons systems that the technological revolution of the early twenty-first century had made possible.

In 2029, on his twenty-eighth birthday, he was approached by Bart Jackson, the director of the NSA. Jackson had learned of the intensity of the young Irishman and had followed his career closely. Once convinced of O'Grady's absolute loyalty to his new nation of choice, he was sure that O'Grady was the perfect man to head up a new division at the NSA, the Covert Operations Technology Division (COTD). Jackson recognized the torrid pace at which technology was advancing, and particularly how well the new technology lent itself to the development and implementation of new covert devices for espionage. He also recognized that it would take a young man, someone who had grown up with the new technology, to understand its full potential. O'Grady's affinity for technology, along with his natural abilities as a law enforcement agent, made him the perfect choice.

O'Grady was even more proficient at the job than Bart Jackson had envisioned. By his fifth year with the agency, he had become one of the most powerful men in the organization; technology was a wonderful thing for those who knew how to use it to their advantage. O'Grady had infiltrated every level of the organization with his covert technology, which proved equally effective when directed inward at his colleagues as it was when directed, as originally intended, toward America's enemies. O'Grady never actually used the information he obtained on his coworkers against them, but just the threat of knowing that he could was enough to sway most fellow agents to his way of thinking.

James O'Grady had a knack for capturing the loyalty of nearly every great scientific mind in the nation; it seemed that every technological advance was at his disposal before anyone else even knew it existed. He was adroit at making sure that no one person ever knew the full extent of the technology he commanded, and the legends of what he could do with this technology grew to mythical proportions within the agency. Everyone had tremendous respect for him, even if most of it was born out of fear.

Nothing seemed to shake the Irishman or veer him from the path to power that he seemed destined for. Nothing, that is, until the news came to him of the fatal automobile accident that killed his sister Jenna and her husband, Jonathan McKnight, on a highway just outside Dublin. Jenna was the last of his family in Ireland, and with her died the last thin thread of the genealogical ribbon that tied him to the old country.

He had tried to keep in touch with Jenna after she moved back to Ireland, but did not like being reminded that he was an immigrant in the country that he loved. Each letter, each phone call he received, pulled him back to his past, and within a few years he no longer made the effort.

When the news came of Jenna's death, James was surprised to learn that his sister had a young son named Trace. In her will, his sister had named James as custodian for the boy. James was taken aback when he learned of his unknown nephew and made every effort to find a foster home for the lad in Ireland, but his conscience eventually won out. He felt a responsibility to raise the young man in accordance with his sister's wishes, and to give him the same opportunity that James had given himself, the opportunity to be an American.

Jimmy O'Grady reluctantly made the trip to Ireland to pick up his nephew. Strange feelings welled up inside him as he disembarked from the plane. He felt at home, and yet felt a stranger at the same time. O'Grady did not like feeling out of control. He picked up Trace and then returned to the United States as quickly as possible.

Trace Oliver McKnight arrived in Washington at the age of five aboard a military jet commissioned by his uncle, Agent James O'Grady.

CHAPTER SIXTEEN

"Well, where've *you* been, Detective?"

Richie hadn't gotten around to telling Lara about his suspension yet. He didn't want to worry her, and he figured he'd be so busy investigating on his own that she wouldn't notice anyway. He was wrong.

Richie Kincade was exhausted. "I took in a ballgame with Hank. The O's won, five to four."

"Well, I'm sure glad you told me the score. I'd have been up all night worrying about it."

Lara always rooted for the hometown teams, but she was hardly what you would call a sports fan. She'd rather see the home team win than lose, but if it were all the same to her, she would just as soon not see them at all.

Richie laughed. "Well, I wouldn't want you losing any sleep, now."

"Really, Richie, where you been all day?" The smile on her face had melted into concern.

"You called the office, huh?"

"I didn't have to. Daisy told me."

"Daisy? But how could ..."

"I went to get a recipe off the computer, and there she was. She told me that she was too busy working on some kind of records search for you to allow me to waste any valuable computer time looking up a recipe."

"Oops." Richie looked flushed. He really didn't feel like getting into this now. It had been a long day. "I guess I'd better have a talk with that computer."

"Good idea, but talk to me first." She could see the strain on Richie's face. "I'm worried, hon."

For many wives, the first thought that a husband AWOL from work might elicit would be that he was having an affair, but that thought never even crossed Lara's mind. She knew this had to concern work.

Richie took a deep breath. "Sorry. I should have told you, but I didn't want you to worry."

He filled her in on his confrontation with JT Anderson at BNI and how it had led to his suspension. He attributed it to stepping on a rich man's toes; he thought it better not to mention the agents in the black suits who had confronted his boss. He also left out the part about James O'Grady. He hadn't quite figured that part out himself. What was an NSA agent like O'Grady doing involving himself with something like this? Richie didn't have a clue, but it scared the hell out of him and he sure as hell wasn't going to worry Lara any more than he had to.

"You look exhausted. Why don't you sit down and I'll fix you something to eat."

Richie waved her off. "Thanks, but I grabbed something at the game."

"Health food, I'm sure."

He looked up at her and raised an eyebrow. "Crab cakes," he said proudly. It wasn't exactly a well-balanced meal, but it was healthier than the hotdogs he usually had at the park, even if he had washed it down with a couple of beers.

"Good for you," she smiled. "Sit down anyway. I'll fix some tea."

Richie acquiesced and settled into one of the kitchen chairs. Lara took his jacket and hung it on the hallway coat rack. It was comforting to sit and have tea with his wife; she brought order to his chaotic life.

"Daisy said the search wouldn't be ready until morning," Lara said as she placed two cups of tea on the table and sat down across from her husband, "so you might as well relax." She reached her right hand toward him and placed it palm up, resting on the table. He smiled and gently took it into his own hand. She knew Richie wasn't telling her everything, but that was OK. She also knew why, and was not going to press him on the issue. She looked into his eyes and smiled. His face started to relax.

—

Richie was up at the crack of dawn. Thanks to Lara, he had managed to put his worries behind him for the night and woke up well rested. He allowed her to sleep in, and for the first time in as long as he could remember, *he* put the coffee up for *her*.

"Computer on."

The hard drive whirred. "Good morning, Detective Kincade."

"Good morning, Daisy." Kincade cleared his throat. "I know that I told you to make that phone log search top priority, but around here my wife has even higher priority. If she needs the computer, take a break and let her borrow some computing time, OK?"

"Understood."

He marveled at the personality that Daisy's programming had taken on. He almost thought he heard a pout in that last response.

"So how's it going, anyway?"

"Excuse me, Detective?"

"The search. How's it going?"

"It was completed at four AM. Would you like me to display the results, or shall I print them out?"

"Printer's on the fritz. Just extrapolate the data and display any repetitive phone or Net contacts between Dr. Fletcher's lab or home and Dr. Hingston's lab or home." Paul Hingston seemed the obvious place to start.

Richie poured himself a cup of coffee, took a sip, and then returned to the table. He sat back in the chair facing the monitor, left hand tucked deeply in the pocket of his flannel robe and right hand gripping the mug.

As he started to bring the mug back up to his mouth, Daisy interrupted. "Extrapolation complete. Sorry for the delay detective, but you really do need to get me that memory I asked for."

"Yeah, yeah. All right. Just display the data, Daisy, would you?"

The data came up on the screen. Richie sipped his coffee as he scanned down the list, eyes widening in disbelief.

"You sure about these numbers, Daisy."

"Numbers don't lie, Detective."

Kincade couldn't believe what he saw. When he had instructed Daisy to do this search, he doubted that any useful information would really come from it. He figured that if someone were going to all the effort to steal Dr. Fletcher's data, they would probably be more discreet than to use Net access or phone lines; even protected lines can be traced with the right knowledge. He was wrong.

The data was as clear as day, but now Kincade was more confused than ever. Every Saturday morning at two AM for the past two years an Internet connection had been initiated with BNI from the same source – the home of Dr. Sandra Fletcher. *What kind of game is the good doctor playing with me?* The only way this could be done was for someone to have access to her personal computer, using her personal codes and accessing her personal data from her own home in the middle of the night...every Saturday for nearly two years without her knowing about it. "What are the odds of that?"

"Of what, Detective?"

"Did I say that out loud?"

"Yes, you did."

"Uh, just thinking, Daisy. Ignore request."

"Consider yourself ignored."

Kincade shot a dirty glance at Daisy, but knew she couldn't see it. He could swear he heard a giggle from the computer.

"Nah." He shook his head.

Why would Dr. Fletcher be giving all her information to BNI? Maybe she was trying to help her old boyfriend, Dr. Hingston, and then got pissed off at him when he left her out of the patents and stole all the glory for himself.

"Man, I hope I'm not in the middle of some lover's quarrel. I hate that." He sat back in his chair and stretched.

The only other explanation seemed even more far-fetched. *How could someone be using her codes and her computer inside her own home for two years without her knowing about it? Unless ...*

"Daisy, see what you can find out about Dr. Sandra Fletcher. See if there is anyone else living at her home address."

That had to be the answer, but for someone to be living there with her and doing something like this for two years without her knowing it... "Man, this must be one trustful woman. Sure knows how to pick 'em, eh Daisy?"

"Excuse me, Detective?"

He forgot for a second that Daisy was only a program after all.

"Man, I've gotta get some air. Print that data up on a disc for me, Daisy, would you?" He slipped a microdisc into the drive slot.

"Uploading data to disc."

The disc popped out in a few seconds and Richie slipped it into the right front pocket of his robe.

"See you later, Daisy. Computer off."

Richie stood and tightened the cloth belt around his waist, grabbed his mug and walked to the front door. The morning paper would be on the front porch by now. He needed a distraction to clear his head.

CHAPTER SEVENTEEN

Friday mornings were always hectic at the lab. Sandi would have to plan her day carefully in order to have time to meet with each of her grad students to review their progress for the week. Unless she was ready to give up her weekend, something that she would often do, she had to make sure that no current experiments were left at a stage that required daily monitoring. This had been a long week, and she looked forward to spending a quiet weekend at home with Guy.

"Sam," she said, "why don't you meet with Randi and go over the spinal growth stimulation hormone work. I'll meet with Robert and check out his progress with oligodendrocyte stimulator sequencing."

"Gotcha." Sam Collier had been nearly as disappointed as Sandi that BNI had stolen their work on the brain nanobots, but he had decided to stay on to work on nanobots designed to repair a damaged spinal cord. Although the work was similar to what they had done before, it was still in the early stages and the details were tedious. It was tough to put in the hours when there was still no end in sight.

Sam was going over Randi's schematics for sequencing the DNA that would allow nanobots to produce a hormone necessary for the growth of new spinal neurons when the phone rang.

"Can you get that, Sam?" Sandi was on the computer going over her student's gene sequencing work and did not want to break her concentration.

"Sorry, Randi," Sam said. He put down his work pad and walked over to the phone.

"Hello?"

"Hi. This is Detective Richard Kincade. Is Dr. Sandra Fletcher there?"
He glanced over at Sandi. "Uh, I'm sorry, Detective …?"

"Kincade."

"… Kincade, but she's tied up at the moment. Can I take a message?"
Sandi looked up from the monitor. "Did you say Kincade?"

Sam was jotting down the number as Kincade gave it to him, and didn't hear her. She got up from her chair and walked quickly across the room.

"Right," Sam said into the phone, "got it. I'll be sure to …"

"Gimme that thing!" She grabbed the phone out of his hand, and Sam looked up, startled.

"Detective Kincade?" she said into the receiver.

"Right. Is that you, Doc?"

"Yeah, it's me. What have you got?"

"C'mon, you know better than that; not on the phone. Can you meet me sometime today?"

"How about back at the market. It's kind of hectic around here, but a girl's got to eat."

"The sooner the better. Same place as before?"

"Perfect. I'll see you there at noon."

"Great. Oh, by the way, Doc, do you have a pocket computer with a microdisc reader?"

"Sure."

"Good. Bring it with you."

"No problem. See you at the Market."
"See you then."

—

As soon as he hung up the phone, Richie thought twice about bringing an unencrypted disc to the meeting. Daisy had already completed her search, and Kincade now knew about Guy Andrews; he was sure that Guy had something to do with stealing Sandi's data. It was the only explanation that made any sense. If Guy were to get hold of the microdisc with the phone log, Sandi's life would be in danger. The best bet would be to encrypt the file, but then he would have to have a computer with decryption software to show it to Sandi.

Richie picked up the phone again, and dialed Hank Holiday.

"Hank, listen. I need for you to check Unit Five out of the garage and pick me up at my place around eleven-thirty. I'll spring for lunch at Pedro's."

Hank agreed without any questions. It wasn't hard to talk Hank into anything that involved eating.

—

Agent Trace McKnight was a sports car kind of guy. He loved his little red Porsche. It was great for picking up women, but it was a little too obvious for stakeout work. That's what the gray Buick LeSabre was for.

Trace sat patiently in his Buick, a half block down the road and across the street from the Kincades' row home. Uncle Jimmy had told him to forget about the cop. He said a beat cop like Kincade was harmless, but Trace thought that his Uncle was a little too soft when it came to taking care of 'problems' like Kincade. Trace had worked too hard on this project to let anyone get in the way, and Kincade had gotten a little too close for comfort when he came snooping around at BNI. Uncle Jimmy didn't have to know about everything. Trace decided that he would handle this by himself.

Hank Holiday drove up in Unit Five at eleven-thirty sharp and parked in front of Kincade's home. He knocked on the door and Richie opened it, already dressed in his Orioles jacket.

"Ahh, paydirt," Trace muttered to himself.

Hank tossed the keys to Richie. "I'm not supposed to do this, you know."

"Thanks," Richie smiled. Hank knew how Richie felt about Unit Five.

"So what's this all about, buddy?"

"We've gotta meet that doctor from Hopkins."

"That Fletcher chick?"

Richie shook his head. "You're the kind of guy that gives guys a bad name."

"What? What'd I say?"

"Just do me a favor. Don't call the doctor a 'chick' when we meet her."

Hank's not so slim belly jiggled a bit as he laughed. "Don't worry, I won't call the babe a chick."

"Thanks...I think."

Richie started the car and they headed for Lexington Market. Neither of them noticed the late model LeSabre following a half block behind.

"So what's all this about anyway, Richie?"

"I told you the doc said BNI had been stealing her data, right?"

Hank nodded.

Richie had his eyes on the road and didn't notice the subtle nod, but continued on. "Well, I had Daisy do a search of all the phone and broadband connections between the doc's place and BNI. It turns out there's been a Net uplink initiated from the doc's house to a computer at BNI every Saturday morning around two AM for the past couple of years."

Hank whistled. "Whew. You mean the doc's been sending the data over to BNI herself? That doesn't make any sense."

"Yeah, well, I've been thinking about that. See, any discoveries she makes in the lab over at Hopkins belong to the university. She gets the credit, but not the cash. That could certainly be enough of a motive to make someone look for a way to cash in on their own work."

"Ahh, I get it. She's selling her own work to BNI on the sly. That way, it looks like BNI made the discovery, but she shares in the dough. Did you check her bank records?"

"Yeah. Nothing. Besides, she's clean as a whistle. Dr. Sandra Fletcher is as altruistic as they come from what I can tell. I had Daisy search her activities all the way back to grade school. On paper, she looks like a saint. Dr. Fletcher committing data theft would be about as out of character as you fasting for a week."

"Hey!"

Richie smiled. "Something else doesn't add up. If the doc were selling her data to BNI, why would she call me in to investigate?"

"Maybe to throw you off the trail. After all, you're the one that stirred things up at BNI. She didn't call you until after that. If she's in cahoots with Anderson, maybe he told her to contact you, try to gain your confidence."

"For what?"

"So she could feed you false information, keep you going in the wrong direction."

"Maybe, but I've got a hunch that it's not her at all. See, she's living with this musician, a fellow named Guy Andrews. He moved in with her just before these Net uplinks started. My suspicion is that he is somehow accessing her computer and using it to send the data to BNI."

"A musician? What's the connection? I mean, why would he be into computer espionage."

"Come on, Hank. You've been in this business long enough to know that people aren't always what they seem. I've got Daisy checking him out now, but so far there is nothing obvious. Four years of college at American University, music major, computer science minor."

"Aha!"

"Aha nothin'. Half the kids in America have a computer science minor these days."

"Yeah, I guess so. But I'll bet he's got some hacking skills."

"Probably, but where's the motive. I've checked out his finances too, at least what little there is to check out. It seems nightclub guitar players aren't in one of the higher tax brackets."

"Lower than cops?"

"Lower than cops," Richie said, shaking his head, "but his accounts are all clean as far as I can tell."

"One way or the other, Richie, you'd better watch your step."

"That's why you're here, buddy. Well, that and the fact that I needed Unit Five's computer."

"What for?"

"I figured the doc's either not going to believe me when I tell her about the Internet links from her house to BNI, or she already knows about them, but will pretend not to believe me. Either way, I wanted to be able to show her the microdisc with the search results. I encrypted the disc, and the only decryption software I know of that can decode it is in Daisy's programming or in the police department computers."

They pulled up to park on a side street near Lexington Market, one of the few with street parking.

"Oh, I almost forgot," Hank said. He reached into his pocket and pulled out a piece of paper, then handed it to Richie.

"What's this? Richie asked as he took it.

Hank smiled. "Just take a look. I want to see if you can figure it out."

"Oh, Christ, Hank. Is this another one of your stupid puzzles?"

"Well...yeah, but..."

Richie stuffed it in his pocket. "Maybe later, man."

"I think you should look at it now, Richie. It's..."

"There she is," Richie interrupted as he spotted Sandi in the driver's side mirror. She had parked a few spaces away and was just getting out of her car.

"Doc!" he called out the window.

Sandi lifted her hand to shade her eyes from the sun and peered into the car. "Well, right on time, Detective."

"Listen, Doc, the burritos are on me today, but before we eat, I've got to show you something first. Hop in."

Sandi stooped down and peered into the car. Hank smiled an annoying kind of smile with one eyebrow raised, contorting his face in a way that he mistakenly thought was attractive to someone of the opposite sex. The usual response from women was either one of disgust or laughter, but Hank couldn't help himself.

"I don't know, Detective. My mother always told me that I should never get in a car with strangers, and you two look pretty strange to me." She held back a giggle as she glanced at Hank again.

Richie looked over at his partner. "Ah, he's harmless. He only looks annoying."

Sandi laughed and got in the back seat.

Richie motioned to Hank. "This is my partner, Hank Holiday." He nodded toward Sandi. "This is Dr. Sandra Fletcher."

"Ma'am," he said.

"You're the one I talked to at the station, aren't you?"

Hank was impressed that she recognized his voice from a single word. "That would be me."

"Thanks," she said.

Hank nodded.

"Look, Doc." Richie said. "I did that phone search I told you about."

"And?"

"And there were no phone calls between BNI or Dr. Hingston and your lab at Hopkins other than the ones that you told me about, but..."

"But what?"

"Well, I think you'd better look for yourself."

Richie put the microdisc into the car computer. The encryption was quickly deciphered and the search results came up on the screen. Sandi peered over the front seat, trying to focus on the screen through the glare of sunlight pouring in through the windows.

"Here," Richie said. He activated the window tinters and the car darkened slightly. "That help?"

"Much better. Thanks." She read the data incredulously. "Jesus! No way! This can't be right."

"Computers don't lie, Doc."

"Yeah, well they can be programmed to lie. There's no way those uplinks came from my computer. Are you implying that *I* sent that data to BNI? My own data?"

"Unless someone else was using your computer every Saturday morning at two AM."

Sandi looked at him, disgusted. "Christ, you know about Guy, don't you? You checked me out and learned about my boyfriend...excuse me, my *live-in lover,* right?"

"Look, Doc, you're the one that asked me to..."

"I didn't ask you to pry into my personal life. Who I choose to share my bed with is none of your damned business." She reached for the door handle.

"Yes you did," Richie said.

She stopped and looked at him. "Yes I did what?"

"You did ask me to pry into your personal life. Somebody stealing data off of your computer is about as personal as it gets."

Sandi was offended, but it was hard to disagree. She flopped back in to the seat. "Besides, there's no way Guy could have done it. I don't give my access codes to anyone, not even my *live-in lover,*" she acerbically directed the last three words at Kincade. "And believe me, Guy may be sweet, but he's no genius when it comes to computers."

"I don't know," Hank said, "I hear he aced his computer courses at AU."

Sandi looked surprised. "Computer courses? Guy hears the word keyboard and thinks piano. He doesn't know a hard drive from a four-wheel drive. What computer courses?"

"He minored in computers at AU," Richie said. "Didn't he ever tell you?"

Sandi sat silently, wondering what else Guy may have been keeping from her all this time. He was just a guitar player, for God's sake...a lover, nothing but a harmless lover.

Richie turned off the computer. "Why don't we go have lunch?"

Hank agreed quickly. They coaxed Sandi out of the car, and headed for Pedro's. Trace McKnight watched intently through a pair of binoculars from the far end of the street.

"I don't get it," Sandi said. "It just doesn't make any sense. My work is always the farthest thing from Guy's mind." Sandi always felt wonderful when she was with Guy. He was good at romance, but in her heart she knew that it would never feel like anything more. He never showed the least bit of interest in her work. Even when he feigned interest to try and be nice, she could tell that his mind was elsewhere. "He wouldn't understand my work enough to sell it to someone at BNI even if he wanted to. Besides, there's no way he could get into my files. Computer minor or not, I'm telling you he's no computer whiz."

"I didn't make the facts, Doc, I just found them. Someone made those calls. If it wasn't him and it wasn't you, who else could it have been?"

Hank watched her closely. She was either a great liar or a really bad judge of character. In either case, she was in way over her head. Guys like JT Anderson and James O'Grady were not the kind of people you'd want to mess with. Hank was sure that her hands were dirty, but he felt sorry for her anyway. This could not end well for Dr. Sandra Fletcher.

"Maybe it was Anderson's henchmen. They could have falsified the records to make it look like I was sending information to them...you know, to make me look bad."

"And frame themselves for the theft of data that belonged to Johns Hopkins University? I don't think so," Richie said. "You may have done the work, but it wasn't yours to give even if you wanted to. They would be implicating themselves along with you."

None of them had an answer. Hank was sure it was Sandi who was the perpetrator, Richie was just as sure that it had to be Guy, and Sandi was sure that she was being framed. They walked quietly into the market and ordered lunch.

"Mind if I come back to your place and have a look at your computer, Doc?" Richie asked nonchalantly as he took a sip of Coke. "Your internal Internet log will tell us whether those calls really came from your PC or if those records were falsified."

"Yeah, why didn't I think of that," she said. "I always shut my PC down when I go to bed. Even if somebody tried to route those calls through my computer from another location, they wouldn't have been able to do it. My PC is always off at night. Those records had to be forged. I'll take you there right after lunch. Sam can handle things at the lab today. I want to get to the bottom of this mess."

They hurried through their lunch and walked back to the cars. The three of them arrived at Unit Five first.   Richie had decided to ride with Sandi back to her place. Hank needed to get back to work.

"Nice to meet you, Doc." Hank extended his hand. "Take care of my boy Richie here." What he really meant was *I don't trust you as far as I can throw you. Watch out, Richie.*

"Don't worry, Hank," Richie knew exactly what his friend was thinking. "We'll be careful."

Hank got in the car. Richie and Sandi waved and turned to walk over to Sandi's car. Hank pulled out the key and slipped it into the ignition. He was just about to turn it, when...

"Hold up, Hank," he heard Richie yell. Kincade tapped on the window. "Hold up a sec. The doc here wants to have another look at that microdisc. She wants to see whether the transmissions to BNI started before or after Guy moved in."

Richie already knew the answer, but Sandi wanted to see it for herself. She slipped into the back seat again. Kincade opened the passenger side front door and got in. He pulled the disc out of his pocket and slipped it into the computer, which whirred on. The patrol cars were equipped with battery back-up that could run the computer for several hours. It wasn't practical to keep the car running for hours at a time while on a stakeout.

Sandi checked the data. Kincade was right. The transmissions started shortly after Guy moved in with her. Could she really have been so wrong about him?

"God, maybe you're right, Detective. Do I know how to pick 'em or what?" She felt so used.

They got out of the car. Kincade wanted to put his arm around her shoulder and console her, but somehow he knew that was not what she wanted. They walked quietly down the sidewalk, Sandi deep in thought and Kincade watching, reading her body language. He was still pretty sure that Guy was the culprit, but he was not ready to let his guard down with the good doctor. The pieces of this puzzle hadn't quite come together yet.

Hank put the key in the ignition and gave it a twist. The engine roared to a start. He turned the wheels sharply to the right and eased off of the brake. As the car moved forward, the left front tire rolled over the trigger that had been set by Trace McKnight. Hank Holiday was dead before the sound of the blast reached his ears.

Sandi and Richie were thrown forward face first into the sidewalk by the force of the explosion. They lay motionless on the pavement, not yet aware of what had just happened.

A moment later, Kincade started to fade back into consciousness. He slowly pushed up from the concrete and glanced back at the blazing hunk of metal that had been Unit Five.

"Hank!" he yelled hopelessly. He struggled to his feet and stumbled toward the car, but the heat forced him back. As he turned away from the car, he realized that Sandi was still laying face down on the pavement. He urged himself over to her as fast as his body could move and kneeled down next to her.

"Doc? Doctor Fletcher?" He gently shook her shoulder.

She slowly turned her head and looked up at him. "I'm OK," she muttered, half-dazed. "What happened?" She hadn't yet realized that Unit Five had gone up in flames.

"I don't know," he said looking back at the car, "but I'm sure as hell going to find out."

Sandi started to get up, and then dropped back down to her knees, holding her head.

"You OK?"

"Yeah. Just a bit woozy."

"We'd better get you to a hospital." He wiped the blood dripping down from her forehead. "You took a pretty good blow to the head."

"It's just a scrape," she said, regaining her strength. "I'm fine." She stood and brushed herself off. "Let's get out of here. Whoever did this might still be around waiting to make sure the job is done."

"Look, Doc, whoever did this isn't after you. They had no way of knowing that you would be going back to Hank's car. That bomb was meant for me. Obviously the NSA was serious about keeping me away from BNI."

"The NSA?"

"I'll explain later. Look, the further away you stay from me the better."

"I'm not so sure of that. If this is about BNI, then I'm in this as deep as you are."

Richie started to protest, but it was hard to disagree.

"At least come back to my place and help me check out the computer. If Guy is involved with this...God, I can't believe I'm even thinking that...then I need to know about it."

Kincade agreed. Sandi took out her keys, but Richie stopped her before she pushed the button to unlock it.

"I thought you said they weren't after me."

"I'm pretty sure."

"Pretty sure. Great." She looked at her car. "I just made my last payment on that thing."

"It's probably fine, but let me get the bomb squad to check it out, OK."

"No argument here." She put her right thumb and little finger to her mouth and let out a loud, shrill whistle as she waved her left arm at a passing cab. "Ready?" she said to Richie.

He admired her grit.

They arrived at Sandi's house about twenty minutes later. On the way in, Richie phoned the department.

"Where the hell are you, Kincade?"

"Minding my own business, Chief. I'm on leave, remember?"

"Yeah, I remember. Do you?"

"Listen, Chief, I need a favor."

"Richie...Hank's dead."

Kincade was silent for a brief moment. It was hard to get the words out. "I know. I was there."

"You what?"

"I was with him, Chief. That bomb was meant for me."

"Don't flatter yourself, Richie. You remember a guy name of Aldo Echeverria?"

"Echeverria...Echeverria...wasn't that some drug dealer Hank busted by accident a couple of years back?"

"Yeah. It was the case of that auto de-chipping ring in Anne Arundel County. Hank was tracking down a rash of de-chipped cars used in petty crimes. He discovered that they were all done at this auto shop in Anne Arundel. Echeverria was the owner of the shop. Turned out he was using the cars to smuggle drugs. Hank stumbled into this department's biggest drug bust of the decade."

"What's that have to do with this? He got twelve years in the state pen, didn't he? He should be safely locked away."

"I just got off the phone with an Agent James O'Grady at the NSA. Apparently, they were keeping an eye on you after your shenanigans at BNI. One of their surveillance teams spotted Echeverria messing around with Unit Five just before the explosion. Seems he just got out of the pen a couple of weeks ago and had Hank in his sights, wanted to send a message. You know how those drug runners are. They don't forget someone who gets in their way."

"So where's the weasel now?"

"In the morgue. The NSA agent chased him down right after the bomb went off, but Echeverria resisted arrest. He took two bullets in the head."

Kincade thought a moment. "Sounds a little too neat to me, Chief."

"Yeah, that's what I thought."

"Listen, Chief. Do you think you can get a hold of that O'Grady fellow? Try and convince him that I'm minding my own business. Tell him that you talked to me and I got the message loud and clear, would you?"

"Did you?"

"Of course, Chief. I'm just using the free time to help out a friend, you know?"

"Yeah, right. Listen, Richie. Watch your back."

"Thanks, Chief."

—

The cab pulled into Sandi's driveway. Kincade paid the fare and they went inside.

"I'm telling you, you're not going to find anything. Maybe Guy's not being totally up front with me about everything, maybe all the sweet talk was just to get into my pants, but he's no super sleuth. He's got the brains of a Neanderthal, but he's real sweet, you know?"

"Uh huh." Kincade was trying to be polite.

Even Sandi doubted the words coming out of her mouth. "Even if he did want to steal the data off my computer, nobody knows my access codes," she said while waiting for the computer to boot up. "Here we go. Let's have a look."

She pulled her desk chair up to the monitor, and Kincade looked over her shoulder. "Computer, access Internet logs. Display all uplinks initiated from this location between twelve PM and three AM for the past two years."

She looked over her shoulder. "I'm telling you, it'll come up empty. Guy never goes near this thing and *I'm* always asleep by eleven."

Within a few seconds, the computer responded. "There are no entries that match the specified search criteria."

Sandi smiled and breathed a sigh of relief. "There, satisfied?"

"Mind if I have a go at it?"

Sandi shrugged her shoulders and stood up, offering the chair to Kincade. "Computer, access OS Internet log, same search criteria."

"Access denied."

"See," he said to Sandi, "the programmers put a hidden file in the operating system that keeps a log of all Internet sites accessed from the computer. They don't really want you to know about it, and even if you do it's almost impossible to access."

"You mean they keep a record of all of my personal use and hide it from me?"

"Yup."

"What for?"

"For security reasons."

"Who's security? Certainly not mine." Sandi was brilliant, but still naive when it came to the ways of the business world. She was offended at the thought of someone recording all of the intimate details of her personal life.

"For times like this," Kincade said as he slipped a disc into the micro drive. He waited for the deciphering program to load.

"Computer, access OS Internet log, same search criteria," he repeated to the computer.

This time the results were different. A large file several pages long came up on screen listing hundreds of Internet sites. Sandi stared wide-eyed at the list.

"Computer," Richie said, "eliminate all entries with the words 'sex', 'babes' or 'hot' in them."

Sandi started to object, but held back, mouth agape, as she watched the list shrink dramatically.

"Well, you sure can learn a lot about someone from this, can't you?" Sandi said, obviously offended at the thought that Guy had been using her computer to frequent adult Web sites.

Richie felt sorry for her. Obviously, Guy wasn't quite the person she had imagined him to be.

The list was considerably smaller. Some of the calls to BNI were now apparent, but numerous other Web sites remained on the list. It was apparent that Guy spent a good deal of time surfing the Web in the middle of the night while Sandi slept.

"Computer, display only sites containing 'BNI' in their name."

Once again, the list condensed quickly, displaying numerous uplinks to BNI's Intranet.

"I'll be damned." Sandi looked at the list on the screen, which was now identical to the file that Richie had shown her in the car. Every Saturday morning at two AM, this computer had called a computer at BNI and uploaded her work files. Every week since Guy had moved in, this computer had been used to give all of her work to her major competitor. "Right under my nose," she sighed.

"How often do you change your access codes?"

"Every month, and I never give them to anyone. Could he have been getting them off the computer somehow?" She was starting to believe that maybe Guy knew a lot more about computers than she had given him credit for.

"Not likely. Even with a program to break the encryption codes, it can take hours to break the encryption system that this software uses. The programmers aren't always up front about what they put on your hard drive, but they do try to keep it safe. If it was easy to steal personal data from a PC, then no one would feel safe using one and the programmers would be out of business."

"Then how is he doing it?"

Kincade walked over to the sofa on the other side of the room and sat next to Sandi. "Tell me about your Friday nights. What's your routine?"

Sandi blushed.

"Sorry to pry, but there's got to be a clue, something that he's using to gain access, and since it's always on Friday nights, that seems to be the place to start looking."

"Well," Sandi thought, "I'm afraid I'm really very boring." She was embarrassed to admit how poor her social life was when Guy was not around. "Fridays are really tough days for me, getting everything tied up at the lab for the weekend. I usually don't get home until about seven or eight, and by then Guy's long gone. He plays down at the club every Friday night. He's usually not back until after one in the morning."

She stopped briefly, realizing that the timing would be perfect for him to go to the computer as soon as he gets in from work, with her sound asleep and unaware of his late night activity. "I just thought he was being thoughtful by not waking me." Her voice started to break.

"Take your time, I know this can't be easy." Richie said, putting a hand on her shoulder.

"Like I said, I'm exhausted when I get in. I fix a quick bite to eat, take my insulin shot and then watch a little TV until I crash at about ten o'clock. That's it, I'm afraid. Like I said...boring."

Richie raised an eyebrow. "Insulin?"

"I guess you don't know *everything* about me, Detective, huh?"

"How often do you take your shot?"

"Oh, it's that new stuff, Synthulin. You only have to take it once a week. It's great. When I was a kid I used to have to take a shot every night. Boy, did I learn to hate needles. But now, with this new synthetic insulin, I only have to take one shot a week. I keep it in the fridge and every Friday night like clockwork, I..."

"Every Friday night, eh?"

"Of course!" Sandi smacked her forehead with the palm of her hand. "It would be so easy for him to...Look, I keep the stuff in the refrigerator. That's no big secret. All Guy would have to do is to slip a little Allohypnol into the vial while I'm at work."

"Allohypnol?"

"Yes. It's a hypnotic drug, real potent stuff. It was developed by the military, but it's not that hard to get, especially for a guy with connections like JT Anderson. Allohypnol renders the subject highly suggestive. With that in my system, Guy could talk me into doing anything."

"Like accessing your files and uploading them to BNI."

"Yup, he could wake me in the middle of the night, get me to upload the files and I wouldn't remember a thing in the morning."

"So why don't we test that insulin vial of yours? Let's see if the drug is in there."

"It's not that easy, I'm afraid. The drug rapidly degrades once injected into an aqueous environment."

"You lost me, Doc."

"Aqueous...water. Once it's injected into the vial containing the liquid solution my insulin is in, it would degrade in a matter of hours.

"So he'd have to inject it into the vial every Friday."

"As long as he does it within twelve hours of the time I inject myself, it would still be active. Once it's in my system, it would stay active for several hours more. I'd be like fruit, ripe for the picking when he gets home at one in the morning."

"Well, it is Friday, isn't it? What time does Guy usually head downtown for work."

"Of course." Sandi smacked her forehead again. "Ouch!"

"I'd stop doing that if I were you. You're going to make it bleed again."

"Bad habit. Maybe that scrape on my forehead will cure me of it." She rubbed gently around the sore on her forehead. "Damn, that hurt."

"Could have been a lot worse," Richie said, thinking about Hank.

"Yeah," Sandi sighed. "Anyhow, Guy usually splits around twelve-thirty or one in the afternoon so that he can grab a late lunch down by the Inner Harbor. He must inject the Allohypnol into my insulin vial right before he leaves."

"If that's the way he's doing it."

"There's one way to find out."

Sandi called next door to Mrs. Flannery. The elderly woman had a ten year old Camry, but hated to drive. Sandi often ran errands for her and she was only too happy to loan the car to Sandi. It was nice to be able to do a favor in return, she had said.

Sandi grabbed the vial of Synthulin on the way out the door. "A friend of mine over at Hopkins can run this through an analyzer in a second."

They drove to Hopkins, and just as Sandi suspected, the vial contained Allohypnol.

"Look, Doc, maybe you shouldn't go back home tonight."

"Don't be crazy. I can handle Guy. Besides, he won't know that I know what he knows."

"And that's supposed to make me feel better?"

Sandi looked at Richie and smiled. "You're sweet. Why can't I find a man like you?"

"Keep your eyes on the road, young lady." Richie was more concerned that she'd catch him blushing than he was about getting into an accident. It was pretty flattering to have a younger woman pay him a compliment like that, especially one that he found increasingly more attractive as he got to know her. With the passing years, his waist was growing faster than the graying hair on his head. It had been a long time since any woman other than his wife had noticed him.

Kincade checked in with the chief as they drove. The bomb squad had checked out Sandi's car; it came up clean. The two of them stopped by to pick up the car, and Richie drove it back, following behind the old, reliable Camry. He tried again to talk Sandi into accepting some protection, but his protests were in vain. They dropped off Mrs. Flannery's car, and then Sandi drove Richie home before returning to prepare for the evening.

CHAPTER EIGHTEEN

Trace McKnight was watching the breaking news on the TV screen in his Buick LeSabre. He had just pulled into his driveway, but left the car running to savor the moment. It hadn't taken the news crew long to converge on the scene of the blazing vehicle just outside of Lexington Market. The smoke from the wreck that had been the Baltimore Police Department's Unit Five billowed high into the sky and out of the frame of the small TV screen. Trace smiled; he was proud of his work.

"One officer is dead," the reporter said, "and another officer injured at the scene. There was at least one civilian reported injured as well, but both the injured officer and the civilian have left the scene. The degree of their injuries is undetermined, and their identities remain unknown. The body in the car was …"

The ring from Trace's car phone temporarily cut off the sound from the TV.

"Shit," he said, annoyed at the interruption. "Answer call," he said to the computerized phone.

The face of James O'Grady appeared on the screen.

"Well, Uncle Jimmy. What a pleasant surprise."

O'Grady didn't look too happy. "What kind of crap are you trying to pull, Trace? I told you to stay away from Kincade. You're gonna take a toothless cop and turn him into a media darling. With press support, this guy can knock our legs out from under us. Use your head, would you?"

"Well," Trace said, "news travels fast, eh? Do you have your TV on? Our problems have just gone up in smoke."

"They don't put everything on TV, you know. The fried corpse in that car was a BPD detective, name of Hank Holiday. He was Kincade's partner."

Trace went white. "But I saw him …"

"You saw wrong, and what's more important is you *thought* wrong. Initiative is only a good thing when it's used at the right time; breaching my orders is *not* the right time."

Trace was fuming. He was sure that he had nailed Kincade. Failure did not come often, and he didn't like the feeling.

"Don't make the same mistake twice, Trace. One dead cop will have the police force on full alert. Two dead cops and we'll be so thick in blue that we won't be able to make a move in this town without them knowing about it."

James O'Grady stared at Trace through the video screen. It was a cold, piercing stare, the kind that made it clear who was in charge. This was Commander O'Grady's face, not Uncle Jimmy's. Trace was not the first who had been frozen by those eyes. He knew better than to speak.

"It's like a chess game, kid. We make the right moves and Kincade gets knocked off the board; everyone forgets a player once he's out of the game. We make the wrong move and everyone on the other side knows just what we're up to. Let's not make a martyr of this guy, huh. We don't want anyone wondering what he was snooping around for."

Trace nodded.

"Nuff said. You're doing a heck of a job, Trace, but you've still got a few things to learn. You stick to the tech stuff and let me handle the chess game."

The transmission clicked off and the TV news came back on screen. "We now return to our regular programming."

Trace reached to turn off the car, then pulled back.

"Phone access," he said.

"What number please?"

"Place call: Guy Andrews, cell phone number."

The TV screen went blank as the number was dialed. After three rings, Guy answered the phone, but the screen remained blank.

"Hello?"

Trace stared at the screen out of habit. "Christ, can't you spring for a video phone, Andrews?"

"Christ isn't home right now. This is his father, may I take a message?" Guy said. He burst out in laughter.

"Cute. Real cute." Trace was not amused. "Listen up, guitar man, I don't have time to waste shooting the breeze with you."

"Irish? Is that you, Irish? I haven't heard from you in ages."

Trace hated it when Guy called him that. He had nothing against Ireland, but he had worked damned hard to erase any hint of his childhood accent. He thought of himself only as an American and was proud of it.

"Good guess, Andrews."

"So, you got some more inside info for me about the doc? I thought you had squeezed just about everything you could out of our boy Hingston. With all the little tidbits you gave me about Sandi, she thinks I'm Don Juan or something. That girl's convinced I can read her mind, star-crossed lovers or some shit like that, but my material's getting a little old, you know? I could use some fresh stuff to butter her up."

"Man, after two years, if you don't know how to push her buttons there's something wrong with you."

"Hey, I've got her eating out of the palm of my hand, dude. I could convince her the Pope is Jewish if I wanted to."

"Well, it's a good thing, loverboy."

"What do you mean?" Guy didn't like the tone of Trace's voice. It didn't take much to spook him.

"Look, I just called to tell you to keep your eyes open. There's some detective that's been hanging around your girlfriend a lot lately, the same guy that's been snooping around at BNI."

"Shit, man. You gotta get me out. Now."

"Relax, Don Juan. If she's as in love with you as you say, a nosey cop isn't going to turn her against you that easy. Besides, there's no way he can tie you into this. He's not that bright."

"Listen, dude..."

"No, you listen, guitar man. I spent way too much time and money setting you up with the doc. You stay put and do your job for now. You're not out until I say you're out."

Guy didn't like risk, but he knew better than to cross Trace McKnight. "So what, then? Do I cancel the transmission tonight? I already juiced the insulin vial."

"No. Don't change the routine until I tell you to. Just watch your back. Transmit at the usual time."

Trace disconnected and went in to pour himself a Scotch. Guy was a natural with women. He had been the obvious choice for the job two years ago when Trace had planned it. He'd seen Guy work his magic time after time in college when they were roommates at American University. While Trace was working hard getting his degree in bioengineering, Guy was busy playing his guitar and working on his smile. Trace spent many nights sleeping on the floors of his other friends' rooms, supplanted from his own by one after another of Guy's sorority conquests.

There was no doubt that Guy could win Sandi Fletcher's trust and gain access to her files, especially with the intimate details of her personal life that Trace was able to get from his connections at BNI. It wasn't hard; Paul loved to talk about Sandi, and the wounds were fresh when Paul started work at BNI shortly after his break-up with her. It was easy getting Sandi and Guy together, but counting on Guy to keep his wits under pressure, this was the part that concerned Trace. He had always suspected that his old classmate didn't have the backbone for espionage, and could only hope that Guy wouldn't do anything stupid.

———

Guy Andrews didn't give the best show of his career that night, but no one really noticed. There was enough liquor flowing around the club to cover more than a few strained chords. He couldn't get his mind off the conversation with his old college roommate that afternoon and was anxious about what he might find upon his return home tonight. He finished his second set, pilfered a bottle of Jack Daniels for the road, and started home in his blue Chevy flatbed. The white side-stripes were covered with scratches from years of backwoods camping trips.

Maybe that sick bastard is just playing games with me, he thought to himself. He never really liked Trace McKnight; the Irishman was always a little too smug for him, a little too military. He never would have worked with him, but when the call had come two years ago, Guy was broke. The owner of The Pendulum Pit, a bar by the Inner Harbor, owed Trace a favor and agreed to hire Guy at three times what he had been earning in sporadic gigs at the time. McKnight provided the funds, which were hard to trace when laundered through the Pit. Guy eagerly accepted. It seemed like an easy job, and although he hated the espionage-like feel to the computer games he played every Friday night, it had been fun. Sandi wasn't his ideal woman, but she was attractive enough and knew how to have fun. He had never really regretted taking this job. Not until this afternoon.

It had been a rough day. Guy tried to forget the tone in Trace's voice, but he couldn't get it out of his mind. He had a few more drinks than usual that evening trying to calm his nerves, and he struggled to focus on the dark road on his way back home. His beat up flatbed truck swerved back and forth, but the security chip kept it a safe distance from the roadside markers, which sent out signals that the car's security system could use to monitor the distance. The safety systems worked quite well and he made it home intact. Guy pulled the truck into the driveway and parked. One last swig from the bottle of Jack was just what he needed to slow his heart, which pounded in his chest at the thought of confronting Sandi, or maybe even an angry cop, when he went through that door.

He got out of the car and ran his hand across the large silver buckle on his belt. Working downtown until late at night had its disadvantages and Guy was not the type to face the darkness of the city streets unprepared. On many occasions he had practiced releasing the catch of the spring-loaded switchblade that was built into the belt buckle, but he had hoped he would never find out if he had the guts to use it. Tonight, it was comforting to know it was there.

Guy walked quietly up the four wooden steps to the front porch, pausing at each step and shifting his weight slowly, hoping that a creak from the old stairs would not betray his presence. The rain fell lightly against his face. He slipped the key easily into the lock above the doorknob and twisted the handle cautiously until the door popped open ever so slightly. Standing motionless in the misty night, he listened for voices. It was a relief to hear nothing but the drops of rain against the roof above his head, to see nothing but darkness beyond the door. Guy stepped just inside the threshold, waiting for his eyes to adjust to the darkness. The lights were staying off tonight. Slowly, the room around him came into focus. Everything was in place, nothing unusual. Maybe Trace was right. Maybe Sandi didn't really suspect anything

Feeling a bit more at ease, Guy made his way to the kitchen, moving easily through the darkness in familiar surroundings. Inside the refrigerator, the insulin vial was in its usual spot. The sharps container, in which Sandi always disposed of her syringes, had been empty this morning. Guy had taken the old one away and replaced it with a new one himself. He picked it up and gave it a gentle shake. He smiled as he heard the rattling of the glass syringe against the sides of the container. Obviously, Sandi had given herself the usual Friday night shot of insulin and tossed her needle in the container.

Guy crept up the stairs and slowly opened the door to the bedroom. He froze as the rusty old hinges creaked and Sandi stretched out an arm, lifting the blanket ever so slightly. Guy held his breath. She gently settled back under the covers, sound asleep, her thick brown hair strewn across the pillow. He smiled; his nerves began to ease.

The familiar smell of home was comforting. He managed to slow his breathing to a near normal rate and slipped past Sandi into the bathroom, quietly shutting the door behind him. The thought of waking Sandi rekindled his anxiety. He'd done this dozens of times before, but it didn't feel the same tonight. Standing over the sink, he turned on the cold water. A few quick splashes to the face helped to counter the effects of the whiskey.

"Show time," he said to the mirror. He left the door ajar to allow the light to spill out into the bedroom, providing just enough illumination to negotiate the room.

Sandi hadn't slept well that night. She kept drifting in and out of sleep, her mind racing with scenarios, each playing out in a different way. The light from the bathroom awakened her from her half-dream state. Her heart raced as she lay motionless in bed.

"Sandi." Guy shook her shoulder gently. "Time to get up, love," he whispered in her ear.

'Love', my ass, she thought to herself. She turned over, stretching her arms and squinting as if awakened from a deep sleep into the

brightness of the faintly lit room.   "Hi, sweetheart. What time is it?" she said, forcing a smile.

"Time to take a walk, dear. I need some help with the computer again."

Sandi wasn't quite sure how to act. She tried to imagine how someone on Allohypnol would react. She had no idea. *God, I hope he goes for this.* Her heart raced a mile a minute, but she concealed it well. She sat up and slipped out from under the covers. It sickened her for Guy to see her nude body. She had never given it a second thought before, but this time was different. She had fought the urge to wear a nightgown to bed tonight, but if she had, Guy would certainly know that something was not right.

As she reached for the nightgown that was draped over the metal bedpost, Guy admired the grace of her naked form silhouetted against the light breaking through the bathroom door. She shivered ever so slightly in the cool night air and Guy reached out to help her on with the robe.

"No," she brushed him away, "I've got it." She was afraid that she may have given herself away and abruptly added, "Thanks, sweetie." She carefully tucked the robe around her slim figure and positioned herself to Guy's right, taking his hand in hers.

"Right then," he said, "let's go."

He led her into the study. They walked hand in hand each wondering if the other knew what was racing through their mind, each trying to conceal the anxiety that drove them forward.

This is the last time, Guy thought. *No way they're going to make me do this again. I'm getting the hell out of here tomorrow, with or without McKnight's help.*

Sandi held her robe tightly to her body with her left hand. Even in the coolness of the night she could feel the sweat beading up on the nape of her neck.

Guy flipped on the light switch and they entered the study. He sat down and booted up the computer as Sandi stood beside him trying hard to take slow deep breaths.

"Here we go." He stood and motioned to the chair. "Have a seat."

Sandi sat down in front of the keyboard. Although much of her work was done with voice recognition entry, a keyboard was still the preferred way to enter codes and passwords. "What now?"

"Key in your Net access password and go to BNI.net."

Guy had given her the same instructions every Friday night for the past two years, but thanks to the Allohypnol she would forget her actions within minutes. She noticed that Guy seemed a bit anxious tonight. It was unnerving to have him standing over her.

"Have a seat, Guy." She pointed to the char next to the desk. "You know I don't like to work with someone looking over my shoulder."

Guy turned his gaze from the monitor, teeth clenched, and glanced askew at Sandi. She was usually in a hypnotic state during these sessions. It was unusual for her to say anything without prodding. Guy ran his fingers along his belt buckle. Sandi bit back the lump in her throat as he hesitated briefly, and then pulled a second chair up beside her. He didn't take his eyes off her face as he slipped past her and into the chair.

Sandi accessed the Internet and went to the BNI.net site. She wanted to take this just far enough to see who it was that Guy was sending the messages to. She had to know if it was Paul.

"Good," Guy said as the BNI site came up on the screen. "Now go to the employee access area."

Sandi clicked on the icon labeled "employees only." A message popped up: "enter ID and password." She looked at Guy.

"You really don't remember, do you?" He laughed. "All right. The ID is "TOM" and the password is "Mindfields." Guy was starting to let his guard down. *Maybe,* he thought, *Trace was just being paranoid.*

Sandi typed in the entry. She had no idea who Tom was, but she was relieved that it was not Paul's site that she was accessing. The site came up with three options: "enter text message," "enter voice message" and "upload file". Once again Sandi looked to Guy for instructions.

"Excellent. Click on "upload file.""

Once again, Sandi complied and a new message appeared: "choose files to send."

"Now unencrypt your office files, the ones with this week's research and select them to send."

Sandi hesitated. She still hadn't found out the name of Guy's contact at BNI, but she knew that she could go no further. The faint ticking of the antique clock on the mantle was the only sound that Sandi could hear in the tense silence of the night; it seemed to grow louder with each passing second.

"Type, Sandi," he said sternly between gritted teeth, the anxiety quickly overtaking him once again.

God, I don't know if I can do this. She held her hands suspended over the keyboard. She glanced at the clock. It was nearly two AM.

"Type," he snapped. His hand cradled the silver buckle.

"I don't think so sweetie," she smiled at him.

Guy's eyes opened wide. The clock chimed, a muffled electronic chime that Sandi normally didn't even notice anymore, but this time it ripped into the tension of the night. Guy jumped up from his chair, clasping the open switchblade in his hand.

"I said type in the God-damned address."

Sandi stood up slowly, backing away. "Now look, Guy. You don't really want to do this."

He stood motionless, more scared by circumstances than enraged. As he had always feared, he wasn't sure if he could use that knife when the moment of truth arrived, and now that moment had come. The fact that the object of his anger was Sandi, the woman with whom he had shared his bed for the past two years, did not make it any easier.

Sandi edged back across the room, hand planted firmly in the right pocket of her robe, cradling the cold metal handle of the pistol that Richard Kincade had lent to her. She froze as her back hit the wall. She and Guy stared at each other, neither recognizing the stranger who now stood across the room. Tears welled up in Sandi's eyes, but did not steal her confidence.

Guy stepped tentatively forward, gripping the knife tightly in his right hand. "I need you to upload that data, Sandi."

"I won't do it, Guy."

"You switched the insulin, didn't you?" She didn't need to answer. "How did you know?"

She stood against the wall, staring incredulously as he came closer, the knife now up in the air.

"Guy, don't," were the only words she could force through her lips.

————

The rain pounded against the second story window of the Kincades' Highlandtown rowhouse. Richie stood by the window staring out at the reflections of the streetlights on the rain-drenched road. He didn't say a word, but Lara could feel his anxiety and lay half awake in bed.

"Come to bed, Richie."

"I shouldn't have left her alone."

"She's a big girl. She told you to leave."

"Still..."

He just stood there, holding the curtain back and staring into the night.

"Call her."

Richie dropped the curtain. "Yeah."

He walked over to his side of the bed and sat. The phone on the nightstand was dimly lit, but he had no trouble seeing the numbers. Richie preferred manual phones to the voice activated kind. He punched in Sandi's number and sat silently as the phone rang.

"No answer?" Lara asked as she turned to face him.

Richie shook his head as he put the phone down. "I'm going over there."

Lara rolled back over so that he wouldn't see the worry in her eyes. There was no point in protesting. Even after all these years she could feel the fear each time he walked out the door to go to work. Times like this were even worse, but she wouldn't let him know. He had more important things to worry about tonight and she wanted him focused.

Richie dressed quickly, walked over to the bedside and gave her a kiss on the forehead. She opened her eyes. "Be careful."

"Always." He smiled and walked out the door.

————

The Chevy pick-up swerved out of the driveway and sped into the stormy night. The bent wiper blade on the driver's side smacked against the hood of the truck with each beat. Guy struggled to see the road through the streaky window as the rain pounded against the windshield. He decided to keep to the back roads, afraid that the police would be out looking for him.

"I can't believe she didn't take the damned drug. Stupid bitch." He took another swig from the bottle of Jack Daniels, trying to soothe his frayed nerves.

Between the alcohol and the rain, it was a challenge just to keep the truck on the road. Every muscle in his body was as taut as an anchor line in a hurricane. He hunched forward peering intently over the steering wheel and gripping it tightly with both hands. His neck and his clothes were soaked with perspiration in spite of the coolness of the night air.

Acorn Creek Road wound through the countryside from southwest Baltimore toward Columbia, rejoining the main road just past the Acorn Creek Bridge about a mile from the entrance to BNI. He was sure that he would be safe once inside the confines of Anderson's well-guarded estate.

Lightning flashed across the sky, briefly illuminating the pitch-black countryside with each strike. He saw the turn onto the Acorn Creek Bridge about fifty yards up the road on the left. He hadn't realized he was quite so close already.

"Shit!" He hit the brakes and turned sharply onto the bridge. The seldom-traveled road was littered with leaves, now wet from the fall storm, and the old bridge was not yet equipped with the roadside sensors which the automobile safety chips used to keep cars from veering off the road. The truck's safety computer chip was unable to detect the boundaries of the road as Guy made the sharp turn. The tires lost their grip as they hit the bed of wet leaves covering the bridge. Guy was helpless as his pick-up truck slid across the road and smashed through the rickety wooden side-rails, plunging twenty feet down into the shallows of Acorn Creek. The Chevy crumpled against the rounded boulders that bordered the riverbed and rolled into the rushing water. The river, swelled from the prolonged storm, quickly enveloped the truck. There was no one to notice the last bubbles of air rising to the surface as it sank.

———

Richard Kincade drove up the Jones Falls Expressway through the pouring rain. Even in good weather, the serpentine highway through downtown Baltimore was not his favorite road, but at three in the morning the traffic wasn't too bad. He soon found his way onto the winding country road north of the city that led to Sandi's home. It was not hard to spot her house, the only one on the block with the lights on in the living room. Richie pulled into the driveway. Sandi's car was still there.

He stared out the window, struggling to see the house through the rain. There were lights on in two of the upstairs rooms. Once more he tried calling from his cell phone and once more there was no answer. Richie put the phone into his pocket and pulled his gray trench coat tightly around his body. He shut the car door and raised his collar up over his neck. The rain hadn't let up a bit.

There was no answer at the door. He turned the handle, but it was locked. The kitchen door proved to be less of an obstacle. It was dark inside and he gave himself a moment to adjust to the light.

"Dr. Fletcher," he called out. He was not surprised when no answer came.

Richie hated carrying a weapon, but at times like this he was glad to have one. Pulling the semi-automatic handgun out of his holster, he inched cautiously across the floor to the living room door. There was an eerie silence disturbed only by the raindrops beating methodically against the windows. The living room was not immaculate; he could tell that Sandi was the type of person who liked to use her living room to unwind in, not as a showroom like so many others did, but at the moment it was unoccupied.

Up the stairs, Richie could see a dim light coming from the bedroom door at one end of the hall and the more brightly lit study at the other end. "Doc?" he called out as he slowly ascended the steps. It was tough working without backup. He tried not to think of Hank.

The door to the bedroom was ajar. Richie stood next to it with his back against the wall. He called out one more time, again answered only by silence. One last look down the hallway at the study door, and then he ducked into the bedroom, gun first. He stood crouched in the doorway surveying the room. The only light visible was coming from the bathroom.

God, I hope she's not taking a shower. This could be really embarrassing. His knees cracked as he struggled to his feet. "Shh," he whispered to them. *I'm getting too old for this nonsense.* Walking towards the bathroom, he stopped periodically to glance back over his shoulder. That light from the study was unnerving. For a brief moment he was convinced that he did hear the shower, but soon realized it was just the rain slapping against the bathroom window. He took a deep breath and ducked in. Much to his relief, everything was in order. No naked woman taking a shower, no sign of violence.

Only one more place up here to look, he thought as he turned back toward the hallway.

Richie rechecked his weapon to make sure the safety was disengaged, wiped the sweat off his palm and slowly made his way back down the hall to the study. He could hear the faint whir of the computer's hard drive as he got closer. The rain had started to let up and as he crouched by the door, listening intently; he could swear he could hear his own heart ticking. He took deep, slow breaths to calm himself and was somewhat relieved as he realized the ticking sound was actually coming from a clock inside the study.

He readied his weapon and leaped in, steadying the pistol in both hands. His eyes darted toward the computer desk and then across the room to the floor by the window, drawn by the glare of light reflecting off Guy's knife. He looked around again to make sure he didn't have any unwanted company, and then walked over to the knife and bent down. The blood on the blade was still sticky. It wasn't until that moment that he noticed the sparse drops of blood camouflaged against the hardwood floor leading out the door and down the hall from where he had just come.

Richie followed the trail of blood, which led down to the kitchen door, the same door that he had entered several moments ago. He hadn't seen the trail of blood in the darkness of the house when he entered. Even now, it was hard to discern in the dimly lit kitchen.

He quickly searched the rest of the house. It didn't take long to convince himself it was vacant. He rechecked the computer in the study, but it provided little in the way of clues. Richie was tempted to take the knife, but thought the better of it. After all, he had been relieved of duty and technically he was presently in the process of breaking and entering. "Better leave this to the boys in blue," he said, this time out loud. It was a comfort to hear his own voice. Creeping around in the dark was not his favorite pastime.

Kincade went back to his car and called the station. "Hey, Jimmy. It's Richie. Listen, I need you to put out an APB on a couple of people for me."

"What's up, Richie?"

"There's a lady friend of mine who's gone missing."

"A lady friend, huh?"

"Not that kind of a lady friend, Jimmy. It's a client of mine and I think she's in trouble. The boyfriend's gone too."

"Hmm, sounds pretty suspicious, Richie. A girl and her boyfriend out late together on a Friday night. Next thing you know, they might disappear for the whole weekend. Should I have the boys check all of the hotels in the Poconos to see if a guy and girl checked in to any of the rooms together last night?"

"Cute, Jimmy. Real cute. Listen, I've been through her house, and there's a bloody knife on the floor."

"What the hell were you doing, Richie? You're on suspension, remember?"

"Yeah, yeah. I remember. Listen, like I told you, she's a friend of mine. She was supposed to call me and when I didn't hear from her, I came to her place to make sure she was OK. The kitchen door was wide open."

"You know better than that, Richie."

"Hey, I was invited."

"Who am I to argue? I'll send a team right over."

"Thanks, Jimmy."

There was not much else to do. Richie headed home to salvage what little he could from the rest of this night.

———

The chief called for Kincade to meet him at the station first thing in the morning. Richie explained the information he had come across that implicated BNI in the theft of Sandi's data.

"Look, Richie," the chief said gruffly, angered that he had to deal with something like this on the weekend, "I told you stay away from this BNI thing. Go take a damned vacation, would you. How am I going to explain what you were doing there last night?"

"Who needs to know it was me."

"Those guys in the black suits have a way of knowing."

"You may be right, Chief, but if they give you a hard time about this, it'll tie them into it. I'm sure they don't want that, even if they are on JT Anderson's payroll. We've got to find out what happened to Dr. Fletcher. She's the key to all this."

"We're on it now whether we want to be or not, Richie, but for Christ's sake, keep your nose out of this. I don't want any more visits from the NSA."

"I'll keep a low profile."

The chief wasn't thrilled with Kincade's answer, but Richie had hung up before he could say another word.

Kincade was tempted to give Paul Hingston a call, but he still wasn't sure who the inside man was at BNI, and Hingston was a prime suspect. Richie decided not to fan the flames. He placed his trust in the police force.

———

By Monday morning there was still no word and Richie was starting to give up hope that they would ever find Sandi alive. Then, at ten AM, the first clue came in. A motorist just outside of Columbia spotted a break in the guardrail of the Acorn Creek Bridge. It took only a few hours to determine the make of the vehicle from the paint on the guardrail. The blue paint was from a Chevy pickup truck matching the description of the vehicle owned by Guy Andrews.

The surging river prevented an extensive search for the truck and its occupants; it would likely be too rough to dredge for weeks. The team focused on the shores of the river downstream from the bridge. A woman's jacket was the only thing found; tucked safely away in an inside zippered pocket was a plastic card, the faculty ID card belonging to Dr. Sandra Fletcher.

The chief had hoped that Sandi might have just left the coat in the truck at an earlier date, that maybe she had not been with Guy when he plunged into the Acorn Creek River. By four PM his hopes faded as a report came in from the forensics lab. The blood on the knife found at Sandi's house, as well as a large bloodstain found on the jacket, were both the same blood type, a blood type matching Sandi Fletcher's. He made the call to Richard Kincade a few minutes after four.

Richie was beside himself. He was sure that Sandi would still be alive if he had insisted on staying with her that night. He was determined to find out who was responsible for her death, with or without the chief's help. For three days he went over every clue that he had, and for three days he continued to come up with the same conclusion: he had to get inside BNI or he would have no chance of resolving this. He went over and over the four cases of the BNI employees that Shelly Lange had told him about. He was sure that BNI was somehow using the neurological nanobots to exert some sort of mind control, but proving it would be impossible without Sandi. Kincade didn't know a nerve cell from a jail cell; he didn't have a prayer of understanding this. There was only one option left to him. He had to hope that Paul Hingston was the honest man Sandi had once loved, that he was not involved in this madness. It was a long shot, but Kincade was ready to take it.

———

"Dr. Paul Hingston?" Richie had been sitting in the lobby of Poe Towers for hours waiting for Paul to come home.

"Who wants to know?" Paul was particularly edgy. He hadn't slept well since hearing about Sandi's disappearance. It was all over the news, and Paul had stopped watching TV a day ago to avoid the pain of seeing the morbid story.

"My name is Richard Kincade. I'm with the Baltimore Police Department."

"What's this about?"

"Dr. Sandra Fletcher."

Paul's eyes turned down.

"See, she was helping me with this case and, well, she spoke very highly of you. I was hoping you might be able to help me out."

Paul was furious. "Jesus, that's what this is about? You sick bastard, they haven't even found her body yet and you're looking for a replacement for your case? Just leave me alone. You got a hell of a nerve coming here and..."

"Look, Dr. Hingston, I'm sorry. I think you've misunderstood me. This is *about* Sandi. I need your help."

Paul was curious. As angry as he was at this intrusion, he was even hungrier for any information about Sandi. "Go on."

Kincade motioned Hingston to a quiet corner of the lobby, and they sat. "I know that Dr. Fletcher was upset with you, that she thought you had stolen some research from her."

Paul was offended. "Where the hell are you going with this, Detective? Surely you don't think...Look, Sandi left me a long time ago, but I never stopped loving her. If you think I had anything to do with her death, or that I even would have considered stealing her research, you're way off track."

Kincade wasn't expecting much cooperation. He suspected that Hingston was just a spurned lover, that he was likely the inside source of the data theft at BNI. But the sincerity in his voice, in his eyes...

"I'm sorry. I don't mean to open wounds. I was just going to say that although she did think you had stolen her data, she was also sure you never would have been involved in any kind of project that included hurting people. She refused to believe that you could have had anything to do with this." He handed Hingston the file describing the four BNI employees with prior brain injuries who had met with strange and untimely consequences.

"What's this?"

"Just read it and then give me a call. Here's my card. Call me at home or on the cell anytime." Kincade stood to leave.

"That's it?"

"I think you'll feel better about talking to me after you've read that."

Paul Hingston looked down at the file in his hand. His curiosity was definitely piqued.

Kincade nodded and walked out the door.

Paul Hingston took the elevator at Poe Towers up to his penthouse apartment. The elevators ascended the outside of the thirty-seven story building overlooking the harbor. The lights of Harborplace Mall, the Museum of Science and the Baltimore Aquarium lit up the periphery of the waterfront; it was a beautiful sight. Paul looked out over the harbor, but barely saw a thing. All he could think about was Sandi.

He walked into his apartment and tossed the folder onto the counter. The bar adjacent to the balcony was well stocked; this was going to be a Dewars kind of evening. He poured himself a glass of scotch. The ice cubes rattled against the glass as he swirled the amber liquor over them. Paul loosened his tie, picked up the file and plopped down on the over-stuffed brown leather sofa across from the glass doors to the balcony.

"Jackass," he mumbled as he read about Lester Hanes smashing his car into a highway lamppost after de-chipping his car. "Serves him right." He flipped to the next folder, the case of Helen Jensen. "Pathetic," he said, shaking his head as he read about her history of childhood seizures and the life threatening episode of severe seizures that she suffered shortly after coming to work at BNI, which left her a mental vegetable.

He laid the file down and took a sip from his glass. "What in the hell did you give me this for, Detective? Did you figure I wasn't quite depressed enough yet?"

Paul put his glass on the end table and turned to the third file. He remembered Billy Jackson. Billy was a high school football star from Harford County, heavily recruited by several top universities. He had NFL prospect written all over him. When he was blindsided in the state championship game and suffered a severe concussion, it made the headlines of all the local papers. Paul remembered the case well. Jackson had suffered a right frontal lobe injury. Thanks to extensive rehab at Sinai Hospital, he made a nearly complete recovery except for some slight weakness in his left leg that dashed any hopes of a pro football career. He came to work at BNI as a programmer right out of college. Paul had met him at the interview; the next news he heard about Billy was when his car slid off an icy bridge into the Middle River.

Paul flipped back over the first two files again. "Shit," he muttered. "Right frontal lobe, all three of them. What are the odds?" He looked at the dates of employment and the dates of the accidents. They all occurred within a two-year period of time, the same two-year period when the Phase Two neuronanobot program was in the testing stages. Each accident occurred within a few months of the victim being hired at BNI. "Now you've got my attention, Detective."

Turning to the fourth case, he immediately noticed that Janice Saint-Martin had suffered a minor right frontal lobe injury in college, when she was beaten by a boyfriend. Although she was still alive, her case was even more puzzling. She swore to this day that she had no recollection of hiring a mechanic to de-chip her car, even though the mechanic had a video of the transaction on his security camera. She also had no recollection, when questioned after her arrest, of having driven her car at one hundred and twenty mph, and everyone who testified at her trial described her as demure and conservative.

Paul put the file on the coffee table, got up and stretched. He grabbed his glass and walked over to the window. As he stared out the balcony trying to make some sense of the four strange cases, his thoughts again turned to Sandi. He took a long, slow sip of scotch, hoping to dull the pain. As he stared out into the night, he remembered his last conversation with her and the packet she had sent him, the one containing the supposed evidence proving that BNI had been stealing her work. It was still unopened in the bottom file drawer of his desk at the office. He had forgotten all about it until this moment. A terrible thought occurred to him. "My God, could I have been responsible for her death?"

Paul was at work earlier than usual Thursday morning. After pausing to pour himself a cup of coffee, he pulled his leather chair up to the old oak roll-top desk and leaned his elbows on the padded armrests. Staring down at the file drawer, head resting on his interlocked fingers, he sighed, half hoping that the packet within was only a figment of Sandi's imagination.

He took another gulp of coffee, and then reached into the drawer and pulled out the envelope. As usual, Sandi's notes were both detailed and well organized. Methodically, Paul made his way through the notes. Nearly an hour later there was little doubt that the work completed in his lab at BNI, the work he had so proudly patented, had been derived directly from Sandi's research at Hopkins. Every detail, every gene sequence that he had programmed into the nanobots was precisely identical to the corresponding one documented in Sandi's notes.

Paul went back through his own notes on the computer. He searched for instances where they had encountered problems with the gene sequencing of the nanobots, and cross-referenced these instances with Sandi's notes. He was shocked to discover that in each case, the solution that he had found to the problem was identical to the one found by Sandi, and in each case, his own discovery had *followed* the identical breakthrough in Sandi's lab by a matter of days. There was no way this could be coincidental; someone at BNI had been stealing her work on a regular basis and feeding it to Paul.

He thought back to the hundreds of hours of research, trying to remember where these answers had come from. The intense work of the past two years blended together to the point where he was convinced that some of these ideas had been his own. He knew, of course, that *he* had not been stealing the research from Hopkins. The most likely prospect was Sean, but as bright as Sean was, Paul rarely remembered him solving any of the major gene sequencing problems; Sean's strength was always in the physical construction of the nanobots.

He sat back in his large, cushioned desk chair, struggling for answers. And then he remembered. "Of course," he muttered, "the meetings." Once a week, during the project, he and Sean would meet with JT Anderson to review the progress. Paul had often admired the astuteness of Anderson to scan the data and come up with seemingly impossible solutions. He had always attributed it to JT's genius. After all, JT was one of the pioneers of nanobotics, and still considered one of the leading experts in the field. But now it all made a lot more sense. JT wasn't solving the problems; he was merely giving Paul and Sean the solutions that he had stolen from Sandi. He certainly had the wealth and power necessary for industrial espionage.

"It had to be JT." Paul thought about how he had chided Sandi for accusing him of stealing her work. "And all this time I just thought she was a paranoid fool, a sore loser," he mumbled under his breath.

"What's that, lad?" Sean was standing in the doorway behind him. "You're a loser? Man, quite an evening you must have had." He laughed. "What's that you've got there?" he asked, spotting the packet of files on the desk.

Paul gathered them up and tossed them in the trashcan. He wasn't sure just how much Sean had seen or heard. "Ah, just a bunch of crap. More letters from those geeks over at Hopkins saying we stole their work. Must have been sent before Sandi died, God bless her. I loved that girl, but she was a sore loser." He turned to Sean. "Did you run the probability studies on those new gene sequences we worked out yesterday."

"I'll get right on it." Sean smiled. "Sorry again about Sandi."

"Thanks." Paul watched him walk away, then gathered the papers out of the trash and put them in his briefcase. Much of the remainder of the day was spent checking into the employee files of Lester Hanes, Janice Saint-Martin, Billy Jackson and Helen Jensen. There was not much to be found, and the absence of information was the most disconcerting evidence that Paul could find.

———

By Saturday night, Richard Kincade still had not heard from Paul Hingston. He paced back and forth across the living room floor, and prayed that he had not made a mistake. If Hingston was the NSA's inside man at BNI, it wouldn't take them long to discover that Richie knew too much, and they would be certain to make sure he didn't tell anyone else what he knew. Everywhere he went, he began looking over his shoulder. He was furious at himself for putting Lara's life in danger.

"For God sakes, Richard Kincade, you're going to wear a hole in my new carpet. Take me out to dinner. I'm in the mood for some steamed crabs. You can take your frustrations out on those claws."

The crabs were running small, but it was still a good idea. After a mug of beer and half-dozen steamed crabs, Richie was feeling a lot better. Lara was relieved to see the tension melting away from her husband's face as he pounded the claws with a wooden mallet and artfully scooped the chunks of meat out with his knife. By the end of the meal, they were reminiscing about the annual department crab feast, and the antics spurred on by the Chesapeake Bay ritual of good friends gathered around bushels of steamed crabs and a keg of draught beer. Lara left the beer drinking to Richie tonight; she played designated driver. They finished up and washed the sting of Old Bay seasoning off their lips and out of the narrow crab-shell cuts that stung their fingers.

Richie fought to stay awake on the ride home, and by eleven they were both in bed, drifting off to sleep. At eleven-thirty, the phone rang, startling Richie from a dream state. He reached out in the dark and knocked the phone off the receiver.

"Shit," he muttered, as he groped around the nightstand.

"Hello?" he said wearily as he managed to get the phone to his ear.

"Detective Kincade?"

The voice was shaky, but there was no doubt who it belonged to. "Sandi?" Kincade said incredulously. "Thank God you're OK. What in the hell happened to you? Where have you been?"

"Can we talk? Is this line safe?"

"Sure, at least I think so." As he thought about the car bomb and the NSA, he realized that it probably wasn't, but if someone was listening, they knew by now that she was alive anyway.

"I'm right out front. I took Mrs. Flannery's Camry after Guy ran off, and I drove to a small hotel off I-95 just outside of DC. I didn't know what to do. I stayed there until my money ran out; I figured they'd find me if I used my credit cards. I'm scared, Detective."

He decided it would be best to continue this conversation in person. "I'll meet you by the door."

Richie hung up the phone.

"Who was that, dear?" Lara turned toward him, half awake.

"Ah, just my mistress. Go back to sleep."

"OK then." She smiled and pulled the covers up over her shoulders, laying her head back on the pillow.

Richie threw on some clothes and went downstairs, trying not to wake Lara again.

Sandi was at the front door waiting.

"Doc?" Sandi's thick brown hair was now short, straight and platinum blond. Her face was worn from the long, sleepless nights.

"You look like hell."

"Thanks," she smiled feebly.

Richie looked around quickly and took her by the shoulder. "Come on in."

Sandi limped as she walked in.

Richie motioned her into the kitchen. "Let me get you a cup of hot tea."

She was shivering from the cold.

"Are you hungry?" he asked.

She shook her head no. "Gas station sandwiches aren't so bad when you're hungry enough."

"What the hell happened?" He sat down beside her and slid a cup of tea in front of her.

"You were right about Guy." Tears started to well up in her eyes, but she fought them back. "I took my shot Friday night from a sealed bottle of Synthulin, not the stuff with the Allohypnol in it. I waited up for Guy. When he came in, I hopped into bed, pretending to be asleep. He woke me and led me into the study. When he asked me to access my Internet connection and dial into BNI, I played along, hoping to find the name of his contact at BNI, but when he told me to upload my research, I refused."

She stopped to take a sip of tea. "He got real mad. I've never seen Guy like that. I got up from the chair and backed away from him. When I told him I knew about the Allohypnol, he pulled a knife on me. I was pressed against the wall and he kept coming at me. That look in his eyes...I knew he would do it." A shiver went up her spine as she relived the terror of that night.

She paused again and Richie put his hand on top of hers. "That pistol you gave me, I hid it in the pocket of my robe. I had my hand on it the whole time. When he came at me, I pulled it out. My hand was trembling so bad it was hard to hold the gun straight. I steadied it with my other hand, just like you showed me. When Guy heard the click of the safety release, he stopped dead in his tracks. I guess he could see it in my eyes too; I would have pulled that trigger, I..." she sobbed. "I can't believe that I could really do something like that."

"You were only defending yourself, Sandi."

"Still..." She took another sip of tea and composed herself. "When he saw the gun, he mumbled something and dropped his knife. He turned and ran out of the room. I was so scared I couldn't move a muscle. I was still standing there pointing the gun at the spot where he had been standing when I heard the truck start. The window was fogged from the cold. I wiped a spot clear so I could see out, and just stood there holding the gun; I couldn't let go. I watched the truck pull away. I couldn't believe he was gone. All of a sudden I felt dizzy and leaned back against the wall. My hands went limp and I dropped the gun as I slid to the floor.

"I just sat there trying to decide what to do, trying to clear my head. I had to get out of there. I was afraid Guy or someone from BNI would come back for me and try again. I rocked forward onto my knees reaching for the gun and lost my balance. My left leg came down right on that damned knife. It hurt like a bitch. I grabbed at my leg; it was bleeding like hell, but the cut wasn't deep. It just scraped off a chunk of skin. I got up and ran down to the kitchen where I keep the first aid kit and wrapped it up. That's when the phone rang."

"That was me," Richie said. "Why didn't you answer it?"

"I was petrified. I didn't know what to do. I was afraid Guy would come back, afraid he'd tell somebody at BNI that I was on to them. All of those people that died...," she shook her head and paused. "I knew they wouldn't be afraid to kill me...   I ran back upstairs, scraped together whatever cash I could find, threw on some clothes and grabbed the keys to the Camry."

"The Camry?"

"Yeah. When I borrowed Mrs. Flannery's Camry that Friday to take you home after Hank's car blew up, she told me that her kids were coming by to get her. She was planning on spending a couple of weeks in the mountains with them and told me to keep the keys in case I needed it again while she was on vacation. I knew no one would miss the Camry, but they might be looking for my car, so I took it and drove off. I've been hiding out in that hotel room ever since."

"Smart thinking." Richie admired her ability to think under pressure. "There's still one thing I don't get, though. They found a jacket downstream from where Guy's pick-up went off the bridge. It had your Hopkins ID in the inside pocket..."

"My ID?" Sandi looked surprised.

Richie nodded. "And a large blood stain on it...your blood. We figured Guy must have forced you into the truck after he stabbed you. When we found that jacket...well, we all figured you were dead."

"Oh God," Sandi rolled her eyes, "So that's where it was. No, that jacket had been sitting in the back of his truck for weeks. I spent hours looking for that damn card. I never thought to look in that cruddy old jacket."

"So how'd the blood get there?"

"Hmm? Oh...we had gone hiking out in the Catoctin's a few months back. We liked to do that whenever we could both break away for the weekend." She hesitated a moment and bit back a tear, then continued. "Well, it was kind of a warm day, so I tied the jacket around my waist. I was just wearing a T-shirt and I slipped on a rock... you know, one of those big boulders."

Richie nodded, but he really didn't know. Hiking through the mountains was not his idea of a good time; he'd never seen the rocky trails in the Catoctin Mountains.

"I skinned my elbow real bad – bled like a stuck pig. The only thing I had with me was the jacket, so I wrapped it around my arm. By the time we got back home, that jacket was such a mess I just tossed it in the back of the truck before I went in the house."

Sandi slumped back in her chair and sighed.

Richie could see the exhaustion in her face. "Come on, there's a guest room upstairs. We'll talk some more in the morning."

Sandi nodded appreciatively and followed him up the stairs.

CHAPTER NINETEEN

Paul Hingston stretched and looked out over the harbor from his penthouse in Poe Towers. The heavy rain of the night before covered Harbor Place with a surrealistic glaze that caught the rays of the morning sun. It was a crisp, clear morning, the kind that invigorated the soul, something that Paul needed desperately. He had struggled through the workday on Friday. Everyone looked a little different to him now. He eyed everyone with suspicion and hoped his paranoia did not give him away.

The thought of someone using his work to kill people sickened him more than it angered him. He couldn't believe that JT would be involved in something like this, but who else could it be? Paul had gone over and over the possibilities in his mind, trying to tie together the theft of Sandi's data with the four cases that Kincade had given him involving the BNI employees with frontal lobe brain injuries. There was only one plausible explanation: JT was so anxious to reap the rewards of the new nanobot therapy that he stole the work from Hopkins to keep his lab on pace, and then authorized premature human experimentation with the nanobots on his own employees, each time with dire consequences.

Paul couldn't believe it. Although no one was around to hear, it often helped him to organize his thoughts out loud. "JT must have been looking to hire people with frontal lobe injuries so he could experiment on them. The early generation nanobots weren't ready for clinical use, and JT proved that the hard way. God, if anyone ever finds out and associates me with this..."

He wasn't sure who he could trust, but Kincade was as good a place as any to start.

"Hello?" Richie was in the kitchen making breakfast when the phone rang.

"Detective Kincade?"

"The one and only."

"This is Paul Hingston. We need to talk."

"Ah, you read the file."

"Yes." Paul wasn't sure it was wise to elaborate on his other discoveries over the phone.

"So what do you think?"

"I think we need to meet."

"Right." Richie could hear the anxiety in his voice, but wasn't sure if it was derived from a fear of what he might be mixed up in at work, or whether he was just trying to figure out how to get Richie off his back. Kincade still wasn't convinced that Hingston was not involved in the theft and murder plot unfolding at BNI.

"Meet me at noon in front of Phillip's at Harborplace." His voice was shaking.

"Noon won't work for me, Hingston." Richie would make sure that this meeting took place on his own terms. "Be at the phone booth across the street from your building at one o'clock today. I'll contact you there." Kincade had jotted the number down when he left Poe Towers after his brief meeting with Paul Hingston the other night. He had a feeling it would come in handy.

"I'll be there." Paul hung up the phone and poured himself a drink. He was disgusted with himself for drinking this early in the day, but his nerves were frayed. He glanced at the clock. He still had four long hours to wait.

———

Sandi slept well for the first time in days. By the time she awoke, Lara had gone to work and Richie was lounging in the kitchen having coffee and catching up on the morning news.

"Good morning," she smiled as she walked in.

"Maybe we should get you to a doctor," he said, watching her limp into the room.

"Nah, it's not that bad, just a little stiff when I first get up. What I could really use is a hot cup of coffee."

"Oh, sorry," Richie said, pushing away from the table.

"No, no," she motioned him to sit back down. "You stay put. Just point me in the direction of the cups."

Richie pointed to the cabinet above the coffee maker. "Help yourself. Can I make you some eggs or cereal or something?"

"Not yet, thanks. I'd just like to sit and talk if that's OK?"

Riche nodded. "Sure."

"I had plenty of time to think things over sitting in that hotel room," she said. "I keep going over and over it in my head, that bizarre scene with Guy. God," she laughed, "you should have seen him. He's definitely not the cloak and dagger type. I think he was more nervous than I was when he pulled that knife out, and believe me I was plenty scared. I'm surprised the two of us didn't both just pass out on the floor together."

Richie smiled, but he could tell that Sandi was still rattled when she talked about it.

"Anyway, like I said, I keep thinking about it to see if there was some hint that I missed, some clue that he might have given me as to who his contact at BNI was. I keep coming up empty except for one thing."

"What's that?"

"The BNI Intranet mailbox that Guy was having me send the information to: the ID was TOM and the password was Mindfields."

Richie didn't want to make her feel stupid, but it sounded pretty obvious. "Well, Tom could be the name of Guy's contact at BNI."

"Duh," she glared at him. "Is that why they call you a detective?"

Real swift, Richie, he thought. "Suppose you thought of that, huh?"

"Uh, yeah. Came up with it right away. Pretty clever, eh?"

"All right, all right. So I suppose you checked it out already, right?"

"No. I was afraid to access the Net. I don't know who these guys are, but I figured it would be better if they really thought that I was dead. If they were monitoring the Internet, I'd give myself away as soon as I linked in. I kept going over and over it in my head, and all I could think of was Paul."

"Paul? Is his middle name Tom?"

"No, but his father's name was Thomas and Paul thought the world of his dad. It would make sense for him to use it as an ID name on a hidden account."

"Except for one thing," Richie said. "If Paul were using that account to steal your data, he wouldn't be hiding it using a secret ID that would be so obvious to you."

"I thought about that too, but it just seems so right. Paul is one of the few people in the world who would know what to do with my data, he works at BNI, his father was named Tom and," this part made her sick, "he could have told Guy all the right things to say to win my trust."

Richie felt sorry for her. It was tough to argue; Paul was the obvious suspect. "I've learned that things aren't always what they seem, Doc. Let's check out all the avenues before we plunge headlong down that road."

She composed herself and nodded.

"Right," he said, "let's get to it then." He motioned for Sandi to sit at the kitchen table by the computer monitor. She nodded and they sat.

The computer was already booted up, displaying the latest network news update.

"Computer, close program." The screen went blank. "Computer, load program 'Daisy.'"

"I'm here, Detective," was the immediate response. "You don't think I'd sleep the whole day away, do you?"

Sandy gawked at the computer. "Wow! What is *that*?"

"Daisy, meet Dr. Sandra Fletcher; Doc, meet Daisy," he pointed to the monitor.

"Pleased to meet you, Doctor."

"Awesome," Sandi gasped. "AI?"

"Yes," Daisy answered. "I have artificial intelligence capabilities, but they're rather stifled in this cramped computer."

"Give it a rest, would you, Daisy? I told you I'll get more memory for you as soon as I can. Hell, if things go right I may even be able to take you back to the station soon."

"That would be a relief."

"Enough small talk. It's time to earn your keep. Access the BNI employee database and show me a list of everyone with the names Tom, Thomas or Tomassina."

Sandi looked up. "Tomassina? I never would have thought about Tom being a girl."

"That," Richie emphasized, "is why they call me a detective."

Sandi grinned.

The list came up immediately. "I already took the liberty of running that search while you and the doctor were talking."

Richie raised an eyebrow. "You scare me, Daisy."

"Thank you."

Sandi and Richie scanned down the list:

> *Thomas Jones, Mailroom Clerk*
> *Thomas Martin, Director of Sanitation*
> *Tom Post, Legal Department*
> *Thomas Richter, Marketing*
> *Tomassina Small, Inventory Management Clerk*

"Pretty unsavory looking bunch, eh?"

Sandi rolled her eyes. None of these people would have the education to understand nanobotic gene sequencing. She sat, staring at the screen, and then a thought came to her. "What if it's not a name?

"Huh?"

"What if Tom is not a name? When Guy had me type it, he had me enter it in all capital letters. Maybe T...O...M are initials."

"Hmm...Daisy, show us a list of all BNI employees with the initials T.O.M."

The list appeared after a brief delay:

> *Timothy Olin Mallory, Finance Division*
> *Thomas Oliver Martin, Director of Sanitation*

"That sanitation engineer is starting to look pretty suspicious, isn't he," Sandi smirked. "None of this is helping dissuade me. It's got to be Paul."

"Daisy," Kincade said, "display all employees with the middle name "Tom, Tomassina or Thomas."

Once again, the list was short:

> *Jason Thomas Anderson, CEO*
> *Harold Thomas Johnson, Marketing*
> *Marsha Tomassina Smythe, Human Resources*

"Bingo," Sandi said. "That son of a bitch. JT Anderson. I never thought about what the JT stood for."

"Anderson? He's a CEO. How would an administrator know what to do with genetic research? Besides, why would he dirty himself with stealing your data? If he wanted it done, he'd just pay someone else to do it for him."

"Maybe, but if you were doing something like this, wouldn't you want as few people as possible to know about it?"

"I suppose."

"And as far as understanding what to do with it, don't forget that JT Anderson was one of the pioneers in nanobotics. Before he was a bureaucrat, he was one of the brightest scientific minds in the world. Believe me, he would have no trouble figuring out how to use my research."

"Well, unfortunately, there's still the matter of proof. The last time I went to talk to him, two NSA agents came knocking at my boss's door within an hour...and that was just for talking to him."

"Our only hope is to go to the press. If we go public with this, they can't touch us."

"Go public with what? All we've got are a bunch of mysterious coincidences with BNI employees, a scientist griping that America's leading medical research company stole her ideas...no offense..."

"None taken."

"...and to make matters worse, the most damning fact we have against Anderson is that his middle name is Thomas."

"Yeah, we'll look like idiots." She had to agree. "We need someone on the inside, someone who can get into the files at BNI."

"Funny you should bring that up."

Sandi looked at Richie and put up her hands. "Nooo. No way. Look, I don't believe for one minute that Paul Hingston would get himself involved with this murder and espionage stuff, but there's no way I'm contacting him again. The last time I called to accuse him of stealing my work he called me a pathetic loser, not in so many words maybe, but I felt about two inches tall. I am not going to let him make me feel like that again."

"What if he feels differently now?"

"I don't care. I am not going to call him. No way."

"Maybe you don't have to." Richie smiled deviously.

Sandi gave him a dirty look.

"He called this morning. He wants to meet with me," Richie said.

"Even if he is being up front, how did he know to call you?"

"Well, when you were missing I was at my wits end. My last trump card was to show Hingston the files on the four BNI cases Shelly Lange told me about. I figured that if he wasn't in on this mind control thing they are working on, it would pique his interest."

"And if he was?"

"Then he'd go to the NSA and we probably wouldn't be here talking right now, but like I said, he called this morning. I guess I piqued his interest."

"Or he just wants to draw you out into the open."

"I'm not completely naive, Doc. I'm going to meet him on my terms."

"I'm going with you."

"No way. If this is a trap, I don't want you there. Like you said, the longer they think you're dead, the better."

"Nobody knows Paul better than I do, Detective. I need to be there to see if he's telling the truth. He won't be able to lie to me. Never could."

Kincade hesitated. "Well... If we're going to do this, we'll do it my way." He proceeded to detail his plan to Sandi.

At one o'clock sharp, the pay phone across the street from Poe Towers rang. Paul Hingston was pacing in front of it and darted forward to answer.

"Yes?"

"Is that you, Hingston?"

"It's me. Where do we meet?"

"Meet me just outside the front entrance at Fort McHenry, two o'clock. Come alone."

"Who in the hell would I bring? I'm not even sure that I trust *you*."

"Don't be late." Kincade turned off his cell phone. He was already at Fort McHenry, positioned with a perfect view of the main road in and the front gate. The backdrop of the Chesapeake Bay made for a beautiful sight. Hingston seemed sincere enough, but Kincade was not about to take any chances. The odds of "TOM" being Hingston's father were just as good as the odds of it being JT's middle name. Kincade sat on the concrete bench and waited. There was little else to do for now.

At one forty-five a cab drove up to the front entrance at Fort McHenry and Paul Hingston emerged from the car. The sun was shining and there were a fair number of tourists out, but it was not hard for Kincade to spot Hingston as he walked up to the main entrance. No one was following as far as Kincade could tell. He failed to notice the gray Buick LeSabre parked a few blocks away, or the high-powered binoculars that its driver had trained on him.

"Christ," Agent Trace McKnight muttered, "is that son of a bitch just going to sit there all day." He still had a bad feeling about Kincade, and despite the warnings from Uncle Jimmy, Trace had decided to keep an eye on Kincade from time to time. He had been tracking Kincade's car with a global positioning system for the past week, and for the second time in the past few days he had traveled to the Inner Harbor near Poe Towers. This was not particularly unusual for a Baltimore suburbanite, but it was enough to make Trace curious, and he decided to check it out. After an hour of watching Kincade sitting on a park bench, he was beginning to doubt the wisdom of his action.

Richard Kincade stood and walked toward the entrance to Fort McHenry. Trace hopped out of the Buick and followed at a safe distance. He could just make out the figure of the other man who Kincade approached, but couldn't see his face at this distance. As he raised the binoculars to get a closer look, the two men disappeared behind a red brick wall.

Paul Hingston held his hand out to greet Kincade as he saw him coming. Richie reached for Hingston's arm instead. "Come on," he said as he pulled him around the wall and away from the entrance gait.

Hingston was too scared to protest. He didn't like these games. "Was I followed?" he asked as he walked quickly by Kincade's side.

"Not as far as I can tell, but I'm not about to take that chance."

Hingston glanced back over his shoulder and tugged gently on his thick brown mustache, as he often did when he was nervous.

Trace McKnight walked rapidly toward the front gate. Running would draw too much attention, but he needed to know who Kincade was meeting. He was still a hundred yards away, and the two men were out of his line of sight.

Kincade motioned toward a small Coast Guard boat waiting by a dock behind the fort. They hurried over to the boat and a man helped them aboard.

"Thanks, Jack," Richie said to the man, "I owe you one."

"You sure do, man. I could have been sailing today. Look at that water, smooth as glass."

"Ah, what fun is sailing without at least a thirty mile an hour wind?" Richie laughed.

They walked into the small cabin of the boat just as Trace McKnight came around the wall. He focused his binoculars on the boat, but the men inside the cabin were all out of view. "Shit." He couldn't get any closer without being spotted. His only hope was to squat behind the hedge near the wall and hope the men would come out on deck. He watched intently through the binoculars.

Jack pulled out an electronic wand and swept it carefully around Paul Hingston. "He's clean," Jack declared, finishing the sweep. "No weapons, no bugs."

"Good," Richie said. "Let's go."

He motioned for Paul to sit and the two of them settled onto facing benches in the small cabin. All Trace McKnight could make out as the boat sped away was a blurry glimpse of Jack's face through the weathered window in the cabin. He went back to his car and waited. It would be too difficult to follow the boat without drawing attention. He could only sit and wait, and hope that Kincade and his clandestine friend would return to the same spot from which they had departed.

The roar of the engine made it difficult to speak and Kincade waited until they were a few hundred yards out in the bay before he broke the silence. He motioned to Jack to cut the engines.

"So, I guess you were impressed by those files I gave you, eh, Doc?"

The boat rocked gently in the still water of the bay, drifting north toward the harbor. Jack walked outside for some fresh air, and Paul waited until he departed to speak. The stillness of the day was disrupted briefly as a pair of seagulls flew by calling out to each other in their high-pitched squeals, which faded into the distance as they glided away from the ship.

Hingston turned back toward Kincade. "Impressed? More like disturbed. As unbelievable as those files were, it made it pretty obvious that there is something screwy going on at BNI. Four new employees, all with right frontal lobe injuries and all having some catastrophic event a couple of months after starting work... Hard to write that off as coincidence."

"Yeah, that's pretty much how I saw it too. Some sort of hypnosis or mind control, don't you think?"

"Mind control? You've been reading too many science fiction books, Detective. It's probably just some shoddy work, somebody trying to speed up the research to get to the pot of gold at the end of the rainbow."

"How do you mean?"

"Well, it usually takes years to get a new medical treatment to market, especially something as revolutionary as nanobots. Once the product has been developed, it has to be tested with computer simulations and eventually with animal studies before you can even hope to get approval for human trials. Those four people that died, their old brain injuries would have made them perfect test subjects. Somebody at BNI was trying to jump the gun. They were all treated with the nanobots during the animal testing phase, I'd bet on that."

"But why? They'd still need to get approval to market it wouldn't they?"

"Sure, but what better way to work out the bugs real quick than to see what happens in a human being. You avoid the risk you usually have to take when problems with human trials go public; bad results with human trials can shelve a new treatment before it ever even gets out of the lab. One mistake could cost millions. Hell, a little bad PR can ruin a company. It'd be nice to have a guarantee of success before you begin human trials."

"So that's what you think they were up to?"

"Yeah, but it gets uglier. After I saw those files, I remembered a packet of information Sandi had mailed to me months ago. She said it was the proof that I had been stealing her files. I figured it was just professional jealousy; it was so pathetic that I couldn't even bring myself to look at them. See, I had this picture of Sandi as someone... well, someone a notch above the rest of us, you know? When I got that packet from her, I just tossed it in a drawer. I didn't want to think of Sandi as petty. I had forgotten all about it until you gave me that file to look at. But after I read about those four BNI employees, I thought maybe there was something going on at BNI that I didn't know about. I couldn't believe somebody was using my own work to do something like that. It made me sick."

Hingston paused and glanced out the window, collecting his thoughts. "I went through that packet of Sandi's. I would never have stolen research from her, but someone sure had. All of my work on Phase Two nanobots...all that time I was developing the bots based on research that someone was feeding to me...Sandi's research."

"Who?"

"My guess is JT."

Kincade thought a moment. "Of course... Jason Thomas Anderson...Tom."

Hingston looked at Kincade with an odd expression. "Tom? Nobody calls him Tom."

"Oh, sorry. It's just that I came across a bit of information I hadn't quite been able to figure out for sure...until now. It seems that Dr. Fletcher's stolen files were uploaded to an employee file with the ID name Tom. I checked out all the Toms at BNI, even those with the initials T.O.M. The only ones that came up as possibilities were Anderson and, well, you."

"Me? My middle name is Milton. How'd you figure me?"

"You were our most likely suspect...nothing personal...and your dad, his name was Tom, wasn't it?"

"Well, yeah, but...hey, you didn't think I was the one, did you?" He hesitated, but only briefly. "And how did you know about my dad?"

Kincade was not ready to answer that question. "Could Jason Thomas Anderson have been stealing the info and funneling it to you through someone else on the research team?"

"Hell, he was funneling it to me himself. After I went through Sandi's file, I thought back over our research protocol. We met with JT every week. He always wanted to know exactly where we were with the research, and I was glad to have his help. He always seemed to have the right answer to every problem that came up. I just figured he was some kind of genius, you know? I mean, his track record speaks for itself, but all he was doing was stealing Sandi's answers and presenting them as his own. Makes you wonder about all of his other great work, doesn't it? I wonder how much of that was someone else's ideas too. It may be that his genius is in knowing how to steal rather than in knowing how to develop nanobots." He shook his head. "Jason Thomas, huh? I never really thought about what the JT stood for."

"And you didn't know about any of this until I gave you that file to look at? For two years this was going on right under your nose and you had no idea?"

"I was too focused on my work. I know it's kind of hard to believe that I could have such tunnel vision."

"I believe him," Sandi said, half in tears as she emerged from the small cabin below.

"Sandi!" Paul couldn't believe his eyes. She looked so different with the short, blond hair, but he recognized her instantly. "But I thought you were..."

"Tales of my death have been greatly exaggerated," she laughed uncomfortably. There was still a connection that was undeniable, but the closeness was awkward for both of them.

Sandi broke the discomforting silence. "All this time I thought it was you. I hope you can forgive me."

"I'm the one who should be asking for forgiveness."

"Uh, Doc," Kincade interrupted, "I thought we agreed..."

"*You* agreed." She knew the tone in Paul's voice well enough to know that he was telling the truth. There was no doubt that he could be trusted, and no need to hide from him any longer. Odds of success would be greater if they worked together; Sandi was sure of it. She looked at Kincade. No words were needed. He went out on deck, where Jack was leaning against the rail, looking out over the Chesapeake.

"Sure is a beautiful day, Jack."

"Yup. Great day for a barbeque. The wife and kids should be firing up the grill right about now."

"Yeah, yeah. You'll be home in time for the steak, don't worry. We're about done in there."

"The lovers make up?"

"I don't know about that, but at least they're not trying to kill each other."

Richie stood by Jack's side and leaned on the rail, the two of them staring quietly out into the day.

"That's a good thing," Jack said.

"Yup."

Inside, the boat rocked gently as Paul and Sandi sat across from each other searching for the right words to say.

"All this time, Paul. All this time I thought it was you."

"You didn't really think I could do something like that, did you? You know me better than that."

"I refused to believe it at first. When I sent you that packet, I was desperately hoping for some other explanation, but when I didn't hear back from you…"

"Yeah, well I was a jerk. What else can I say? I was so excited when you called me that day, and then when I realized that the call was just to accuse me of stealing your work, well, I was fuming. It hurt in more ways than one."

"You deserved it."

"Not that, I didn't. Look, we each made our own choices. I don't regret having joined the private sector; it has a lot of perks. I'm not fighting for grants all the time and I'm not struggling just to pay the bills at the end of each month. You can do just as much good in private industry as you can at the university, but…man, I never thought I'd get tied up in something like this. Anderson's a shark, but he's always seemed so up front about everything."

"You've got to help us, Paul. If we're going to stop them, we need something solid, some hard evidence tying them into the murders. If you can get a hard copy of some kind of proof that the 'TOM' mailbox on BNI's Intranet belongs to JT Anderson, then we've got him."

"Hey, I'm not going anywhere until I figure out what's going on. It's my reputation on the line; they're using my work to do this. I'm sure Sean feels the same way."

"Sean?"

"Yeah, Sean Lightbourne, my lab assistant. He's in the same boat I am now. Our fingerprints are all over this project. I'll get him to help me tomorrow. He was a computer minor at American University; he can hack in to anything. I'm going to get those bastards, whoever they are."

"Just be careful."

"Hell, they won't kill me. They'll need me to blame it all on when it goes public." He laughed half-heartedly.

"Yeah. Like I said."

They looked at each other briefly, then turned away in an awkward moment of silence.

"Well, I'd better get back," Paul said.

"Yeah. I'll get the captain."

Paul watched Sandi as she opened the door. It was painful to be with her, and yet to not *be* with her. He had forgotten how much he missed her.

Jack started the engines up and the ship motored toward Baltimore's Inner Harbor. The boat pulled up to the Coast Guard dock by Federal Hill at about three-thirty. Paul thanked Jack for the ride. It was a short walk home to Poe Towers from there. Kincade watched him walk away and hoped that this had not been a mistake.

"You really think he's with us, Doc?"

"I'm sure of it, Detective."

He shook his head. "Hope you're right." He thought of the consequences if they had misjudged Dr. Hingston, but there had been little choice. There was really no place else to turn.

They took the boat back to Fort McHenry, where Jack dropped off his passengers.

"Thanks, Jack. Enjoy those steaks."

"You bet I will."

"And tell Ellie I'm sorry I dragged you away today."

"Why don't you and Lara come on over tonight. You can tell her yourself."

"Thanks anyway, but I'll have to take a rain check. I'll tell Lara about the invite, though. She'll appreciate that."

"Anytime, buddy. You take care."

Richie nodded and helped Sandi off the boat. They watched Jack pull away, and then Richie put his arm around Sandi's shoulders and walked her back to the car. He could see that the encounter with Paul had taken its toll.

"You OK, Doc."

"No," she reached up under her sunglasses to wipe the tears from her eyes, "but I will be."

They walked in silence the rest of the way.

Trace McKnight had listened to the entire Raven's game on the radio. It was a good thing the LeSabre had comfortable seats. He glanced over toward the fort, as he had done periodically for the past two hours, and this time he was relieved to finally see two figures emerging from around the wall where Kincade had disappeared with his mystery man. He pulled his binoculars out.

"Shit. It's a broad," he yelped as he saw Kincade with his arm around a petite young woman with short blond hair and sunglasses. "I've been sitting in this damned car all afternoon waiting for this? The guy's having a God-damned affair, and I just pissed my whole day away to make this great discovery. Damn, I could have sworn it was a *guy* that he got on that boat with. It was probably some bimbo in disguise, and I fell for it."

He took one more look through the binoculars, then tossed them in the back seat. "Christ. Enjoy your midlife crises, Kincade." He fired up the LeSabre and sped off.

CHAPTER TWENTY

A gray pall hung over the sky and pervaded the mood of the employees at BNI. Paul nodded to the lobby guard as he passed. The excitement that he once felt coming to work each day had turned into resentment. He had given up the lab at Hopkins and the only woman he ever loved to pursue a dream career, and now he found himself fighting to escape the vacuum of deceit into which he was being sucked. He knew that if he did not find a way to distance himself from BNI now, his integrity would be stripped from him even if he somehow managed to survive the scandal that was sure to ensue.

It had been a long, sleepless weekend. Paul languished at his desk, trying to decide the best way to approach Sean. He knew that JT had to be behind the data theft and the illegal human experimentation with nanobots, but there surely had to be others. Paul could only guess at who they might be. He was sure that Sean couldn't be involved in something like this...well, almost sure. It would be difficult at best to get the evidence without his help.

"Mornin' Paul. Looks like you had one heck of a wild weekend," Sean called from the office door. He wasn't used to seeing Paul looking so haggard.

"You don't know the half of it."

"Are we meeting with JT at the usual time?"

"As far as I know. We've got to update him on the spinal cord project." Since the completion of the brain injury project, the lab had turned its attention to developing nanobots designed to repair an injured spinal cord.

"Damn, I forgot that was this morning. I've got to get my notes together." Sean glanced at his watch. "Gotta hustle. I'll meet you up there at ten."

"Say," Paul said as Sean started to turn away, "can you break away for lunch today?"

"Sure. I never miss lunch. You know that. Priorities, man." Sean laughed.

"No," Paul said. "I mean get out of here for a couple of hours. There's something I need to talk to you about."

"A girl, I hope." Sean smiled mischievously.

"You might say that."

"All right. Way to go, man. For this, I'll make time."

"Great."

"See you up at JT's office at ten."

Paul nodded and watched Sean walk away.

Richard Kincade was getting used to being on suspension. It wasn't so bad sleeping in every day. He rolled out of bed at about nine and went downstairs. Lara was already off to work and Sandi, still catching up on a week of sleepless nights, was sound asleep in the guest room.

He peered out the bay window as he came downstairs. "Yuck," he muttered as he saw the gray stillness of the morning. "Looks like a great day to stay home." He put up some coffee and went out to get the paper. Internet news was great for a quick update in the morning, but when the luxury of time presented itself, Richie always preferred rumpling through the Sunpapers. He grabbed his Orioles jacket out of the closet and opened the door. The chill of the morning air surprised him. He shoved his hands into his pockets to keep them warm. On the right side, he felt a crumpled piece of paper pressed up against the lining, and pulled it out to take a look. It was the note that Hank had handed him in the car that day they went to meet Sandi, the note about James O'Grady. He had forgotten all about it. It was hard not to think about what had happened to Hank that day. Richie bit down on his lower lip as he opened the paper.

Richie,

I called in a favor from a buddy of mine at the CIA. Not surprisingly, they didn't have a whole lot of info on James O'Grady, he's pretty well protected by his own people, but here's what they do have:

  Name: James Carlton O'Grady
  Born: Baltimore, 11/19/2001
  Aliases: Ian Blane Nielsen
     Karl Damon Potter
  Current Position: Director of Covert Ops Technology, NSA
  Address: 142 Old Court Avenue
     Potomac, Md.
  Next of kin: Trace Oliver McKnight
  Born: Ireland, 1/19/2029
  Address: unknown
  Current position: unknown. It is suspected that he works with the NSA under an assumed identity, possibly with the initials SNL or UPN, based on the pattern used by O'Grady.

Hope this helps,
H. H. (but you can call me G.G. or I.I.)

Richie smiled and sat back in his recliner. "Always a puzzle with you, buddy." Hank was always a bit of a jokester. Richie was going to miss that.

He looked back at the letter again. "G.G. or I.I.?" he muttered to himself. "What in the hell does that mean, Hank?" He read over the letter again, looking at the aliases more carefully. "You picked a great time for this, friend." Hank had a knack for codes. It was something he was good at – breaking them or making them. Richie was not in the mood right now. He stared at the paper until it looked blurry.

"Hell, let's let Daisy do this." He read the names into the computer. First James O'Grady and his two aliases, then Trace McKnight and the two sets of initials that the CIA suspected he might be using, and finally, Hank's initials, H.H., along with G.G. and I.T.

"You're slipping, Detective. This is too easy," Daisy answered immediately.

"I'm not in the mood, Daisy. I just want answers."

"Answer displayed now." Daisy sounded almost disappointed as the screen displayed the names in a new order:

```
Ian     Blane    Nelson
James   Carlton  O'Grady
Karl    Damon    Porter

S          N        L
Trace      Oliver   McKnight
U          P        N


           G    G
           H    H
           I    I
```

It was not until he scanned down to Hank's initials that he saw the
pattern. He was impressed that Hank had figured it out without the
benefit of the isolated initials as a clue.

"Daisy, display all capital letters in bold print."

The screen updated to meet his request:

```
Ian     Blane    Nelson
James   Carlton  O'Grady
Karl    Damon    Porter

S          N        L
Trace      Oliver   McKnight
U          P        N


           G    G
           H    H
           I    I
```

"Now delete all lower case letters."
Once again, the screen updated:

```
I        B        N
J        C        O
K        D        P


S        N        L
T        O        M
U        P        N


         G    G
         H    H
         I    I
```

"Of course...consecutive letters."

"Painfully obvious, isn't it detective," mocked Daisy.

"Watch it. I just might need to reprogram you, Daisy," Kincade snapped.

"A bit touchy, aren't we? Can't a computer have a little fun once in a while."

"How am I going to explain what's happened to you when we get back to the station?"

"Not to worry, Detective. I'm not stupid. My personality program is just for your ears."

Kincade just shook his head and refocused his attention on the screen. His eyes were immediately drawn to the center set of letters, particularly the initials in the middle: TOM. Tom was a very common name; maybe it really *was* J. Thomas Anderson who was receiving those messages from Sandi's boyfriend, but Richie knew that O'Grady was knee-deep in this, and he didn't believe in coincidence. He scanned the initials above and below TOM.

"SNL...Shit," he smacked his forehead as he remembered Hingston talking about his lab partner. "Sean Light...something."

He looked up at Daisy. "Daisy, access a list of employees at BNI and display anyone with the initials SNL or UPN."

"Accessing...List now on screen."

Only one name appeared: Dr. Sean Lightbourne, Nanobotics Lab. No middle name available.

Kincade picked up the phone and dialed Paul Hingston's cell phone.

———

It was nearly noon, and Paul had wasted away most of the morning. He had managed to make it through the meeting in JT's conference room, but was sure that his anxiety was obvious. He returned to his office and stared at the computer monitor. Solitaire was about the greatest challenge he could face this morning; it helped calm the nerves.

"You about ready, buddy?" Sean came to the door at twelve sharp and saw the screen with a half-finished game of Solitaire. "...or do you need a little more time to work on that top-secret project you've got going on there?"

"Ah, hell," Paul said, "let's get out of here."

"Must have been some wild weekend, huh? I can't wait to hear about this one. What do you say we figure out women over a couple of burgers."

Paul laughed and grabbed his coat. It felt good to laugh again. "Come on." He slapped Sean on the back and they walked toward the elevator. Just as they stepped in, Paul's phone rang.

"Hello?"

"Hingston, thank goodness I found you. Listen, have you talked to Lightbourne yet?"

"No." Paul looked up at Sean. "Why?"

"Don't."

"OK then. Can I pick it up Friday?"

"Can't talk now, eh?"

"I was really hoping to have it by this weekend. Did the stain come out OK?"

"Just listen then. The Tom we're looking for is not J.Thomas Anderson. In fact, it's not anybody named Thomas. The guy we're looking for is TOM, as in the initials T...O...M. They are the initials of an NSA agent named Trace Oliver McKnight."

"Great. I really don't need all of the details. As long as you got it clean."

"He uses an alias with the initials S.N.L. According to my computer, your lab partner is named Sean Lightbourne. You wouldn't happen to know his middle name, would you?"

"Thanks, Nathan," Paul said.

"Shit. That's what I was afraid of. Be careful."

Paul was trying hard not to stare at Sean too long and hoped that the sweat on his forehead wasn't too obvious. "I sure will. See you Friday." He disconnected and put the phone back in his pocket.

"Damned good laundry service," Sean said. "Who do you use."

"Some little place that my doorman recommended near Poe Towers. It looks like a dump. I can't even remember the name, but they do a hell of a job."

"Oh well. That wouldn't exactly be convenient to my house anyway. It's a long haul from Columbia. I don't know how you do that drive everyday."

"Ah, it's not to bad. At the hours I'm on the road, most people are still asleep."

Paul wiped his brow. He'd have to think of something else to talk about at lunch today. He could hardly believe that his best friend, Sean Lightbourne, was an NSA spy, much less the kind of man who could perpetrate the kind of crimes that Richard Kincade was implicating Sean in. Sure, he had the means to misuse the nanobot research, and he certainly had the knowledge, but... It was just too hard to deal with; he would need more evidence that Sean was really doing this before he was ready to give up on his friend, but he knew better than to do anything foolish until he was sure.

They went to lunch as planned, and Paul managed to divert the flow of the conversation by appealing to the well-ingrained machismo of the suave Sean Lightbourne. He didn't have to stray too far from the truth in telling Sean that the girl he wanted to talk about was Sandi Fletcher. Sean wasn't too surprised. In fact, Paul's obsession with her was something that Sean had counted on through the years, and he was rarely disappointed. But this time, Paul explained, the news of Sandi's death had changed things. He just had to find a way to get her out of his mind and get on with his life. He asked for Sean's advice on how to pick up women, something that Paul had to admit his partner excelled at. Sean carried the bulk of the conversation throughout the remainder of lunch, just as Paul had hoped he would.

After nodding in admiration for an hour, not all of it feigned, Paul thanked Sean profusely and they returned to BNI. Paul realized that it would be hopeless to try to get into the computer system without being detected during daytime hours, and was able to redirect his attention to the spinal cord project. No matter the distraction, he usually found work an interesting enough diversion to lose himself in. This time was different.

The afternoon seemed to grind by more slowly than any that Paul could ever remember. He could not help but wonder if Sean was into something far less altruistic than anything he himself would want to be associated with, but he could not afford to let his newfound knowledge surface today. He went about his work and kept any further conversations with Sean centered on the Ravens upcoming match-up with the Redskins. Sports was a topic that most men could discuss passionately, unencumbered by their true feelings for one another. He did not want Sean to notice the tension that welled-up inside every time he thought about the consequences of what Kincade had said.

Paul knew his computer skills were not adequate to bypass the company security that protected the BNI Intranet. There was only one way he might be able to find out if Sean was really performing illegal human experimentation with the nanobots: Paul would have to get in to Sean's computer.

The day came and went. Paul found himself alone in the lab by eight PM and discreetly closed himself into Sean's office. It wasn't difficult to gain access to the computer sitting on his desk, but the files were encrypted in a multilayered format that only served to heighten Paul's suspicions of his younger research partner. Not many people knew Sean's full name, Sean Nathan Lightbourne, and that knowledge helped Paul break into the main file listing. He scanned down the list, stopping periodically to glance back toward the door.

Halfway down the screen was a folder containing the neuronanobot research project. He opened the folder. There were three subfolders, one for each of the two phases of the project that they had developed together, and a third, labeled "Phase Three".

"Phase Three? What in the hell is Phase Three?"   He clicked on the folder and a listing of files was displayed. The first file was entitled "Bionic Properties" and the second "Genetic Coding". Paul was unable to break through the encryption for either, but on the third, listed as "Subjects", he got lucky.

A listing came up: LH, JSM, BJ, HJ, RS and HB. The first four, he recognized as the four BNI employees from the file that Detective Kincade had handed him last night. He was unsure about the other two, and was unable to open the files to gain any further details.

It was nearly midnight by the time he had made his way to the list and he was exhausted. Between the lack of sleep and the eyestrain of staring at that monitor for the last four hours, he was starting to have trouble concentrating.

"I guess that's all I'm going to get out of you tonight," he said to the computer as he shut it down. He had seen enough to confirm Kincade's suspicions, but he wasn't sure what he was going to do about it. Implicating Sean Lightbourne and BNI would be implicating himself, not only in data theft, but also in murder. Of that much he was sure. He couldn't believe the web that he was trapped in. If he helped Kincade, his career was over and he could end up in jail. On the other hand, this was not something he could live with; there was no way that he could continue to help Sean, knowing what he was doing with their work, and if Sean were to discover just how much Paul knew...these were people who killed without regret.

Richard Kincade grabbed the phone quickly, hoping to keep from waking his wife.

"Hello."

"Christ, you were right."

Kincade recognized the voice. "Do you know what time it is?" He checked the clock on his nightstand. It was two AM.

"How did you know it was him?"

"Listen, this isn't the time or place..."

"It's OK, I'm calling from a payphone. I'm not stupid enough to use the phone at my place."

"No, just stupid enough to call me on *my* home phone."

"God, you're right. I didn't think of that. I'm just so rattled right now."

"Yeah, well listen, get some sleep. I'll get in touch with you tomorrow."

"Right."

Kincade hung up the phone. He was pretty sure it wasn't tapped. Richie had checked the lines himself, but the NSA has its ways. He just hoped that if someone was listening in, they didn't recognize Paul Hingston's voice.

Tuesday, September 17, 2051 —

Paul couldn't face Sean this morning. He had called in sick; the raspy voice was pretty convincing, at least *he* thought so. When he walked into the kitchen, there was a message on his fax machine. "Be at Pushnik's at ten sharp...R.K."

The aroma of freshly brewed coffee poured out the open door of Pushnik's Bakery on Lombard Street. It was one of the most popular spots for a quick breakfast in the Inner Harbor area. Even in the middle of the week, it buzzed with activity. Paul followed the allure of the coffee in through the front door, and pushed his way through the crowd. Dozens of simultaneous conversations merged into a din, broken only by the frequent clanging of plates against the tables.

"Just one, hon?" the hostess said as he made it to the front of the crowd.

"Actually, I'm meeting..." He spotted the platinum blond Sandi sitting across a table facing Detective Kincade in the far corner. "Oh, there they are," he said, brushing by the indignant, gum-chewing redhead who was trying to keep order amidst the chaos.

"Sure, just walk right in," she sniped as he knocked her ever so slightly off balance.

"Oh. Sorry, miss."

"Sure." She turned away. "Two of ya, hon?" she said to the young couple who were next in line.

Paul made his way to the back of the restaurant and sat next to Sandi. They were facing Richie, who had positioned himself strategically where he could watch the room.

"So, I take it you had quite a day, eh Hingston?"

"Yeah. Sorry about the wake up call." He smiled at Sandi. "Hi."

"Hi," she said. "You OK?"

"For now," Paul said. "But I don't know for how long. You've got to help me, Detective. I can't believe what I've gotten myself into."

"What do you mean?"

"It's worse than you thought…a whole lot worse. See, after I got your call, I decided it might not be such a good idea to try and get Sean to help me hack into BNI's Intranet to find that TOM mailbox."

"Good decision, Sherlock." Kincade couldn't help himself.

"Yeah," Paul gave him a dirty look. "Well anyway, I knew there was no way I could figure out how to hack in to something like that myself, so I decided to check out Sean's computer instead. I hung out until the place was deserted and hacked the PC in his office."

"Good work, Doc." Kincade decided to be a little more cordial. "What did you find?"

"More than I cared to know. I found a reference to those four BNI employees that you had the file on. Not only was Sean experimenting on them before the human trials were approved, but he was doing it with Phase Three nanobots."

"Phase Three?" Sandi yelped. "What in the hell are Phase Three nanobots?"

"Exactly," Paul said proudly.

"God," Sandi said, shaking her head.

Kincade was lost. "Want to let me in on this, professors?"

"Oh, sorry," Sandi answered. "See, the neuronanobots were developed as a two phase system. Phase One fixes the damage to the brain after an injury, and Phase Two bots turn into new brain cells to replace the damaged ones."

"And what do the Phase Three bots do?"

"That's just it, there aren't any Phase Three bots. At least, there aren't supposed to be. What are they, Paul?"

"I'm not exactly sure. I couldn't get into all his files. See, *we* never developed any Phase Three bots either. Whatever they are, Sean was making them and using them without my knowledge."

"Got any theories?"

"Well, it seems pretty far-fetched, but…"

"Let's hear it."

"Well, we had talked a couple of years ago, just theoretically of course, about whether it would be possible to make nanobots that could be resequenced… reprogrammed, if you will…after they were inside of the human body. I didn't think it was possible, but maybe he found a way."

Sandi couldn't believe what she was hearing. "Brain cell nanobots that can be reprogrammed by remote control? My God, Paul. What have you done?"

"Hey, I didn't even know about it."

"Hate to interrupt boys and girls," this conversation was way over Kincade's head, "but could you give me the English version of that explanation."

"If Lightbourne really did this," Sandi said, "then, in theory, he could play with anyone's mind once the nanobots were in their brain. See, if he could figure out a way to send the right signal to one of these Phase Three bots, he could make that person do whatever he wanted them to, whenever he wanted them to."

"Mind control." Kincade got it.

"*In theory* is the key phrase," Paul said. "Even if he has come up with a way to control the bots with some kind of a remote control, the complexity of the programming that would be required to get a person to perform a specific action would be almost impossible."

"But it fits," Sandi said. That's why they were experimenting at BNI. The employees who were implanted with the Phase Three bots were each given increasingly complex tasks. The first guy... what's his name?"

"Lester Hanes," Kincade piped in.

"Right, Hanes. All they had to do to him was get him to make a sharp turn of the wheel while he was driving - one simple action. Then there was that poor girl with the seizures. She was just a mistake, I assume. Then that football player..."

"Jackson."

"...They repeated the same task they gave Hanes, getting that Jackson guy to drive off a bridge, maybe just working on controlling him at a greater distance. Then came that woman who de-chipped her car. With her, they had to program her to get the car de-chipped, then go out and drive it a hundred and twenty miles an hour. That would involve an awfully complex set of tasks to program into her brain. I'd say they're getting pretty damned good at it. Who knows how many others they may have practiced on in between that we don't know about."

"This is all just theory, right?" Kincade asked, glancing back and forth between the two scientists.

"Absolutely," Paul said. "It's pretty far-fetched stuff."

"Got any better theories?" Sandi said. No one did.

Hingston sighed. "Well, if they really did do those things, there's more to come."

"Obviously," said Kincade. I'm sure their end goal was not to make some poor lady get a speeding ticket."

"Brilliant deduction, Detective," Sandi said sarcastically.

Kincade glared at her. "Thanks."

"Right," Hingston interjected. "Well, what I meant was that there were two other names on Sean's computer under the Phase Three Project list."

"What names?"

"Well, initials actually — R.S and H.B.."

"So, who are they?"

"Hell if I know," Paul said.

"I don't suppose you got a hard copy of those files you hacked into, did you?"

"Hell no. I was scared enough as it was. If I tried to copy to disc or print from a protected file, I may have set off some kind of alarm. Sean's pretty computer-savvy, you know? I'm surprised I got as far as I did."

"Any chance we could find some of these Phase Three bots in the bodies of those BNI employees?"

"Not likely," Paul said. "If they were inorganic, they would have shown up in the MRI scans they did on that girl with the seizures. Assuming they are organic, like all the other bots we've developed, there's not a chance you'd find them without an autopsy. Hell, even with an autopsy you probably wouldn't be able to tell the different bots apart after death. The difference between them is more physiologic than anatomic."

"Moot point," Sandi said. "There are no bodies. The two guys from the car accidents have been cremated and I don't think the two women who are still alive would consent to an autopsy."

"Then I'd say we better find out who R.S and H.B. are. If they're not already dead, whoever they are, they may be our only way to stop this thing. I mean, who in the hell is going to believe us if we try and go public with this? We're going to need some pretty convincing proof."

"Y'all ready to order?" The waitress came up behind Sandi and Paul.

"Just some coffee for me," Richie said, "cream and sugar."

"No cream for me," said Paul, "but lots of sugar. "I like it sweet and black."

"I'll bet you do, honey," said the waitress coyly.

Paul turned to look over his shoulder. The waitress was a tall, slim African-American woman by the name of Wanda, which was marked clearly on her nametag.

"Whew! Look at those bags under your eyes," Wanda said. "How 'bout we make it *tall*, sweet and black for you, honey? Looks like you need all the caffeine you can get."

"Sounds good, Wanda" said Paul sheepishly. He wasn't sure which embarrassed him more, the "sweet and black" remark or the bags under his eyes.

Sandi laughed. "Just some O.J. for me."

Wanda winked at her. "Watch out for this one, now," she said, nodding toward Paul. "Y'all let me know if you get hungry. The blueberry muffins are awesome here."

The power of suggestion is a mighty thing. Wanda brought out three muffins, fresh from the oven. They *were* good.

The TV mounted in the corner of the room was inaudible over the clamor of the brunch crowd. Richie glanced up as CNN was broadcasting coverage of an impromptu press conference on the steps of Walter Reed Hospital, where President Huntley Forsyth had just been visiting with his chief of staff, Harold Bradley, still recovering from the injuries sustained in his Labor Day weekend accident. The president was answering questions from reporters, as Bradley's picture was superimposed in the bottom right corner of the screen. He was due to be released within a couple of days and his miraculous recovery was big news. One of the reporters apparently asked a question about the driver of Bradley's vehicle, as a second picture was briefly displayed on the bottom left corner of the screen. It was a picture that looked familiar to Kincade from an article in the Sunpapers, but he probably would not have been able to put a name to the face if it weren't for the caption underneath: "Rocky Stankowski."

"Hey, Kincade?"

Richie ignored Hingston, his eyes fixed on the TV.

"Kincade!" Hingston reached over and tapped Richie's arm. "You want any more or not?"

Richie looked up and saw Wanda standing there with a pot of coffee. "Oh, sorry. No thanks, I'm fine."

"You don't look so fine. You look kind of flushed," she said. "You sure you're OK, honey?"

"Yeah, I'm fine. Thanks." Richie was still staring at the TV. He watched Wanda walk away, and then looked back across the table at his new friends. "I know who R.S. and H.B. are."

CHAPTER TWENTY ONE

President Huntley Forsyth was distraught over the accident of his chief of staff and good friend, Harold Bradley. They had first met at a party Forsyth's parents had thrown in honor of his graduation from Harvard Law School. Bradley was a close family friend of one of Forsyth's classmates. He was so impressed by Huntley's valedictorian speech that he had to meet the young man, and crashed the party with the blessing of Mr. and Mrs. Forsyth.

Huntley vividly remembered the first time they had met. He was having a glass of champagne with his girlfriend when a slightly graying and very distinguished looking gentleman approached him. "Young man, your sharp wit is exceeded only by your uncanny ability to connect with your audience. Your speech was truly inspiring. It is quite a shame that you have chosen to waste all that on a career in law."

Bradley was a political analyst for the Boston Globe, well liked and respected by many of the nation's leading politicians. Forsyth recognized him instantly. "But, sir," he responded, "surely you would not have me waste it on the septic tank that is politics."

Bradley smiled. "Well, somebody has to clean out the septic tank."

It was not long before the two were good friends. Bradley gradually swayed the interests of the brilliant and charismatic young lawyer toward a career in politics, and several hard-fought campaigns later, Forsyth was elected as the President of the United States.

"You look like hell, Harry," President Forsyth said as he stood over Bradley's bed at Walter Reed.

"Thanks, kid."

"Kid? Geez, Harry, nobody calls the president 'kid.' It ain't fittin', it just ain't fittin'."

They both laughed. Gone With the Wind was one of their favorite movies. They had discussed it often.

"It's good to see you laugh, Harry."

"Thanks...kid." He winked. "I'm going to play this brain injury thing out for all it's worth."

"Don't want your job back, then?"

"Hell, yes, I want it back...Mr. President. I'm sick of this hospital food." Bradley hopped out of bed and walked over to the window.

The president laughed. He pointed to the hospital gown as Bradley looked around. "Enjoying the breezes, are you?"

Bradley, realizing that his gown was open in the back, reached around and pulled it together. "And I'm sick of these God-damned gowns." He walked over to the closet. "Where the hell are my clothes?"

"Relax. It's not everybody who gets to moon the president, you know?"

Bradley smiled. "Yeah, you're right. There are a few other presidents I'd rather have mooned, though."

"And just which ones would those happen to be?"

"Mostly the Republicans, Huntley. Mostly elephants." He pulled on his pants and grabbed his robe. "Let's take a walk. I've got to get out of here."

The president glanced over at the security guard by the door, who shook his head in the negative. "I'm afraid you've got to stay put a couple more days, Harry." Bradley gave him an icy stare. "Tell you what, how about we walk down to the lounge at the end of the hall. I think I can talk my way past Jack, guarding the door out here, but I doubt the two of us could take on the Secret Service contingent by the elevators."

"I'm willing to give it a try."

"Let's just settle for the sofa in the lounge, shall we."

Harold Bradley nodded. He was grateful just to get out of the room for a while.

"Looks like you're getting along pretty well, old man."

"Who are you calling old, sir?" Bradley forced a lilt into his step.

"All right then. I'll tell you what. You and me at Windsong Meadows, one week from Saturday."

"One week!"

"Hell, man, you're getting out of here the day after tomorrow."

"Yeah, but..."

"You chicken?"

Bradley glared at him.

"Besides, I want to get you while you're down. Heck, I haven't beaten you in what, two years?"

"Two and a half."

"Right, but who's counting. I'm gonna whup your ass a week from Saturday, Harry."

"Fat chance...sir."

"So we're on?"

"We're on."

President Forsyth smiled. He could see the fire return to the eyes of his old friend.

"Mr. President?" One of the guards tapped his watch.

"Right. My public awaits. I promised the administrators I'd do a little press conference on the front steps of the hospital on my way out."

"You don't want to disappoint your voters, sir," Bradley said. They shook hands and the president turned toward the elevators. "Sir?"

"Yes?" Forsyth looked back at his friend.

"Thanks."

President Forsyth nodded. "See if you're still thanking me when I sink the winning putt next Saturday." He smiled and walked into the elevator.

———

Richie Kincade settled into the family room sofa to watch some TV. It had been another frustrating day. Once again, he had uncovered new clues, only to find himself in a new quagmire.

"It makes perfect sense," he said to Sandi, who sat on the other end of the tweed sofa. "R.S. and H.B. are Rocky Stankowski and Harold Bradley. I mean, they both had head injuries and they were both treated with nanobots."

"Yeah, but...the White House Chief of Staff? I mean, if you were trying to work out the bugs for a new secret weapon you were developing, especially one that you want to use for covert operations, would you test it out on one of the most public men in the country?"

"It does seem kind of dumb when you put it that way," Richie had to admit. He sat, sipping on a glass of tea, staring at the television screen but not really watching. "But what if they were finished with the testing?"

"I don't follow?"

"Well, we don't really know for sure how many tests they've run or how far they've gotten with the Phase Three nanobots, but we do know they've gotten pretty darned good at getting their subjects to do what they want."

"Yeah?"

"Well, what if Stankowski and Bradley aren't test subjects at all? What if they're not just *part* of the game, but they're the *objects* of the game?"

"I'm not sure I follow you."

"Look, Stankowski got jumped by three hoodlums with baseball bats, but the only place they hit his head was directly over the frontal lobe, the *right* frontal lobe."

"Not so strange. Most guys are right handed. If they came up behind him with a bat and swung high, they'd hit the right side of the victim's head. One blow like that is about all it would take. Even a bull like Stankowski would go right down. They wouldn't need a second swing."

"Spoken like a true detective, Doc. But still... And what about Bradley? A focal right frontal lobe injury again. No other brain damage."

"How could anyone have controlled that? It happened in a car accident."

"There are ways, believe me. Hell, he could have even been bopped over the head before the accident. Maybe Stankowski was taking him to a hospital for help."

"Without calling ahead to report it? Why wouldn't he have called for the paramedics to come and help?"

"Yeah, you're right. A guy like Stankowski would play it by the book. But someone could have rigged the car and staged the accident, set it up so that when the car swerved, Bradley's head would smack into the door at just the right angle. It wouldn't be easy, but it could be done."

"Do you realize what you're saying?"

Kincade nodded. "Afraid so. The NSA could be trying to infiltrate our own government."

"But to what end? They *are* the government."

The CBS evening news was coming back on the TV, which Richie had kept muted through the commercials. "Shh," Richie said, as video of the afternoon press conference from the steps of Walter Reed Hospital came up on the screen. "I want to hear this." He turned up the volume.

———

"I sure do," the president responded to a question from the crowd of reporters. "In fact, I'm so convinced he'll be fit for duty that I've challenged him to a round of golf a week from this Saturday."

"Do you think you can take him, sir?" joked the reporter from NBC. President Forsyth's mediocre golf skills were a matter of public knowledge.

"I'm hoping he's still rusty," the president chuckled. "I know he hasn't swung a club for at least a couple of weeks, anyway. I think I might be able to take him on the front nine if I don't let him warm up too long." Forsyth smiled his election-winning smile. The reporters laughed.

"Where is the match going to be held, Mr. President?"

"You'll have to try and convince one of the Secret Service boys to reveal that, ladies and gentlemen."

Press Secretary Gracie MacNeil tapped President Forsyth on the shoulder.

"Well, folks. My boss here," he nodded toward Ms. MacNeil, who rolled her eyes, "says it's time for me to go, and I know better than to argue with the boss. Thanks for enduring me." He waved to the crowd, and then winked at MacNeil as he handed her the microphone.

"I'll be glad to answer a few more questions," MacNeil said as the president was escorted to a waiting car.

———

Kincade hit the mute button. "Golf, huh?"

"Yeah," Sandi said. "It'd be nice to have time to play golf once in a while, wouldn't it? Busiest man in the world, my ass."

"What's that about your ass, dear?" Lara Kincade had just walked in the room with a cup of tea for Sandi.

"Oh," Sandi said, blushing, "I am so sorry, Mrs. Kincade. I didn't mean to..."

"Relax," Lara laughed. "You're at home here. You've got enough things to worry about without having to worry about your ass. I'm sure Richie will be glad to worry about it for you. Isn't that right, dear?" she asked Richie.

"Uh... yeah. Right," Richie mumbled. His mind was obviously elsewhere.

The two women laughed. Sandi appreciated Lara's ability to put her at ease.

"Huh?" Richie chirped. "What? What'd I miss?"

"I believe Sandi was talking to you about her derriere."

"Lara!" he said. "Really, now. You don't think that me and the doc here are..."

"Oh, Richard. Don't be so up tight. I'm just having a little fun." She turned to Sandi. "It *is* comforting to know that he's so harmless."

"Hey," Richie protested as Lara left the room, "you don't have to insult me."

Sandi took a sip of tea. "I hope I can have that someday."

"What? A nagging spouse."

"Unconditional love."

"Yeah," Richie said, glancing back toward the door that Lara had just walked out of. "I am pretty lucky."

"So is she," Sandi smiled.

Richie's blush was barely perceptible, but Sandi noticed. He looked away without a word.

The ring of the telephone was a welcome break from an awkward moment. "I've got it," Richie called out as he picked up the receiver.

"Kincade? Is that you?"

Richie recognized Paul Hingston's voice. "Yeah. What's up, Doc? It's late."

Sandi burst out laughing.

"Hang on a sec," Kincade said into the receiver. He looked over at Sandi. "What?"

"*What's up, Doc?*" she burst out laughing again. "Who're you talking to, Elmer Fudd?"

Richie shook his head, and brought the receiver back up to his mouth. "Uh, sorry. I think your girlfriend needs a little sleep. So, what's up, D...uh, Doctor Hingston?"

"Just call me Paul."

"Right."

"Listen, ...can we talk?"

"Yeah. Some of my boys swept the phone lines for me just this afternoon; they're clean."

"Good. Well, I was thinking about our conversation at lunch. If R.S. is Rocky Stankowski and H.B. is Harold Bradley, then this thing is even scarier than I thought."

"Yeah, Sandi and I have just been talking about that."

"Well, I thought of something else that might just rattle your nerves a little more. On my way home tonight I was listening to NPR. They were running a story on the campaign. It seems that Russell Stetson is the only Republican of any consequence with the balls to try and take on President Forsyth next year."

"Balls? They can say that on NPR?"

"I think so, but they probably used another word...guts, or something."

"Probably."

"Anyhow, the analyst said it's tantamount to political suicide to take on a guy as popular as Forsyth, and he can't understand why an up-and-comer like Stetson would do it."

"Yeah, well, I try not to think about politics too much. So just why is it that you thought I'd be so anxious to get a campaign update at ten-thirty at night? It's past my bed time, you know."

"Oh, sorry. I'll get to the point."

"Fine idea."

"Well, that story got me thinking. You see, last October at Anderson's big Halloween bash, I stumbled across Sean and Senator Stetson talking out on the patio. It was a cold night and they were off by themselves, which I thought was kind of odd. Sean... or Trace, if that's his real name... never impressed me as the kind of guy who's real interested in politics. If he's really NSA, I'm sure he's just in it for the action. Hell, I was surprised he even knew who Stetson was. Anyway, I popped out to say hi. I was obviously interrupting a pretty heated conversation, but they both brushed it off as idle party chat. It struck me as being pretty strange, but I just shrugged it off. I didn't really make anything of it...at least, not until today when I heard that broadcast."

"So what about it? What does Stetson have to do with all of this?"

Sandi perked up. She remembered having to face Russell Stetson at the Senate Nanotech Committee meeting when she was lobbying for authorization to begin the human trials for the Phase Two nanobots.

"I'm not exactly sure," Hingston said, "but he's knee deep in the political end of nanobot research. He's the vice-chairman of the Senate Subcommittee on Nanotechnology. He knows more about it than just about anybody in Washington, and he's a strong advocate for biotech research. Maybe he's working with Sean to help the NSA develop this mind-control thing as a weapon in exchange for their support for his campaign. The NSA would be pretty darned good guys to have backing you."

Kincade nodded silently.

"But I still don't see why he'd take a chance on messing with a guy like Harold Bradley. I mean, he's a pretty high profile kind of guy, and if Stetson gets caught, he's toast. Not just his career either."

"Maybe it's not just about political support."

"What then?" Sandi had picked up the line in the kitchen.

Richie looked over his shoulder. "I didn't even notice that you walked out of the room," he said to her through the phone.

"You seemed pretty engrossed. I had to know what you guys were talking about," she said.

"Sandi?" Paul said.

"Hi there," she answered. "So what, then, Detective? If not for political backing, what would the motive be?"

"How about a guaranteed victory in the next presidential election?"

"Against Forsyth? How?"

"Take him out," Kincade said.

"Murder! Even JT Anderson wouldn't be so bold as to try and murder the President of the United States."

"Not by himself, no. But for an NSA agent, it would just be another target as long as he was convinced that it was in the interest of national security. President Forsyth is not an ally to those who promote the use of biotech weapons, and right now he's a lock to win re-election. On the other hand, if something were to happen to Forsyth, the Democratic Party would be thrown into turmoil. Vice President Addison is a political lightweight; he'd never be able to carry the party. The next election would be easy pickings for the Republicans, and Forsyth would be the clear favorite to get the nomination."

"If the NSA could get a man like Stetson elected, they would have carte blanche to develop all the biotech weapons they could get their hands on. Not only is he on their side now, but with the NSA possessing evidence tying Stetson in to the murder of President Forsyth, they'd own his soul. It would be a bonanza for men like James O'Grady and Trace McKnight. For Anderson and BNI, it would be a windfall; they would have a long term customer with the deepest pockets in the world."

"Jesus, Kincade. Do you realize what you're saying?" Paul couldn't believe how this had snowballed. How he had ever gotten himself into the middle of a plot to kill the President of the United States?

"Think about it. Why go to all the trouble of getting the Phase Three bots into the brain of the White House Chief of Staff? Who else has better access to the president?"

"Why not just put the bots into the president himself?" Sandi said.

"Not so easy," Paul answered. "Setting up the accident would have been tough enough with a guy like Bradley, but with the president...forget it. The odds of pulling it off without getting caught would be astronomical." He sighed. "I hate to admit it, Kincade, but you're making a lot of sense."

"So how do we stop this thing from happening?" Sandi said. "With no evidence, who in the hell is going to believe us...a plot by America's most prominent entrepreneur and a presidential candidate, conspiring to carry out a mind control experiment where they use the White House Chief of Staff to kill the president."

"They'll lock us all up in a loony bin," Paul said.

"Look," Kincade said, "you two sit tight. I'm going to take this to my boss. Hopefully I still have some credibility with him, because this is really going to test it. I want you staying out of sight, Sandi. The longer they believe you're dead, the better. And you, Hingston, you've got to just go on about your business. If you can't face your buddies at work without giving yourself away, then take a few days off and go on vacation. Just make sure you actually go where you tell them you are going, because these kind of guys check things out when they get suspicious, and believe me, you don't want them getting suspicious about you."

———

"Hey, Maggie. It's Richie Kincade. Patch me through to the chief, would you?"

"Is he expecting you?"

"Don't start with me, Maggie. I'm not in the mood." Richie had slept poorly wondering how he was going to convince the chief that the NSA was plotting to kill the president.

"He doesn't talk to anyone without an appointment."

"Put me through now, Maggie, or I'll make sure his wife finds out who sent him those Godiva chocolates last Christmas."

"Detective Kincade! You wouldn't dare."

"And I'll make sure *he* knows, too." Everyone in the office knew about Maggie's crush on the chief and her anonymous Christmas gift. Everyone except the chief, that is.

"You rat. Hang on, I'll see if he'll talk to you."

"Thanks, doll."

There was a click, and the line went dead for a few seconds. Just as Richie was about to hang up and call Maggie back to give her hell, Chief Hartner came on the line.

"Kincade?"

"Yeah, Chief. It's me. Listen, I've got to talk to you ASAP. I'm on my way in now. If you've got any meetings out of the station, cancel them. This can't wait."

"What's this about, Richie?"

"I'll tell you when I get there." Richie knew that if he started to spout out a theory about the NSA using mind controlling miniature robots to force the chief of staff to kill the President of the United States, he wouldn't make it to the end of his first sentence before the chief hung up on him.

"Listen, I..."

"This can't wait, Chief. It's a matter of national security."

"Just be here by ten, Richie. I've got to be downtown for a meeting with the mayor at eleven."

"I'll be there."

"And Richie...this had better be good."

"Right." *If he only knew...*

———

Kincade rushed into the police station with a box of Godiva chocolates under his arm. "Here, sugar," he said as he thrust them in front of Chief Hartner's secretary, Maggie. She gave him a dirty look as he brushed past her to Hartner's office.

"Godiva, eh Maggie?" Larry Welch winked at her, and a few of the other guys snickered as they looked over at the box on her desk.

"What?" she sniped, glaring around the room. "So Richie's a nice guy. Wanna make a federal case out of it?" She shoved the chocolates in her desk drawer, seething at the opportunity to get Richie back someday.

"Come on in," Hartner said, as Richie knocked on the glass door.

"Thanks for seeing me, Chief."

Hartner motioned to a chair, and Kincade sat. "I'm not quite sure where to start," he said.

"Well, you'd better start somewhere, 'cause the clock's ticking. I don't intend to make the mayor wait."

"No, of course not. Well," Richie took a deep breath, "you remember that BNI thing?"

"Aw Christ, Richie," Hartner lifted the file that he was holding and slapped it down onto the desk. "I told you to let that go."

"I know, but..."

"But you didn't."

Richie shook his head no.

"I am not going to butt heads with a guy like Anderson. Not again."

"I don't blame you, Chief, but at least listen to what I've got to say, then if the answer is no, I'll understand."

"The answer is no."

Richie glared at Chief Hartner with one eyebrow raised.

"You aren't gonna let this go, are you?"

Richie shook his head ever so slightly. "No, sir."

"Shit." The chief let out a deep sigh of resignation. "I know I'm going to hate myself for letting you do this," he said, "but go on, I'm listening."

"Well, a researcher from BNI named Paul Hingston has been helping Dr. Fletcher and me..."

"Dr. *Sandra* Fletcher?" the chief interrupted. "The *late* Dr. Sandra Fletcher?"

"Not so late, I'm pleased to say."

The chief sat back down behind his desk and folded his arms over his chest. "Well, now you've got my attention, Richie."

Kincade proceeded to explain the sequence of events of the past week that had led to his conclusion that JT Anderson was working with the NSA on a plot to kill the President of the United States and help propel Senator Russell Stetson into the presidency. The chief became increasingly restless as the implausible story unfolded.

"A couple of weeks ago," Richie said, "I wouldn't have believed it any more than I imagine you do now. It still seems pretty far-fetched, I've got to admit. But every fiber of my gut tells me I'm right, Chief."

Hartner sat in silence for a moment, digesting the information, then stood up slowly. "If you were anybody else telling me a story like this...Hell, even if I do believe you, what in the heck can I do about it? You don't have one lousy shred of evidence, Richie, nothing but a trace sample of Allohypnol from an insulin vial. You've got cremated corpses with no trace of these so-called mind-control nanobots, two living victims who have been scanned to the hilt with no sign of these nanobots showing up on any of the tests, and secure files from the BNI Intranet system that you never could have seen, at least not legally speaking...nothing we can use as evidence. But," he paused for effect, wagging his index finger in the air, "you *do* have a *gut instinct* about all this. Am I right?"

"Yes, sir. That about sums it up."

"All right then." Chief Hartner grabbed his jacket and walked toward the door. Richie was about to say something when the chief turned to him. "So I'm going to go the Secret Service, tell them to beef up security around the president and to be particularly suspicious of the president's chief of staff, who just happens to also be his best friend. Is that about right?"

"Yup." Richie smiled.

"I'm gonna look like a complete idiot, Richie."

"It'll be good to have company, sir."

Hartner shook his head and walked out the door.

———

"Maggie, get in touch with the White House. Find out who's in charge of the president's Secret Service detail. I need to talk to him." The meeting with the mayor had been more boring than usual, and Hartner was glad to get back to the station. He was anxious to nip this thing in the bud. Over the years, he had learn to respect Kincade's instincts.

"The White House, sir?"

"Yeah. You know, the big white house on Pennsylvania Avenue in Washington. You probably read about it in school."

"There's no need to be nasty, sir. I mean, it's not like you're on a first name basis with the big guy or anything."

He had to admit she was right. "Sorry. Just find out for me, would you...please?"

"Sure, Chief." Maggie sat up a little straighter and accessed the phone listing in her PC. She loved a challenge.

Chief Hartner was sitting at his desk, nursing a hot cup of coffee when the intercom buzzed. "Yes?"

"Jacques Fleurian."

"What?"

"Jacques Fleurian. That's his name, Chief, the head of the security detail for President Forsyth. He's in for another ten minutes. Are you available to talk to him now?"

"I suppose I'm as ready as I'm going to be. Ring him in, would you, Maggie."

"Sure thing."

"And Maggie..."

"Yes?"

"Thanks."

"You got it, boss."

The phone line rang and Chief Hartner tapped his screen. The face that appeared was that of a middle-aged man with rough-cut features and short graying hair, held tightly in place by a touch of gel.

"Looking mighty dapper there, Jacques." Chief Hartner recognized Jacques Fleurian from his brief stint on the Baltimore Police Force. Fleurian had started in Hartner's department fresh out of the academy along with Richie Kincade nearly two decades earlier before moving into the security work that eventually landed him in the Secret Service.

"Thanks, Chief. Been a long time."

"Sure has. How ya been?"

"I've been getting along OK, Chief. Listen, I don't mean to be rude, but I've got a meeting to get to. What's the urgent news you've got to get to me."

"Yeah, about that. Well," he stammered, "you're probably gonna think I'm nuts..."

"Spit it out, Chief."

"I've got reason to believe the president's life may be in danger."

"The president's life is always in danger, Chief. That's why I've got a job."

"Not this kind of danger. I hear from a reliable source that Harold Bradley is going to make an attempt on the president's life."

"Harold Bradley! Chief of staff, best friend to the president and all around good guy, Harold Bradley?" Fleurian laughed facetiously. "You've got to be kidding. Look, I've got better things to waste my time on. It's not April Fools Day already, is it?"

"I'm serious, Jacques, and I'd advise you to take this seriously too."

"Alright, I'll bite. Who's your reliable source?"

The chief bit down on his lower lip. "Detective Richard Kincade."

"Kincade?" Fleurian burst out laughing. "You can't be serious. Is that bag of hot wind still working there? I'd have thought you would have wised up and put him out to pasture by now."

"Richie's a good man. I know you two have had your differences, but..."

"Our differences? That sonofabitch tried to get me kicked off the force. From the day I first put in for transfer to enter the Secret Service, he started cooking up that story. Don't you remember? He tried to ruin me."

"He was only doing what he thought was right."

"Give me a break. It was jealousy, plain and simple. He wanted the promotion that I got and that he never deserved, that's all."

The chief did remember; he remembered the case like it was yesterday. It had been Fleurian's first day on the street. A call had come in about an armed robbery in progress. Fleurian and his partner were in the closest patrol car to the scene; they were there when Kincade arrived. Feurian's partner had been shot and killed. There were two hostages, teen-aged girls, guarded by one of the perpetrators just inside the store. The second man was out in front, arms in the air, but with the gun still in his right hand as Kincade drove up with his partner. Fleurian was squatting behind his patrol car, yelling at the man and poised to shoot.

Kincade's partner, the only experienced officer of the three, recognized the potentially explosive situation and jumped out of his car to intervene. The man spun and aimed his pistol at Kincade's partner. "Shoot, Jacques," Richie yelled as he scrambled out of the car, reaching for his own weapon. Fleurian stood there, motionless in his squat, while the man pulled the trigger and killed Richie's partner. Richie shot twice and killed the man. The second perpetrator inside the store was unarmed, and came out with his hands up. Kincade and Fleurian were decorated for bravery. It turned out that one of the two hostages was the governor's daughter.

Kincade had kept his report vague, but he met privately with the chief. It was obvious that Fleurian had frozen under pressure, as lots of men do. He just wanted to make sure that Fleurian wouldn't be the cause of any more officers losing their lives. Fleurian adamantly denied the allegations, and used his newly acquired medal of valor to gain entry to the Secret Service, where his career would flourish over the years; he had learned from his mistake. Kincade tried to stop the transfer, afraid of Fleurian's new position creating a danger for the president, but he was rebuffed and accused of acting out of jealousy of his comrade's promotion. Kincade never fully came to terms with having to kill a man at such close range that he could see the piercing agony in his victim's eyes as the bullet struck; he vowed to keep himself out of that situation in the future, and put in for transfer to the Motor Vehicle Tech-Tampering Division.

"That's all dead and buried, Jacques. Let's not dig it up. You've both grown since then, and you're both damned good at your jobs. Give him that at least."

"Do you have any evidence, anything hard that implicates Bradley."

"Nothing hard." The chief relayed the information that Richie had told him, including the theory on the NSA's nanobot mind-control project. "I know it sounds kind of crazy, but I trust Richie's instincts."

"I'm not going to stake my career on one of Kincade's hunches."

"At least keep an eye on Bradley. If nothing else, he is coming back awfully quick from a serious brain injury that could affect his judgment, experimental treatment or not, and he'll have optimum access to the president."

"I'll do my job, Chief."

"I have no doubt of that."

"Take care, old man." The line went dead.

"Screw you, Fleurian," he said to a blank screen.

CHAPTER TWENTY TWO

Dust swirled around the low-flying Hawk D-46 helicopter as it traveled across the arid Arizona desert toward the Bush Army Base System. BABS, consisting of five desert army bases, had been established in the early part of the twenty-first century as a training ground for American military personal likely to see action in the Middle East. Trace McKnight stood just inside a Plexiglas barrier at the helipad of BABS-5 watching the D-46 swoop in from the south. The noise was deafening, but the barrier protected his eyes from the swirling sand.

The helicopter landed gracefully, but no one disembarked from the craft until the blades stopped churning.

"Welcome," McKnight shouted as James O'Grady hopped down from the chopper. "Welcome to BABS-5, Uncle Jimmy. How was your trip?"

"You don't have to shout, kid," he said. The air was still, but McKnight's ears still felt the effect of the helicopter engines.

"Oh yeah, sorry. Takes a few minutes for my hearing to return to normal."

"So this is BABS-5, huh?"

"Yes, sir."

It was O'Grady's first trip to the desert complex, but Trace McKnight had been coming here twice a month for the past three months. He led O'Grady over to a waiting jeep.

"Looks like hell," O'Grady said. "Feels like it too." It was ninety-eight degrees in the shade.

"Ah, you get used to it. It's a dry heat, not so bad."

"It's still heat." O'Grady preferred the D.C. climate.

The jeep pulled up in front of a two-story non-descript-looking building, classic army architecture. "This is it."

"Pretty impressive," O'Grady said facetiously.

"Like they say, it's what's inside that counts, Uncle Jimmy."

He led O'Grady into the biotech research facility at BABS-5. "Without civilian red tape to worry about, we've been able to get twice as much done here as we could back at BNI. It's a whole lot easier to get 'volunteers' out here," he laughed. "We've run a dozen simulations in the past three months."

"A dozen? You've had that many head injuries on a base this size? You're going to get us investigated, Trace. Even for an Army base, that's going to stick out like a sore thumb."

"Brain injuries? We don't need no stinkin' brain injuries," he said in a poorly imitated Mexican accent, a twist on one of his favorite lines from the movies. "That's the beauty of it." He led his uncle into an operating suite. A faint smell of disinfectant hung in the air. "We use this," he said, pointing to a stainless steel drill that was suspended from a swing arm at the end of an operating table. "Our volunteers are given a vague description of the study. They're told they'll be treated with a new type of implant that will enhance their ability to perform in a combat situation – not totally untrue, really. We bring them in here and inject the Phase Three nanobots directly into the right frontal lobe."

"My God, you're creating an army of human robots."

"Precisely," Trace said proudly.

"This could backfire on us, Trace."

"Life is full of risks, Uncle Jimmy."

"I don't know..."

"Take a look at the test results before you make up your mind."

"I intend to."

There was a knock on the open door and both men looked over. "Yes? What is it, Private?

"They're ready for you, sir," the young man said.

"Excellent," Trace said. "That'll be all, son."

"Yes, sir." The private turned and walked away.

"Follow me, Uncle Jimmy. I think you're going to like this."

Trace led his uncle back outside to a waiting jeep. "I'll drive, Private. You're dismissed."

"Yes, sir. Thank you, sir." Anytime a drive into the desert on a summer's day could be avoided, it was a welcomed dismissal. He hurried away quickly.

"Guess he was afraid you'd change your mind. You're not really going to drive me out into the desert on a day like this, are you?"

"Aw, don't be such a wimp, Uncle Jimmy. Besides, it'll be worth it. Believe me."

O'Grady reluctantly climbed into the open jeep. Trace took the driver's seat, then activated the automatic roof, which closed in over their heads from the rear of the vehicle. He started the engine and turned on the air conditioner.

"I may like the desert, but I'm not stupid," he said.

"Thank God for small favors," O'Grady said.

They drove off into the desert. About fifteen minutes from the camp, Trace pulled into a sparsely wooded area at the foothills of a mountain range and followed a dry riverbed in toward the mountain. The foliage was sparse, but increased as they penetrated further into the park. A couple of miles in, he turned up a winding road that ended on a bluff overlooking a valley with a small stream running along the base, and bordered on the far side by a small grove of palm trees. Trace parked the jeep between two trees that had camouflage netting draped between them. The holes in the net allowed the two men to see out across the vista, but shielded any light reflecting off the jeep from prying eyes.

"See there?" Trace said, pointing at the grove.

"Just beautiful, kid. This what you brought me out here to see? You're mom would be proud."

"Maybe not," he answered, looking sullen for the first time today. He hadn't thought about his mother in a long time.

O'Grady could see the pain on his nephew's face. "Sorry, Trace."

"Yeah..." He stared blankly out the window for a moment, and then reached across the dash to pull a pair of field binoculars out of the glove compartment. "Try with these."

O'Grady looked through the binoculars at the grove area down by the river. Two men in uniform were sitting by the stream, fishing and dangling their feet in the water.

"I still don't get it. I mean, it looks like a hell of a way to spend an afternoon...better than what we're doing, anyway...but what am I supposed to be looking at here?"

"You're looking at Tommy Philkern and Joey Carson, a couple of privates who joined the army about eighteen months ago. They grew up together in Blue Ball, Pennsylvania, best friends. They played on the same high school football team, enlisted together and volunteered for assignment at BABS-5 together."

"Very touching. Really."

"Thought you'd like it," Trace continued. "And they both volunteered for the new combat performance enhancement project back at the base." Trace pulled a small electronic device out of his shirt pocket. It looked like a TV remote control. "But only Tommy, the one on the left, has been injected so far."

He lifted the remote control and typed in a series of digits.

O'Grady glanced over at the device. "Is that what I think it is?" It looked strikingly similar to a device that he'd seen Trace use years earlier in Italy to activate a mind-control motorcycle helmet.

"Just watch and enjoy." He lifted his hand, pointing his index finger up in the air and then emphatically plunged it down onto the remote control, activating the 'send' signal.

O'Grady scrambled to get the binoculars up to his face and focus on the two men again. Tommy Philkern put his fishing pole down on the ground and walked back to a tree where the soldiers' backpacks were resting. He reached into one of the packs and pulled out a pistol. As he cocked the gun, Joey Carson looked around, apparently roused by the noise. O'Grady could see the cold, lifeless stare on Tommy's face; he could only imagine what was going through Joey's mind. Tommy fired the pistol; the sound could be heard reverberating through the desert a split second after the gun kicked back ever so slightly in the soldier's hand. He turned, walked to a wooded area about fifty yards from where Joey lay, paused to wipe the gun down carefully, and then tossed it into the brush. Tommy walked over to the backpack, kneeled down and closed it. He seemed to freeze for an instant, and then slumped slightly forward, dropping his head down into his hands as he was released from the programmed actions of the nanobots. After a moment of disorientation, he turned and saw Joey lying on the ground. Tommy ran to his best friend's side and turned him over. He jumped back from the body as he saw the wound, then quickly scanned the area, eyes darting wildly in all directions. He stayed low and scrambled back to his pack. Tommy rummaged frantically through the pack, then tossed it aside and reached into the other pack, retrieving Joey's pistol and taking cover behind the tree. O'Grady could see him peering out from behind the trunk of the tree intermittently.

"What in the hell is he doing?"

Trace was looking through another pair of binoculars at the proceedings. "Darned fool has no idea what happened. One minute he was fishing, the next he was sitting under the tree looking at his dead friend. He's looking for a sniper, but wondering why he didn't hear the shot and how he got over by that tree." Trace snickered.

"He doesn't remember anything he just did?"

"Not a bit. Ain't it beautiful? He just shot his best friend at point blank range without hesitation and doesn't remember a thing."

"You're a cold hearted bastard, Trace."

"Thanks, Uncle Jimmy."

"Then it's a go?"

"It's a go," O'Grady nodded.

CHAPTER TWENTY THREE

"It's for you, Richie," Lara Kincade called from the upstairs bedroom.

Richie had heard the phone ringing, but preferred to let his wife answer it. He sighed and struggled out of his easy chair by the TV. "Got it, hon," he called up to her as he reached for the phone.

"Yeah?" he said into the receiver.

"It's me, Richie." Kincade recognized Chief Hartner's voice. "Afraid I've got some bad news. The head of the president's security detail now is an old buddy of yours."

"Say it ain't so," Richie muttered. He only knew one man in the Secret Service. "Jackass Fleurian, huh?"

"'Fraid so, Richie. I talked to him, did my best, but I don't think he'll bite. My guess is that he's going to have a good laugh at my expense..."

"At our expense."

"At *our* expense... and do absolutely nothing about it."

"I can't say I blame him really. To come to him with a story like that and not one lousy shred of evidence to implicate Bradley..."

"Yeah. Thanks for making me the messenger."

"Cheer up, Chief. Maybe Bradley really will kill the president. Then you'll turn out to be right. Just think what it'll do for your credibility."

"Some consolation, Richie."

"Thanks for trying anyway, Chief."

"Right. Well, let me know if you've got any more ideas. I don't feel right about this."

"Yeah. Me neither. Thanks." Richie hung up the phone.

"No luck with Washington, eh?" Sandi said. She had been watching from across the room.

"Nah. I didn't expect any, really."

"How about the press? It'd make a great story, and if you can get this to go public, the NSA will have to delay their plans. It'll be too risky."

"Would you run that story? No editor worth his salt would risk running that story in his paper. No, we've got to figure out what they are planning to do. We need something concrete, and it's too dangerous to let your boyfriend keep digging around at BNI."

The evening news was on the TV. Richie had the sound muted, but Sandi was watching none-the-less.

"Isn't it just beautiful?" she said. They were showing the rolling hills of the Windsong Meadows Golf Club. It was the president's favorite place to play, and the location that most members of the press were guessing the match with Harold Bradley would take place next weekend.

Kincade looked over at the TV. "Yup. Looks like a great place to spend a day — quiet, pristine, wide open space with...of course," he whispered, interrupting himself.

"Of course what?"

"It's the perfect place for the chief of staff to blow out the president's brains."

"Of course," Sandi said, nodding agreement as she realized where Kincade was going with this. "There's got to be a million ways for Bradley to sneak a weapon onto a golf course, something he'd never be able to do in the White House."

"And," Kincade added, "Lot's of wide open space with clear line of sight to the course from a thousand well concealed hiding places, where an NSA agent could watch the match and wait for the perfect opportunity to activate the nanobots that will turn Harold Bradley into a killing machine."

"Great," Sandi said. "Now all you have to do is tell your buddies at the station so they can stop it."

"Not that easy. This will be a federal operation. The president will have his own men there. The local cops will only be patrolling the streets around Windsong Meadows. Besides, the BPD has no jurisdiction there."

"Then go back to the Secret Service guy. What's his name?"

"Fleurian. Jacques Fleurian," Kincade muttered with disdain.

"Talk to him. Make him understand."

"Not a chance. Me and him go way back."

Sandi knew not to pursue it any further. "So what, then?"

"I've got a friend who can get me the plans to Windsong Meadows. Maybe I can figure out where the strike is going to take place."

"Good idea, but you might make someone suspicious if you start asking around for those plans. Why not just get it off of the Internet?"

"You can do that?" Richie didn't spend any more time on the Net than he had to.

"Sure. Easy."

Sandi, along with Daisy's help, pulled up the topographical map of the golf course. Kincade spent the next couple of days studying it, trying to figure out exactly where on that course James O'Grady was going to carry out his plan to kill the president. There was no 'if' anymore, not in Kincade's mind, anyway. They were going to force Harold Bradley to kill the President of the United States, and it was going to happen next Saturday at Windsong Meadows.

CHAPTER TWENTY FOUR

The third fairway at Windsong Meadows was custom-made for President Huntley Forsyth – literally. In a moment of marketing genius, Eddie, the groundskeeper, had convinced the owners of the club to let him modify the third fairway to accommodate the president's famous slice. He turned it into a two-hundred yard, par three hole, with the straight and narrow fairway yielding to a gradual dog-leg toward the right, beginning one-hundred and thirty-five yards from the tee and ending in a short, straight run to the green.

"OK, boys, watch and learn."

The president had played this hole at least a dozen times before, each time with the same result. It was the one hole in the D.C. area where he didn't have to fight his natural slice. He took his practice swing as the other members of his threesome looked on. Chief of Staff Harold Bradley had already taken a two stroke lead over the president, and led Senator Stanton Cole by one, but Forsyth was confident he would pick up some ground here; he always did on the third tee at Windsong.

The two elder statesmen and two young Secret Service men looked on in silence as President Forsyth eased into his backswing, and then accelerated the head of the club through the ball in a picture-perfect swing. His head followed the ball's low trajectory, and he smiled broadly as the flight path mirrored the contour of the fairway's dog-leg, disappearing behind the trees. He didn't have to see his ball land to know that it was on the green.

"Home field advantage, gentlemen." The president smiled as he walked past his two colleagues and slipped the three-wood into his bag. He never used a caddy. One of the things that he enjoyed about golfing was getting away from White House protocol. It was one occasion during which he didn't have to have someone trailing at his heels, other than the obligatory Secret Service, of course, but he had long ago learned to ignore their presence. It wasn't that he didn't appreciate them, he did, but until he learned to ignore them, he could never really relax.

"Not bad, Mr. President. Not bad." Harold Bradley walked up to the tee, determined to defend his lead.

———

Detective Kincade made his way onto the course from a side street that abutted Windsong Meadows. Access was strictly limited when the president was on the course, much to the chagrin of the club members. Kincade hid his car in the low-lying brush of the dense forest that surrounded Windsong Meadows, and crept silently through the woods. He was sure that today was the day Anderson had planned to activate the nanobots in Mr. Bradley's head, that today was the day the president was to die.

The bushes rustled as he made his way toward the forested area that skirted the third green. Kincade knew virtually nothing about golf, but the president's propensity to ace the third hole at Windsong was common knowledge; it's the kind of story that the press loves. Eddie, the groundskeeper, had achieved his goal of garnering publicity for the club.

Richie Kincade counted on the president being the first man to the green, and hoped he would have a chance to get there in time to warn him. Even if those blithering idiots in the president's security detail had dismissed Kincade's hunch about the BNI plot to kill the president as self-aggrandizing paranoia, he hoped that President Forsyth would be more reasonable. The tough part was getting the president's ear. Richie knew that he'd look even more crazy popping out of the bushes at the third green, but there was no choice. Today was the day; Richie was sure of it.

———

Hap Wilson had been with the president's security detail for over a year now. He was hired in part for his knowledge of golf courses. Hap had been a semi-pro golfer after a stint with the Marines. He realized after a few months on the tour that he'd never be able to make much of a living hacking away against more skilled players, and when his buddy Marty Zelig at the Secret Service contacted him about joining the president's detail, he figured it was a no-brainer. Marty explained to Hap that the president loved to spend a good deal of time on the golf course, and that they needed someone in the Service with an intimate knowledge of how golf courses were laid out and run. Hap jumped at the opportunity.

"Damn," Bradley grumbled as his ball bounced down the fairway, "shanked it."

"Gotcha," gloated President Forsyth.

"It ain't over till it's over, Mr. President," said Stanton Cole, still waiting to tee off.

"Yeah, yeah. Take your best shot, Stan. I want to get out there and see how close I am to the flag."

Bradley muttered to himself as he walked over to the golf cart. He shoved the club into his bag in disgust and plopped down in the cart.

Senator Stanton Cole strode up to the tee. He had been around too long to take this game seriously and nothing bothered his swing anymore, not even the swagger of a young president. He eyed the fairway, tucked his head, and lifted his club with the grace that came from thousands of practice swings and an uncanny ability to shut out the surrounding world for a brief moment. *Thwak.* The ball lofted high over the trees on the right edge of the fairway. It would put him in position to reach to green with one easy pitch.

The president put an arm around him as he walked back to the cart, gracious in the knowledge that the beautiful drive would still be positioned well behind his own. "Picture-perfect swing, Stan, picture-perfect."

"Thank you, sir." He'd grant the president his condescending demeanor for now. By the ninth hole, he would be back on top with the president saying how he almost had him this time. It always ended that way.

Hap Wilson and junior agent Dennis McLaughlin were standing by the president's golf cart, wearing black golf shirts and trousers. They weren't the typical black suits that Secret Service men were notorious for wearing, but it made them conspicuous none-the-less. Nobody would have a hard time figuring out which men at the tee were Secret Service.

The earpiece attached to Hap's black plastic sunglasses beeped softly, and he reached up and gave it a tap. "Wilson here," he said just loud enough for the microphone concealed in the frames to pick up.

"Crowley, Captain." Jay Crowley was a junior agent assigned to perimeter patrol. "There's a late model blue Ford Taurus parked along Ridgeway Road. I followed some tracks in the grass and found it just inside the woods. Looks like it's been intentionally camouflaged with some leaves and branches."

"How long's she been there, Crow?"

"The engine's still warm. Couldn't be more than fifteen, twenty minutes."

"Get some back-up and follow his tracks in if you can. I'll take it from this end."

"Right, sir. Crowley out."

Hap pulled out his palm-tracker. It displayed a map of the golf course and the location of each agent by GPS. He narrowed the search to Crowley's beacon. "Shit," he said, realizing that the car in the woods was just a short distance from the third green. *I sure hope this is just some asshole paparazzi with a camera.*

Hap approached the president as he was walking past his two tee partners, still gloating from his perfect slice down the third fairway. "We've got a problem, sir."

———

Richie Kincade heard the men rustling in the leaves as they entered the woods, and knew that his car had been spotted. No matter, he was already tucked in by the third green, well camouflaged between a small grouping of bushes.

Hell of a shot, he said to himself as he eyed the president's ball teetering just an inch from the cup.

He held his breath, listening for both the oncoming agents trudging through the bushes and the sounds of the president's two golf partners hitting up to the green. He hoped their aim was good. It would be kind of embarrassing to be found lying there in the woods unconscious, struck in the head by a stray ball.

———

Agent Wilson explained the situation to the president. "Better to keep you gentlemen here until we have the situation in hand, sir."

"Ah, hell, it's probably just some kid lookin' for a picture to sell to the tabloids." President Forsyth continued toward the cart. "Nothin' you guys can't handle. I've got great confidence in you, Hap." He hopped into the cart.

"Thank you, sir, but I must insist ..."

"Now look, Hap, I know you're just doing your job, but you're not going to cheat me out of my birdie. Hell, who knows, maybe I even got a hole-in-one this time." He smiled and the cart lunged forward as he pushed the accelerator.

"Christ, stay with him, Denny."

Agent McLaughlin nodded and hopped onto the back of the cart.

This was the part of the job Hap could do without. He didn't mind dealing with the riff-raff or even the thought of throwing himself in harm's way to save the president, but these egos ... "Man, what a jackass," he muttered. He stopped abruptly and glanced around. *Did I say that out loud? Shit, I need a vacation.*

Kincade had a twenty minute start on the agents. They were still at least ten minutes behind when the threesome reached the green.

"Darn!" he heard the president yelp as he spotted his ball. "One more inch!"

Kincade smiled. It was nice to see the president acting like a real person. This was the first time Richie had seen him other than on TV, an icon of America.

He stayed nestled in his hiding place, still not sure exactly what he was going to do. You don't just go jumping out of the bushes and running up to the President of the United States. Not unless you have a death wish, anyway. He just knew that he needed to do something. He could feel it in his bones.

The president was focused on his ball, Kincade was focused on the president and the Secret Service agents were focused on trying to find Kincade. Everyone was so focused, in fact, that no one noticed the glint of light reflecting off a pair of binoculars on the roof of the clubhouse overlooking the third green.

Trace McKnight had made his way into the clubhouse the evening before, and was camped out on the rooftop terrace. He knew the clubhouse would be deserted on a day reserved for the president's threesome. He had come in on foot in the dark of night. The routine security checks would begin in the morning, and were not particularly hard to evade if one knew their routines. The president had played here at least a dozen times before, and the sequence of the security sweep at Windsong was always the same. A few casual questions to the right staff members at the club revealed enough information to tell McKnight that the rooftop terrace would never be checked. Its entrance was always locked, except during special club activities. *And this would surely be a special activity,* mused Trace, thinking about that wonderful little tidbit of information the bartender had passed on to him one Sunday afternoon following a round of golf with JT Anderson.

The nanobot activation transmitter would easily work at this distance from the third green, and with field glasses, it would be simple to see when Bradley would be in position to take the shot. One simple code sequence entered into the transmitter would start the cascade of events that would propel BNI into the future.

McKnight peered through the field glasses, and patiently waited for the threesome to take their places on the third green. He hadn't counted on the angle of the sun, which was reflecting off his lenses directly toward the third green. But fortunately, he had a very determined Richie Kincade unwittingly running interference for him. No one noticed as McKnight kept vigil over the scene.

President Forsyth waited patiently by his ball as Cole and Bradley made their way to the green. Much to his chagrin, they had each made it in two strokes. The most he could hope to gain would be one stroke on each.

"About time, gentlemen."

Bradley eyed the president's ball, sitting near the lip of the cup. "By all means, Mr. President. Take a gimme."

Senator Cole nodded his approval. "Heck of a shot, Huntley." Not many people called the president by his first name, but Stanton Cole and Huntley Forsyth's relationship went way back, beyond the days of their lofty titles.

"No way, gentlemen." He strode up to his ball. "But with your permission, I'll clear the green for you." Without looking back for their consent, he lifted the flag out of the cup and laid it on the fairway, just off the green. He knelt down behind his ball and eyed the terrain as if studying the slope of the green. He then licked his thumb and held it up to check the wind direction, paused for a moment, shook his head, and then carefully placed one foot on either side of the ball to line up his shot. He methodically took a practice swing as Cole and Bradley looked at each other and sighed audibly.

"Quiet now, gentlemen."

"Now look here, Huntley. I don't care if you are the president ..."

President Forsyth lifted his right hand toward them without taking his eye off the ball. They fell silent. He placed his hand back on the club and proceeded to sink the one-inch putt.

"Thank God," Cole said. "The suspense was killing me."

Forsyth just smiled, pulled his ball out of the hole and went to get the flag. Stanton Cole had overshot the flag wide to the right, and walked over to his ball after "admiring" the president's shot. As Forsyth placed the flag back in the hole and held it for Stanton Cole's shot, Harold Bradley went to the cart, parked to the left of the green, to pull out his putter.

It was just the moment that Trace McKnight had been waiting for. He activated the nanobots in Bradley's brain, which had been carefully programmed to guide the actions of the White House Chief of Staff for the next few moments.

Harold Bradley went limp for a split second as he slid the putter into his bag. He reached out with his left hand and steadied himself against the bag, quickly regaining his composure. His next movements became mechanical as he slowly unzipped the ball pouch on the side of his bag and reached deep down to the bottom. Devoid of any emotion, he pulled a loaded pistol out and slowly turned, pointing it in the direction of the president.

Hap Wilson was scanning the woods for signs of the intruder, who his men had failed to locate.

Richie Kincade, well camouflaged only about ten yards from the green, had been watching the proceedings intently. He alone had noticed the glint of a reflection from the rooftop of the clubhouse, but it wasn't enough to blow his cover for. He could tell by the double reflection that it was binoculars and not a gunsight. He would not risk giving up his position for what was likely to be nothing more than a Secret Service agent overlooking the scene. When Kincade saw Harold Bradley pull the gun out of the bag, he couldn't believe his eyes. This was the White House Chief of Staff, for God's sake, one of the president's most trusted men. He hesitated briefly, but then remembered the nanobots that had been placed in Bradley's brain. *So, they really* can *do it,* he thought to himself. His worst suspicions had been realized, and although this would exonerate him, it was little consolation.

Kincade jumped from the bushes, pointing at Harold Bradley. "Look out, Mr. President!"

Hap Wilson pulled out his pistol and swung toward Richard Kincade in the same motion. In a split second, he saw that Kincade did not have a weapon and followed Kincade's pointing arm toward Harold Bradley.

In less than one second, three shots had been fired. The second shot had come from the pistol of Bradley, who looked down in horror as the nanobots released his mind just long enough for him to realize what he had done. The third shot, a blink of the eye later, came from Agent Hap Wilson, and ended the brief misery of Mr. Harold Bradley.

The first shot had been fired by Agent Dennis McLaughlin, who had not summed up the situation as rapidly as Hap Wilson had. Denny looked at Bradley, lying on the ground, then over at Hap, and finally back toward the limp body of Detective Richard Kincade, who Denny had felled with a single shot to the chest. Nausea overtook him as he realized that he had just shot the man who had saved the life of the President of the United States.

It all happened so fast that President Forsyth never turned around. He was still looking squarely at Stanton Cole, who now lay face down on the green, blood seeping into the ground by his side. The second shot, the one from Bradley's pistol had whizzed by the president and hit Stanton Cole as he was lining up his putt. Hap rushed to the president and whisked him into the shielded back seat of the golf cart. The agents who had been scouring the woods for Kincade had come running out when the shots were fired. Hap directed Crowley to take control of the scene. He motioned Denny into the cart and they sped back toward the clubhouse.

President Huntley Forsyth was the winner, and only man of the threesome left standing on this beautiful day at Windsong Meadows.

Forty-five minutes after the fatal shot was fired, the president was safely back at the White House, paramedics were attending unnecessarily to the corpses of Harold Bradley and Senator Stanton Cole, and Hap Wilson's boss, Special Agent Jacques Fleurian, was on the scene.

"But really, sir, I must insist," one of the paramedics pleaded. "It's protocol."

"Hell's bells," sniped Richie Kincade. "I'm fine, kid. I'm fine. Richie had wrangled his way out of the bulletproof vest he had donned for the occasion. "Just a little bruise, see?" He opened his shirt and let out a poorly muted yelp as he tried to sit up. "Well, maybe a big bruise. Give me a hand, kid, would ya?" He held his left hand out to the young paramedic, who hesitated and looked around for anyone who might be able to convince his patient to lie still.

"No use, kid. Your buddies are all busy trying to save the dead guys. Now let me off the ground, would ya?"

The young man hesitantly relented and helped Kincade to his feet. They were both too busy to notice Special Agent Fleurian approaching.

"Puttering around in the wrong place at the wrong time again, eh Dick?" he said to Kincade with an unmistakable air of disdain.

Richie gently pushed the young paramedic aside, revealing a man about his own age, in the requisite G-man garb: black suit, black tie, white shirt and classically U.S. Government issue sunglasses with a black plastic frame. Richie squinted briefly, more out of pain from his freshly bruised chest than to focus through the glare of the sunlight. That voice was unmistakable, visual confirmation merely a formality.

"Don't call me *Dick,* Jocko."

Fleurian sneered. "Tell you what. I won't call you Dick if you don't call me Jocko."

Richie nodded. "You got a deal, Jock."

"Jacques," he snarled through clenched teeth, enunciating the proper French pronunciation of his name.

"Oh, well excuse me, *Monsieur.* I guess my French is a little rusty."

Special Agent Fleurian was losing his patience. "Don't be such an asshole ... *Dick.*"

Kincade smiled. "Just having a little fun with you. Figured I could use the sympathy thing to get in a few jabs. I did just get shot, you know." He winced as he tapped the spot on his chest were the bullet had struck the vest.

"I don't do sympathy, Kincade. You should know that." Fleurian glared at him.

"Geez, who's the asshole now?" Richie burst out laughing, then grabbed at his chest. "God, don't make me laugh, man."

Fleurian looked at him warily. "You haven't changed a bit, Richie."

"Ah, if that were only true," Richie said, shaking the slight roll of fat around his belly with his right hand."

"Could be worse," Fleurian said, smoothing his hand along his receding hairline.

Richie chuckled again, and this time Fleurian joined in. A much relieved young paramedic left the two of them to reminisce.

Over the years, Richie and Jacques had run into each other from time to time even though their lives had gone in drastically different directions. Kincade was put off by Fleurian's superior attitude, especially given past circumstances, but he eventually learned to see past it. With experience comes wisdom, and as time passed he came to realize that it had just been a rookie mistake Fleurian made those many years ago, no malevolence intended, and the years had proven Fleurian to be very adept at his job.

For his part, Fleurian had been furious at Richie for almost ruining his career, but he eventually came to understand that Kincade's intentions were not personal.

Deep down inside, the two men harbored a mutual admiration. They were both damn good at what they did. The friction between them was only skin deep now; they both knew it, but neither wanted to admit it.

"I thought you were just crazy, Richie. You know, about the mad scientists' plot against the president."

"But you knew better, right Jacques?"

"Oh, yeah. I *knew* you were crazy."

Kincade just shook his head.

"Seriously though, Richie. I did think you had gone off the deep end on this one," he glanced back at the corpses being carted off into the ambulances, "but obviously, I was wrong. I think we'd better have a talk as soon as you're up to it." He could see the pain in Richie's eyes. Fleurian signaled to the young paramedic to come back over, then turned back toward Richie, grabbing his arm to help steady him. "Do what the young man says, huh? Get on the stretcher and go get yourself checked out." He reached into his pocket and grabbed a business card, handing it to Kincade. "Gimme a call as soon as you're up to it. I know have been a little slow on the uptake, but I'm ready to listen now."

Kincade nodded, relieved to be helped onto the stretcher by the young paramedic and his old classmate. The pain was catching up with him as the adrenaline rush, sparked by the events of the day, began to wear off. He slipped the card in his pocket and laid back, eyes closed.

Fleurian stood over him and nodded to the paramedics to cart him off to the ambulance. He watched them drive off, then rejoined his men, who were finishing up their inspection of the crime scene. The bodies were long gone.

"Let's go, boys."

Windsong Meadows was desolate that afternoon, save for the reporters buzzing like bees around the locked gates of the main entrance, struggling to suck the last bit of sap out of the enigmatic story that had unfolded on the third green.

CHAPTER TWENTY FIVE

Two weeks later —

"And on the continuing investigation into the assassination attempt on President Huntley Forsyth at the Windsong Meadows Golf Club two weeks ago, speculation continues to mount about the motives that former Chief of Staff Harold Bradley may have had for trying to kill the president. The FBI is pursuing all leads, but continues to maintain a complete blackout of the press, claiming national security reasons. For his part, the president maintains that Mr. Bradley was clearly affected by his recent head injury, and asks that the American people refrain from condemning the former chief of staff until all the facts are in."

Richard Kincade was watching the Internet news update on the computer as he ate his sandwich. "You're a hell of a friend, Mr. President. That SOB aimed a gun at your head and pulled the trigger, and all you can say is that it wasn't his fault."

Kincade was itching to go to the press and let them know what had really happened, but Fleurian had warned him to stay quiet. He didn't want anyone mucking up the investigation, and certainly did not want to have to deal with the media circus that Kincade's story about little mind-control robots would create. Richie decided that he'd stepped on enough toes for a while and agreed to stay quiet...for now. Besides, he still had no hard evidence to tie BNI or the NSA in to the murder. He decided to take the chief up on his offer and return to work in exchange for keeping a low profile while Fleurian's investigation proceeded.

"In business, the Dow Jones Industrial average is up one-hundred and thirty-two points at this hour, led by biotech giant BNI." Kincade glared at the screen. "The stock is up ten percent on news that the Senate has just approved a five-hundred million dollar research grant, to be used in the development of nanobots, miniature robots that cure human disease from inside the body."

"Son of a bitch," Kincade muttered. "As if the bastards don't have enough money already."

The phone rang, and the message "incoming call" flashed up on the monitor.

"Computer, mute volume and display caller on screen." He missed having Daisy around to help out at home, but she was happy to be reinstalled back in Richie's computer at the station, where she had a lot more memory and processor power to do her work.

"Message is audio only," the computer said dryly.

"Answer call."

"Line open," the computer said.

"Hello?"

"Detective Kincade?"

"Hey, how you doing, Doc." He recognized Sandi's voice. She had been staying at her aunt's home in Aspen at Richie's advice. She knew too much about BNI's operations for the NSA to ignore, or at least they would presume so. He had convinced her that her life was still in danger and she should continue to "stay dead."

"Well, it's getting pretty cold out here, but I'm doing OK. Did you see the news today?"

"Yeah. Just watching it, as a matter of fact. Why?"

"The BNI grant. You know who heads the committee that determines where those grants are awarded?"

"No idea."

"It's the Chairman of the Subcommittee on Nanotechnology."

"Fascinating, Doc. I was just thinking to myself, 'I hope someone calls me up and tells me who is in charge of doling out government grants for biotech research.'"

His facetious tone was unmistakable even through the phone line. "You haven't changed a bit, Detective Kincade."

"And that's a bad thing?"

"Not at all," she laughed, "but your sarcasm is a little frustrating sometimes."

"Sorry. Go on. I suppose you had a point, right?"

"Right. The former chairman of that committee, Stanton Cole, was not a big proponent of human nanobot research, especially the research being done by the private sector. He felt that big business should fund their own research."

"Damned right."

"Yeah, well anyway, that five-hundred million dollar grant to BNI would never have been approved if Cole were still in charge of that committee. I'll give you two guesses who took his place after he was shot, who controls that committee now."

"I'll be damned," he said, starting to realize where she was going with this. "I don't suppose it would be a promising young senator by the name of Russell Stetson, now would it?"

"Bingo. And you only needed one guess."

"Hell, you don't suppose..."

"I sure do."

"Gentlemen," Russell Stetson raised his glass, "to a job well done."

The private dining room at Flanagan's assured anonymity, as usual. Anderson and O'Grady raised their glasses. Trace McKnight had begged his uncle to include him in the meeting as well, but O'Grady preferred that Anderson continue to believe that Trace was Sean Lightbourne, family friend of the O'Grady's, rather than the NSA agent that he really was.

"So what's your plan for getting Forsyth out of the way? I assume you still want me as your next president." He grinned broadly.

"That goes without saying, Russ," O'Grady said. "I believe that tomorrow morning's Washington Post will be running a story about the investigation into Cole's murder. It seems that an unknown source has given some evidence to a young reporter named Molly Woodward regarding the little known fact that Mr. Forsyth had written some wonderful letters to Mr. Cole's granddaughter, a twenty-three year old law student who had interned at the White House. The content of those letters was, shall we say, disturbing to the morality of Senator Cole. Mr. Bradley became aware that the senator was about to go public with these scandalous letters and decided to stop Mr. Cole from ruining the president's reputation. Mr. Bradley's unfortunate lack of judgment in carrying out such a public assassination was due, of course, to his recent brain injury."

"Wow," JT said. "The president was having an affair with Cole's granddaughter?"

"Well," O'Grady snickered, "no, not really, but by the time anyone realizes that, our boy Russ here will be the next President of the United States."

"You're the master," Stetson said, raising his glass once again.

"All in a day's work, gentlemen. All in a day's work."

The meeting adjourned, and O'Grady placed a call to the BABS-5 facility in Arizona from his cell phone.

"How did it go, Uncle Jimmy?" Trace McKnight was out at BABS-5 running some routine checks on the Phase Three Project.

"You missed a hell of a lunch."

"Damn. I love their crabcakes. Sure can't get a decent one out here."

"I suppose not. Listen, there's just one more loose end to tie up."

"Kincade?"

"Yeah. You know what to do. Get your ass back here as soon as you can. I want this taken care of, and I don't trust anyone else to do it."

"I'll give you a call when it's done."

"You won't have to. Just don't botch this one, kid. There' a crabcake in it for you if all goes well."

"Make the reservation at Flanagan's for tomorrow at eight. See you then." Trace hung up the phone and hurried to the chopper. He had an hour and a half to make the plane out of Phoenix for BWI.

———

Richie was glad to be back to work. It didn't even seem so bad getting up early on Monday morning.

"Oh," Lara said as a car horn beeped, "that's my ride." Her car's battery was dead when she went out to start it earlier that morning, and she had called Martha Richards for a ride in to work. She gave Richie a quick kiss on the cheek and ran out the door.

"Have a nice day, hon," he called out after her.

Richie glanced at the wall clock. As usual, he was running late. He finished his coffee, grabbed his jacket and locked up. It was a chilly morning and he hurried to get into the car and get some heat on. He pulled the door closed, blew some warm air into his hands and rubbed them together, keys dangling from his index finger. With a quick twirl of the finger, the car key flipped into his grasp. He slipped it into the ignition and gave it a twist.

"Shit," he said as he heard the silence. "Not you too. What are the odds? Two dead batteries in the same morning." It was too late to call any of the guys for a ride in, so he pulled out his cell phone and called for a cab. The driver was in front of his house five minutes later.

"Damn, that was quick," Richie said to the driver as he got into the back seat.

"That's my job, buddy," he answered without turning around. "Everybody's in a hurry these days. Got to be quick if you want to make a buck in this line of work. So where to?"

"The police station on Howard Street. Know where it is?"

"Sure thing. I'll have you there in ten minutes."

"Great."

The cab sped off toward the station. The driver glanced in the rear view mirror and saw Richie reading the morning paper; he felt no great need to disturb him with idle banter. Rush hour traffic was heavy as usual. As the cab made its way slowly toward Howard Street, neither the driver nor passenger noticed the black Lincoln Continental following closely behind. Roadwork was obstructing the turn onto Howard Street and they followed the detour signs around the block, stopping at a red light just a few blocks from the station. At first, Richie kept his head buried in the paper, but the long delay distracted him.

"Everything OK?" he asked as he glanced out the window.

The driver didn't answer. Richie looked out the left rear window at the car next to them. The man in the back of the black Lincoln looked over at him and held up a small object that looked like a TV remote control. He lifted his right index finger and smiled. He pointed at Richie, and then down toward the little box. Just before he pressed a button, Richie recognized the face from the BNI files he had reviewed. It was tough to be sure through the car window, but he could swear that it was Sean Lightbourne grinning at him through the back window of the Lincoln.

"No!" he shouted. "Driver!" he frantically looked up toward the front seat. The driver, looking out the windshield with his head tilted slightly toward the right, continued to ignore him. The car jolted forward through the red light into the crossing rush hour traffic. The last thing that Richie remembered seeing was a large scar on the right side of the driver's head.

———

Two days later —

"Jesus," Paul said as he answered the door to his Poe Towers apartment. "Are you nuts? What are you doing here?"

It was already dark outside, but Sandi was wearing dark glasses and a red floppy hat, trying to conceal her face as much as possible. "Trying to get into your apartment," she said. "Do you think we could take this conversation inside?" She glanced over her shoulder as one of the elevator doors opened down the hall.

It caught Paul's attention too, and he reached out to put an arm around Sandi's shoulder, pulling her in. "Of course, of course. Come on in." She walked inside, and Paul poked his head out once more, looking right and then left down the hall before closing the door. "Let me take your coat."

"In a couple of minutes, when the chill wears off," she said.

"Please," Paul motioned toward the living room couch.

"Wow," Sandi said, looking around the penthouse apartment. "Nice place."

"Yeah, well, the private sector does have its advantages. I can't argue with the salary at BNI."

"Yeah, but look what you have to do to earn it."

"Can't argue with that either," he said, hanging his head. "You were right about that."

"Uh uh." She shook her head. "I was talking philosophical differences. Nobody should have to expect to fall into the rattrap you've fallen into. You're not like them, Paul. I know that."

"I should have seen it coming. I should have been able to tell that something..."

"Give it a rest. These guys are professionals; it's what they do."

"I guess your right, but still..." Paul plopped down next to her on the sofa. "So what are you doing here anyway? It's much too dangerous. Didn't you hear what happened to Kincade?"

"Ah, so you don't think it was an accident either. *That's* what I'm doing here. Kincade put his life on the line for me, for *you*. We've got to do something to help him."

"Look, he's getting the best care money can buy. The best thing you can do for him is to stay out of sight. The last thing he needs is to wake up and start worrying about you."

"Where's he at?"

"He's over at Harborview. It's the best hospital in the city. Word is, he's doing OK."

"Word is? You mean you haven't even gone to visit?"

"The only thing he needs less than seeing you at the hospital is seeing me. The only chance we've got to get any hard evidence against these guys is if I can dig up something at BNI. I figure if I lay low until things blow over, maybe they'll let their guard down a little. But if the NSA ties me to Kincade, they'll be on me like white on rice. I'll never have a shot at getting out of BNI with anything."

"Probably not even your life." She had to agree.

"Look, San, I'll keep an eye on him somehow, but you've got to get out of here. If someone were to recognize you..."

Sandi reached out and took his hand. She knew how hard it was for him to ask her to leave. "How about I go in the morning," she said as she looked deeply into his eyes.

"Nighttime would be safer," he said, squeezing her hand gently. He couldn't believe he was asking her to leave.

"It'll still be dark in a few hours," she said, rising from the sofa and pulling Paul up by the arm.

They kissed, and she felt more at home in his embrace than she had ever felt before. Her hand slipped down his arm and found its way into his; hand in hand they walked to the bedroom. Paul dimmed the lights as they entered.

"I don't want to go, Paul," Sandi said, waking from a light sleep. She glanced at the clock; it was two AM.

"Believe me, I don't want you to go either, but I want to know that this will be here for us for the rest of our lives. If you stay, I may lose you forever."

"I want my life back, Paul."

"I want *our* life back. Look, I've been thinking about this every waking moment. If the NSA finds out you're alive, they aren't going to be too happy about having you around, knowing what you know. If you try to go to the press, you're going to have a hard time convincing them that Guy did anything more than get drunk and drive off a slippery bridge on a dark, rainy night. You're likely to disappear long before any story gets run. We still don't have any hard evidence against them, and the only way we are going to get our lives back is if I get some. If I do and we go public with it, they can't touch us; it'd be too obvious."

"So what then," Sandi asked. "You can't just waltz in there and ask for a copy of the killer nanobot files."

"I don't know," Paul said. I'll dig around at BNI until I come up with something."

"Are you nuts?" Sandi said. "You know what these people are like. You're going to get yourself killed."

"What the hell," he shrugged. "I'm tired of living without you anyway, San. I'm not going to lose you again"

Her eyes swelled with tears. "God, Paul. These are not amateurs. They *will* kill you."

"Yeah, probably, but only if they catch me," he feigned a smile. "Look, if I can't do this thing, if I can't find something that will keep them away from you, then I don't really care what happens to me."

"But I do. I do care."

———

"So, you've finally decided to rejoin us." The voice was ghost-like.

Richard Kincade tried to focus on the face in front of him as he squinted against the bright, thick haze. "Where am I?" he asked the ghost.

"Honey, you're in Harborview Hospital. I'm your nurse, Loolie," she said in her lilting Jamaican accent. "You were in one hell of a crack-up last week."

"Last week? How long have I been here?" His mind was still clouded, but his vision began to clear.

The nurse in front of him was a heavy-set Jamaican woman, neatly dressed and wearing latex gloves. She reached forward and smoothed the bandage on the right side of his head.

"Ouch!" he reached up to feel the bandage. "How bad?" he asked.

"Real bad. You were lucky, though. Not one broken bone except for that little crack in your head, and that was hardly anything to brag about. You're wife says it was that thick skull of yours that saved you."

"Lara? Is she here?"

"She's been here all week; hasn't left your side except when I come in to change that dressing. I sent her for some lunch. She'll be back in a minute."

The nurse prepared a syringe and walked around the bed to the IV line.

"What's that?"

"A miracle in a bottle. That's what I call it, anyway. See," she said as she injected the liquid into the IV line, "you're getting this new treatment for that bash on the head you got. It's a brand new therapy using tiny little robots that go inside your brain to repair any damage from the injury."

"God, no," he said, bolting up in bed. "Ah," he grabbed his head to support it against the throbbing pain.

"Whoa now, honey," Loolie said, gently pushing him back down. "The miracle doesn't work that fast. You've got to rest and let the treatment do its work. Here, this will help," she said as she injected a second syringe into the IV. "It's a mild sedative; it'll help calm your nerves."

"But...no, don't let me fall asleep again." His thoughts were foggy; he desperately tried to remember what Sandi had told him about the nanobots...Phase Three bots...something about Phase Three bots... "I need to make sure they don't give me the Phase Three bots. Don't let them give me Phase Three bots," he muttered.

"Phase Three?" she said, shaking her head. "That mind of yours is playing tricks on you, Mr. Kincade. There's only two shots, the one you got last week when you came in through the E.R. and the one I just gave you now."

"But..." His thoughts were clouded in a half-dream state. It didn't make any sense to him, but he could feel the fear welling up inside.

"Look," the nurse said, pushing the play button on the videodisc player under the TV. "This will explain it all."

The TV screen lit up with the bright blue logo of BNI.

"My God," Richie muttered as he began to remember. He tried to sit up again, but the sedative Loolie had given him began to take effect. He fell back against the pillow and was sound asleep when Lara came in.

"How's he doing," she asked.

"He woke up for a minute, but he was pretty restless. I gave him something to help him rest. He's going to be fine, ma'am." She smiled and walked out the door.

Lara sat next to Richie and held his hand, watching the video explaining the miraculous little robots that were working to repair her husband's brain.

———

Sandi sat in the waiting area staring out the window at the British Air jumbo jet being prepped at the gate. On the way to the airport, Paul had taken her by a studio run by Donny Austin, an acquaintance who prided himself in making false ID cards. Paul had often heard him brag at parties, but never thought he'd be glad to have this low-life as a friend. "I guess every profession has its place," he had said to Sandi as they walked in. They each had a false driver's license made, and Paul gave Sandi his emergency supply of cash before dropping her off at the airport.

"I'll meet you at the Kensington Gate Hotel as soon as I can," was the last thing he had said to her before he drove off.

"Last call for British Air Flight 6897 to London," came the announcement.

Sandi grabbed her bag and boarded the plane, wondering if she would ever see Paul again.

CHAPTER TWENTY SIX

Jack Tarrington had the most boring job in Baltimore, and he loved it. For the past year and a half, Jack had worked the early morning weekend shift as a security guard at the main gate for BNI. The guardhouse was small, but comfortable. It was a great place to kick back and read a book. He could usually count on one hand the number of cars that passed through the gait on a Sunday morning, with a couple of fingers left over, and the only one that ever rolled by on a regular basis was a beautiful emerald green Jaguar sportster driven by Dr. Paul Hingston. Jack loved that car; he even talked the doc into letting him take it for a spin around the lot once. Dr. Hingston was about the only BNI employee Jack knew other than his counterpart Harry Finch, the early morning weekend guard in the main building of BNI's research facility.

———

It was an overcast Sunday morning, a typical early fall day for the Baltimore-Washington area. The windshield wipers beat rhythmically against Paul's Jag, fending off the light drizzle of a cool October morning. He had driven to work a hundred different ways over the years. The monotony of the drive from Baltimore to suburban Columbia was abated by the challenge of finding new routes, most of which were far more picturesque than the convenient highway that attracted rush hour drivers like flies to a lantern.

The countryside of Howard County was beautiful, even on a rainy day. A layer of morning fog hung over the valleys that rolled between the gentle slopes of the Maryland hillsides, still rich with the greenery that mother nature would soon steal away with her harsh winter frosts. Paul made the turn into the BNI complex, almost disappointed that his commute was at an end. Jack Harrington waved to him as the Jag rolled by. Paul parked in the garage next to the employee entrance and swiped his ID card through the security lock. The door clicked open and he entered.

As expected, the lab was empty. He'd been here by himself a hundred Sundays before, but with his senses heightened by an almost palpable tension, things looked a little different this time. He could swear he was being watched. Paul rubbed his palms against the sides of his pants legs, trying to keep them dry. Sean's office was locked, but Paul's card opened all the locks in the lab. He entered and pulled the desk chair out from under Sean's workstation. The worn wheel bearings struggled against him, emitting a loud squeal that seemed to shoot right up his spine. He glanced around the room, even though he knew there was no one there to hear it. Slowly, he sat down and cautiously swiveled the chair back toward the monitor, bracing for another squeal, one that never came.

Paul breathed a deep sigh of relief. "Well, here goes."

He booted up the computer and inserted a microdisc into the optical recording drive. Much to his relief, Sean had not changed any of the encryption codes. Paul's fingers moved deftly across the keys; he enjoyed the feel of using a keyboard for data entry, and his years of practice had made him much more adept at it than most of his generation. He worked his way through the files until he came to the Phase Three Nanobot Program. Like before, he was not able to penetrate the individual files, but he was able to download the encrypted files to his disc. Even if the authorities were never able to crack the codes to get all of the information of the Phase Three Program, there would be plenty of evidence to tie Sean Lightbourne and BNI to the murders.

———

Personnel at the BABS-5 facility had gotten over the death of Joey Carson. Tommy Philkern had returned with his friend's body after the shooting. No one who knew the two men could have imagined that Tommy could have brought himself to shoot Joey under any circumstances, and had no reason to doubt his story that someone had apparently sneaked into their packs while they were out fishing and taken Tommy's gun. The weapon was found in a wooded area not too far from where he was shot, with the fingerprints wiped clean.

An exhaustive search yielded no other clues as to the identity or whereabouts of the shooter, and the investigation was suspended. Tommy had a hard time adjusting to the loss of his best friend, but he was a BABS soldier; he would deal with it.

Trace McKnight was pleased with the work that was progressing at BABS-5. Not only was the work here advancing his research far faster than he would have been able to accomplish at BNI, but he was also creating a new generation of field soldier, one that would allow a field officer to truly orchestrate the actions of his troops.

Trace was up early, still on east coast time, and looked out over the military complex, faintly lit by the light of the full moon.

"Computer, log onto the Net and link with BNI.net." He decided to catch up on his e-mail while he waited for the sun to rise.

"Accessing... Link established."

He typed in his ID and password to access the BNI system.

"Accessing... Unable to establish connection. User Sean Lightbourne is currently logged on."

"That's not possible," Trace said to the computer. I *am* Sean Lightbourne. Try again."

"Accessing... Unable to establish connection. User Sean Lightbourne is currently logged on."

"Where is Sean Lightbourne logged on?"

"Sean Lightbourne is logged on at his BNI primary CPU."

"Shit. Computer, place call to JT Anderson, 7-420-555-5989."

The computer dialed the number. "That line is on privacy protection and is not accepting calls at this time."

"Interrupt privacy protection, authorization TOM-beta-14, notify receiver that message is urgent."

The computer put the call through once again, and the phone in JT Anderson's bedroom rang.

"What time is it?" Anderson muttered as the phone awakened him.

"The time is five AM."

"Five AM! Why the hell did you wake me? Didn't I set you on privacy mode last night?"

"Yes, sir," the computer said, "however, the caller has authorization for emergency bypass. This call is listed as urgent."

"Christ, must be O'Grady. Put it through."

"That you, O'Grady? What the hell is going on that you had to call me at five in the morning, and on a Sunday no less? You're inhuman, man."

"No, it's me. It's Sean, JT." Sean was staring at a blank screen. "Is your video out? I can't see a thing."

"That because it's *five AM,* boy wonder. The sun ain't up yet and I stopped using a night light a long time ago. Why in the hell are you calling so damned early?"

"There's been a breach in my office. Somebody's hacked into my PC and accessed my files. The Phase Three files are in there."

"Christ!" JT yelped, jumping up out of bed. Who is it?"

"How the hell do I know? I'm half way across the country, but I suggest you find out...fast."

"Right." JT disconnected the call.

"Computer: Tie in to security at BNI."

The computer used a voiceprint ID to authenticate Anderson's voice and access security at BNI. "Connection completed."

"Security," the night guard answered with a yawn. Harry Finch had been working the early morning weekend shift at BNI for over a year and this was the first time the phone had ever rung.

"This is JT Anderson."

Finch sat up in his chair and straightened his tie. "Yes, sir. Finch here. What can I do for you Mr. Anderson?"

"Close down all access in and out of the Nanobot Research Unit. Lock it up tight. Someone's broken into Dr. Lightbourne's office."

"But, sir, no one's come by here this morning except for Dr. Hingston."

"Hingston?"

"Yes, sir."

"Look, Finch. Lock up that lab and shut down the elevators. Lock down access to the stairwells too."

"Can't do that sir. Fire Department regulations; the system won't allow us to do that."

"Shit. Then make sure you deactivate Hingston's ID badge. Don't give him access to anything, and make sure you watch the stairwells. I don't want him leaving until I get there, understand?"

"Yes, sir."

JT wasn't going to be called a wimp by O'Grady, not this time. He could handle Paul Hingston. He dressed quickly and grabbed his semi-automatic 22 pistol. *What the hell are you doing, Paul?* he thought as he ran out the door.

———

"Got it," Paul said as he grabbed the microdisc out of the disc drive, stuffed it in his pocket and shut down the computer. As he stood, he heard the click of the deadbolt locking the door to the lab.

"Shit," he muttered, realizing that he was not alone. He hurried out of Sean's office and over to the double glass doors at the entry to the lab. He gave them a tug, and as he suspected, they were locked down tight. He fumbled through his pockets and pulled out his ID badge. It slipped easily through the optical scanner, but with no results. After three tries, it was obvious that this was not a coincidence.

Through the glass doors, Paul could just make out the numbers above the elevators to his left. Under normal circumstances, unoccupied elevators would all be down at the lobby, but the numbers indicated that they were all stopped on the top floor of the building, a security precaution used during a manual shutdown of the system. He glanced nervously toward the stairwells at either end of the hall; they were his only way out...if he could just find a way to get out of the lab. Paul shook the doors, but they were latched tight. His eyes darted around the room, searching desperately for another exit, although he knew there was none. A steel-legged stool next to the workbench caught his attention and he raced over to it. Grasping it tightly in both hands he paused briefly. Taking a few quick, deep breaths to focus his mind and body, he hoisted the heavy stool up into the air and let out a roar that crescendoed as he raced toward the entry and hurled his makeshift battering-ram at the glass doors.

The steel legs hit the right hand door squarely, and it shattered out into the hallway. Paul picked up the stool, wedged halfway through the door, and used it to bang out the remaining shards of glass that stuck to the metal frame. He tossed the stool aside and darted through the open frame of the door, then ran down the hall to the left, past the elevators and toward the stairwell. Opening the door slowly, he held his breath and carefully listened for footsteps. In the silence, all he could hear was the pounding of his own heart.

Paul was sure the guard would be waiting for him in the lobby, keeping an eye on both stairwells; they were the only exits to the building. He stopped at the second floor and exited into the dining area, which looked out over the grounds of BNI. Floor to ceiling windows wrapped around the room. The one on the far left was directly over the roof of the overhang that connected the parking lot to the main building. Paul picked up one of the chairs and threw it at the window, turning to shield his face from the flying shards of glass. He hoped that the guard waiting vigilantly in the lobby below wouldn't hear the high-pitched rattling of glass against the marble floor. Paul was no athlete, but it was a short drop to the flat asphalt shingled roof below, made easier by the adrenaline rushing through his system.

Harry Finch waited nervously in the lobby by stairwell B, holding his gun in both hands to steady his grip, trying to remember whether the safety was off when it was up or when it was down, Harry had only shot at a man once, and that was a dummy in a firing range. He was hoping that JT would arrive soon. Glancing frequently toward the front entrance and then over at the doors that led in from the parking garage, he saw Paul Hingston drop from the top of the overhand and duck into the walkway that connected BNI to the employee garage.

Anderson's car screeched to a halt just outside the main entrance. "Have you seen him yet?" JT yelled as he ran through the front door.

"Out there, Dr. Anderson," he motioned toward the double glass doors leading to the garage. "He just dropped down from the roof; must have busted out a window on the second floor."

"Go!" JT yelled as he ran toward Finch and pointed to the door.

The two men burst through the door simultaneously as Paul was opening a door at the other end of the walkway leading into the garage.

"Freeze," yelled Finch, struggling to steady the gun that he was pointing at Paul Hingston.

Paul glanced over his shoulder and saw the gun. He hesitated briefly, but he was not ready to die. Slowly he let go of the door and raised his hands.

JT walked up to Paul, puffing to catch his breath and grinning like the Cheshire cat. "Well, well. I guess I was wrong about you, Paul. I'm disappointed. I was sure that I could count on greed to sway your conscience."

"This is just too wrong, JT. This whole Phase Three thing, it goes against everything we've been working for."

"You're looking at it all wrong, Paul. Don't think of it as medical research, think of it as national security. This will give us an edge unlike any we've had since Oppenheimer came up with the A-Bomb. It'll strike a blow for democracy."

"It'll strike a blow *against* democracy."

JT shook his head. "Like I said, you're looking at this from the wrong side, my friend. Just give me the disc."

Paul hesitated.

"I know you downloaded Sean's files. You're hacking skills could use a little polish. Now give me the disc."

Finch, standing just behind JT's right shoulder, waved the gun slightly in Paul's direction.

Paul sighed and reached into his pocket.

"Hold it," Finch said nervously, thrusting the gun forward.

"Whoa, trigger-boy," Paul said. "Take it easy, it's only a disc." He raised his hands again, realizing that his life hung at the end of a sweaty trigger finger.

"Shirt pocket," he said to JT. "Why don't you get it?"

Anderson reached inside Paul's jacket and pulled the microdisc out of the left shirt pocket. "Let's make sure this is the right one. You wouldn't be trying to pull a fast one on me now, would you, buddy?" He chuckled.

JT reached into his jacket and pulled out a pocket computer. The microdisc slipped into the side slot and a list of files came up on the screen.

"Pretty impressive, Paul. I guess your hacking skills are a little better than I gave you credit for."

Paul watched Harry Finch closely. It was unnerving being at the business end of a loaded pistol. As Anderson perused the list of files, Finch looked over to see what was on the screen. Paul seized the moment and lunged at Anderson, knocking him back into Harry Finch, and the two of them sprawled over backwards onto the ground, Finch inadvertently squeezing off a round of ammunition as he fell. The bullet ricocheted off the ceiling of the overhang, causing the two men on the ground to squirm like freshly dug earthworms. They struggled to untangle themselves from each other, Finch desperately trying to discern where his gun had landed.

Paul Hingston didn't stay to find out. He bolted through the door into the garage and pressed the keyless remote to his Jag. The engine roared to a start and the driver's side door slid open. Paul threw himself into the driver's seat and watched the two men scrambling to their feet as he desperately tried to get the car into gear.

"The door is open," the pleasantly feminine computer voice reminded him. "The drive gear cannot be engaged until the door is closed."

"Well close it, God-damn it. Close it."

"The door is closing," the voice announced as the door slowly slid shut.

"Christ, technology," Paul muttered. As soon as the door latched, Paul shoved the lever into drive. The gears engaged just as Harry Finch pushed the doors open and raised his pistol. Paul jammed his foot down on the accelerator and the Jag raced off, tires squealing, as Finch pulled the trigger. He got off two shots, neither of which hit their target, before the Jag was around the corner and out of range.

Anderson and Finch stood helplessly amidst the smell of burnt rubber from the tires that had just carried away their prey. Finch pulled out his cell phone and dialed the guardhouse at the front gate.

"Jack?"

"Yeah. That you, Harry?"

"Yeah. Listen, close the gate...now!"

"But Doc Hingston's on his way out. Look's like he's in a mighty big hurry, too."

"No shit. Just close the damned gate. Don't let him out."

Jack didn't understand, but he could tell by the stressed tone in Harry Finch's voice that there had to be a darned good reason. He pushed the button and the main gate started to close. Paul saw it closing and jammed down harder on the pedal, racing toward the exit. Jack saw the Jag coming his way and ran out of the guardhouse to get as far as possible from the inevitable crash. The gate was nearly closed and about to engage the latches when the Jag hit it at ninety miles per hour. The iron gates flew open and the badly scraped green Jaguar raced away.

JT Anderson had run out of the garage, hoping to see Hingston's car stopped at the gate. A black sedan, waiting at the main entrance to the building lurched forward and accelerated toward Anderson and Finch. JT jumped back as the car squealed to a halt next to him.

"Was that him?" the driver yelled out.

Anderson didn't recognize the man, but his demeanor had federal agent written all over it. Obviously, Sean had called O'Grady after he called Anderson. This had to be O'Grady's man.

JT nodded to the driver. "But I've got the..."

The car sped off after Paul Hingston's dented Jaguar before JT Anderson could finish the sentence. JT figured Hingston was harmless without the proof that was on the disc, now safely inside of Anderson's pocket computer, but the NSA wouldn't want any loose cannons. Hingston knew too much, and was obviously playing for the other team.

Paul Hingston knew these roads better than anyone. When Kincade had first convinced him that he was in over his head at BNI, Paul pulled out a map and went over possible escape routes, roads that he had driven dozens of times over the years. One route in particular had the most promise. Over the past few weeks, he had driven it several times; he had every twist and turn memorized, and one of the fastest road cars on the planet to negotiate it with.

Paul sped away from BNI into the Maryland countryside, looking back in his mirror frequently. He spotted the black sedan in the distance and figured he had about a half mile on it. Paul drove the winding country road with as much speed as he could handle, but the sedan was gradually closing the distance; the NSA agent was not new to this sort of thing and it was easier to negotiate a new route when one had a pace car to follow.

The Jag made a sharp left, then about a quarter of a mile up the road, turned back to the right, heading up an unpaved switchback on the hillside. Paul slowed as he passed a familiar section of the road, a small clearing on the left used as a parking area for day hikers. On the right, there was a sharp drop-off leading to a creek fifty yards below. He stopped just past the passage, where a trail led off the road into the woods, and carefully backed the Jag down into the trail. He had staked out the terrain just two days earlier and knew that the ground was solid enough to ride on. Maneuvering the car about fifty yards into the trail, Paul angled in behind some low-lying tree branches to provide camouflage, then turned off the engine and waited.

The driver of the black sedan negotiated the hilly terrain cautiously, no longer able to see the Jag he was chasing. He drove slowly by the spot where Paul had turned off, then stopped. As Paul held his breath, hoping the deception had worked, the sedan slowly backed down the road and stopped at the end of the trail. Paul could feel his heart pounding in his chest. He strained to see the driver through the branches. The man was rather large, and from this distance, Paul could swear that he had no neck. The man peered out the window, using one of his massive hands as a shield against the sun, straining to focus his vision down into the shaded trail.

Paul felt like a fawn being hunted by a tiger. The sweat made his hands slip ever so slightly along the steering wheel, which he was unwittingly grasping like a vice. He tried to wipe them dry on his jacket as he kept vigil, hoping the man with no neck would not spot him, and move on. He felt helpless, backed into the woods in a parked car.

The man in the black sedan pulled his hand back into the car. A moment later, it emerged back through the window. A glint of sunlight reflected off the barrel of the gun in his hand, as No-neck turned to point it down the trail.

Paul's mind began to race. It was foolish just to sit there; he would be no match for No-neck. Should he get out of the car and run through the woods, or start the engine and race against the gun? Neither idea was particularly appealing.

The NSA agent struggled to focus, squinting into the sunlight. He tried to get his left arm up out of the window to use as a sun visor, while he brandished the gun with his right. He couldn't quite twist his large body enough to accomplish the task, and reached down to unfasten his seatbelt, trying to give himself more slack.

Paul saw No-neck pull the gun back. Quickly, he reached down and turned the key in the ignition. The engine of the Jag roared to life. No-neck looked up, startled. Paul shoved the gearshift into drive and jammed the pedal to the floor. The Jag lunged out of the woods like a tiger pouncing on its prey. No-neck raised his pistol in the direction of the oncoming car and fired off one round, piercing the windshield and narrowly missing Paul, who flinched ever so slightly, keeping focused on his quarry. The hunted had become the hunter. Before the man with no neck could get off a second shot, the green sportster slammed into the sedan at full speed. Paul could see the driver's face, a trained assassin, never turning from his target. No-neck lurched toward him as the speeding Jag rammed the sedan. The pistol flew into the air and bounced off the roof of Paul's car.

Paul was stunned by the impact as his head ricocheted off the air bag, but kept his foot pressed to the accelerator, tires burning as the Jag struggled forward, forcing the sedan across the narrow dirt road toward the precarious drop-off to the creek below. No-neck pulled himself back into his seat and hit the gas, trying desperately to regain control of his car, just as it began to slip off the road. The rear wheels spun aimlessly as the black sedan rolled down the hillside, plunging into the rocky creek.

Paul hit the brakes and pawed helplessly at the airbag, trying to clear his view. Groping with his right hand, he managed to open the center console and retrieve a small pocketknife. He flipped it open and tore into the side of the airbag; the gas hissed out as it shriveled into his lap.

Through the partially shattered windshield, there was nothing to see except for the sky and the trees in the distance. He was unaware that his car was precariously balanced over the precipice at the edge of the road. Momentarily disoriented, he looked around for a point of reference. Glancing over his left shoulder out the driver's side window, he could see the creek flowing in the distance beneath him, and the black sedan resting on the boulders of the riverbed. His mind began to race again, pulling him back into the life or death confrontation he had just escaped. His gaze fixed on the mangled car, looking for any motion, unsure if the relentless agent was really finished hunting him.

As time passed and the sedan lay motionless amongst the rocks, Paul began to let his guard down and he became aware of his predicament. He held his breath, realizing that his car's front end was protruding off the edge of the road, and that any shift in the center of gravity might send him toward the same fate as the man with no neck. He slipped the car into reverse and slowly gave it some gas. Nothing. The wheels were spinning in mid-air. At that moment, Paul was thankful that the Jaguar salesman had talked him into forking over the extra two grand for the four-wheel drive option. He pressed the button on the side of the gearshift lever.

"Four-wheel drive engaged," the car's computer announced pleasantly.

"Thanks, sweetheart," Paul said. He pressed the pedal again and the Jag's rear wheels began to pull it back onto the road. A few minutes later, Paul was driving home, thankful to be alive.

Agent John Mason was awakened to the trickle of cold water across his face. The lullaby of the creek meandering past his car was calming, yet disorienting. Still dazed, it took a few minutes for him to focus on his surroundings. The black sedan was lying sideways at a forty-five degree angle in the shallow river, the water just barely deep enough to find its way in through the shattered driver's side window.

Mason tried to open the door, but even the powerful body of the man with no neck was no match for the gnarled steel doorframe. Struggling against the newly deformed car, he tried in vain to free himself from the seat that wedged him against the steering column. Lightheaded from the exertion, he slumped back into the seat. Mason was not used to failing at physical contests; he let out a roar of frustration and grabbed for the phone in his pocket.

"Yeah?" the voice on the other end answered.

"It's Mase. The son of a bitch blindsided me."

"He got away?" O'Grady said incredulously.

"He got away."

"Where in the hell is he?"

"Well, he ditched me at the bottom of a hill, knee deep in a river. Last I saw, he was heading north on State Road 437. It's a little dirt road off of Scarborough Boulevard about five miles from BNI. His Jag's got to be pretty banged up. Shouldn't be too hard to spot."

"Right. I'll get somebody on it."

"And I could use a hand here." He glanced down at the water trickling into the car. The level had risen about two inches since he had awakened. "Is my GPS beacon still working?"

"Hang on." O'Grady turned to his computer monitor and pulled up the GPS system. He scanned down a list and clicked on John Mason. A blip registered on the screen. "Yeah, I've got you, Mase. I'll have somebody there as quick as I can."

"Sooner would be better than later."

"Hang tough," O'Grady said. He felt foolish as soon as the words left his lips. They didn't come any tougher than John Mason, and Jimmy O'Grady knew it.

———

Paul's nerves were frayed. He could still feel his hands trembling as he grasped the wheel. He rolled up to an abandoned farmhouse about five miles up the road from where he had rammed John "No-neck" Mason into the river. The Jag wobbled in along a dirt road into the dilapidated barn. Steam was hissing from the hood as he rolled to a stop next to a white Ford Taurus.

The keys to the Taurus were tucked safely into Paul's pants pocket. He opened the trunk; his briefcase was still there. After checking to make sure the Ford would start OK, Paul pulled out his cell phone and dialed Anderson's number.

JT was still at the office checking out the damage that had been wrought by Hingston's getaway when his phone rang.

"Excuse me," he said to Harry Finch. He pulled out the phone and walked away from the BNI security guard.

"Hello?"

"How the hell are you, JT?"

Anderson recognized Hingston's voice. "What're you sounding so smug about? I've got the disc and all you've got are a bunch of very angry, very dangerous men on your ass. I'd say you're up the proverbial creek without a paddle."

"Yeah, well about that...you see, before I made a copy of those files, I e-mailed them to my computer...you can check that out if you want, and then I had my computer send those files to a couple of dozen other computers around the globe. Hard copies of those files are being produced as we speak, and the discs will be tucked safely away. If anything ever happens to me, those files will be released to the press. There's some pretty damaging stuff there, JT. If I were you, I'd do everything I could to make sure that Paul Hingston lives to be a very old man, or at least that he outlives you."

"You son of a bitch. After everything I've done for you."

"Everything you've done? You've stolen my life, my career. You've killed the love of my life. You've made me an accomplice to a heinous crime against humanity. Oh yeah, I'd say you've done plenty, JT, and believe me, I won't forget it."

"So why don't you just turn those files over now? You want money, don't you? How much?"

"Damned right. I'm gonna need something to live off of. Those bloodsuckers you work with will never stop coming after me. You don't really think they care about you, do you? They could care less whether that disc can ruin BNI."

"Maybe not, but they don't want to lose the nanobots, and they sure as hell don't want the kind of publicity those files can generate. They thrive on anonymity. No, you've played a good game, Paul. Looks like you hold all the cards."

"You don't think I'm really stupid enough to stay on this line until you can trace me, do you? Look, check your e-mail when I hang up. There's a Cayman bank account number there. If you want those files of yours to stay buried, make sure that fifty million dollars shows up in that account by five PM."

"Fifty million! Now look here, Paul..." Anderson stopped as he heard the line go dead. "Son of a bitch," he muttered.

Paul Hingston drove off in the white Taurus. It took him twenty minutes to get to the Baltimore Washington International Airport. The fake ID's had been surprisingly easy to get, and he was on his way to London by midnight.

———

Donny Austin was sleeping in the apartment over his studio in downtown Baltimore. The Austin Photo Studio was a popular place for yuppies to bring their kids for the traditional annual birthday photos. Donny had built quite a reputation as a children's photographer and had many high profile clients, the kind that brought him the occasional invite to holiday parties of the rich and famous. He had met Paul Hingston at one of these parties about a year ago. Donny was quite charismatic, and took full advantage of these parties to market his business. It was no big secret amongst this crowd that his photography skills were equally effective at producing high quality ID cards as they were at shooting pictures of toddlers. Donny was the man to come to if you needed a new identity and had the money to pay for the very best.

The reputation of Donny Austin was not unknown to James O'Grady. In fact, Austin had done some fine work for him over the years. Agent John Mason was only too happy to check out the lead from his boss. Hingston had vanished after he left Mason for dead. There was no trace of his Jag anywhere. O'Grady figured that if Hingston was looking for a new identity, he'd find his way to Donny Austin. Hingston had made Mason look like a fool, and this was one agent who wasn't about to let a few broken ribs keep him from tracking that weasel down.

One swift kick from the tree-trunk leg of John Mason brought down the front door of Austin Studios. The shattering wood broke the silence inside the darkened building. There was a brief pause, then a frenetic clatter from an upstairs bedroom; a few seconds later Donny Austin appeared at the top of the stairs with a shotgun in his hand.

"Who the hell's there?" he barked out. As he reached to flip on the light, Mason's arm stretched out and ripped the shotgun from Donny's grasp before he even saw his assailant. Mase was amazingly quick for such a big man, and had been at the top of the steps waiting before Donny had time to get his gun and come through the door.

Donny's eyes bulged from their sockets as Mase dragged him back into the bedroom by his neck.

"What say we have a little talk, photo boy."

Donny tried to answer, but couldn't get a word through the tight grip around his throat. He nodded in agreement as he held onto Mason's forearm with both hands.

"Good boy," Mase said as he tossed Donny into a chair.

After that introduction, it was not hard to pry Paul Hingston's new identity from the lips of the photographer. He was also only too happy to provide the new name of the woman that Paul had with him, along with the digital photo still stored in his computer.

———

Sandi Fletcher had been waiting at the Kensington Gate Hotel in London for two days. She was too scared to venture out and had plenty of time to think about all of the terrible things that may have happened to Paul. She had decided that she would give him one more day. If he hadn't shown by then, she would move on. She stood by the window, grasping the drapes and staring down to the street below, desperately hoping to see Paul at the entrance of the hotel. Her nerves were frayed and she ripped the curtain off of the first three hooks when the ring of the telephone tore into her concentration. She ran to grab the receiver.

"Hello?" she said, hopefully.

"San?" It was Paul's voice.

"Thank God. I was afraid you wouldn't make it."

"I'm in the lobby. I'll be right up."

Paul knocked gently on the door of room 205 at about the same time that No-neck Mason was boarding a plane at BWI bound for Heathrow. O'Grady had arranged for Trace McKnight to meet him there.

Sandi hesitated on the other side of the door.

"It's me, San. Open up."

Sandi opened the door and threw herself into Paul's arms. She grasped desperately to his body, afraid to let go. Tears streamed down her cheek as the tension of the past three days burst free.

"It's OK," he said softly. "Everything is going to be OK." He said it in a way that convinced her that she was safe now, though he wished that he could feel as secure.

"God, I can't take any more of this," she said to him as she wiped the tears from her cheeks.

They walked into the room and closed the door.

"Listen, San. I hate to have to do this," he said, "but I don't know how much time we have."

"What do you mean? You said it was over." She clenched her fists and pounded them against his chest. "I can't do this anymore," she cried as she backed away and fell onto the edge of the bed, dropping her head into her hands.

"I'm sorry, Sandi," he said, pulling back the curtains and glancing out the window.

"But how could they possibly find us here? We're half way across the world, with new identities, no credit cards to trace, and...Hell, they don't even know I'm alive." She looked up at Paul. "They don't, do they?" she asked hopefully.

"I don't think so, but they will find us, I'm sure of it. If I knew about Donny Austin, I'm sure Sean did too. It's not like it was a big secret. Sooner or later they'll go to Donny, and I doubt that they'll have much trouble getting him to talk. Once they know our new ID's, it won't take them long to figure out where we went. In fact, I'm counting on it."

Sandi looked up incredulously. "You're counting on it? Look, if you've got a death wish you can count me out. There are still a lot of things I want to do with my life."

"Me too, San, and I want to do them with you."

Sandi was totally confused; Paul could see it in her face. He placed his briefcase on the bed next to her and opened it. It was padded with thick blue foam on the inside, protecting two small vials and syringes.

"What's this?" she asked, hesitantly.

"A little something I've been working on. All those weekends at BNI that they thought I was working on the Phase Two nanobots, I was really working on this. Nobody was around to notice. The weekends are dead quiet around that place and I had free run of the lab."

Paul pulled out one of the vials and held it up to the light. It was a lime green liquid with a faint iridescence. "I haven't been able to do any human testing, but I've tested it on a half-dozen chimps with the same result every time."

"What is it, Paul?" she asked again.

"It's our ticket out," he said. "It's the Fountain of Youth."

Sandi was speechless as she stared at the glowing green liquid.

"Aging is a simple matter of genetics," he said. "I was sure that if I could come up with the right gene sequencing, I could find a way to program nanobots to reset the cells in our body to a nascent state; we could start our lives over with all our knowledge intact, but without the ravages that time has wreaked on our bodies."

"Let me get this straight," Sandi said slowly. "You sent me off to London, lured the goons who want to kill us here, and now you want to shoot me up with an untested mutagen?"

"Yup, that about sums it up," Paul said.

"OK then. And to think, I was worried that we might be in trouble."

They both laughed. It was a nervous laugh, but a cathartic one nonetheless. Paul carefully put the vial back into the case and closed it up. He sat next to Sandi on the bed and took her hand. "Look, if you don't want to do this, I'll understand. We can just try and outrun these guys, hide out in Africa or something. I've got enough money to last a lifetime."

Sandi was tempted to say yes, but she knew that their chances of staying hidden from a determined NSA agent were slim.

"So if this thing works," she said, "we'll be a couple of kids and they'll be looking for a couple of adults, is that it? I guess youth is the perfect disguise. I mean, lot's of people change their appearance, maybe make themselves look older, but nobody can fake youth. Is that the deal?"

"Well, something like that. The bottom line is that they'll be looking for us in London, and the trail will end here. We can start our lives over anywhere, even back in the States. They'll never think to look for a younger couple. We can have our lives back again. Better yet, we can even have our youth back again."

"OK," she said.

"OK?"

"OK," she repeated.

Paul prepared the syringes and injected Sandi first, and then himself. They pulled down the covers and went to bed. It was mid-day London time, but they were both tired. They were fast asleep by the time Trace McKnight arrived at Heathrow. No-neck Mason was there waiting when the plane pulled up to the gate.

———

A horn sounded on the street below and awakened Sandi from a restful sleep. She stretched her arms out over her head.

"Ouch," she winced, grabbing at the pain in her right shoulder. She massaged it gently and rolled over to look at Paul. Fear shot to the core of her soul as she saw the face of the old man lying next to her. With a shriek, she jumped out of bed and stared at him.

Paul was awakened by Sandi's cry. He peered up at her naked figure in the dimly lit room and smiled. "It's nice to know you'll still look that good in thirty years."

"Paul?" she said, as she studied his face. The loose wrinkled skin and sunken eyes belonged to the face of an old man, but the mustache and wavy brown hair was his, and the voice...it was a bit raspy, but unmistakably Paul's. "My God, what happened to you?"

"To me?" he laughed. "I wouldn't talk, old girl."

Sandi looked down at her naked body. "Jesus! They're down to my knees," she said staring in disgust at her sagging breasts.

"You wish," Paul said, still laughing. In a rare moment of vanity, Sandi had once lamented that she was not more well-endowed in the bust line, but to Paul, her figure was just right.

Sandi grabbed the blanket and pulled it off the bed, covering herself. "This is your Fountain of Youth?"

"Step one," he said. "This is why it's so perfect. See, the chronobots – that's what I call these de-aging nanobots – they first age all the cells in the body to a chronological age of roughly sixty-five, then reset them. The whole process takes about seventy-two hours."

"So I'm gonna look like this," she rubbed at her sore shoulder again, "and *feel* like this for three days."

"Yup."

"Lovely. And tell me again why this is so perfect."

"Why, did you forget already? Oh, yeah. You're probably just getting a little senile, now aren't you dear?"

"Cute. Just talk old man. I want to get dressed."

"All right, all right. Think about it. We're going to waltz right out of here this morning. Even if those guys are down there in the lobby right now, they'll never recognize us. If they so much as suspect it may be us, one close look and they'll see this stuff isn't make-up." He tugged at the baggy skin on his neck.

"In the lobby? How could they know we're here? You don't think you were followed, do you?"

"I don't think so, but these guys are professionals. Besides, like I said yesterday, I'm pretty sure they'll find their way to Austin. Hell, if I know about his fake ID operation, you can bet your sweet ass they do too, and I doubt it'll be very hard to get old Donny Austin to give them our new ID's."

"Jesus, Paul. So they could be here right now?" she said, pulling the curtain aside just enough to see out the window.

"I sure as hell hope so."

"You really *want* them to find us? I thought you were just kidding when you said that."

"You don't kid with these guys. Believe me, I don't want them to find *us*, just the trail to London that we've left for them. See, when we walk out of here looking like this, they won't recognize us even if they're standing right next to us. Their search will come up empty and they'll assume we're hiding out somewhere in Europe."

"And won't we be?"

"Nope. Before we left Baltimore, I stopped by to see an old friend of mine. He spent a couple of years working with Austin. His work's not quite as good as the old master, but good enough to pass through most security checkpoints, and nobody but a few close friends knows about this little hobby of his. See, he's too timid to sell the stuff; he just does it for fun, but I was able to talk him into showing me how to make a blank set of documents. He set up the computer for me, and I put in the names myself. Even he doesn't know the names I used, so if by some long shot they figure out that I went to him for help, they still won't know what names we're using. All I've got to do is insert the photos," he pulled a digital camera out of his briefcase, "with this, and we're all set. We walk out of here and fly anywhere we want. Three days from now, we'll be a couple of teen-agers. We can be whomever we want and go wherever we want. Imagine being eighteen again, with all the money you'll ever need, and armed with the knowledge that a couple of extra decades of life has forced into us."

"Yeah," Sandi muttered as she looked into the mirror on the bathroom door, "it will be nice to be young again." She ran her fingers through her hair, looking for gray roots.

"You're probably wondering why there's no gray, huh?"

"Not really," she said, "just looking to see if it's starting. I mean, all the hair I had on my head last night is still here. It's just a bunch of dead cells, so your little chronobots wouldn't affect them, right?"

"Right. Only the new hair that's growing now will be gray. That's why I brought some of this along." He tossed a tube toward her. It fell on the floor as her slowed reflexes failed to grasp it in the air.

"Ugh," she grunted as she bent over. She picked up the tube and tried to read the label, but it was all blurred. "My God, what's happening? I think your chronobots are malfunctioning. My vision is starting to blur."

"Look over here," he said. She looked at him. "Can you see me?"

"Well...yeah," she said hesitantly, and then looked back down at the tube, "but I can barely read the label on this tube.

Paul laughed and walked over to her. "Here, try these," he said, handing her a pair of reading glasses.

Sandi took them and slipped them on her face. She looked back down at the tube again and saw the label: "Actor's Theater Gray Hair Dye"

"You're just a little far-sighted old girl," he said, smiling.

"So this is what the Golden Years are going to be like, huh?"

"Yeah. Some treat," Paul said. "Now get in there and dye your hair gray. I don't know how long we've got, but we'd better be ready before any NSA agents show up looking for us." He walked over to the window and peered out toward the street below as she went into the bathroom and turned on the shower.

An hour later, they were ready. Paul had picked up some age appropriate clothing. They had both dyed their hair and the thick mustache that Paul had sported since high school was gone. Even Sandi barely recognized him. They stood side by side, studying themselves in the mirror.

"Pathetic," Sandi said, shaking her head side to side.

"What?" Paul said, "I think we make a cute couple."

"We look ridiculous," she said. "Where did you get these clothes?"

She was wearing a flower-print dress, slightly tattered around the hem. He was wearing plaid pants and a red shirt.

"From a thrift shop. I think it's perfect. We look like tourists."

"We look like a circus act. Go down to the lobby and pick up a couple of sweat shirts, the ones that say London on the front. But first," she started to unbutton his shirt, "get that bull-fighter's flag off your chest. Anybody who spots you in that won't be able to stop staring. That's the last thing we need."

"Wait a sec," he said pulling away. "This works out better anyway. Let's shoot the passport photos with these clothes on, and then we'll change. That way we won't have the same clothes on in the photos that we're wearing today. It'll be less likely to arouse any suspicion." He pulled a digital camera out of his suitcase and took a mug shot of Sandi, and then had her take one of him. Then he reached back into his bag to get a mobile printer. It was about the size of a cell phone, and interfaced with the camera via a wireless RF port. Paul downloaded the photos from the camera into the printer, and then lined the printer up on the photo page of the passport. He printed his picture into the square where the official photo needed to be placed, and then did the same with Sandi's passport.

He changed into the shirt that he had worn last night and went to the lobby. By the time he returned, Sandi had changed back into her jeans. She was bare up top except for her bra. Paul tossed her the sweat shirt.

"Don't ever buy clothes for me again, OK?"

He nodded sheepishly and changed shirts. They checked themselves in the mirror again.

"That's better," Sandi said.

Paul had to agree. Even the plaid pants didn't look too bad with the sweatshirt hanging over them a bit. He walked across the room to the window and glanced down again. "Time to go," he said. Trace McKnight was across the street getting out of cab. "We've got company."

Paul tossed their things into a laundry bag and checked the room quickly. He wrapped the briefcase in a towel, and put it into a second laundry bag. Sandi cleaned the bathroom, removing all signs of the hair dye. She tossed everything into the trashcan and pulled out the plastic bag, stuffing it into one of the laundry bags in Paul's hands.

"Ready?" she asked, walking over to the window to take a look. She saw Trace McKnight accompanied by a large man with a bandage on his forehead. "Jesus. Who's the big thug?"

"It's Sean, or whatever his real name is. Don't you recognize him?"

"Duh." She smacked him lightly on the side of the head. "I know who Sean is, but who's the monster with him?"

Paul looked out the window, stunned by what he saw. "Shit. It's the frickin' Terminator," he muttered.

"The what?"

"The Terminator. You know that old movie, "The Terminator?" The guy never dies, he just keeps coming back."

She had a blank stare on her face.

"You know, the one with Arnold Schwarzenegger."

Still a blank stare.

"You're a deprived person," he said. "It was a classic."

"So you pick now to do movie reviews?"

"That guy," he said motioning toward No-neck Mason, "is the Terminator. He's the guy I killed, the guy I pushed off the road into the river."

Sandi looked out the window. "You didn't do a very god job."

"I guess not."

Trace and No-neck were crossing the street toward the entrance to the Kensington Gate Hotel. Paul picked up the laundry bags and led Sandi out the door. They tossed the bags into a utility closet down the hall and took the elevator to the lobby. Trace was talking to the front desk clerk as they walked by, turning their faces away.

"Excuse me folks," the clerk said to them. They tried to ignore him and kept walking. "Excuse me," he repeated a bit more loudly. Paul turned toward him. "We keep the keys at the desk while you're out, sir."

"Of course," Paul said in a raspy voice, walking over to the clerk. "I haven't traveled out of the States too much." He placed the key on the counter next to Trace, who looked up at him.

"American, huh?"

"Yes, sir, young fella," Paul said. "From Dayton, Ohio." He knew that Trace had never been to Dayton. "How about you? Where are you from?"

"Uh, Maryland," Trace said, looking strangely at the old man. "Do I know you? You look awfully familiar."

Paul looked him over. "Don't think so. Ever been to Dayton?"

"Nope."

"Doubt it, then."

Trace shook his head. "You sure look familiar."

"Ah, I get that all the time," Paul said with a wave of his hand. "I guess I've just got one of those faces."

"Yeah, maybe," Trace said, pulling out a picture of Paul. "I'm looking for a buddy of mine. I could have sworn he said to meet him at the Kensington Gate. You seen him around here by any chance?"

He glanced over at Sandi, who turned away from him, and then he stared intently at Paul as he handed him the picture.

"Ah!" Paul winced as he took the picture with his gnarled left hand. "Damned rheumatism."

Trace looked down at the deformed joints in Paul's hand. The fingers angled unnaturally, not the sort of thing that could be done to a hand with make-up or synthetics. "Pretty painful, huh?"

"Just one of the joys of aging." Paul put on his reading glasses. "Now let's see that picture."

Paul looked at the picture that Trace had just handed him. It was a photo that they had taken at a department party a couple of years back. "Can't say as I've seen him around here. Good looking fellow though, eh?" Paul smiled as he handed the picture back to Trace.

"Uh, yeah, I suppose so," Trace said.

"Harry," Sandi called over. "We're gonna be late, Harry."

"Coming, dear," he called back. "You married?" he asked Trace.

"Nope."

"Harry!"

"Thank God," Trace added, looking in Sandi's direction.

Paul smiled. "Ah, it ain't so bad..."

"Come on. Let's go, Harry. We're going to be late."

"...most of the time," he muttered, rolling his eyes. "Good luck, mister. Hope you find your friend."

"Thanks," Trace said as Paul walked away.

As they got to the door, Sandi whispered to him. "Are you nuts?"

"Just having a little fun," he said with a glimmer.

They walked out the door and Paul signaled for a cab. Sandi's knee started to buckle as she walked down the steps. She reached for the handrail and a massive hand grabbed hold of her arm, steadying her. She looked up into the eyes of John "No-neck" Mason and started to tremble.

"You all right, ma'am?" he asked with a deep, soothing voice.

"Yes, sir. Thank you." He made her feel strangely at ease. Mason was intimidating to look at, but to his friends, he had the manner of a gentle giant.

He helped her down the stairs. "Ma'am," he nodded as he let go of her arm and leapt up the stairs two at a time.

"Terminator, huh?" she said to Paul, who was relieved to see Mason leave.

They got in the cab.

"Heathrow, please."

CHAPTER TWENTY SEVEN

Wisps of cottonwood silk floated through the air and danced like dandelion fluff in the warm summer breezes, swirling down along quaint residential streets and fluttering into the heart of Aspen. The skiers were long gone and the excitement of renewal coursed through the city, invigorated by the festivals of summer. The town pulsed with the influx of locals and visitors alike, who were enjoying the festivals that celebrated the picturesque mountain village. The convergence of the Summer Wine Festival, the Aspen Summer Words Literary Festival and the Summer Concert Series created a particularly vibrant undercurrent meandering through the city.

Jessica Ryan sat on the quiet patio of the Mogul's Edge Hotel at the base of Aspen Mountain, basking in the warm dry air and sipping a lemonade, enjoying a respite from the festivities.

"There you are," her husband Taylor said as bent to give her a kiss on the cheek and sat down beside her. "You missed a great presentation. Hector Gonzalez from the Travel Channel showed some of his stuff that never made it to the airwaves, the real juicy stuff, you know?"

"Sounds like a guy thing."

"Not that kind of stuff, Jesse. It was wildlife footage, not *wild* footage."

Jesse giggled. She enjoyed Taylor's sense of humor.

"I've never felt so free, Taylor, and...God, I love that name...Taylor."

"Well, you should. You picked it."

The wealthy young couple had been in Aspen only a few short months, but they were at home here. Sandi felt like she had been on the run for months, and always far from home. When she had first suggested to Paul that they move to Aspen, where she could be near her Aunt Darcy, he thought it was a lousy idea. "Any thread of our past could be used to hang us, Sandi," he had said to her. But he couldn't stand to see her so despondent, and eventually gave in. They took the names of Jessica and Taylor Ryan and moved to Aspen in time to enjoy the last month of ski season. It was great to be young again.

Darcy Fletcher nearly fell off her horse the day her niece walked in. Sandi looked exactly as she had after her senior year in high school; it had been the last of her summer vacations in Aspen. Darcy didn't pretend to understand the chronobot theory, and at first was sure that Jessica Ryan was just a young woman who bore an uncanny resemblance to Sandi, but before long the young girl had convinced Darcy that she really was her niece. Sandi knew she could trust Aunt Darcy with her secret. Paul prayed that she was right...for all of their sakes.

"Do you miss it, Taylor?" Sandi asked Paul as she sipped her lemonade. She glanced around to make sure no one was close enough to eavesdrop. "The work, I mean."

Paul let out a deep breath. "Sure, sometimes. But this," he raised his arms toward Aspen mountain and held them wide, "this is the stuff that dreams are made of." He leaned over the table and smiled at her. "To be young, rich and living in Aspen... We're living a dream, Jess."

She smiled whimsically. "I only wish we could share it with the world."

"Maybe some day, Jesse, but not now."

Sandi understood completely. They had this discussion before. If they were to bring Paul's chronobots to the world, the NSA would surely find them. Even more worrisome was the thought that humankind was just not ready for the chronobots yet. It upset her, the thought that they were playing God, deciding what humanity was or was not ready for, but the thought of what people like Trace McKnight and James O'Grady might do with the chronobots was enough to convince her that Paul was right. She did not wish to contribute any further to the atrocities that men like those two could wreak on humanity with the technology that science could create. Aspen had helped to restore her own sense of humanity, to bring her a little closer to God.

"I feel alive, Taylor. For the first time in a long time, I feel alive."

Paul smiled. He loved to see Sandi happy, but still...he couldn't help thinking that Trace would find them; he couldn't stop looking over his shoulder.

"Me too, Jesse. Me too." He would do his best to make sure that she would never know how he felt, never feel the tension that he was cursed to endure.

Paul and Sandi drove up Cemetery Road toward the Fletcher Ranch. They enjoyed their quaint Victorian home near the center of town. It afforded them easy access to the gondola in ski season, as well as the run of Aspen's wonderful shops and restaurants, but come summer they loved to ride the trails. They asked Aunt Darcy to save their two favorite horses for a trek up to Maroon Bells, and she insisted that they join her for breakfast before the ride.

It was a glorious summer day, and Paul opened the top of his Jeep to let the wind blow through. He loved the feel of the dry wind whipping through his hair, but Sandi was sure that she'd look like a clown by the time they got to Aunt Darcy's, with her thick brown hair sticking straight out in all directions. Paul glanced over as she struggled to hold her hair in place; he couldn't help laughing.

"Sure," she shouted above the wind noise, "laugh now, but when you get on that horse, you're mine, wise-guy." Paul wasn't quite the rider that Sandi was.

Paul could tell by the look in her eyes that he was in for a tough day, but it was worth it. He stepped on the gas.

Darcy was sitting on the porch when they drove up. Sandi got out of the car, patting down her hair.

"Well, look at you," Darcy chuckled. "Just like the old days, huh?"

"Oh, please," she sniped, glancing toward Paul with laser eyes.

"Don't you worry now, dear," Darcy said, nurturingly, "A brush will fix that. You're beautiful. You look like a part of nature."

Somehow that didn't sound so bad to Sandi anymore. It had driven her nuts when she was a kid, but it seemed like a compliment now.

"Thanks, Darcy," she said, and she ran inside to use the mirror.

She looked back at Paul as he came walking up the porch steps. "I don't suppose I could talk you into giving me some of those little Fountain of Youth robots of yours, now could I?"

"Now, Darcy," he said, glancing around nervously, "we've talked about that. It's too dangerous. We still don't know what the long tem effects will be, and," he looked around again at the surrounding countryside, "if those goons find us..."

"Aw, hell's bells," she said, "there's no one as far as the eye can see. Anyone within a half mile of this porch would be trespassing."

"These men don't care about trespassing. Hell, they don't *need* to trespass. They could be listening to us, watching us from miles away, even from a satellite. You can't even imagine what these guys can do."

"I've got a pretty good imagination, young man."

"I'll bet you do." He had no doubt that Darcy had led an interesting life of her own. "Listen, when the time comes, we'll take care of you. I promise." Paul took her hand; he knew what she meant to Sandi.

"I appreciate that...Taylor. I really do." She knew what he meant. One day, she *would* feel the power of the chronobots. Staring out across the mountains toward Snowmass, she hoped that day was still far off in the future.

They both turned as Sandi walked out the front door, every hair in place.

"Well," Darcy said, "much more presentable, young lady. Now we can eat."

Sandi glared at Paul. She wasn't quite ready to forgive him just yet.

The three of them went inside. Sandi helped scramble the eggs while Darcy put up the bacon and Paul started the coffee.

"So what's happening in the world today?" Paul said as he flipped on the TV.

"Three months here and you still haven't left the big city, eh?" Darcy said. "Who cares what's happening out there. We're in here, in the shelter of the Rockies, in our own little world."

"Ah, but if it were only that easy," Paul said. "God, how do you find anything with this," he asked Darcy as he played with the remote control. You need a new TV, one that understands English."

"I'm not going to start talking to a TV," she said.

"Ah, here we go," Paul said, ignoring her, as he found CNN and put down the remote control.

"Ohh, that coffee smells good," Sandi moaned. "I could really use some right about now."

"Shh," Paul said, trying to concentrate on the TV.

A picture of President Huntley Forsyth appeared on the screen. "President Forsyth officially announced his withdrawal from the '52 presidential election today, citing peace of mind for himself and the American people. He still adamantly denies any wrongdoing in the death of Senator Stanton Cole, and both he and Natasha Cole, the granddaughter of the deceased senator, deny having had any sexual relations. However, a smattering of evidence strongly linking the two romantically continues to arouse — no pun intended," the reporter snickered, "suspicion amongst the American people. Mr. Forsyth has vowed to defend himself vigorously against the allegations, and has chosen to drop out of the race in order to give this matter his full attention."

A video clip of the president played in the inset on the screen: "I regret that I must withdraw from the campaign, but the American people deserve a president who can devote his full attention to the matters of state. They do not need the distraction of a distasteful case like this. I am therefore withdrawing and throwing my full support behind Henry

Addison. I am quite confident that the vice president can continue to lead this country forward in the direction established by the policies of this administration."

"But," the reporter resumed, "the American people don't seem to share the president's confidence in Mr. Addison. Polls show that if the election were to be held today, Russell Stetson, the young senator from Maryland would win in a landslide. With the election only a few short months away, it appears certain that the Republicans will retake the White House next year."

"Christ," Paul shook his head. "And so it continues."

Sandi handed him a cup of coffee.

"Thanks," he nodded. "Maybe all this was never really about a plot to kill Forsyth, Jess."

"What do you mean?"

"The whole thing. The NSA, the neuronanobots, the mind-control...maybe it never was about killing the president."

"What then?"

"Power. It was all about power. Five-hundred million dollars funneled into BNI as the NSA's private slush fund for tech research, government control of the top tech research facility in the world, and this," he said, motioning toward the TV set. "The ultimate power, their own puppet in the White House. It's all so clean. If they had killed Forsyth, the investigations would have never ended. Sooner or later something would have tied BNI or the NSA into the crime, and even if they had gotten away clean with it, there would always have been a sense of mistrust for the man who rose to power on the heels of a presidential assassination. But this way, Stetson comes off as the proverbial knight on a white horse, the man who sweeps in to bring decency back to the Oval Office." He took a swig of coffee. "It makes me sick."

"I'm telling you," Aunt Darcy said, "shut it off, and shut it out. You're in Aspen now. Leave the worries to the rest of the world and just enjoy life. You've earned it," she said, scraping the bacon and eggs into the serving dishes. "You've both earned it. Now come sit down and have your breakfast. It's a beautiful day for a ride."

Paul turned off the TV, and they sat around the table. The clanging of the serving spoon against the plate replaced the drone of the television news reporter, and the smell of freshly crisped bacon brought Paul's senses back to the present. Washington faded further away with each passing minute, and the placid smile on Darcy's face pulled Paul into a new sense of well-being. Aspen was starting to get into him.

Sandi trotted her horse, Feather, up the trail toward Maroon Bells. The granddaughter of Sandi's pride and joy, young Feather bore an uncanny resemblance to her namesake.

"You two be careful now," Aunt Darcy said as the two of them rode out that morning.

"Don't worry, Darcy," Sandi called back, taking care never to address her as "Aunt" again, "I'll watch out for him."

They rode up the valley toward Maroon Bells, trotting along the wildflowers and breathing in the life that coursed through the peaks and valleys of the Rocky Mountains.

"Slow poke," Paul called as he raced past her.

Sandi frowned as he blew by. "Come on, Feather," she said, prodding the young mare on, squinting to shield her eyes from the dandelion-like fluffs of seeds that floated down from the cottonwood trees. She giggled as she whisked past Paul, and turned back to taunt him with a smile.

That was the moment. It was as if life itself suddenly shifted into slow motion as she slipped out of the saddle. Feather could sense that something was wrong as he felt Sandi slipping from his back, but unlike that dream those many years ago, this time Feather slowed and steadied her pace, allowing Sandi to regain her balance and right herself on the saddle.

"You OK, Jesse," Paul said as he pulled up next to her.

"Never better." She smiled serenely.

VALLEY OF THE ANJELS

the first volume in a new fantasy series by best selling author
Judith Tracy

Three magical sisters searching for their hearts' destiny find themselves in a battle to save their world

ISBN 1-890096-23-7, $14 US

<u>Praise for Judith Tracy</u>

"INVENTIVE, WILLING TO TAKE CHANCES... AND A CLIMACTIC TWIST." -Paul Di Filippo, **ASIMOV'S**

"A REMARKABLE SCIENCE FICTION NOVEL." -Leann Arndt, **BUZZ BOOK REVIEW**

"ELEGANCE, A REALLY GOOD COMMAND OF BASIC STORYTELLING... AN AUTHOR TO WATCH." -Andrew Andrews, **TRUE REVIEW**

DESTINY'S DOOR
The bestselling novel from Judith Tracy

Here's to those that hope and pray.
Fate has led you here today.
Have we the power to grant you this,
Search your heart and make one wish.
Click here to Enter

ISBN 1-890096-08-3 $14.00 US

THE STARSCAPE PROJECT

BRAD AIKEN

The Teconean Empire, a civilization of Neanderthals, is determined to retake Earth, their homeworld. The rogue starfighter pilot that once stopped their plans, is now framed and running for his life over a crime he did not commit. Danny Stryker finds himself on an unexpected path that will alter the balance of power in the galaxy, and forever change man's definition of life.

$14 US ISBN 1890096202